THE
COTARD
DELUSION

DANIEL J. BURKE

MINDSTIR MEDIA

Published by Mindstir Media, LLC
45 Lafayette Rd | Suite 181| North Hampton, NH 03862 | USA
1.800.767.0531 | www.mindstirmedia.com

Printed in the United States of America
ISBN-13: 978-1-958729-83-0 (Paperback)

Cotard Delusion: when one believes with absolute certainty parts of their body become nonexistent. Limbs vanish, organs decay, and on rare occasions, a soul disintegrates, creating the perception of death.

Since first discovered in 1880 by Dr. Jules Cotard, the most profound records document an alive, breathing person convinced they have died.

I investigated this delusion further as a lieutenant of the Haddon County Police Department. In the early phases, I learned my old partner Max Vale had a particular tie to the case, and I requested his help.

This story is our recollection from the living and the dead.

PROLOGUE

Diary entry written by Max Vale

THE LITTLE GIRL'S stomach was nauseated.

Her pale fingers shined a laser around her new pet. The kitten stared at the red dot encircling its body and lowered its back as if the rug was tall grass, calculating the moment to attack.

Why? What is this urge?

Ragg kept telling the little girl something was off with it. The kitten looked functional but not quite put-together, like a few pieces were in the wrong places.

She stood behind the kitten and gently swung the laser point. Its golden eyes tracked the red dot... calculating.

In a flash, the kitten flung itself towards the light, its muscles tensed.

Somehow, the dot resurfaced on top of its paws and moved back onto the carpet. In response, the kitten turned to the dot. A crinkling sound came from its neck.

The little girl stood up, bewildered. Her muddy hair flipped behind her shoulders, uncovering her dark brown eyes and roman plug nose. Her features scrunched, highlighting her prominent cheekbones and bushy eyebrows. She wore a blue-flowered sundress.

Of course. There is something wrong with the neck, she thought.

The kitten sunk into the rug again, waiting for the next opportunity to strike.

The little girl reached out her bony hand.

She was not sure what was so obtuse with the neck, but something needed to be fixed. Her fingers skimmed the hair up the kitten's back.

"Marie?"

The kitten jumped, alarmed by the voice, and darted behind the loveseat.

Marie's mother stood at the doorframe. Beautiful locks of black hair plummeted from the sky over her pale skin, and her green eyes gripped Marie with a little more shine than normal. She bent her arm back and pinched her necklace. "Marie, darling." She hugged Marie and kissed her on the forehead.

"Yes, Mommy?"

"Are you feeling any better today?"

"No, Mommy, my stomach's still hurting."

The mother pressed her cheek on Marie's forehead. "You don't feel warm."

"I've felt sick all morning."

"Where does it hurt?"

"Here!" Marie rubbed the center of her tummy.

"How do you feel compared to yesterday?" The mother went on one knee and placed Marie on top.

"Much worse."

The mother's hair blanketed Marie. "How's the kitten?"

"Wonderful."

"A little kitten for a little girl." The mother placed Marie back on the ground, then kissed her forehead once more. "Call out if you need me, darling. I'm in the kitchen with Nana."

"Okay, Mommy."

The kitten stared from under the love seat.

"Would you like some tea?" Nana said, pouring hot water from the kettle before she allowed time for her daughter to answer.

Shyla sat at the kitchen table, pinching her necklace.

"Dear, you must get rid of that habit at some point in your life; it's very unattractive."

"Thanks, Mom."

Nana sat down and stared at her daughter with her brilliant green eyes. Shyla could always tell it brought great joy that she had her eyes. Nana was across the kitchen table, separated by an assortment of flowers gifted from her husband. Her gray hair was pulled back into a ponytail, and she wore a white top.

Nana smiled a lot. She had a way of enlivening everyone around her, of seeing the bright side of life. Shyla missed that trait. She knew she had a backbone stronger than most, something Nana was visibly proud of, but she just always drifted to the negative—the pessimist of the two. That being said, they were always protective of Marie. She was their baby.

"I got a call from Marie's teacher," Shyla said.

"Is this that two-nose, half-witted…"

"No, that was last year's language arts teacher."

"Oh right," Nana laughed to herself, "silly me."

"This year's teacher, one you would like, called me this morning while you were out with your granddaughter to tell me Marie had been getting bullied a lot lately."

"Oh my!" Nana furrowed her brow, having the gift of looking both kind-hearted and furious. She would pet your back before breaking it. "Don't mind me asking, dearest, but is this when all her other school problems started?"

A wave of emotion smacked Shyla. First in the eyes, but she could hide her tears well. Next, the warmth drained from her face; she knew that made her look paler—if that was even possible. Fortunately, she was pale enough that no one could ever tell except one person…

"Oh dear, I didn't mean to upset you." Nana shook her empty teacup. "Please, drink up. It will make you feel better."

It was not the first phone conversation Shyla had with the teacher. Marie's grades plummeted over the last few months. She always earned straight A's without showing much effort. But recently, like a switch, her grades dropped. Her attitude changed. She became more paranoid, and Shyla was becoming the enemy.

Tears formed, and this time, she couldn't hold them back. What ate her up the most was that she did not see this downfall coming and felt helpless. Anything she tried failed—kindness, punishment, mother-daughter dates. Marie had been growing more indifferent, and she could not figure out why.

"I just feel things are starting to make sense. And there's nothing scarier to me than the truth."

"Dear, chin up. There's plenty of beautiful things around you, including your daughter. She is still a sweet loving girl. I had trouble with you and your brother at times." Nana poured more hot water into her cup, then nudged the drink to Shyla.

"Mom." Shyla shook her head. "I'm just afraid…" Her words got caught.

"Oh?"

"I'm just…" Caught again.

"Shyla, you are an amazing mother that would do anything for her daughter."

Shyla broke down; the tears flowed onto her sundress. She kept quiet so Marie would not hear.

"A bad parent wouldn't be questioning; I did it many times myself with you."

"But am I really doing all I can? She's only eight, and she is already angry at me and probably angry at herself." Shyla could not remember the last time she cried.

"She'll come around, just as you did. And I have something to remind you of that," Nana said. She reached her hand below the table and pulled out a white rectangular box.

"What's this?" Shyla took a deep breath, and the tears slowed to a halt.

"Open it and find out." Nana made room on the table and placed it down.

Shyla put her hands on the lid and lifted it off. She gasped at the black silk cloth was folded in the box. "Where did you find this?" Shyla asked.

"I suppose you know your father and I have the tendency to keep everything."

Shyla's eyes widened. Nana had never admitted her hoarding before.

"Once in a while, a treasure reappears when you least expect it."

Shyla took out the cloth and unfolded it, watching it dangle in the air. "How old was I?"

"You were eight, just like Marie. I was working on what ended up being the most influential dress I would ever design. And I remember having to decide between two sheets of silk—a Prussian blue or black—and decided to have tea to debate. And what a surprise it was, when I came back to my mannequin to see you, wrapped in the black silk, taking a nap. You never looked more at peace during that rough time in your life."

Shyla stared at the cloth and felt warmth cover her heart in a way she had not felt in ages. A teardrop trailed down her cheek.

"So you made the decision for me, sweetie. I would use the Prussian blue on the dress and, most importantly, wrap the black silk around you every night and sing you to sleep until your cancer went away."

Shyla closed her eyes. Her hands shook in the air, rippling the cloth.

"You're a more beautiful soul than ever, and I know through this tough time, your love will ultimately get through to her," Nana said.

Shyla pulled down the sheet and revealed the tears that had formed. "I wish you could stay longer."

Marie dangled her feet off the edge of the Earth. She did not like the idea of swinging, but she enjoyed sitting on the seat and listening to the noises of the surrounding pine trees. The whistling from the wind smacked the branches, and the drips of water from last night's rainstorm trickled off the needles and pattered onto the sand. It was calming. But her favorite sound would always be listening to the birds chirping. It made her think, and that was the purpose of this meeting.

She held Agnes and Clarabelle in her left hands, both hand-me-down lifelike dolls Nana had named. They both had brown hair down to their chins in gray dresses from the old times that she had read about in school. Their mouths were slightly open, attempting a smile, and exposed a few teeth.

Ragg rested in her right arm. It was her favorite doll. She made it in the first grade—exhilarated with each stitch. The doll was perfect: blonde hair with pigtails, black dots for eyes, and a long curved line to represent a slight smile from cheek to cheek. All the kids at school said it was creepy, but what did *they* know? They couldn't differentiate their nostrils if she wedged a peanut in one. She held Ragg closer. The beautiful purple-cloth dress and shoes completed the perfect doll.

"You were right," Marie said to Ragg. "Something is not right with Graylin's neck."

"I always said something was wrong," Clarabelle said.

"No, I did. You were the one who said she was cute," Agnes said.

"You always try to take my credit!"

"You good-for-nothing…"

"Please," Ragg said. Its bass voice filled up the surrounding air, making Clarabelle and Agnes shiver. Marie loved that about the doll. They kept quiet. "Tell me everything, Marie."

"Every time I had tried to come close to the kitten, it would nip at my toes. So I took out my laser and distracted it to get a good look at its neck like you said."

"And what did you see?" Ragg asked, its voice shaking the swing set.

"It isn't right."

Agnes and Clarabelle froze.

"What isn't right?" Ragg asked.

"Her neck's broken. And every time I stare at it, I get that same feeling in my stomach."

"The nauseous one?"

"Yes."

Ragg thought for a moment. Its black eyes caught a bird flying by. "Of course, there's something wrong with the neck," it hissed. "Something is very wrong with the neck."

"We need to fix the neck," Agnes said.

"The neck," Clarabelle repeated.

"It's been ten days, *ten days*, since that kitten has appeared here," Ragg said, "and the neck has made it a broken toy the whole time."

"The neck," Agnes and Clarabelle said, their hum engraving the words into the back of Marie's skull.

"Something needs to go in the neck. Something cold, something has to go in there."

"Something cold? Should it be sharp?" Marie asked.

"It doesn't have to be; it just has to go in there. Something else has to belong in there."

"What will come out?"

"Your nausea. It will leave you for good." Ragg twitched.

"Are you okay?" Marie asked.

"I think I'll be fine, once the neck is fixed." Ragg fell into Marie's bright blue-flowered sundress.

"What do you think I should do?"

"Do exactly what you have been doing," Ragg said, "but fix the problem."

Marie smiled like Ragg.

"Have you been extra nice to Mother lately?" Ragg asked.

"Yes, extra."

"Great, continue as planned."

"The neck," Agnes and Clarabelle said, "the neck, the neck, the neck."

The dolls became quiet as the front door opened to the yard.

"Marie," said Mother. "Come say goodbye to Nana."

"Yes, Mommy," Marie said. She hopped off her swing and carried her friends inside.

The sun settled behind the pine trees, and the remnants of light lingered, leaving a reddish sky.

Marie sat in the main hall, a room with a long history of banquets. The piano would entertain guests with snappy tunes for each birthday, decorations covered the wood-log support beams for all the matches, and art conventions were often held due to the intricacies of the flawless molding to set the stage, a proud feat for the Daltons. But as generations passed, family members moved, communications broke, and hostilities worsened, leaving the room with just a piano, tables of unoccupied seats, and portraits of these alienated relatives along every wall. It was Marie's favorite spot, so her father made it her lavish toy room.

They scattered the floor as Marie sat at a table playing with a coloring book, waiting.

At last, underneath the tabletop, the kitten nipped her toes. *Finally.* The kitten had remained hidden all day in the shadows. Marie lifted the tablecloth and peeked.

Her stomach grew nauseous again.

The neck, her stomach said. The voice was like a hand grabbing her brain and pulling it down to her stomach so it could get a clearer listen: *The neck, the neck, the neck. Look at how imperfect it is.*

Marie reached into her pocket and brought out her laser. She drew a circle on the floor.

The kitten ignored it and kept nibbling her toes.

In response, Marie nudged the kitten to the red dot. Only then, its golden eyes became interested in the light once more and followed its usual motion—stiffening and sinking into the rug, ready to attack.

Marie brought her hand to the top of the table, and amongst her arts and crafts, she grabbed her scissors.

Something to fill the hole.

The blades were dull, and the handle was pink, her mother's choice. A chill rose from her stomach. *Yes, this moment is perfect.*

Marie sunk under the tablecloth.

The kitten was turned away, eyeing the laser dot. Her nausea grew. Nothing felt right with the kitten. Everything was wrong. Marie started to sweat.

The neck, her stomach said again. Its voice became lower.

"Ragg?"

"Yes."

"I need help."

"Why, whatever do you need?"

"How do you stab?"

"Without breathing."

Marie paused. "Is that all?"

"Yes, Marie, just hold your breath and go."

Marie stared at the neck, robotically swirling the laser around. She raised her scissors in her left hand and held her breath.

She lowered her arm. The metal felt heavier than usual, causing her to slow down. The scissor blades skimmed the hair on its back, but nothing more.

The kitten perked and darted from under the table, still broken.

Marie's nausea worsened.

Shyla lifted her side of the covers and climbed into bed. Dean turned from his side and kissed her on the cheek. He smiled, revealing the wrinkles that had been appearing over the past year. Fortunately, aging had not hit his hair yet, still gelled back from a day's worth of work. He placed his hand on hers.

"Should she go?" Shyla asked.

"She's a Dalton. If she wants to go…" Dean lowered the tablet and looked at her through his reading glasses. The screen illuminated his pale features.

"Of course she doesn't want to go, but should she?"

"You're the wife. I think she should do what you want her to do."

"What kind of answer is that?" Shyla said with a snarl. "Just once, I wish you'd give me a direct answer."

"I'm not talking about this. Not now."

"Do you think Marie should stay home tomorrow? Yes or no."

"I already said, you're the wife. Do what you think is best. I thought you wanted this freedom from me."

"I don't know what is best!" Shyla yelled. The words echoed in the master suite, it made the air difficult for Dean to take in. He stiffened.

Shyla lay on their bed and tried not to cry. Dean attempted to pat her on the back, but Shyla swatted his hand away. She lifted her body and glared at him. "I just wish you showed you cared a little more."

"Of course, I care! I wish you would notice that once and a while. Don't be selfish. There are other people that care. Why do you think I put up with all of these hours at the university?"

"I know you care! I just want you to show it more at home! Why do I have to explain this!"

"Maybe if you asked me how my day was."

"Ask me about mine for once! Do you even know how hard it's been to sit around this place?"

"It must be so hard working part-time."

Shyla's eyes shot ice and froze Dean. They both knew that was the wrong thing to say. Every word stuck onto Dean's tongue and refused to leave his mouth until he slouched his shoulders and said, "Sorry."

Shyla pinched her necklace. "No, don't be. I'm just being too angry."

"You're not. I need to be... I need to be more around."

They both sighed, drained.

"What is with me lately?" Shyla asked, staring blankly at the wall behind him.

"Hell if I know." The silence dragged his voice.

"Oh, Dean, what do you think I should do? I'm being a wuss about this."

"You're not; you're just being a caring mother."

"That's what Nana said."

"I know. She called me three times at work until I picked up."

"*You* talked to Nana?"

"Don't worry, she was her curt self."

Shyla shook her head.

"I think you should talk to her. Mother-daughter, tell her she needs to go to school tomorrow and face her fears. Show some guts."

"Are you sure?"

"I think that would be nice. If you need me to be the arm-and-hammer, you call for reinforcements?"

"Okay... I can do that. I think that sounds right. You're right."

"Of course I am." Dean brought Shyla close and gently kissed her on the lips. "How has she liked Graylin?"

The trap had been set for two hours.

Marie lay in bed. Her nausea was stabbing her stomach. It continued to spread around her abdomen, making her feel like someone was pulling her hair to the floor. The stutter continued. *The neck. The neck.*

Sleep could not happen until things were fixed. Dark things should never be contained because they stay in your stomach and swish around until you're nothing.

The door nudged open. It was only a matter of time.

The past three nights, the kitten found a comfortable nook at the edge of the bed. Little footsteps climbed the cat stairs; fur brushed Marie's toes.

The nibbling started.

Marie sat up and took out a laser she hid under the covers. She shined the light. The red dot stood out in the darkness and caught the kitten's attention. The dot slowly waved from one side of the bed frame to the other, and the kitten turned its head to expose what was broken.

Shyla crept down the hallway and passed a nightlight of a cross.

What is going on with me? she thought. She had always been even-keeled and enjoyed listening to people's problems, so much so that she made a living off of it. She walked past her office and gazed. Part-time was okay; the private practice was friendly, but she missed her research. Too many fun nights wondering about the mind. Nothing allowed her to explore those thoughts like the freedoms of academia—at least when the funding allowed.

She sighed. If she had spent a few more nights with her daughter, maybe she would not be here. Maybe she would have a stronger backbone. Shyla always had one because Nana would not allow otherwise. Was she too soft? Or too hard?

For what felt like the millionth time in her life, she was stumped, but never in a worse way. She stopped by the mirror and stared into her green eyes, eyes that she would get lost in on many late nights.

"I need to accept that Marie will have to make her own decisions in life, but as long as she is young and willing to listen, I will set the best example I can, and I can only hope that one day, she will be happy to talk about her life over tea."

She pinched her necklace. *Nothing really calms an anxious mother.*

Marie's nausea caught on fire and rose to her brain.

She zoned into a trance. *Something has to go in there. Something needs to go in there.*

"The neck," Agnes and Clarabelle said by the window. "The neck, the neck."

She focused on the kitten and grimaced. She reached out her hand to the end table for the pink scissors. But they were not there. She gasped. The nausea stabbed her insides. She turned left and right.

Where were they? Where did I have them last? she thought.

They were supposed to be there. They *had* to be there.

The neck. The neck.

Marie scanned her bedroom. Toys covered the windowsill, the dresser, the closet—but no scissors.

"Just hold your breath," Ragg said louder from the toy chest by the window.

Where are the scissors?

The neck.

She scanned the room again. The kitten started to look bored with the laser.

Her nausea spread to her limbs.

There they are! Near the toy chest—an arm's length and a stretch away, they sparkled in the moonlight.

She needed to get up, but she couldn't. Nausea weighed her down.

The neck. The neck.

She stretched out her left arm and leaned toward the scissors, but she was not as close as she had expected. Her hand felt heavy, like it was anchoring her to fall off her bed and drown in the carpet. Her world was crashing. The blades went further away.

The nausea crept down her arms.

Please! Please, come back...

She extended her body as far as possible to the scissors in desperation. Then the anchor dropped. Marie gripped the kitten's neck and snapped it sideways like a twig.

It cracked.

"Marie Dalton!" Shyla gasped. She ran to the bed, denying what she had just witnessed. "What—what in the world... You did this?"

Marie gazed up and hinted a smile.

She never held her breath.

Months later...

A loud clang shook the main hall, the room where Marie would play with her dolls. To the sound of Dean's footsteps, Shyla jumped out from a cluster of Nana's mannequins and a couple of boxes. "What's going on here?" Dean asked, entering from the hallway.

The back of a large portrait lay on the ground.

"Grandpop..." Dean said under his breath. He sprinted over and blocked Shyla from getting close, as if it was a crime scene. He turned the painting over and studied its detail.

"I'm sorry, babe, I must have bumped into it moving Nana's boxes around."

He sighed. "You're lucky he's okay." Dean picked up the portrait and hung it back on the wall. "I once promised this man I'd keep all these portraits pristine." He left Shyla and inspected the other portraits of his family that surrounded the room.

"What are the heck are you doing?" Shyla asked.

"Seeing if you or your daughter messed up any others while I was gone."

"Seriously?"

Dean walked to the other side of the hall and scanned the portraits. "You're going to be up here one day, you know, " he said.

"That's really at the front of my mind right now."

"And Marie, one way or another..." He turned to Shyla and sunk his eyebrows, glaring down at his wife. "Are we actually helping her?"

"What do you mean?" Shyla asked protectively.

"Marie won't talk to me about her episodes. She's harder to crack than most of my court cases."

"Of course, she's your daughter."

"But you feel what I feel around her, right? The way the house chills… it just sucks the life out of you. Hell, I can barely breathe around her. The doctor seems willing to work with us."

"She doesn't know my daughter like I do. They ruled out any tumors and blood clots. What else would a neurologist do that I couldn't? Marie's not made for a hospital, not with the care we can provide and the privacy we have. There is something wrong with our daughter that requires more psychoanalysis from me before I figure out what to prescribe."

"You're sure as hell taking your damn time."

"Screw you."

"I'm just saying, please realize you're doing your best." Dean wrapped his arm around Shyla and kissed her on the cheek.

"No." Shyla stepped out of his reach and glared at him. "It's our daughter, Dean, there's no *best*. I have to do better."

Dean shook his head in disagreement, exhaling. He stared at Nana's mannequins and asked, "How is sorting through her items?"

"Terrible. I wished you would help."

"It's not my business," he said. "Plus, I don't think Nana would have wanted me to."

"I think she would have liked you to give me support." Shyla put her hands on her waist.

"That's what I'm doing."

"No, you're not. Like, what am I supposed to do with these?" She pointed to the six old papier-mâché mannequins against the wall blocking light from the window.

"Toss them."

"I'm not tossing those mannequins. Nana spent a lifetime on these."

"Then what do you want me to do?"

"To not ask me a question when all I want is support."

Dean held his hand up, stopping Shyla. He pointed out a window behind the mannequins to the backyard, where Marie sat on her swing and talked to her dolls. His features darkened as he said, "I don't want her to be outside by herself. You should be out there too."

"She's not going anywhere. You're the one that always tells me she's a Dalton and to give her some space. And you do that well every night you get home late."

"Don't antagonize me. I keep us alive."

"Whatever," she said, taking a step away from him. "You know it's her favorite spot. We just had a math lesson, so she's relaxing."

"Fine. I just don't want her hurt. That's all," he said.

They looked out at Marie sitting on her swing. She rarely swung; instead, she liked to dangle her feet and play with her dolls on it. "She's been good for three days. That's pretty long."

"The longest," she agreed.

"A sign she's getting better?"

"Who knows."

Shyla and Dean stared at each other for a few seconds, and each felt a wave of confusion press on their chest.

The wind wrapped around Marie. Dalton Manor was the lone empty circle within a field of pine trees, which at times created strong vortexes. She liked to kick out her legs and let them blow through her hair. She closed her eyes. Agnes and Clarabelle hung in her left arm pressed against her stomach while Ragg leaned onto her wrist front and center.

"It's all about control," Ragg said. Each word slithered like a snake.

"It is?" Marie asked.

Agnes and Clarabelle looked at Ragg dumbstruck. For the first time in months, their conversation had picked up about the kitten's neck. They could never decide if it was fixed or more broken.

"When I tried to reach for my scissors, it started to feel farther away."

"The scissors felt further because you lost control of your emotions. Emotions are everything with control," said Ragg. "Just like how a car ride to a new location always seems longer on the way there compared to on the way back. Anticipation slows down time, dear, and that has deep emotional ties to your perception of distance traveled."

"I still should have gotten up and grabbed the scissors; no emotion was needed. The kitten wasn't going anywhere."

"You're judging your control based on tangible objects. A scissor... a cat... your hand... look deeper."

Marie dangled her legs for a minute and focused on a few birds hopping around on the sand, looking for bugs.

"Control can be complicated, but it can be made simple too," said Ragg. "The art is making complicated scenarios simple. That's the secret."

"The secret?"

"Oh yes, a powerful secret. Look at the robin on the lawn."

Marie stared at the bird. She couldn't help but focus on its small yellow beak poking around between the dead pines on the ground. "It's searching... frantically... for food."

The bird looked at Marie, tilting its head.

"There's so much emotion in that bird, so many thoughts," Ragg continued. "How will it eat? Can it find food for its family? It probably has little ones by the look of desperation on its face. Should it fly away and start over at a new spot? Are its children okay? Those fears are all instinctual, most are... and I'm just cracking the surface."

"That's complicated."

"Yes!" Ragg's stitched mouth curled. "You can't control all of those feelings. And believe me, you want total control to make them move."

"Is that why I see colors when I look at the bird?" Marie asked.

"Go on…"

"A mesh of colors. It's not like there are splashes of blue or green in front of me, but it's like the colors are *there*, surrounding me. I feel it in my tummy. Sometimes I get nauseous and want to throw up. I see those colors right now when I look at the bird. I think I was starting to do that with the kitten. But after I cracked its neck, I *felt* the kitten turn red."

"Interesting," Ragg said excitedly.

"Very interesting," Agnes and Clarabelle said.

"Darling, what you are seeing is control," Ragg said.

"I'm seeing control?"

"Sure, a rare gift to see something so intangible…"

"I don't know if I totally get it."

"How do you control that robin?"

"Make her complexities simple."

"Exactly. Birds are the classic example of control."

"Really?"

"Yes!" Agnes and Clarabelle laughed.

"Shut up, you two!" Ragg said.

Agnes and Clarabelle hid, squishing into Marie's side.

"What is their most instinctive resource in an emergency for them?"

"Flying."

"Right… the wings." Ragg licked the stitches around its lips. "You can control birds like a switch, because you can control how fear blankets them."

"But how?"

"Snap two wings, the bird fears imminent death and comes to accept it quickly, some control, but it doesn't last very long—so that's *the color red* you felt with the kitten in your case. Snap no wings, and it will fly away unharmed. No fear, no control, like that bird… *a blue color*. But if you snap one wing, that's when you have complete control because the bird will try and fly away. It will try many times. But you know it can't. You know there's nothing it can do about the circumstance. Its fears will creep up, and it will accept death. But until it does, you can play any game you want with it. That is *yellow.*"

"It's all about snapping a bird's wing?"

"And every other runt."

"Like who?"

"Marie!" Shyla yelled hysterically from the front of the house. Dean sprinted out just behind her. "Marie! Darling, speak to me."

"I told you she shouldn't be out here!" Dean yelled, sprinting right behind her.

Shyla ran across the lawn and went down on her knee.

"She just dropped all her dolls and stared straight ahead—like nothing was going on!" Dean said.

Shyla kissed Marie and wrapped her arms around her. "Marie, darling, talk to me." She sat emotionless on her swing. "Please, honey, talk to me... Please, say anything... *I'll do anything.*"

Later that evening, Shyla softly opened the door to Marie's bedroom.

For a minute, she watched her daughter.

Marie rested under pink floral covers and snuggled up with her dolls. Even asleep, she appeared more alive than in the last few hours of the day. Shyla tiptoed over to the side of the bed, holding the black silk cloth Nana gave her.

Shyla kissed her daughter on the forehead and then unfolded the black cloth. She carefully removed each blanket until Marie's body lay half-curled into a ball.

She did not move.

Shyla spread the black cloth over her daughter and tucked it in. Then automatically, Marie nuzzled deeper into the bed with the cloth. Shyla carefully placed each blanket back over her and stroked her daughter's hair.

Shyla's eyes closed, and she relived those fearful, tired nights in bed as a child, not being able to sleep until her mother came in to sing. That very love poured out in melody.

"Say goodnight, and fall yourself to sleep, little child.
Kiss goodbye, dream up in the clouds with your smile.
Cheek to cheek. Fly in the sky. No matter how far you go...
My love is in your heart as your home."

Shyla watched Marie in silence, unaware her daughter had heard the entire song. Through Marie's closed eyes, she could see yellow swirl around her mother.

It's all a game of snapping a wing, Ragg said.

The yellow molded an outline of her mother's shape and flew through her.

That's control, Ragg said. *And once we develop your gift, we can fulfill my vision.*

End of diary entry

*   *   *

I remembered the day I first learned of this journal entry. How could Max Vale, my dear ex-partner of all people, have captured the internal dialogue of a young girl and her parents with such clarity, with such respect to their emotions, and spit out verbiage from their perspectives? Had he gone mad?

To be blunt—yes. I would even argue Vale is the craziest man I have ever met. And I will come to learn in time that thought was the ultimate compliment.

For as we sink deeper into this case, it is our definition of madness that will be our source of orientation—time and location would leave us alone. Besides, they're just a product of our perception anyway, and our senses can only detect a fraction of what is around us. At least that was true until Marie came along, and for the first time in human history with such definition, we began to detect more…

Up to that point, humans were not built to process the original universe because we did not have the molecular capability to sense it. But make no mistake, our home—all billions of lightyears—evolved from the original universe. What we perceive as scientific law exists because of its evolution.

I felt insignificant when I first learned the news.

But thankfully, I was wrong. Because I then learned the original universe is not in parallel with us but intertwined. I am saying that by living in our dimension, we live with the original one—what created us.

Call it God, science, or what you would like, I was taught to call it *the Deus*.

Thanks to Vale, and with the guidance of Marie, we once again will redefine just how little we know, exploring all corners of the world in this dimension and the original, with, of course, madness as our compass.

Near the start of the case, a good friend would tell me, "All great challenges are psychotic; only this awareness reveals a man's true sanity."

At this phase of my life, as I near the end of my days, consider me cured.

PART I

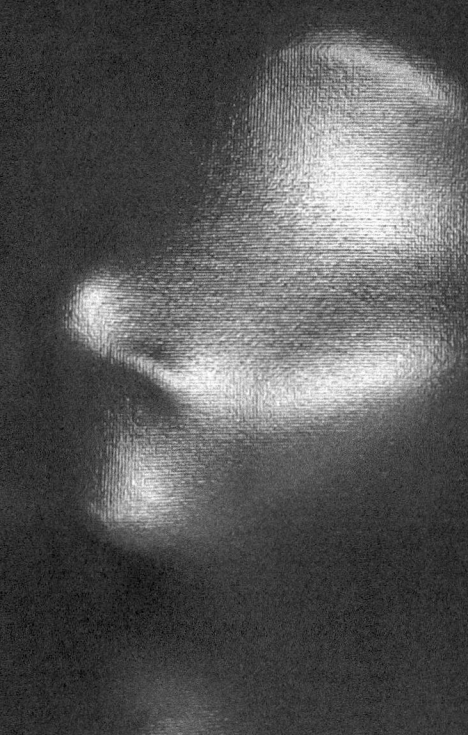

*"There is no greater agony than bearing
an untold story inside you."
~ Maya Angelou*

FOG

"THERE'S BEEN NOTHING from her in over forty hours," I said, speeding the Crown Victoria down the lone county road to Dalton Manor.

In the rear-view mirror, the remaining streetlights from civilization revealed wrinkles around my turquoise eyes. Blades of sandy hair were shortened to unshaved bristles, carpeting my pale jawline.

I watched Max Vale. His wiry contour pressed against the passenger window. The outside abyss of the pine trees highlighted his browline glasses that rested on his pointed nose. Still drenched from entering the cop car, the drops rolled down his bronze skin. Underneath his unbuttoned trench coat, I noticed a gray flowered vest, one he had been known to wear.

"You've added some more of these guys," Vale said in his posh accent. He grabbed a sleek and silver toy robot I had taped to my gray dashboard. He scrunched his forehead, and his hazel irises intensified, lost in thought. I never understood where his mind wandered, blazing his own path in verbiage, drooling cynicism. It was a road no map could guide me toward. But at the time, I would never in my right mind suspect he wrote a diary entry about Dalton Manor years earlier. Why the hell would I?

"Don't touch, I spent days making that one," I said, referring to the robot.

"Are they even in any order?" Vale shook my creation.

"Date of purchase… but come on, you know the rules."

Vale studied the robot's arm motion, and I clenched my jaw. "The paint job's a bit spotty," Vale said.

"Will you put that back?" I swatted at him.

"And the Crown Victoria has become a garbage can—a rule of mine you clearly broke since I left."

"It's not messy…" I scanned the gray interior, acknowledging the piles of food wrappers and receipts resting on the center console that I meant to throw out.

Vale's brow rose.

"I suppose I could vacuum at some point." I recomposed and hardened my tone. "But galactic travel is cool, got it?"

"I'll defer to your expertise, old man."

I snagged the robot out of his hand and stuck it back on the dashboard. "Jesus, Vale, you're not worried about your twin sister?"

"I gave up worrying about her a long time ago. I haven't even talked to her in a decade."

"But she's up for her tenure in two days."

"I get that."

"And you're her emergency contact."

"I didn't even know she went to grad school."

"Doesn't matter. You're what we have to work with."

Vale tucked his lips to a corner.

"Elara isn't just going anywhere for her tenure," I said, "it's Dougray University. They are not giving me any leads with this one, and you have the best insight into her past."

"If you say so."

I spun the steering wheel at the first intersection we had seen in miles. Vale gripped onto the door handle for dear life. He had never been a fan of my driving and was not afraid to protest. After the Crown Victoria straightened onto a road bordered by sand against the pine tree lines, Vale relaxed his hand and said, "I suppose it has been forty hours since her disappearance. But every other detail before that fact... I am not so sure."

"What are you saying?"

"While I am appreciative of your suspects, especially since you were willing to drop names the moment you picked me up from the train station... I must decline further discussion of these people."

"*Decline?*"

"I need more physical introduction, Price. What a man suspects about the world will not prepare one for what lies ahead, but rather what is caged deep inside."

"That's a new one," I said, used to Vale's peculiar jargon.

"Just hold your gossip for tonight. We'll discuss people and motives when the time comes. A lot has changed. For now, I want to hear what you know to be absolutely true."

I tapped my dirty finger beds on the steering wheel for a minute, biting my lower lip until I said, "All I can guarantee is that your twin was hired as an assistant professor at Dougray, and her research focuses on relativity."

"Lovely."

"I assume you remember your physics from high school?"

"Why, I had planned to lean on the world's leading experts..." Vale pointed to my row of robots on the dash, all staring at us as if they were listening.

"That's what I thought," I said. "From what I have taken notes on, the basic idea is a person's perception of time changes when they travel faster than the speed of light. I just skimmed her old dissertation. It is... complicated, to say the least."

"Complicated? Who, Elara?"

"She's just like her twin."

"And what's that supposed to mean?"

"You're not the easiest person to figure out yourself."

"I'd be insulted if you thought otherwise." Vale's eyes pierced me, and just briefly, all the skeletons I knew that rested in his closet surfaced, chilling my bones. He noticed the crack in his wall and quickly patched it.

Then Vale became silent, and I imagined he was processing the attempts to reconnect with his twin sister due to his many oral histories with me over whiskey. The numerous unanswered phone calls, the false promises… Vale had little hope for their relationship. I understood his frustration. Why was he—of all people—her emergency contact?

"I suppose there's a reason we cannot just go to her lab?" Vale asked.

"It's locked. Dougray's working on it."

"Then why don't we break in?" Vale joked—at least I thought he was.

"Her lab is in the newer building at Dougray. We might as well rob all the banks up the East Coast."

"We're playing with a wildfire."

"It at least brought you in on the case. A consult with a private investigator would not fly most days with the Haddon Police."

"Ah yes, the beloved Haddon Police," Vale mumbled. An empty moment dragged into silence, and he went back to staring out the windshield to digest the information. The silence began to crescendo, but then Vale started muttering to himself. He tended to do that when he was left to his own thoughts. When I was first assigned to be his partner, I did my best to try and connect the fragments, but after a few years, I concluded it was a waste of time. He brewed in isolation, regardless of my presence.

Until then, I forgot how much I missed those disconnected ramblings of his. So, I let it fill the Crown Victoria as background music.

It was nice to consult my old partner for this case. I had wondered how long it would be before his eventual return, especially because I never fully understood why Vale chose to leave the force—

his unexplained departure broke my heart a little. He had not been back to Haddon in well over a year. And I would have never expected his estranged twin sister to be the reason for the visit.

Perhaps he was more afraid to return than I realized.

I pondered over that notion as the rain pattered on the rooftop, dragging time, and the surrounding forest darkened. The Pinelands, as the locals called them here, always played with my imagination. The trees mutated. Each leaf shriveled to a needle, and the soil dried to sand. I avoided this place when I could in my youth. But now, as a lieutenant, a fog covered the Pinelands, one my subconscious created to help this memory cope, blurring my vision, sucking the air out of my lungs. I feel lost every time I relived this evening. Conversations and poignant details remained, but their connectivity was distorted.

This recollection I share is my best effort, and my disorientation, I later appreciated, would be essential going forward. A sane mind could not handle the upcoming journey.

At some point, after we tacked on the miles, a trivial detail about Vale's life surfaced. "How's the coastline been treating you?" I asked.

"A breath of fresh air. How it should be."

"Anyone new you're dating out there?"

Vale raised his brow.

"Hey, it's my job to keep tabs on my prodigy's well-being," I said, grinning.

"I'm doing well." Vale laughed. "The bigger question is—how's your granddaughter?"

"Novah has never been better... going off to school soon."

"You know, she still owes me money for spilling her OJ on my slacks."

"I'll be sure to forward the bill her way."

Vale's lips curled.

I slowed the car down to a stop by what appeared to be a small series of houses through the headlights. After passing the final house, which was in ruin, I stopped the car and glanced to my left. On the edge of the pine trees was a one-lane muddy road. Even aware of its existence, the road blended well into the shadows. It looked abandoned, but I noticed a set of tire tracks.

Vale scrunched his forehead and looked at me as if he was asking whether this path was correct. My response was to turn onto the road. We kept silent and cautiously drove. The road was unkempt by the tree roots that stuck out of the dirt like mini speed bumps.

A minute later, two stone pillars covered in weeds stuck out on each side of the small road. On top of both, a two-foot stone lion stood, stuck in a roar, showing off its claws. *DALTON MANOR* was engraved in stone on each pillar. Several feet further, a metal fence wrapped in barbed wire started from each end of the road and traversed the pine trees.

"What's this place again?" Vale asked.

"I believe Elara's experiments were done here," I said. I was unwilling to reveal who gave me the information because it would have opened a can of worms about my own dating life.

Vale did not respond. After a minute, a small field appeared to our left. "This can't be it," Vale said.

"Where?" I asked, slamming on the breaks.

"A few feet away, past the first layer of pine trees."

I stared into the darkness outside my driver's window, and then as my eyes adjusted, I felt like a hand grabbed my heart and pulled it to the floor.

Dalton Manor appeared as deformed as the pine trees. The building was a rectangular rancher. And even with the headlights beaming, the manor blended into the background and tucked under the tree line. I didn't recognize what the house was made of, but it reminded me of unfinished wood, making the manor look more like a project than anything. Behind the pines, the manor rested on muddy sand, with weeds covering several walls, some so overgrown they looked like small trees had gripped onto the manor's side and climbed up to its flat rooftop. There was no noticeable door and only a few small windows, each a different shape and height on the walls.

"There's no other building around here?" Vale asked.

"This should be it," I said, bewildered.

"I suppose it's time to play Detective again, just like the good old days."

"We certainly had a good run, didn't we?" I asked.

Vale chuckled. We pounded each other's fists, then snapped our fingers. I smiled. It had been over a year since we last did that ritual. But then Vale's lips tightened, noticing through the downpour another police car that was tucked away on the far-right side of the structure.

"Ah, that explains the tire tracks. Looks like Lieutenant has given you some sway. But how were you able to get backup?"

"A good question," I said, hesitant to reveal more. I opened the door, and the downpour sounds filled the car. I raised my voice to avoid feeling the total force of what was going to be his reaction. "Took a little kicking and screaming... but it comes at a cost."

"I don't like that tone," he said.

"Your other former partner is one of the officers."

Vale's face hardened. After I had been promoted to lieutenant, he was reassigned to a younger cop in my quadrant. "I like how I find this out once we get here," Vale said.

"He was on a leave of absence. The department pulled him back in to join us," I said, avoiding my belief Vale would have not even come if he knew his newest ex-partner was here.

"I see the uppers are thrilled to have me back." Vale stepped out of the Crown Victoria and joined me on the muddy lawn.

The wind picked up, and I stuck my hands inside my trench coat pockets. I focused on the surroundings through the darkness and buckets of rain, seeing nothing but those shriveled pine trees. We took out our flashlights and fought the weather to meet the patrol officers who had positioned themselves to the right of Dalton Manor.

I could not make out their faces through the storm, but once we were closer, I first recognized the frame of the officer Vale did not want to see.

"Carl Moreno," Vale said, laughing to himself in the rain.

"Max Vale, how has the last year been?" Moreno said in his standard egg-headed tone. He was young and muscular with the bone structure of an ox. His facial features were chiseled, and a thick wave of hair escaped from under his peaked cap.

"Not too shabby, Officer," Vale said.

I recognized the other man, Martin Brezniack, but had never worked with him and was glad I never had. The man was scrawny, no more than five feet high, with a buzz cut. He was a family hire, nephew to the chief of police. He was pale and had a few lone blades of hair around his chin in an attempt to look older. I knew the officer worked downtown and was unofficially demoted to a parking patrolman. He was best known for all the odd tinker toys at his desk at the station, one of which clipped to the side of his pants.

I nodded to both men. "None of this crap from you two," I said with a bite, more to Moreno than Brezniack. "I don't want to hear anything. I would never put you both here unless I had my hands tied behind my back."

"Hey, I got nothing to hide, Lieutenant," Moreno said, glaring at Vale. "Whose brilliant idea was it to have us out here?"

"The powers that be," I said. "You can go if you'd like."

"Don't be messing with me now. And did I hear we are looking for an Elara *Vale*—"

"My twin sister," Vale said.

Moreno's eyes flared with excitement. He said, "After all this camaraderie, you never mentioned you had a sister."

"They might give you a loaded weapon, but I won't."

Moreno tucked in his lips, pronouncing his rigid chin.

"Now, what the fuck are you both doing standing around?" I asked, distracting Moreno.

"We found the entrance, Lieutenant. There's only one way in, and it sort of blends into the background," said Brezniack in a soft, high-pitched voice that battled the downpour. "You got the warrant?"

"I do. Would you tell your uncle otherwise?"

"Just checking, that's all."

I bit my tongue and had Brezniack guide us to the entrance in the back corner.

"I hear you are enjoying life on the coastline," Moreno said, pressing into Vale's ear but still loud enough that I could hear him through the storm.

"You heard right."

Moreno grabbed his shoulder and said, "Congratulations, you motherfucker. I won't ever forget what you did, and I will do everything in my power to fuck you."

"You missed me that much?" Vale turned to Moreno and swatted his arm away.

"Go choke on a dick."

I stepped in between them and pressed my nose to Moreno's. "We don't know what's in this shithole, and you're badgering about some bullshit from a year ago? So help me God, if you bring that up at all tonight, I will make your career a living hell." My rule of thumb had always been to let my officers work their own spats, but I felt guilty for blind-siding Vale.

I must have been angry because neither one responded; perhaps they were surprised as well. They had worked with me long enough to know that response was extreme. Or so I thought.

I looked at Vale for backing. He nodded smoothly, relaxing like he was in meditation. Moreno, on the other hand, looked emotionless. It was then I noticed behind the stylish head of hair and spotless outfit just how off he appeared. I was not sure what to make of him yet. After his and Vale's falling out, he was transferred off my team into a different quadrant.

At the time, I thought I understood their situation, since I knew why there was tension between him and Vale, and I was aware Moreno had a troubled past of his own. But in reality, I had no idea how deep their issues ran. I was clueless—so I turned my clueless eyes to Dalton Manor, unprepared for what lay ahead that night.

The entrance was an unassuming wooden door. I nudged Moreno over, and he clenched his fist, then banged twice. We waited for half a minute getting no response. He repeated the motion with the same result.

"Well then, the fun begins," Moreno said, acting like my tirade did not happen. But, as long as he stayed out of Vale's way, I was okay with the response.

"Once we break in, follow my lead and be on your guard," I said.

Moreno stood sideways several feet from the entrance and took a deep breath. He kicked the wooden door below the doorknob. On the second try, it flung open and banged loudly against the inside wall.

Darkness greeted us. We swiftly stepped inside.

Our flashlights revealed an empty wooden foyer and a rustic chandelier that dangled at its center. The walls looked torn up as if a tornado had gone through, and a musty smell pinched my nostrils.

Breathe and slow down the case, I thought. It was part of my regimen with every search—if I didn't make a strong effort to let the case present itself gradually, my world would crash. I took that deep breath and observed how the storm seeped into the stillness of the manor. The power was out. *Of course.* My palms began to sweat.

I surveyed the paths from the foyer. There were two options to choose from: a hallway straight ahead or a room to the left. I directed Moreno and Brezniack to the former, the hallway directly in front of us, while Vale and I darted into the latter—the left room.

We entered. A chill blanketed me. And for a moment, I froze. I had never seen anything like it. I learned later it was called an "Artistry Room." It looked much larger than I expected—as if it could not possibly fit into the run-down rancher.

Every wall was filled with canvases of humans, their bodies penciled in black and white, with a consistency that reminded me of television static. But the texture was so fine I was surprised at the excruciating detail of each person, down to the crevices on their fingers and the wrinkles in their clothing. Their eyes had incredible depth, yet an eerie emptiness to their glares, as if each one had the energy drained out of their soul, leaving only a mold of their carcass.

I squinted. The contour of each television-static human was odd. Random parts of household items such as jewelry, utensils, or cars would stick out of the person as if they were in the process of emerging from their figure.

Even weirder, streams of color swirled around the static subjects like a breeze.

As a whole, the individual paintings blended into a bigger collage—like the room was an entry into another cosmos. I was disturbed and had no idea what to make of it.

In the corner, several easels held canvases. Brushes rested on each ledge. One of those canvases in particular grabbed Vale's attention. I crept over and stared dumbfounded.

The painting was his twin sister in this television-like static. I barely recognized her from the photo I had seen, but in my gut, I knew it was her. Vale looked mystified. The only characteristics I felt were on point were her accentuated dimples and powerful eyes that popped out of the canvas. But even with those eyes, her face looked drained of life. She had a few piercings on each ear. A thick head of curly hair tumbled down to her waist, where at least half a dozen necklaces dangled with charms off chains. Similar to the other portraits, parts of items were trying to break out of Elara's body. Studying the objects closer, I could distinguish glass jars and computer chips that reminded me of a science lab, but there were other items I had never seen before but looked just as technical.

She was with two other women around the same height. They all wore similar bizarre outfits. It was a static cloak that fluffed by her shoulders from scrunched, excess fabric. From there, it stretched tightly down the sleeves and was left unbuttoned, revealing what I expected to be skin from her chest to her stomach. The skintight pants completed the look, while similar scientific objects broke their contour. Light orange and red lines of paint circled around them like the wind.

My stomach squeezed. I turned to my old partner, and I could hear the gears turning in his brain. *What the hell is this?* I thought. But I did not have the time to fully compute until I addressed my top priority—clearing Dalton Manor.

I moved on, growing more anxious with every step, and felt the paintings disturb my psyche, as if they fell off the wall, burying me. I needed to get out. Panting, I thought once more, *Slow down the case.* But it was then that my mind started to get foggy. As if the clouds had emerged from the pine trees into Dalton Manor. I pushed on.

We found nothing else of importance and impatiently darted into the next room. It was clearly the kitchen. To the left, dishes dried on a rack atop a counter. I brought my focus to a window behind the sink, where the downpour echoed against the glass. I turned to my right and shined my flashlight underneath a round wooden table that pressed against an indented part of the room with several chairs. There were crumbs.

Someone was here recently, I thought.

A faint odor of urine pitched my nostrils.

Vale waved his flashlight to grab my attention. He nudged his head to a pantry across the kitchen, near the entrance to the next room. I crept over. A bloom of heat cut across my face as the stench appeared localized to what was behind the pantry door.

I gestured Vale to the doorknob. The floor creaked with each step. Vale gripped the handle. My heart pounded as he waited for my signal.

One... two... three... He swung the door open.

Past the entrance, Professor Elara Vale sprawled on the empty closet floor.

"Oh my God," Vale said.

My eyes widened. I was not anticipating a corpse, especially not this early in our search, but within minutes of entering Dalton Manor, the damn shack gripped my skull, forcing me to look at her body.

I was disgusted.

The skin on her face was carved away, exposing her muscles, eye sockets, and teeth. All of her fingers were cut off. Her black curly hair fell over her cloaked shoulders like in the living room painting. There were three stab marks on her neck, and the floor was stained with her dried blood. Vale fixated on her body.

"Vale... I'm so sorry," I said as sincerely. My hands were shaking by my side.

Vale did not respond, instead fixated on the pantry. It went further in, filled with boxes and cans of food; some of them had fallen onto Elara. A light bulb dangled in the center of the ceiling.

Once more, I needed to investigate, but for now, I had to keep searching to see if the killer was lurking.

We jumped. A scream came from the foyer, from where we entered. It sounded like Brezniack.

Clouds formed around me.

At once, I backtracked in my mental fog, dashing back through the Artistry Room to the entrance of Dalton Manor, Vale fast on my heels. *This is all going too fast*, I thought. But I knew I didn't have a choice.

We arrived back in the foyer. It was empty, and the voice had stopped. The silence chilled my spine.

I turned to the lone hallway I had assigned Brezniack and Moreno to search, adjacent to the Artistry Room we just explored.

The hallway extended far, bending out of sight into darkness. Lamps were nailed onto the wall, and the wallpaper looked like a pack of wolves clawed through it. Two doors were halfway down, across from each other.

The one on the right was ajar, and there was no sight or sound of Brezniack or Moreno. Vale darted to the lone cracked door on the right. I followed, concerned for his mental health. He had been hit hard. I knew he was trying to push forward to block the weight of his sister's death. If time had allowed, I would have preferred he sat outside a little while to decompress and keep guard at the door.

Vale turned to the doorframe, and I glanced at him. His eyes revealed a mind going a hundred miles an hour in all directions. His anxiety spread to me. Against my will, I relived the crime scene. The dead body from the pantry plummeted my sensorium, and the hack job on the face grimaced at me—I shook and repressed the terror. I needed to push through and feel later.

I had no choice. Yet, on a subconscious level, I was already losing.

We entered. The moonlight from the window revealed a master suite with a made bed at its center. Vale and I searched opposite corners. I scanned behind the door and found an antique desk. The top shelves contained various pictures and magazine clippings but nothing of importance.

From the other side of the room near Vale, a whimper broke through the rainstorm.

I turned around, and Vale stopped in his tracks at the sound.

My neck hairs spiked.

It came from the closet door, in the opposite corner of me, by the lone window. Vale crept around the bed to that door. He pressed his ear on the wood.

He glared at me.

Goosebumps grew on my arms.

Vale placed his hand on the knob, pointing his pistol forward.

He opened the door, and my jaw dropped.

Inside the closet, a woman trembled.

She pressed a gun to the side of her head. She had locks of dark hair that flowed down to her waist and wore the same black cloak as the static painting from the Artistry Room.

What the fuck? I thought.

Vale looked into what appeared like his sister's bright green eyes. They looked haunted. Her mouth twitched, and her legs shook. Sweat dripped down her pale, light skin.

I thought I was in a nightmare.

"Max, it's in your hands... I'm so sorry," Elara said, sounding relieved and petrified.

"It's okay... I'm here," Vale said, barely audible.

She then whispered a few words that sounded foreign.

"Just hand me the gun..." Vale brought out his shaky hand.

Elara closed her eyes and pulled the trigger. The bullet went through the side of her skull, and brain matter splattered the closet wall.

Vale screamed. His face froze in a state of horror, focused on the blood. It oozed out of her head. It was everywhere—on the walls, on the floor, on the ceiling... his sister's blood.

Terror gripped me, forcing me to stare. At some point, I walked to Elara's body.

Vale had yet to move, petrified.

"Take a deep breath," I said, placing my hand on his back and knowing that would do nothing. I grabbed a handkerchief from my trench coat and wiped the blood from Vale's frozen face.

He pulled his eyes away from the suicide. "This is her."

"How..." I said, helplessly entranced by the crime scene of the second body.

Vale did not answer. I felt he was trying to rationalize who was the other person in the kitchen pantry, and I didn't know. Hell, at this point, I had no idea what the fuck was going on. The case had zipped passed me, dragging my legs in the process. But of course, I didn't believe it.

Twenty-nine and a half years as an officer made me hard-wired to appear stoic until the evidence gave an explanation. Though I had a horrible feeling in my stomach that I tried to ignore. Much worse, I could not stand watching Vale's reaction, now twice, to what appeared to be his twin's murder… or suicide? He was a son to me. His pain had and always will feel worse than my own.

At this juncture, I thought Vale would be unable to continue the search. But to my surprise, he said, "I am thankful you brought me on this case." He smiled deliriously.

"How can you possibly think that right now?" I asked, noticing a spot of blood I missed on his chin.

"We need to keep searching."

"*What?*"

Vale darted out of the room back to the hallway.

"What is wrong with you?" I was not ready to keep going. I needed to pull myself together, to tell my mind to be numb just for a little longer. How could my old partner, who just witnessed his own sister commit suicide, be this disconnected?

I decompressed by radioing in for an ambulance. After I put away the walkie-talkie, I wanted to crawl into a hole and leave this nightmare. But once more, I found my adrenaline pushing my body forward, acknowledging I was not safe here.

I went back into the hallway and stopped in my tracks. There I saw the Vale I knew, standing in front of a door across from where we exited. A tear trailed down his face. I went over to comfort him, but he waved his hands to dismiss any fear, accidentally pushing the door open, revealing a stairwell descended to a basement.

"Sorry about that." Vale was unclear if he referred to the door or his teardrop.

I stared down a decrepit stairwell, once more the sidings torn and scratch marks plenty. At the bottom, a door cracked open.

Vale, already done crying, crept down the stairs, following the end point of his flashlight.

I followed, each step dipping into the depths of my memory only years of therapy could bring to the surface.

We reached the bottom and stood by the slightly ajar door. There, Vale took a deep breath and nudged it. His pistol and flashlight followed its swing. It felt like an eternity.

As the basement was unveiled, a chill shot down my spine. In the center of the room, Vale's flashlight caught the stillness of long soaked hair on a couch. The person sat, facing away.

"Freeze! Put your hands in the air!" I said with force, trying to overpower my heart pounding out of my chest.

The back of the person made no reaction to our entrance. Droplets of water trailed from the couch to a lone basement window on the right wall near the ceiling. I fixed back on the guest's hair. I needed to see if the person had a weapon and cautiously stepped around the couch. I paused when the side of the guest's face appeared.

As I would later learn, the woman was Marie Dalton, who Vale depicted in his diary entry about her childhood. Her eyes were empty, face pale, and a bent roman plug nose shot out. She seemed alive... at least not dead.

I walked into her field of vision and crouched to her eye level. She looked right through me. Fear squeezed my heart. For several seconds, the only sound was rain. Words left me.

"Lieutenant Price, Haddon Police," I finally said, falling back to routine.

She remained expressionless. There were no noticeable wounds or bruises, no blood, and no weapons in sight.

"Ma'am, what happened to you?" I asked.

Her face remained frozen.

"I want to help you. But I need you to communicate in any way you can."

She said nothing.

"Can you move?"

She did not.

Footsteps echoed from upstairs. I grabbed my walkie-talkie and pressed it to my lips. I paused, then clipped it back on my belt, concluding no one would listen to me tonight.

We needed to search the rest of the room to make sure it was safe.

"I'll trust you to stay here as I quickly peek around the place."

I was so captured by the frail woman I had not realized Vale stood right behind me. He did not appear terrified like me but instead curious. He always had the strangest ways to compartmentalize his emotions.

We walked to two closed doors in the far corner while keeping one eye on the woman. I gripped the closet doorknob. Sweat covered my palms.

"Some kind of situation we are in," Vale said casually, as if we all met for a cup of tea.

I swung it open—a power generator. I turned back. She remained on the couch.

"I will have to bring you downtown for questioning," Vale said, standing by the second closet door and opening it. A detached arm fell out.

I gaped, and my intestines twisted. I sprinted over.

All of the third body's fingers were cut off. And behind the curly black hair, once again, the skin of the face was carved off, just like the first body in the pantry. She also wore the same dark cloak. A pool of her blood covered the closet floor and pushed up against the ledge. This murder just happened. She again looked like Elara…

I stuck my head out for air, gasping. Marie stood six inches in front of us. Her eyes were now filled with life. My heart pushed to my throat, and we jolted back and drew our pistols. My leg brushed up against the detached arm. "Freeze!" I yelled.

She remained still. Then slowly, her face lost all emotion.

I swiftly took out my handcuffs and placed them around the woman's frail wrists. She provided no resistance. Slowly, she spun her head left to a corner. There, the wall had cracked open.

Vale raised his brow and glared at me. All our years as detectives had not prepared us for this moment. There was no protocol for this woman. "Excuse me, miss, I would like to take a tour," Vale said. He grabbed her by the wrist, and to my surprise, she effortlessly moved her limbs.

I pointed the gun at the opened wall. "You try to escape, and we will be forced to fire," I said.

The woman slowly walked over. The handcuffs rattled with each step. She pushed the wall open like a door. The opening led to a narrow hallway bordered by cinder blocks and a concrete floor.

I did not know where I was in the beat-up rancher anymore—I was just a lost soul in a labyrinth.

We stepped in. A wave of heat smacked me, and a musty smell grabbed my nostrils. Wires dangled from the ceiling and the sound of rain echoed down the hallway. We followed her and occasionally checked behind us. Sweat trailed down my face. We reached the end of the path. It broke left and expanded into a square room no more than fifteen by fifteen feet.

I stared in horror.

Hundreds of small dead birds were wedged along the border of the room, some skeletons, others still rotting.

The woman guided us to the center near a beat-up bed. She turned to the opposite wall of the dead birds. We shined our flashlight.

Blood blanketed the wall.

Each cinder brick had scribbles of symbols I had never seen before. Every mark was crisp. They paradoxically disconnected in an orderly fashion like a stack of abstract thoughts quarantined to their appropriate houses in a neighborhood.

When connected, a common theme appeared from the blood: *Vale's face.*

In fact, his face was the only detail I could recognize. The longer I stared, the more I could see his face appear through the drawings because my eyes needed adjustment to the different layers of blood. He existed in different forms. Some drawings were in excruciating detail; one even looked detailed enough to be confused as a red-tinted photograph. Others buried him in different shapes, contorting his body in positions I would expect to find at an art museum. I could not identify what he was doing in any of the drawings.

At this point, I could only be a witness to what was going on. My legs felt light, and my head disconnected from my body, dissociating from Dalton Manor. The case had won—and with such aggression. I had never been beaten mentally like this. I was merely a fly on the wall.

Vale, on the other hand, was more focused than ever.

He turned to the frail woman and straightened his browline frames. He studied her. She appeared decrepit. Her eyes stuck on him, and I could feel them crawl through his brain and rest in the back of his head.

Somehow, he remained composed.

"Impressive details, must have taken months to complete," Vale said in his smooth voice. He walked close to the wall of blood and pointed at what appeared to be a random symbol. "Any idea who the artist might be?"

The woman stayed silent.

"Miss, there's no need to be bashful." Vale walked over to the broken bed frame and sat on the post. I stood stunned. "Why does it appear like I am on this wall? On a normal case, that would be an excellent question to start with."

Vale smiled, but I could tell inside he was terrified and torn up. At least, for the sake of his sanity, I hoped he was. He continued, "But I don't think this is a normal case. Just like my partner whom you've met, I am a detective... of sorts. I used to be a cop, but now I tackle odds and ends in my own business venture." He made sure to stare into the depths of her dark eyes. "*Especially the odds...* and if you want to be specific, *the oddities.*" Vale let the word hang in the air. "There's something interesting about this drawing that I'm afraid I just need to get some clarification about. That is, of course, if you have an answer. If you don't, that's completely fine."

I furrowed my brow. I had no idea what he was talking about.

Vale rose and walked to the drawing. He said, "When I look close enough, I notice that every part of the drawing is painted with little straight lines. There are no curves in any stroke. I'm not an artist, and I can't interpret styles well, but when you combine that detail with bird's blood, there's a deliberate message you are trying to say. Would you happen to know what that is?"

Before the woman had the opportunity to answer, a scream echoed through the ceiling.

Once more, it sounded like Brezniack.

Vale reflexively gripped the woman's handcuffs. He smiled. "If you'll excuse my manners, miss. I will need you to follow us," Vale said, sprinting with her back into the cement block hallway.

Technically, I followed them. But at the time, I felt like I glided. Room to room, in a fog, a man lost. Somehow, we arrived back at the entrance of the manor. Brezniack had his hands on his knees, panting.

"What happened?" Vale asked in a concerned but soft voice.

"In the library at the end of the hall," Brezniack said in a high-pitched squeal. His features twisted in fear at the sight of the woman in handcuffs.

Before I could comment, Vale and the frail woman led the charge down the hall. I followed in a daze through the clouds. Once again, how we got there, I could not say. But after following the grimy head of Marie for a minute, my senses awoke. And the clouds parted, unveiling a library with towering bookshelves around the periphery.

Horror seized us—at least Vale and me.

In the library's center, Officer Moreno had bugged eyes and a wide-open mouth, like he was speaking at a different frequency than us, yet we still felt the effects of his words. He sucked the life out of the room, welcoming us to hell.

He held a shard of glass in his hand. A desk was overturned, several lamps knocked down, and a bookshelf had fallen. Slash marks were made around the room. And right below his feet, a white powder marked many lines over the top of each other.

And as if our entrance disturbed Moreno's trance, he passed out. We stepped closer.

"I beg you not to move," Vale said to Marie. He put his gun away and released her. To my surprise, she listened. Vale felt Moreno's pulse on his wrist and observed his breathing. He found nothing remarkable. "We must go upstairs, so if you'll please follow my lead."

"We can't just leave him here," I said.

"We won't… for long." Vale grabbed her arm.

The three of us dashed back through the haze to the entrance of Dalton Manor once more. There, at the edge of the foyer, Brezniack remained, now vomiting. He leaned his head outside into the night, where the pine trees watched. "I quit," Brezniack said in his high-pitched voice.

You're not happy your uncle got you this wonderful opportunity? I thought, too fried to speak.

"Take a deep breath," Vale said.

"Nothing will change my mind."

"Maybe take some time here; think about what you're doing."

"No. It's time to go…"

"First, your boss needs to file a report, and you're the only one who saw what happened," Vale said.

"No," Brezniack said. He gripped Vale's wrist and stared with his gray eyes. "We are not welcomed here."

I studied Brezniack. Anxiety filled his face, and sweat plummeted from his short black hair down to the spikes on his chin. He looked behind Vale at the frail woman, filled with terror.

"Explain yourself, Officer," I said, finally contributing something.

"I already quit. I'm leaving. I don't want to be seen anymore," Brezniack said.

"Tell me what I asked, then you can leave. You are a witness."

"Not with the air this thin. Demons weigh you down in these parts," Brezniack said as his eyes grew so wide, they appeared to be popping out of his sockets. He darted into the rain.

"Officer!" I yelled.

"I can't be seen, I can't be seen…" Brezniack said over and over, vanishing into the storm. In the distance, I heard a faint sound of the car engine starting and a car speeding off.

I turned to Vale. He had a concerned but energetic look on his face. "What in God's name is wrong with you?" I asked. This side of Vale was one I had never seen.

Vale did not answer and studied the frail woman in handcuffs. He was preoccupied, and I feared it was with all those skeletons of his, all the baggage about this one topic I hoped we would avoid on this case.

"Is your cult responsible?" I asked, holding my breath.

Vale manically chuckled and turned to me. His eyes once again stabbed me. He said, "It was never my cult, Price, or Elara's… That was only a word to help you understand where I came from. It is far more complicated—a world I tried to protect you from."

"What do you mean?" I asked, sighing.

"I need time... What a lovely night."

"How can you be so positive right now? This is madness. I'm terrified, I can't think straight, and none of the victims is even my twin sister. How are you standing?"

"With my legs, old man," Vale said, sticking out his fist.

I studied his steady hand, unmoved and in complete control. I noticed how my hands were still shaking.

Breathe and slow down the case, I thought in desperation, but on the contrary, I became dizzy. I decided never to use that damn saying again.

Our fists pounded, and we snapped our fingers.

Vale smirked. "Let's get to work."

THE BOARD GAME

THE REST OF the search was a blur. I appreciated, after years of therapy, how my recollection of that night became choppier with each death. Emotions left the further I entered Dalton Manor, and I was lucky to remember the key facts by the time Brezniack quit. After Vale's peculiar remark, all I recalled was that we searched the rest of the manor as well as the outside property and found nothing else important.

Everything else left my mind.

Until that point, I took pride in handling difficult cases. I prefer to observe how I feel and leave it alone. A craft I had carved over my years on the force.

As a result, the next memory I recalled came as no surprise. It was later that evening. And it involved the source that tipped me Dalton Manor's address, making me aware of Vale's title as Elara's emergency contact. I kept the name hidden on purpose, but I could tell Vale had already connected the dots. There was no need to bring my ex-wife up at the time.

I felt little around neurologist Dr. Madelyn Katz—indirectly dulling the aftereffects of Dalton Manor to let my memory properly function. I knew the case piqued her curiosity. She had loved challenges, which was why she originally chose neurology. She used to tell me there was no system in our body more misunderstood and untapped than the brain.

And over the past four years, her interests shifted to policy, earning a seat on the Dougray University Board of Governors.

In case those words are now obsolete, "The Board" ruled the city of Haddon. It was a proud creation by Washington. And I was born under the Board's jurisdiction in their earliest days, shortly after its approval to become the first test site for experimental diplomacy.

Madelyn was an example of the Board's ability to break the mold. She was the first woman in generations to get a seat in power—especially despite me. Yet, throughout her entire four years, people questioned her loyalty because of our divorce. And as a product, she tried to distance herself from me even more than usual. But for some painful reason, we always found a way to cross paths.

I knew Madelyn's goal well—she had repeated the same rhetoric to me many late evenings when we were married. Women needed to be treated as equal to men. Looking back, I never appreciated what she meant because I loved her and thought that was the same thing.

Madelyn was ahead of her time, and I was with everyone stuck at a standstill. I did not realize then how different equality and love were—both separate games. The latter I had lost.

I remembered hearing the sporadic sounds of machines and disarrayed voices in the emergency room hallway, oversaturated with citizens of Haddon from the storm. I left the sounds and walked down a series of hallways, each one emptier than the prior.

I reached my end goal, tucked away somewhere in the hospital. I was alone, no one in sight, and for a minute, there was silence.

Then the clang of footsteps caught my ear.

Madelyn walked down the empty hallway. Her hair was braided, shining against her radiant dark skin, and she wore a black turtleneck dress.

I tried to look away casually.

"Lieutenant Price."

I turned around and saw those eyes that had fooled me many times. I wanted her to go away, for her to just get out of my life. But it would never happen, even after being divorced for eleven years.

"Madelyn, just as beautiful as ever."

"Cut the crap."

I grinned.

"They are waiting on the MRI of your officer's brain to rule out any tumors or strokes, but I think both are unlikely. This is probably a psychiatric issue," Madelyn said, looking down at the ends of the hallway.

In the distance, I recognized several of her guards out of earshot.

"I believe you," I said, remembering all the medical rabble she would throw at me back in the day.

"Tell me everything about the injury."

I answered as thoroughly as I could, reciting my police report from the moment I heard Moreno scream until the EMTs came.

"Are you okay?" she asked, trying so hard to show empathy.

"Of course not."

"But you didn't actually see what happened?" Madelyn asked, already tired of being thoughtful.

"Just the aftermath, the only officer who did quit."

"You couldn't use that charm on him to get some info?"

"You give me too much credit."

"You know, this case is starting to get the Board's attention." Madelyn tapped her left foot.

"Clearly not enough of them. Maddie, no other officers came—a double homicide and a suicide. Seriously? This case is unreal. I'm lucky to walk out unharmed."

"Of course no one else came."

"What do you mean?" I asked.

"I did it behind their backs."

I dropped my jaw.

"Liam… someone on the Board is responsible for those deaths."

"Why didn't you tell me?" I asked.

"Because you wouldn't have taken the case."

"Why not any of your men?" I gestured to the guards at the end of the hallway, who stared away.

"We are a little busy with your quadrant," Madelyn said. "The Board wants to focus solely on what to do there in this storm, and you know how the dominoes fall from there."

"I hear it's already flooded a foot."

"It will only get worse," Madelyn said, unraveling the frustration I felt she meant to keep hidden.

"You predicted this would happen years ago. I bet you can use that to your advantage."

"No one cares at this point. All I'm doing now is counting down the days until I'm relegated off the damn Board. This case is all that's left. They made the first woman in decades a puppet…"

"No, they didn't," I said.

"Excuse me?" Madelyn glared and chilled my spine.

"You were praised for making it to the table your entire time."

"Liam, after all this, you're so thick sometimes… I was used to make the other six men look nobler and have one less person to negotiate with. When did anyone take my women right's platform seriously?"

I garbled.

"Never."

I paused, admitting defeat, then asked, "Any idea who else knows?"

"Not yet, but someone has to."

"How can you be so sure I didn't tell anyone?"

"Because you'd rather crawl halfway around the world than ask for a ride. If you'd like, I can certainly request for assistance."

"Appreciate the concern. But I think Vale and I will figure out a way to make it work."

"And how has the infamous Vale been doing?" Madelyn asked, her eyes burning through my skull.

"I'll be sure to send him your regards."

"You certainly have it all figured out. I swear, if you would just look at the world around you beyond a case."

"I'm a cop."

"Sometimes. Whether you want to believe it or not, there are other parts of the day you are just Liam Price. Yet you always tackle these big life cases, push everything else aside, and will not question anything unless it interrupts your personal objectives."

"Perhaps if you could do me a favor to help me down one of those cases?"

"Never," Madelyn hissed.

"I meant for Carl Moreno."

"Then yes?"

"Can you put him into a secure location?"

She stepped back into the fluorescent lighting and said, "I'll make sure it is done with people I trust within the hour."

I wrinkled my nose.

"Or again, I could have others search Dalton Manor."

"I dare not test your limits."

"Yet you always find a way."

I stared into her eyes and smiled. They looked like the autumn sky. I never hid how much I loved those eyes, if nothing else. I wanted to be mad at Madelyn for assigning me the case, but my mind was already too locked in. I needed to know who did this.

"But while we're here, I found something about Dalton Manor that might interest you," Madelyn said. She brought out a piece of paper that had a photo titled "A MANOR FOR ONE." "Once I found out we were meeting, I decided to wait until we were in person to show you. I found this in Dougray's Department of Journalism Archives."

I furrowed my brow.

"I guess you couldn't find anything about Dalton Manor online either?" Madelyn asked. "I made you a copy. It basically says Dalton Manor is a mental institution."

"But how?" A sinking feeling swirled in my stomach.

"The manor belonged to a medical lawyer in this hospital actually—his name was Dean Dalton. You can read the exact details, but he found a way through Dougray's system to privatize a manor a while back through a loophole. The Board fixed the error the next day. This was six years ago."

"Why would a man create his own mental hospital?"

"He designed it for his daughter," Madelyn said.

I scratched my chin. I did not know how to handle the news.

"Where's the girl?" she asked.

"At the station in her own cell. I don't plan for her to be there long."

"You're an idiot. You left her alone? You can't just keep her there."

"I interrogated her for a good hour at the station, but she said literally nothing. Maybe if I had some real help with men I trust, this wouldn't be an issue."

"Make it work, or else I will have to reconsider."

"Vale does not even have the luxury of a police officer's rights."

"And where even is Vale?"

"He insisted I drop him off at my townhouse before I went to the station."

"How is he handling her suicide?"

"I'm surprised you had enough interest to ask."

"If you're going to be an ass about it…"

I hesitated because I was not sure. He had been in an oddly calm state since his sister's suicide.

"You don't even know," she said, catching onto my thought process. I hated she could still do that.

"I will. We are working on a plan."

"Sure you are. You always are. Just keep me posted."

"Yup."

She turned to leave without saying goodbye, then stopped. "Hey, Liam."

"Yes?" I had not moved.

"Since we are actually somewhat agreeing today, I just want to make sure that neither of us knows what is going on, and moving Carl Moreno is a precautionary measure for something bigger."

"Want to grab a soda later?"

Madelyn shook her head. "Your granddaughter's back to school."

"I'm sure she's excited."

"You should have said goodbye."

"Novah didn't want that," I said, trying not to reveal I mixed up the dates. "I thought if I left everything alone with her, it would be easier on everyone."

"Whatever fits in that grand scheme of yours." Madelyn turned away, pressed the entrance button to open the doors, and left.

I sighed. *It's great when you are a brilliant neurologist and know everything about the brain, but frustrating when you have to actually use it for human contact. Especially when you live with someone for twenty-five years, sometimes showing emotion can lead to empathy—a foreign concept to some.*

I decided to gaze at the empty hallway for a moment, but it quickly turned into minutes where I rotted in the hell I had created.

For what felt like the thousandth time already, I reviewed the three dead bodies—I would never forget them. How could I? The way the two murder victims' faces were skinned off so brutally. Then the suicide... I had only witnessed a suicide one other time, but it was from a distance and from a separate room—this was front and center to a poor mind that would rather explode into smithereens than remain intact. And the body in the basement with the detached arm... I wanted to throw up.

But I suppressed the urge until Marie Dalton plagued my mind. I felt like she was watching me, and, on a normal case, I'd be okay with that. Cases had that effect on me. But I felt weaker thinking of her, more helpless, opening up all my flaws. Some people were just evil to me—call it a hunch. She certainly felt evil, more than anyone I had ever met—a black hole, a darkness I could never have fathomed, even in my own hell.

But was she the root of it, or someone else? I could not say. Regardless, her mental presence sucked me further—and finally, I entered the source of my own evil. *Please, not now...* I thought. But I knew I had no say. Over and over, I replayed the single night that had shaped the rest of my life.

The memory involved Novah's mother... my deceased daughter. In a flash, my body left the hospital and teleported to the mahogany wood at my local watering hole. I remember tapping my fingers on it with great anxiety.

I took my daughter out that night. I told her everything about her mother and me and why I needed to get a divorce. I told her it was all my fault, and if there was anyone she should be mad at, it was me. I was a complete mess.

And you know what she did?

She told me she was proud of me and that all she ever wants is for me to be happy, and that I am an amazing grandfather. My daughter was an angel before her death.

I never like to think about how much I had to drink that night because the sad answer was, I did not down much compared to normal. I had sobered up that day to tell my daughter, my dear sweet Sarina, and it was the first time I had done so in months. I was planning to go back to my usual pace when I got home. So I just had those two glasses of whiskey or whatever, just to keep the shakes off. *Sarina...*

I paused and opened my eyes, realizing I was alone, standing stoic in an abandoned hallway. I wanted to lose the thought and run away from this place, but the pause was just a speed bump. I rolled onward.

Sarina had offered to drive. But I was too stubborn, or perhaps she didn't know me any other way to tell the difference. The crash didn't even require drinks; black ice covered the road. We were going to drift off anyway, but those two whiskeys were enough to delay my reaction to slow down, but not close to numbing me. I was too awake. I was too aware. I watched the entire thing happen.

Just like the bodies from Dalton Manor, Sarina's has never left me. She twisted to the conformity of the tree… Mother Nature won. She couldn't even scream.

How do you recover? It's simple. You can't.

All I could do was promised myself I'd never leave whiskey again.

I would have done anything that night to be plastered in that crash. I could have hated myself in the most blinding way possible, but the details are too real to face. My family was too real to face.

So I cut off any chance of a friendship with Madelyn—I couldn't face her. I left my granddaughter, who was only two. And worst, I made Madelyn tell Novah her mother died in a car crash because I couldn't stomach it.

That was eleven years ago. At the time, I thought I was a good man. I saw the world my own way, and that was it, trapped in the illusion that every action I took was an attempt to do the right thing. I now know that's impossible and the exact way you kill people.

Shortly after my life crumbled, I was assigned to break in a younger cop, "the infamous Max Vale," as Madelyn had said.

Somehow he turned my world upside down even more. His upbringing just touched the surface.

I stopped. *What am I doing?*

Marie Dalton, my biggest lead, was alone in a jail cell at the police station, and an officer I was to guide through Dalton Manor lay unconscious in the emergency room. But here I stood, internally groaning over my life. The realization snapped me back to the present.

I paced back through the hallways into the pandemonium in the emergency department, packed full of people. I slid into a room that Madelyn had requested to keep open for just Moreno.

The walls were made of glass. The back one curved outward, overlooking a parking lot—at least that was what you would see if the curtains were open. I had shut them the moment the doctors left. I sat in a chair by the door with my pistol in my pocket. I only met with Madelyn in a secluded part of the hospital at her request. She had a way of twisting my arm.

I did not know what was going on with Moreno or if anyone had an interest. But Vale's arrival rebirthed my paranoia. Someone was watching me. I needed to keep my eyes open, but darkness blanketed me, tempting rest. I drowned out the beeping heart monitors and oxygen levels and whatever else those machines were. They stared at me. Within a minute, my vision adjusted, and Moreno started to appear from the nothingness I had been studying. His spiffy hair now sprawled over his face, something I had never seen. At least he looked healthier in the dark and at peace.

But I did not sit in there for Moreno. In fact, I cared little for him anymore.

I hid in there because of Vale. He was my biggest asset in solving the case, and I knew the inner workings of his approach. The man needed space at times. He used to sit at his desk at the station in the late hours of the night once everyone left, moving his pen cap on and off, cleaning his browline glasses, reordering his files for the hundredth time. The repetitive motions helped him think. Though he did not formally ask, he wanted to treat my townhouse as home base during the case.

Is Vale okay? I thought. Like Moreno, he was a changed man over the past year. And his ties to the case darkened my imagination.

I decided to investigate the matter further. I brought out my phone and called a person I had built trust with the past few years to investigate Vale behind the scenes. I left a brief message, one of many I had done to that point in time, but I knew the person would help even if he didn't already have the answer.

"Well… we'll see where that one goes…" I said, staring into space.

My mind drifted for a while, decompressing the horrors of the evening. I was not ready to look at the article Madelyn handed over. I needed to relax. So I did the one thing I always resorted to, contemplate what space model I was going to purchase next and which book about intergalactic travel I was going to read.

My mouth morphed to a smile; I couldn't help it. There was this new book about the potential of building a portal from Earth to Mars as a potential way to expedite civilization.

It was a fan-freaking-tastic book. I loved the detail of the technology theorized to stabilize a transfer while maintaining the cellular integrity of humans. I had been obsessed for years. Vale always thought it was odd, but he never appreciated the sciences—and in all honesty, he might be the last person to decide what was weird and what was not.

I continued to get lost in space, and unintentionally, I dozed off into it. Time ticked by as I slept. At some point, Moreno mumbled. I shot my head up, recalibrating. He remained motionless. The machines from the hallway and the room continued their long-fought battle of which sound could be the most annoying.

Then Moreno's words became audible. I did not recognize what he was saying. A chill shot down my spine.

"Moreno, can you hear me?" I asked.

He spoke louder in the same gibberish, enough for me to notice anger in his tone.

I rose from my seat and walked to his bedside. I pressed the page button next to the bed for a nurse.

He became quiet. Only the machines had their opinions to share.

"Speak to me if you can," I said.

In response, Moreno sat up. His eyes rolled behind his head and his body shook, banging the bed against the floor.

I yelled into the hallway for assistance and became nauseous. I sprinted back to him.

His heart monitored buzzed.

"*The neck. The neck. The neck,*" Moreno said. His voice was deeper than I had ever heard.

"Wake up!" I yelled and shook his shoulders. I immediately regretted the decision.

He placed his hands on my neck. I gasped.

"*The neck. The neck. The neck... Something to fill the hole...*"

I grabbed his wrists, trying to make breathing room. But his grip tightened, and he grimaced. His white eyes stared at me, possessed. "*The neck. The neck. The neck.*"

I was petrified. Seconds passed.

Right before I turned blue, Moreno's hands released. I tossed my body to the wall out of his reach, panting.

Moreno flopped back onto the mattress and passed out.

A short while later, I stormed into my townhouse's living room, where Vale had situated himself, and described the details of Moreno's attack.

"You keep yourself busy," Vale said in his usual elegant, lyrical flow. He readjusted his browline glasses and rolled up the sleeves of his sleek navy dress shirt under a gray floral vest.

"How do you find Moreno strangling me anything but terrifying?"

"It is terrifying. Does that make you feel better?"

"Well, no."

"Terror rules my body only when I allow it to. I see the terror in your story, Price, just as with this whole night. I cannot control those feelings. But what I can control is my response."

"Why not be scared like the rest of us?" I asked, annoyed. I scratched my chin and scanned my living room for the first time, alarmed but not surprised by the appearance. I had walked into my townhouse so fried and ready to ramble to Vale that I did not process how peculiar it now looked with my guest's new arrangements.

It was as spotless as it had been in a long while.

The furniture had been pushed to a side of the room ordered by size from left to right. A folded-out table was pressed against a wall covered in photographs, cutouts from textbooks, and old newspaper clippings. They were in evenly spaced rows. Books covered the surface to the left, and one was open in the center. On the ground next to the table, a small red paint bucket was unopened near a brush. Fresh tulips were in a navy rectangular vase at the far corner of the desk next to a white tragedy mask I had seen in Vale's old home.

"I need to stay for a few days," Vale said.

"Where are my spaceship models?"

"They're in your bedroom, along with all those Dougray University signs of yours—don't worry, they're all intact." Vale lifted his arms at the sight of my shoulders tensing. "Is that all you've been doing since I left?"

"Seriously?"

"You're more of a sailboat in the bottle type of fellow, no?"

"Come on, Vale," I said, quivering. "You know that was Sarina's hobby we'd do together."

"I'm just checking on my mentor's well-being."

"I am doing great," I said with a snarl. "Now stop playing games. Tell me what the hell you have been doing since you left our quadrant. You have been acting strange this whole evening, and you keep putting the question off."

"I'm sorry to have blown off your curiosity. I just thought we had enough stresses for the evening."

"Why would I find your answer stressful?" I asked.

"Price, I am a private detective who focuses on specific cases due to my expertise. I rule out the unexplainable activity. Ghosts, spirits... whatever you want to call them. I prove they are not real."

I froze. I still was not sure if he was serious. But after each passing second of his hazel eyes waiting for my reaction, my uneasiness turned to concern. "Are you sure that's a good idea?"

The change in my tone startled Vale.

"Come on. I know where to look better than anyone to disprove those theories."

"I'm just worried about you. Why do that to yourself?"

"Because no one should live the life Elara and I did." Vale slammed his fist on the table he had set up.

"It's your life. I won't ever stop you. I just know how it scarred you."

"I promise you I am well."

"Then what can I say, Vale? I am happy you have found work you are passionate about."

"You've always been a terrible liar."

"I care, that's all. I honestly was not suspecting your childhood cult—or whatever you want to call it…"

"Those bizarre static paintings were reminiscent… but it was not until those drawings in the basement where I scratched my head. The painter used birds' blood and constructed it in a way that makes me very suspicious. Growing up, we were taught birds' blood symbolized elevation from our world into the next, like a portal. And the way the painting was constructed was with only straight lines. That might appear to be an ordinary detail, but I promise you it is much more complicated, with a terrible dark history. But in short, it's a symbol we grew up using. In fact, it is used throughout most cultures and religions."

"Do you think the woman is responsible?" I asked, unsure how much I wanted to go into "terrible dark histories" this evening.

"I cannot say."

"And do you know why your face is on the walls?"

"An even greater mystery. One I must sleep on."

"Her name is Marie Dalton," I said and took out the article copy Madelyn gave me. "Found a few trails to lead me to her name."

Vale snagged the paper from my grasp. And read the article in great suspense over the next minute. Once finished, he stuck out his arm and let the paper dangle. "Hello, Marie."

"I was hoping you could ask her a few questions tonight," I said.

Vale pressed his browline glasses up the bridge of his nose. He stuck his hands in the pockets of his flowered gray vest and paced the room. He stopped by the curtains of the front window and closed his eyes. "Tomorrow. You need rest, Lieutenant."

"Don't we all. We need to jump on this now."

"At this moment, I'm afraid I do not know what to ask her. I need to do more research." Vale shifted his attention to his newly made workspace.

"What's all of this?"

"The literature I keep in my luggage. It is the latest news on hauntings around the country, an extensive history of the ever-evolving and fading cults in our world, and of course, many scriptures from my upbringing."

"I thought you burned all those books," I said, noticing the top one on the pile looked like a children's novel for nursery rhymes.

"I left that world, and I never will be part of that group again. But these books belonged to deceased family members I inherited over the years. We owe it to ourselves to never burn history."

"Jesus, Vale, you're worrying me. I mean, you're actually fucking making me scared. What the hell are you looking for with this shit?" I asked.

"A starting point."

"She's waiting for you at the station."

"I bet she is. But, how will I know what she is saying without studying the language?"

I furrowed my brow.

"Get some rest, Price. I promise we will start early."

I felt too tired to argue, and little did I know at the time, the Deus—the original universe —wanted Vale to be left to his craft...

III
ABERRATION

Diary entry written by Max Vale

"GOOD AFTERNOON, SWEETIE." Shyla flipped through some papers on her desk.

"Good afternoon, Mommy," Marie said.

"How has your week been?"

"Fun. The weather has been more humid than normal this time in August."

"That is... true," Shyla said. She felt Marie sounded more like an adult over the past few months since her ninth birthday. As if after each silent spell, her vocabulary improved by another grade level. At the same time, there were certain intricacies Marie found enjoyment in that made her still seem like a child. "What did you do that was fun?"

"Played around the sprinkler, watched a few cartoons, ate an ice pop... oh! I also read a few magazines you had from your old office's waiting room."

"Oh my, I didn't realize I had any more of those. I guess I must have brought a few back over the years for Nana..." Shyla said.

"Yes, Mommy, there were some with pretty buildings in this one magazine. I really like the decorations."

"Nana would be so happy to hear that. You sound just like her!"

"I understand why she loved designing. The way the colors work off each other with an actual purpose really opened my eyes. I guess I always thought colors just existed. I never got to choose what was yellow, what was blue. But for the first time, I am learning there can be a way to choose colors that best suit you." Marie caught her breath.

Shyla was floored. She had never heard Marie talk with this much energy. And she never mentioned anything about liking art before. Shyla wanted to harness this energy. "That's wonderful you liked the art so much! But I'm still having a little difficulty understanding what you mean, sweetie."

"It's the organization behind the colors."

Shyla paused, and scribbled on her sheet, then asked, "When you say organization, you mean the arrangement of the colors?"

"Yes, Mommy," Marie said. She had not moved since the beginning of the session.

"A very interesting way to put it."

"What about you?"

"Me? When I see a painting I like? The first word that comes to my mind would be 'beautiful'… the organization you enjoy comes from endless hours working towards a vision."

"A vision?"

"Yes, you need a goal to work towards when you are painting. At least that is what Nana did when she designed clothes."

"Other people feel colors too?" Marie asked.

"That's a fun way to look at it. They create a vision in their mind and work towards it."

"I thought it was just me who can feel colors…" Marie started to breathe faster. "They come and go all around me."

"What do these colors feel like?"

"Heaviness, they make me feel like I have been swallowed. Like I'm sinking to the bottom of the ocean. The only problem is in darkness, there's no way to tell if there's a bottom. All I feel are the colors that appear around me."

"When do you feel this way?"

"A few times a week."

"How do you know you are going into this darkness?"

"My stomach gets nauseous. Then I sink into the darkness."

"Why do you use the word darkness?"

"Nothing else is there besides the colors."

"You get nauseous then feel like you are losing consciousness?"

"No. That reminds me of a nap. Like the time I fell off my swing when I was three. This feeling of nausea removes me from the world."

"You cannot recognize the world around you?"

"Not the way we see it now."

"But you told me it was all darkness."

"Darkness is just as much a feeling, Mommy. I feel darkness, this heaviness… this sinking… with the colors. You know what I'm talking about, right, Mommy?"

"I do now, sweetie. How long do you have these feelings?"

"I never know. I have no time there," Marie said. Her voice was becoming empty. "Time does not exist the same way in darkness."

"You feel nauseous. Then have a sinking feeling for an unknown time, then you wake up?"

"Yes."

"Do you remember when the darkness began?"

"I never thought about it… I guess the kitten dragged me down there."

Shyla's shoulders tensed. It had been the first time Marie mentioned Graylin on her own since therapy started. "How?"

"There was something not right about her."

"What do you mean?"

"You, Papa, and Nana were different colors than her. She was always blue."

"And what are we?"

"Shades of yellow and green mostly."

"Why did it matter that the kitten was blue?"

"Because she needed to be part of the family," Marie said flatly. "You told me she would be, and she wasn't. I needed to open up her neck and figure out why her head was not like the rest of the family. She was detached."

"Detached…" Shyla's voice was quiet.

"Yes, Mommy. Her wiring was not connected to me. I needed a closer look."

"Then why did you break her neck?"

"Because I felt the darkness swallow the kitten, and it brought me in with her. It had been knocking."

"Knocking?"

"Yes, Mommy, the darkness had been knocking. It felt like someone was waiting on our doorstep, and once in a while, it knocked to remind me that it should come inside."

Shyla paused for a long moment. "Did the knocking start the day you slipped into the darkness with Graylin?"

"For a while, I thought so. But then I realized it happened before."

"When?"

"With Papa."

"What do you mean?"

"The way you and Papa talk to each other. The knocking gets especially loud when Papa yells. I never thought of it like knocking before Graylin. I just thought I had a tummyache… but now I know."

"I'm sorry you heard us, Marie… Papa and I love each other. And we need to work on talking to each other." Shyla's hands shook.

Marie kept quiet.

"That's when it started?" Shyla asked.

"I don't think so. Before then, Mommy," Marie said, shaking her head. "That's just when the knocking was the loudest."

"Oh…" Shyla said, empty.

"I remember the knocking when Jimmy Balego pushed me into the bathroom door when I was six."

"Marie, I had no idea."

"I was afraid to tell you."

"You can always tell me anything, baby."

"But actually… that's not it either." Marie shook her head. "Come to think of it, maybe the knocking started even before then. Maybe it was when I was four, and you and Papa told me I wasn't getting a younger brother after all."

Shyla became rigid, unable to speak.

Marie scrunched her face for a long moment, then said, "Maybe the knocking was just always there." The intensity in her eyes faded with the realization.

Shyla's shoulders sank into the chair. She dropped her papers on her desk and stared at her daughter. "The darkness was always there?"

"Don't worry, the knocking stopped once the darkness came in with the kitten."

"When you don't feel the darkness, where does it go?"

"I don't know where it hides."

"Do you feel the darkness now?"

"Not yet. But I am becoming nauseous. That's how I know it's coming." Marie was pale.

Shyla rose from her chair and walked around the large desk. She sat on one knee next to Marie. Tears trailed down Shyla's face as she hugged her daughter and stroked her cheek for a minute. "Marie."

"Yes, Mommy?"

"I love you. More than you will ever know. No matter how dark you feel your world gets, I promise you you're never alone. I will always be here. We're going to find out why this is happening, baby. I promise."

"My friends know why. I keep trying to get it out of them, but they said they can only guide me to the truth." Marie turned her head to the chair next to her. Agnes, Clarabelle, and Ragg stared back, lifeless.

In the evening, Shyla peeked into Marie's bedroom. Marie lay in peace under her pink floral covers, snuggling with her dolls. She smiled. Through all the chaos the past year had brought, she found peace singing to her daughter. It was a constant that she leaned on as a crutch.

She walked into the room. And a chill raised her neck hairs from a gust of wind. Shyla walked to the open window above the toy chest, intending to close it, but froze. A piece of black cloth stuck out of the chest. She quietly lifted the lid.

Her heart crumbled.

The black silk cloth was cut into pieces amongst Marie's toys. Shyla picked up a square of it and let the smooth texture slide in her hands, remembering all the years she slept with it as a child. The wind blew on her face, numbing her even more.

Shyla turned back to her daughter and jumped.

Ragg's head stuck out of the sheets, staring at her with its beady black eyes.

End of diary entry

*   *   *

I awoke in the middle of the night to the sound of footsteps in the hallway.

They belonged to Vale. He had the tendency to walk with his heels, like an elephant stomping. I tracked the sound. He went into each room for several minutes at a time. Once in a while, I heard the clang of objects being bumped or moved.

What was he doing? I thought. *Maybe he entered my whiskey collection after I dozed off?*

Then he lightened his steps as he approached my door. For some reason, I closed my eyes like I was pretending to sleep.

The door creaked open.

What the hell is going on? I thought.

Footsteps tiptoed into my room. I heard the familiar whisper of Vale, lost in his own conversation. I was paralyzed but not worried. I felt he was awake and consciously aware of what he was doing. I could have awoken and demanded answers, but I thought observing would shed more light on his motives.

Vale opened and closed different shelves around my room for the next minute, and he lifted different models of spaceships and space civilizations I had spent years assembling.

He better not drop those, I thought, acknowledging the absurdity of my priorities.

He then shuffled through the giant stack of my *Haddon Herald* newspapers I had in piles around my room, flicking through the many pages. At one point, he opened my closet door and checked under my bed. He never came close to me. In fact, I swore I heard a sigh of relief when it seemed his full attention was on me. Once he left my room, I traced his footsteps to my bathroom. The faucet turned on for several minutes. Then the water stopped, and I heard no sound.

I decided to lay motionless for a long while, waiting for more footsteps. But no such noise came. I was confused and felt the need to investigate. I opened my eyes and quietly slid out of bed. I briefly checked my entire room to find a clue as to what Vale was doing. Nothing appeared taken.

Then I cracked my door open and slipped out. The bathroom light was on at the opposite end of the hall. I crept down, dodging areas of the floor I knew creaked. I passed Vale's bedroom and noticed nothing out of place in his room. When I reached the bathroom door, I placed my ear against the wood.

I heard breathing and had a terrible flashback to the night prior. Elara's eyes appeared in my head, then she shot herself, turning into television static.

I came back to the present. I knocked on the door. Vale did not answer. So I nudged it open and peeked in my head. Vale lay on the bathroom rug, still. His eyes were wide open, body rigid, fingers clenched. My heart sunk. "Vale…" I said, weakened.

He did not respond. He was breathing.

I was paralyzed. I wanted to help yet was afraid I was interrupting him—I didn't know what he did anymore since he left Haddon. So, I decided to watch him for a short time to make sure he was okay.

At first, he did not acknowledge my presence, but then I stepped into the bathroom. "Go away," he said faintly.

My heart skipped. I felt like I was caught. I closed the door and went back to my bedroom. The longer I thought about what I had just witnessed, the more I was convinced he was having an anxiety attack.

He never had one when we were partners, I thought. *How do I mention this to him?*

I reentered my bedroom and made sure all the models Sarina and I assembled were not broken—and they were fine… thank God.

I then turned to my piles of *Haddon Herald* newspapers in the corner. They were in a mess, just like how I left them. But the piles seemed larger, and a corner of bookbinding stuck out. I moved my hands through the papers I'd collected over the years and noticed several hardcover novels were buried and spread open.

I picked up one.

The Life and Philosophy of Os, the title said. And a picture of a handsome, well-put-together male I'd seen many times. He had a buzz cut, olive skin, and an infectious smile that complimented his three-piece suit and gentle green eyes.

The man was my inspiration, and soon, he would replace Madelyn's seat on the Board.

Even though I was proud of what Madelyn had done, I counted the days until she left in secrecy. At the time, I thought no one was better suited to be on the Board than Os.

Why did Vale search through these? I thought.

I turned to my bookshelf. It was such a mess I had not noticed on my initial scan that all five of his autobiographies were taken out. I gathered the books—each completely covered in my notes and highlighted phrases—and placed them back in their respective unorganized piles on my shelves.

I turned back to my spacecrafts and figurines again, feeling antsy, and this time verified all the ones I had built on my own after Sarina's death were intact. In the background, a poster of Haddon was taped by the moonlight from my window. My gaze eventually wandered to it, and I sighed.

It highlighted the neighborhoods. Once the Board took over, they merged a struggling city, back then called Camden, and its surrounding towns into the foundation of what became a metropolis. Then they redistricted the sections into four quadrants as a nod of respect to the layout used in Washington. The Northeast—my and Vale's old quadrant—was by far the most notorious for crime.

But damn, did I miss those days together. We knew every back road, alleyway, and hellhole in that place. On the other hand, the other three quadrants had undergone massive gentrification since the Board began, with pockets of neighborhoods showing extreme growth—like where Dougray University existed along the river against the Northwest portion. Vale liked to say the Board quarantined. But I disagreed with him and thought growth was good for the city. What was originally Camden had never been better.

In all, a majority of the crime moved into the Northeast. And at the moment, I rationalized that the wall and turret guns they built were a necessity to keep felonies out of the other quadrants. At this stage of my life, I am ashamed to think that was my rationale back then. But I understood why I felt that way. No further than a foot away, a badge hung next to the map, my Haddon Child Army Badge—my inspiration for being an officer. Those summers I spent incognito in the Northeast. My job was to overhear rumors for the officers in Haddon.

Vale was quick to call out these summers as heinous. I always disregarded the notion.

My mind wandered back to Vale as I drifted to bed.

I then noticed underneath the frame a giant stack of all the posters I had of Dougray University. I collected these throughout my life and hung them all over my townhouse. Vale must have not just taken the posters down in his temporary office but throughout my entire residence.

What is going on with him? I thought.

I lay back down in bed and closed my eyes, confused.

I strategized when would be the right time to talk to him about what I just witnessed, if anything, to take my mind off Dalton Manor—the carved corpses and the static paintings kept flashing into my conscious.

I could not sleep for those reasons and because, above all, I worried for him.

Hours later, to my surprise, my alarm woke me up. It blasted a news segment I would listen to every morning.

I lifted my body, beyond tired, and zoned out to the voice as I tried to get out of bed. It belonged to the very man of the autobiographies that Vale searched.

The Os Daily Science Blast—oh, did I love his passion for pushing the boundaries of space philosophy. It made me excited for what he could do with the Board. It would awaken my mind every sunrise into a different world and get me elated to start constructing the next space model of his that would be coming out.

On a normal day, his smooth deep, presidential voice relaxed me and filled a part of my soul, but not today. I needed to check on Vale. My worry made me feel like a needle pricked my spine. And instead, Os's voice sounded more on edge and paranoid than I was used to.

I walked out of my bedroom and back to the bathroom door. I had not heard any footsteps in the night. I pressed my ear against the door and heard no sound.

You fool! I thought. I worried the rest of the night he was overdosing or seriously injured—and still, I stupidly fell asleep. I had no idea what he could have gotten himself into in the past year.

I shouldn't be this worried about giving him space. I needed to take action, I thought. I opened the door. And Vale was not in there. *How could that be?* I thought. *Did I not hear his loud footsteps when I was asleep?* I couldn't believe it.

I heard movement from the front of the house. I followed it down the hallway into the kitchen. It was there I heard a faint radio voice that I concluded to be from my living room across the way in Vale's temporary office.

I grimaced. Unlike the calmness Os provided to me on a normal day, this voice did the exact opposite. At once, I was agitated, as if I could feel the tension through the speaker grabbing my face. It was a grimy voice, and it completely cut me out of my world without warning.

"Sixty-five years ago, I mean sixty-five years ago now! We all know the story. We all know those several leaders from Dougray who wrote this so-called evidence-based review that 'claimed' to have projected the stagnation of democracy was unfixable without radical action. It was this core journal review those monsters used to request a test city to experiment on how to optimize our government's efficiency. Of course, even with the extreme partisanship, they voted yes—the one thing they could agree on was their inability to agree—to grant that seventy-year window to exercise this idea."

I trudged my way to the source of the voice in the living room.

"Then, just like that, the infamous Board was created. We all heard what it was supposed to become... It was supposed to put Haddon at the forefront of experimental diplomacy—a think-tank for democracy. But we know what it is—unconstitutional! Sixty-five years of this! And now the national media is finally noticing this unacceptable flooding in the Northeast, sourced not from a storm, but rather from neglecting the same issues in the infrastructure that were always there! Only this time, we have strayed further from what the Founding Fathers intended than ever!"

Finally, when I reached the doorframe, I managed to block out the radio—because I saw Vale. He scribbled away in a notebook. I did not make a sound and studied him. He occasionally glanced upward, pointing to pictures he had taken of different rooms in Dalton Manor. Several more rows of newspaper articles and pieces of paper were added to my wall. Another table appeared, perpendicular to the other table wedge in a corner. A really old beat-up laptop and printer sat on it. Each wire had a bread tag clamp and was taped to the table edge.

"Did you sleep well?" Vale asked as if he had eyes in the back of his skull.

"I've had better."

"Appreciate these moments of lost sleep. One day, that is all we will do."

"How was the rest of the evening?"

"Reviewed our search, took detailed notes on our timeline, made countless failed attempts to find more information about Dalton Manor."

"And after that—"

"Reflected." Vale turned around to me. His eyes looked awake, but the dark circles revealed how little sleep he had gotten.

"Are you okay?"

"I'm well. In fact, I have rarely been better." Vale did not give me time to ask a follow-up question. "I think I have a lead, but it's not where you would expect."

"We need to question Marie Dalton, and we don't know how much time we have with her." I decided to avoid talking about his anxiety attack while he was working and guide the conversation about the case.

"We will. But there is a detail that drastically changes my approach with her…"

"Okay…" My jaw stiffened, and a question popped into my mind.

"What?" Vale asked, picking up my glare.

"What's this crap on the radio?"

"The news."

"I've just never heard you listen to this before."

"A lot changes your perception when you leave this city, Price. Now come, we must follow this lead."

We went back and forth a bit more. Then I gave in. And with a sense of urgency, we dressed for the day. I decided to wait to discuss what I saw last night, hoping he would confess to me about his anxiety attack soon enough.

To my surprise, in the matter of a half-hour, we found ourselves in the Medical Examiner's office.

"Quite the interesting case. A fugue in many ways," Dr. Sarkis, the coroner, said. He grabbed a pot of coffee off the burner and turned to Vale.

"You know I don't drink coffee," Vale said.

"Thought a year off might have changed your mind." Dr. Sarkis poured his own cup and mine. He was a large man with a square chin and a long white ponytail draping over his teal scrubs. The steam fogged up his dark-rimmed glasses as he took a sip. He guided us out of his kitchen and into the coroner's office.

I wrinkled my nose. The smell of formaldehyde was distinct, one I never grew fond of over my years visiting our old friend. A long row of metal beds traversed a never-ending ledge off the wall. Some beds were occupied and blanketed. Pipes covered the ceiling, and the absence of windows made the artificial light gloomy. Dr. Sarkis led us to the covered hills in the middle of the room.

"For someone who does not see much light, you're always a ball of sunshine," Vale said.

"Life is brighter when you choose to surround yourself with the dead. Like that storm, it will already be over by the afternoon! It changed its course out to the Atlantic."

"True, the rain will stop. But no one told my quadrant that. We're flooded nearly a foot and a half now," I said, sipping my coffee from a mug. My team had been messaging me all morning with updates.

"And that news is problematic, I give you that," Dr. Sarkis said, "I hear we will have to use Dougray's gymnasium for beds; I'm always on edge with mixing. And to think the Board had the option to prevent this if they just paid attention to the Northeast infrastructure."

"They're shooting themselves in the foot," Vale said with a hint of sarcasm only I could detect.

"They will hear it from me. This is embarrassing!"

"Happy to see we can affect your spirits."

"Didn't take long." Dr. Sarkis winked and sipped his coffee.

"What with the case did you mean by 'fugue'?" I asked.

Dr. Sarkis shook his head, flicking his ponytail once back and forth to shift gears. He pressed his hands together. "Most bodies come in here boding a few questions that only an examination can answer. But this one has many layers; I'm still working out the parts… Three bodies. One I'm sorry to say was your twin. Coincidentally, she was the only body not dismembered."

"Not counting her head?" Vale asked. I was surprised by his apathetic tone.

Dr. Sarkis made no response to his comment, as if he did not hear it, and swiftly snagged each sheet to expose their bodies. Weirdly, they were all around the same height and had similar body shapes. Each had a separate sheet covering their head. Dr. Sarkis stood in front of Elara's body—the only one with intact hands. "Self-inflicted, and the angle of the bullet was forgiving enough to make a positive ID match from Ted Billars since you were a bit busy last evening."

My ears perked. The name was one of the two suspects I had at the start of the case, and I had explained that in great detail to Vale right after I picked him up from the train station. Before he shooed the name away, if I tackled this case on my own, I would replay Ted Billars's interview, in aim for the suspect to provide direction, getting lost in his dialogue, calculating any angle to go against his story.

But Vale's entrance into the case stripped my usual process—just like the old days. As he suspected on the initial car ride, the name "Ted Billars" would hold greater value to me as opposed to the case.

Because the case will go against the standard dimension of investigation.

At the time, I could not realize that, for I had not yet plunged into the darkness. Though it was knocking, waiting to drag me down... I think it had for decades.

I simply chose not to listen.

Dr. Sarkis continued, out of my mind.

"The other two, we'll have to wait a good seven to ten days easily for the DNA results because they are missing their fingers, their skin to their face, and each has three lacerations on the right lateral part of their necks. Whoever did this was kind enough to do a hack job around the eyes and mouth to leave me a few eyelashes on each body. You know I like to use those for DNA."

"You hinted about their backs during your coffee break," I said, bringing him back.

"Why, one of the strangest things I have seen..." Dr. Sarkis tipped the corpse of Elara Vale to her side.

I froze.

"The level of her C8 to S1 vertebrae is completely covered in scars. An uncomfortable amount overtopping each other in all directions—I counted eighty-two distinct markings on this one. There's probably more."

Vale's posture straightened, exuberating renewed confidence for reasons I was not sure. At least I could not see a connection.

"Not all the markings are similar widths, so different sources caused them," Dr. Sarkis said.

"How bad are the other two?" I asked.

"The one on the left... sixty-four. The one of the right one hundred and eighteen."

"You have that much time on your hands?" Vale asked with a smirk.

"No, I am just meticulous and try to look for patterns."

"Any luck?" Vale asked.

"None, I'm afraid. But those stab marks in the neck of the two homicide victims are even more out there."

"What do you mean?" I asked.

"I can't piece together a single likely weapon for those particular markings, and the way the tissue in each stab wound is rotten... I haven't seen anything like it." Dr. Sarkis brought us to the front of the body with most back scars and showed us the stab marks. In each laceration, the cuts were black and released a sulfurous odor.

"What the hell..." I said.

"Nothing notable on the lab tests. We'll see where that goes."

"Anything else stand out to you?" Vale asked.

"Why, yes." Dr. Sarkis walked to the edge of the bed of body on the left, with the least number of back scars. He lifted her ankle and pointed to a tattoo on the back of the thigh. It was the shape of a letter "X" in black; the four edges looked torn, giving the appearance of duct tape.

"I've counted eight more of these on just her body, the first one you and your fellow officer found in the kitchen. I cannot make out a sensible pattern. They were a bit tucked away from the exposing skin just like those back scars... guys?"

Vale and I glanced at each other, backing up each other's observation. "We know who this person is," I said.

"Really?" Dr. Sarkis asked.

"Her street name was Crony. She was a retired drug lord in our quadrant," I said, at a loss for anything more constructive.

We finished our conversation with Dr. Sarkis, unable to unveil any further details. Over the next hour, we located Crony's current address as I wondered how in the world she, of all people, could be connected to this case. Shockingly, we found her current address registered under her legal name back in Pinelands.

I remember driving the Crown Victoria down the side of the dirt road, blasting acoustic synth. The rain had already started to lighten. At some point, Vale turned off the music. "Never liked my taste," I said.

"I prefer songs without singing. We talk to ourselves enough as is."

"Did you find the detail you were looking for?"

"I did. The back scars verified why we are dealing with my childhood society, and that's what I'd like for you to call from now on, Price. A Society—not a cult, consider that knowledge a welcome package."

"Umm... okay. I thought we knew this?"

"It was only a suspicion, perhaps even a wish... now I'm sure."

"Then why are they involved?"

Vale's lips migrated to the side of his face, and he stared at the windshield to organize his thoughts. He said, "I think investigating Crony's home will shed some light."

"You're not going to tell me?"

"If I told you, you wouldn't believe me. Some things you just have to see."

I didn't respond, frustrated. And instead, we drove in silence for another few minutes as I tried to wrap my head more around Crony's involvement. I still had no clue as to why.

Then against my will, that curiosity diminished, as once more Elara's suicide recaptured my attention. I repeatedly watched her brain splatter onto the closet wall. Everything else became numb as I mindlessly drove the Crown Victoria. Though with every reconstruction of her skill, an observation emerged, surfacing a quandary about Elara and Vale. Over the years, I hinted at my desire for further explanation but never received a direct answer. And with each failed attempt, I buried the thought deeper. But the brute force of her repeated suicide finally brought its ugly head to light.

"I need to entertain you with a silly question," I said, feeling the words prick my tongue on the way out.

"There's no such thing, but you can certainly try," Vale said.

"Why did you join the force with your genes?"

"To serve and protect, just like you," Vale said without hesitation. He nodded and smiled to show he was not affected but rather accepting of my question.

"Oh… okay," I said shortly.

"Has it been weighing on you that long? I'd expect the whiskey would have talked."

"I was just curious why Elara didn't have any issues," I said, daring not to speak of the issue head-on.

"We all have aberrations. Normalcy is just a sum of such. Twin or not, Elara has her own." Vale traced his finger around the robots on the dashboard.

"You know, you do look alike."

"We used to…" Vale said. His eyes became preoccupied. He stared into the round lens of one of the robots shaped like a helmet.

For several minutes, I waited to see if there would be more substance. But nothing came. I wanted to respond, but instead, my shoulders tensed. I felt guilty for not knowing, even with his nonchalant reply. But then Vale's features lightened, and he did something I had not expected, distracting my remorse. He asked, "Remember that time we chased Crony down into that alley off of Vine Street?"

My shoulders relaxed.

"And I told you to hide behind the dumpster," I said, grinning. It was the start of a story we had recalled many times in fondness. I was not anticipating his remark, but the memory filled the car at once.

Out of nowhere, we chuckled.

"Crony was hiding in the dumpster the whole time, and Price, I swear when her knife poked through the side panel at me, I screamed so loud."

"I'll never forget that high-pitched screech. Had never heard you scream in—what was that?—a good four years at that point."

Vale cracked up. I was taken aback.

"Hell, I thought you stepped on a cat," I said.

"I was so surprised by my sound, I barely got out of her way. She still got me good all right." Vale rolled back the sleeve of his navy dress shirt, revealing a well-healed scar sliced around his forearm. I had seen it many times.

"And your manly scream made me hesitate just a split second, enough for her to dart out of my grasp."

"Son of a bitch," Vale said. "All these endless days we spent on her..."

"And those 'X' marks she'd have her soldiers spray on the west side gang's targets."

"Gruesome." Vale scrunched his nose. "Those haunted me for years."

"Made us better police, though."

"Just we what needed."

We laughed with more exuberance. Nostalgia filled the car as we relived some of our craziest memories. It warmed my heart, and it was a laugh we needed after the horrible night prior. I missed these talks. Vale had always enjoyed bringing them up. He had an innate ability to make light of dark situations, and I learned it kept my mind strong during our years on the police force. I knew that was true. Once he left a year ago, I felt that lightness drain from my world.

I was not sure what to expect when Vale came back the day prior. It was the first time we talked since he had left, for reasons I wish I could explain, but to hear that spark in his voice for the first time on our visit made me feel better. Until that point, he acted stranger than normal, like he was in a different gear. The stories brought out the complete Vale I knew. But when our laughs finally calmed down, I could feel that part of him leaving. I wish I knew how to bring it back.

A few minutes onward, I parked the car on the side of the dirt road.

"This is where she ended up?" Vale asked.

"That's what she has on public record."

We stepped out into the rainstorm. And Vale's foot landed in a puddle filling one of the many potholes on the road.

"Doggone it." Vale hopped onto a dryer patch of the road.

In the distance, I saw a trailer park blend in with the Pinelands. Some had tipped over from the storm. Two beat-up ranchers were straight ahead. Their front lawns looked like dunes with occasional patches of weeds and pine trees. The rain had reshaped the lawn surface into mud puddles, making it difficult to distinguish what was the driveway.

Crony's rancher was the teal one to the left. We walked through the terrain towards it. The rancher was in ruins. The siding was chipped, and the windows had noticeable scratches. Pillars supported the house, and a white diamond mesh wrapped around them. Several gaps were cut through the mesh that I suspected had been from rodents over the years. The only close neighbor was a broken-down red rancher in a similar style directly next door to the right.

We walked up creaky steps to reach a wooden door with notable scratch marks and cracks along the edges. I knocked. To my surprise, my tap swung the door open.

I raised my gun. We darted into the rancher, entering a little square foyer covered with wooden panels. No one was in view.

I pressed against the inside wall and peeked into a large room. Mold stung my nose. The carpet had been gutted, and the walls were covered with streaks and holes.

We entered the large room. A divider split the space in two. We darted over and pressed our bodies against the divider. When we hovered in silence to listen for several moments, all we heard was rain. We counted to three, then threw our bodies into the other half of the house.

We saw each other and nothing more. It was just as empty, except for three doors in the back corner. I walked towards each and swung them open, praying for no dead bodies. I found a water heater, a bathroom, and the backyard all undisturbed, to my great relief.

I stepped out the back door. A dense wall of pine trees was close to the house. The outside stairs led down to a small empty pit of sand. If there were any footprints, the rain had washed them away.

I raised my brow.

"Someone gutted her house before we could search," Vale said.

"How does a retired drug lord become a victim?"

"Not by chance." Vale studied the divider in the center of the rancher. After several seconds, he took out his phone and snapped several pictures of scratch marks.

"What do you see?" I asked, staring at the markings as if words would appear if I squinted long enough.

"These symbols are drawn hundreds of times in that blood painting of me."

"*What?*"

Vale brought out a pencil and traced the marking. Tick marks were on a single horizontal line. Vale's fingers felt the wood, and he counted out loud over a dozen ticks, some I did not see at first. "These markings were drawn by a member of my childhood Society. Deciphering the message will be a game of symbols."

"Well, what does it mean?"

"That we come from different backgrounds." Vale pointed to the tick marks. "Each mark represents a religion on this line. I grew up Catholic, just as you grew up Protestant. We each have our own tick."

"Okay." I was unsure what else to add.

"It depicts how our world was before this society came around. Religion was celebrated linearly. I will use you as an example. You were born Protestant and, for the most part, have felt spiritually connected to the Protestant faith."

"That's true," I said sluggishly. I did not know where he was heading. And I was not looking to bash billions of people with a fatuous claim.

"See that cut in the wood near the ground?"

"Now I do." I had not associated the marking with the other lines.

"That is supposed to represent the Society I was born into."

"Does it have a name?"

"It does," Vale said, flinching without an answer. "Its members are from your religion, my religion, and many others, searching to understand each other's religions to collaborate for a greater chance to contact the higher powers we pray for."

Little did I know at the time, Vale was referring to the Deus, the original universe… He was born into his particular life to view it in that unique way, similar to how I was born into a family that worshiped a higher power.

It was my first exposure to the idea of the Deus.

"Where are you going with this?" I asked.

Vale used the pencil to gently trace lines connecting the slash near the floor to all the little ticks on the long horizontal line. "I was taught to believe the Society I was born into is the one all religions were meant to be built upon."

"But they weren't," I said.

"Of course, the Society is only sixty years old, but you must understand, Price, the way each member worships has existed for millennia through their own religions. Practicing faith has been around since the beginning of man. The Society was supposed to integrate all practices, like turning strings of yarn into a cloth. All the members were recruited within their own churches, mosques, synagogues... It targeted people who felt their religion could offer clearer explanations as to why we all exist. Members of my congregation recruited my parents with the pitch that joining would enhance their Catholicism. That is why I am partially the man you see today."

"What are they searching for?"

"A connection to the spiritual realm." Vale erased his pencil markings.

"That sounds like it could be peaceful." My mind hurt a bit, wrapping around the idea, as far-fetched as it sounded in today's world.

"It was supposed to be..." Vale stood and walked around the room, taking photographs of more carvings.

"What happened?"

"Time. Humans bring darkness into all things beautiful. The fact this symbol is here is not a good sign. It's used, along with other symbols, to perform dark rituals."

"Vale, you need to tell me what's going on."

"I can't. With the house gutted, I can only pick up a few markings. I need to see more to know what exactly happened."

"What was the Society called?"

"It is in a language believed to be ancient, one meant for spirits. If I told it to you, you wouldn't know how to repeat it. But any member was called a Morte. One I took the liberty to nickname a Mad Morte." Vale walked to the front of the rancher, mumbling to himself. I took the cue the conversation was over, left with more questions than answers.

I wanted to inquire more, but I did not know where to start. So we searched the rest of the property as I processed Vale's answers about the Society. I felt sad for him. It appeared no matter what he did, the past had never left him.

The search of the Crony's property came up empty, leaving us without a clue as to why these markings were in her rancher. Our attention shifted to the lone neighbor in the red rancher. On our way over, we noticed the curtains moving in the back window. We walked to the door, and I knocked, hand on my gun.

The door opened, revealing a pale woman with light sandy brown hair in a messy cloud around her head. She had a light touch of lipstick and a long neck coming off her skeleton trunk. Her outfit was skimpy, revealing her bony frame and worn skin. She moved to the edge of the doorway, holding her hand against the frame to block us from entering. The neighbor started to yell profanity at us.

We brought out our Haddon Police Badges, and her hostility lessened.

Vale and I immediately took our old roles when we used to interrogate together. "Listen," Vale said, "I couldn't care less what you've done. That's not important to us."

"Can't trust law like you," the neighbor said.

"You don't need to trust, miss; just inform the law, then we leave. We all know the black hole here."

"I don't want anything to do with that woman."

"That's not why I'm here, but should I suspect you to be? Is it that leafy perfume I'm smelling off of you, or is it the needle marks on your arm and toes? What's got you going today?"

"I'll close this door on you in a heartbeat."

"Ma'am, we're only here to help. When did you see Crony last?"

"Who?"

"Don't play like you don't know who she was," Vale said.

I pulled a fifty-dollar bill out of my trench coat pocket and shoved it in her hand.

"Two days ago. We don't talk much," she said.

"You ever buy off her?" I asked.

The neighbor looked at me.

"I told you we don't care today," Vale said.

"Back when her soldiers were selling. But she didn't live here then… This belonged to her parents. She only came four years back. Never saw her deal from here."

"She lived here?" I asked.

"She still does. I saw her two days ago." The neighbor stopped herself from talking. I handed her another fifty. "I was still coming out of a bad dose of smack that night, but I heard a lot of strange sounds coming from her place."

"You didn't look?" Vale asked.

"No, I never look. I'm afraid to know what happens there. I know what she was like, I never wanted to put myself in harm's way."

"Ever see anyone else go in there?" I asked.

"One lady many times."

"About the same height?"

"I don't know. I just saw someone else."

"Anything else you remember about her?"

"Long black hair. Pale."

"You never once saw anyone else by chance?" Vale asked, sounding unimpressed.

"Never. I swear."

"Ma'am, are you sure you don't remember anyone else?" I brought out another fifty, but the woman did not accept.

"I stayed away from that place, you hear?"

Behind her, a small child road by on a rusty tricycle—her eyes bulged. "Boy! I told you to stay out of sight and let Mama handle this." She slammed the door on us and locked it.

I looked at Vale, flabbergasted. He made no remark.

We walked back to the car. "Fucking Pineys…" I said, near the driver's door.

"You've always liked that word," Vale said.

Piney was a derogatory word against the few citizens of the Pinelands. It was rooted in a misrepresented article centuries ago. But, misrepresented or not, the negative connotation stuck. Even though the area chilled my body, most people I had met here were prideful and good-natured. In reality, this woman represented the minority, but it didn't matter. She was the majority of the Pinelands' people in the eyes of Haddon because they were like me, unwilling to explore the land's beauty. To this day, I still catch myself using the word.

Once we sat inside, Vale turned to me and said, "I tell you what she really was… a Mad Morte."

"From your Society?"

"Of course, Price."

"How in God's name could you tell?"

"I could see a good twenty scars at least creeping out of her back when she turned around to check on her boy," Vale said.

"I didn't see any."

"They start in your lower back. You'll get an eye for it."

"Do you know why Crony was involved?"

"Can't say yet. But those X's she had tattooed were painted over the eyes of Society members during rituals—except with bird's blood, of course."

"Uh, okay. You wouldn't have noticed her involvement after all that time?"

"She covered herself well. But, I admit, I wondered about her all the years we tried to corner her."

"Why didn't you tell me this?"

"There was enough darkness around us those days."

"Could she have just simply joined the Society after she retired?"

"Unlikely. We need to rule out all other options. Something's not right."

"You mean just one thing?" I asked.

"Something… everything… It's all wrong in this world of ours. We just are finally getting to see it."

"Now, what the hell is that supposed to mean?"

"I don't like the way we've lived, Price."

"And how do you suppose we live better?"

"A little less like our friend." Vale grabbed the silver robot off my dashboard.

"Drop it. Sarina built that one."

"Clean your car. I've already cleaned your townhouse."

"Just don't bring my models into this. You've been acting all crazy since you've come back from the coastline."

"I just need to make sure you're ready to go into this next world with me."

"Of course," I said. "Now knock that shit out."

Vale grinned, but in a more somber manner as if all the laughter he could muster for the morning had already left him. He leaned over and turned on the radio, tuning the dial.

"Do we have to?" I asked.

"You get your Os fixes every day," Vale said. "This is mine."

"Why did you take all his autobiographies out of my bookshelf?" I asked, hoping it could stem the conversation towards his anxiety attack and away from the radio.

Vale smiled instead of responding. A trait he picked up from me over the years. He turned the radio knob to the station, and I at once grimaced.

The same grimy voice I heard in my townhouse filled the car, and I felt my head detach, sinking into the ground.

"*I refuse to normalize the Board's power and give those assistant professors freedom from most laws,*" the grimy voice said.

"*Dougray's journalist will report them if they're out of line, though!*" a squeaky voice said. "*Look around Haddon, the Professorial Act for Tenured Candidate has clearly helped Dougray make historic discoveries no one could have done otherwise. They can't stand for the law to be spun in a negative light. And besides, the assistant professors are not free from every law, so get that fantasy world out of your head!*"

"*A fantasy world? Great, they can't murder anyone. Glad you can sleep well.*"

"*It's just while they're assistant professors. Then they go back to society's standard laws once they're done.*"

"*I believe you call it freedom. You know they carry guns into most places now?*"

"*But that's not common!*" the squeaky voice said.

I cracked open the driver's window, distracting my mind with the whistling of the wind. But it did not work. I felt stuck, as if the paranoia through the speakers tied me to the car seat.

"*Of course, they don't flaunt a gun. They still need to go under review to make tenure, can't exactly wave it out in a mall,*" the grimy voice said.

"*Then why have it in this fictitious picture you have in your head?*"

"*To help get data for their publications. The assistant professors are extra careful. And Dougray's journalists would never report it. Many are under the PATC as well in the Department of Journalism! No one wants to be the one to mess up the PATC's positive relationship with Haddon's public. They'd be tormented by every other genius for risking their future.*"

"*Cybernetics, Microbiotics, Wave Power… There's a long-documented list of life-changing discoveries that came from the approval of this PATC,*" the squeaky voice said. "*Haddon would be nothing without this law!*"

"You know, Price," Vale said over the radio's voice. "Elara was under the PATC as an assistant professor… that damn law. It reminds me of the years we've wasted to get search warrants in our own quadrant. It drove me nuts… especially when I got to watch these PATC professors—like my dear twin—search and seize whenever they felt like it. What was it supposed to be, freedom above the law? For their own data? That's illegality, my friend."

"They keep us safe. Haddon makes its money off their research," I said and reached for the dial, already having enough.

Vale grabbed my hand. "So you know what I asked myself? Why give this case to us? You don't have the authority of the PATC Criminal Justice Department, and I'm nothing in these parts. That is where the true issue of the case lies. Makes me think something big is at play here with the Board."

"Come on, you know Madelyn tipped us."

"Why? I bet whatever Elara was doing was at the forefront of her research. And this clearly involves my Society… Someone on the Board must be in it, and Madelyn knows who."

"I mean, possibly—"

"Plus, the PATC couldn't have funded this all by itself."

"Dalton Manor? I don't know, Vale, the PATC can fund any amount to assistant professors if it's for their tenure review. A beat-up shack like that is pennies to them."

"No, I bet my Society is providing the funding in secrecy. I know they have the ability to."

"Vale, there was nothing expensive in that place."

"Not that we found. Plus, Crony's ties to the drug lords can't be overlooked either…" That fact was true. I could not piece together how Crony's drug ties fit in with the case. It seemed out of place. "Maybe they're both involved," Vale said.

"No way. We are dealing with some dark motherfucker. Not the entire world."

"Just observe, Price. Don't react."

Once more, I was frustrated, staring off into the pine trees on the outskirts of Haddon.

What world does he live in? I thought. Then my mind shifted to Sarina's death, as always. *Hell, where do I live?*

I drove in silence, at last blocking out Vale's radio and my own dark thoughts, drifting my mind to the spacecraft model I had leaned towards purchasing.

Though after a while, I couldn't help but digest the possibility of Vale's rationale, a part of me felt that way. Something was very off. But the enemy was an evil person, someone like Marie Dalton, right? I didn't know what she was capable of—after all, that was why I had Madelyn move Moreno into a secure location. Though is she really the culprit?

"Or maybe I'm just full of it," Vale said, breaking our silence, "and this world is what you picture it to be."

"It is," I said automatically. I had no desire to fuel his imagination.

"Still, every millennium's genius becomes obsolete the following cycle. What does that say about everyone else?"

"Nothing. It doesn't say a goddamn thing about anyone except you." I turned off the radio, and Vale did not respond. We drove in silence, and in my peripherals, I watched him battle the world, mumbling to himself.

Vale stood on his soapbox again. "There's this other society out there besides my own, Price. The Board, the PATC—they're all structures to help us advance how we live, just like how my Society was supposed to advance our faith, but I promise you, it's just made us more lost."

I did not respond because, at the time, I thought I knew the exact purpose of the Board and all its laws like the PATC. I was not observing. I was just a man in the mutated Pinelands listening to the sounds of the animals. I was comfortable hearing about the Northeast Quadrant and every institution Vale despised—because those words were the just calls of the wild.

And when they screeched at me, I was alert, but in my heart, I knew I was safe. It didn't affect me.

So I let the beasts roar, assuming I would never see their teeth up close.

I was dead wrong.

GLITCHES

MILES LATER, VALE again denied the importance of interviewing Marie. He did not give me a reason, but I was not surprised. When we were partners, he would act peculiarly when he could not investigate a fixation of his. He would tremor, and his mind would be foggy when taking on other tasks. Granted, he tended to be right in the end. But I found we would get into riskier situations this way—some I would have never done on my own—and they especially went against everything I trained in him.

I always made sure to question his methods because in the rare moments I was right, and he noticed, our lives became much less endangered. So I grilled him to confront Marie, if anything, for old times' sake. Of course, he did not budge. And I once more struggled to follow his judgment but agreed, given his unique qualifications for this case.

I dropped him back at my townhouse. In the back of my head, I hoped he was not dodging a visit to the station for his own personal reasons. I refused to believe that was the issue. No officer there would treat him like Moreno had.

But as I arrived at the station, I wondered how true that thought was. As it turned out, his absence did not matter.

"What do you mean she's not here?" I asked.

"Marie Dalton left with one of those professors," Dreymond said, a stubby man with a beer belly that had slowly mushroomed over his pant line the past few years.

I groaned. I could not do anything. My role as a lieutenant was clear. Whenever any program in Dougray hopped onto my case, I got the runt of the litter. Over my career, I have had to drop many cases because I hit these roadblocks. I had hoped Madelyn's reference would have given us a leg up. "Any name?" I asked.

"No, but the mystery man said he is expecting a call from you."

I furrowed my brow. I turned around to the jail cell in the back corner of the basement, already replaced by three grown men. "What did the man look like?"

"Short, bearded, wore this weird golden blazer. And he kept drinking from this thermos the entire time," Dreymond said, slightly confused by my indifference to the Northeast.

Dr. Arnold Darwinn, I thought. He was the second suspect from the start of the case. Vale had requested I refrain from discussing him on the car ride to Dalton Manor, labeling it as "gossip." Darwinn researched relativity as well. And they discussed their theories every week, so he told me before I picked up Vale. But he denied having any knowledge about her research.

Once again, on a regular case, I would analyze Darwinn's interview ad nauseam. But with Vale's dismissal of suspects, he remained a name for now.

"Did he say why he wanted Marie?" I asked, returning to the moment.

"I guess you'll have to find out."

I tucked my hands into my trench coat. In a trance, I studied the other jail cells down the hallway. I asked, "How was she?"

"Same as the other ten times you called me. She hasn't done shit since you brought her in. In fact, it's all the other mates who were getting really batty with her here."

"Have you seen the commissioner?"

"No, he's been barely around the station since this flooding went down."

"Of course he is! I need to find this man. Looks like he is still good at disappearing when I need him," I said, grinning.

"Popping up when we don't want him around like the old days. And hey, sorry about your boy."

"Vale is doing okay. A bit shaken from it all," I said, assuming he read the report.

"I meant Moreno," Dreymond said sharply. "Not that Mad Morte."

"What did you call him?" I asked in disbelief.

"Lieutenant, Vale might have been your old partner, but no one on the team thought Mad Morte fit the bill of a cop."

I scrunched my forehead.

"Come on, Price, you've heard us call him that. We'd find him at his desks some mornings asleep, mumbling that to himself."

"If I listened to what each of you said about the other, I would think you're all a bunch of dipshits."

"Your team is concerned he is the reason you're not helping us with the flood."

"Of course not! The Board has me tied up! And besides, I only picked favorites when our lives were on the line. Vale is one of the most competent men I have ever worked with," I said, getting into Dreymond's face.

"Just saying, your quadrant is going through one hell of a time right now with all the theft from the flood. They need their Wheeze King, speaking of nicknames."

"They can't go a day without me?" The Wheeze King was my nickname in the Northeast. Vale despised it, but I was given the name long before he was on the force. We agreed outside of the Northeast not to bring up the origin of the name.

"You know what they say about the Wheeze King?" Dreymond nudged me.

I raised my hands and smiled to accept the compliment and signal I was done. Dreymond laughed in approval. We ended the conversation shortly after, shifting the topic to his retirement plans. I wanted our talk to end on better terms.

I walked out the side entrance of Haddon Police Headquarters, by several stone pillars along the brick building side, into the parking lot. The Crown Victoria was parked on the opposite end. The walk across the asphalt felt off. I looked around. For the middle of the day, I was alone amongst the cop cars. Then, out of the corner of my eye, I turned to the side entrance I had just left.

A short man turned to the back of the building. From behind, his gray hair frayed around a prominent bald spot. I swore the man wore a gold jacket.

"Professor?" I yelled, thinking I saw Dr. Arnold Darwinn, but the man was already gone. I sprinted back to the back of the building, which led to an alleyway. No one was there. *Was he following me?* I thought. My gut told me yes. But then, where was Marie? For a moment, I stood in silence, dumbfounded. *I'm getting paranoid.*

My phone rang, and my heart skipped a beat. I had been expecting the call.

I darted back to the car, forgetting about the man, and answered. It was in response to a voice message I left while in the emergency room last night. The voice belonged to the PATC journalist I knew had a history with Vale. The call was brief but alarming.

My jaw dropped. A detail about his health floored me. I could not even say the news out loud. I did not believe it to be true. It made no sense. But when information came from a PATC journalist, I tended to trust it. They were the main writers for the *Haddon Herald* and had access to resources that overstepped legal boundaries over any other journalists.

That was why the *Haddon Herald* was the only paper I read. At the time, I thought it was simply the best. But the journalist I had talked to had gone rogue, willing to question the Board's success and if it was really an appropriate model for Washington. So it was no surprise he knew Vale rather well. I was hesitant about bringing such a man on, but I knew he, of all people, could get the answer.

I made my way to Dougray University Hospital, looking for an explanation.

On the drive over, I became nervous accepting Marie Dalton was out of jail. It perturbed me. I might not have known how exactly to tie her into this case, but she terrified me enough to know she was an integral part of the equation.

Then I wondered if I had truly seen Darwinn at the police station side entrance or if my mind was playing tricks. *What if Marie already killed Dr. Darwinn and was roaming around Haddon? Or maybe she was already following Vale.* A wave of nausea took over, and I made sure she was not hiding in the back seat. My overactive imagination brought me back to Dalton Manor, and the terror of the night weighed upon my chest. For the rest of the ride, I thought of Sarina's death.

Once I arrived at Dougray, I met with the one person I could trust with this information and painfully asked for insight. But before I could bring up the question, she grilled me about Marie Dalton.

"Of course, she's not there," Madelyn said. She sat on her cushioned throne in her office.

"I tried to get Vale over."

"Sit down."

"You look tired." I sat in not nearly as luxurious a guest chair.

"Three hours of sleep will do that. Now give me a minute to finish what I was doing before you barged in."

I twiddled my thumbs overdramatically and glanced around the room. Several photos were of Madelyn with her boyfriend. I rolled my eyes; I didn't even want to look at the loser. A couple of pamphlets for cancer rehab lay on an end table in the corner. I raised my brow.

"What do you want?" she asked before I could bring the topic up.

I hesitated. A rush of emotions slapped me. And like so many times in our marriage, I jumbled out different questions, much smaller than anything I wanted to ask. "There was seriously nothing in Elara's lab?"

"Nothing but dust. That's why I texted you earlier. I hope that's not all you came by for."

"Actually, not quite," I said, relieved of the verification. Vale banked on nothing of value to be in her lab in the Dougray Buildings because he felt if Elara's dying wish were to have him on this case, she would not leave clues in areas we would have great difficulty getting into. I had yet to share the news. It came after I dropped him off.

"Any real leads?" Madelyn asked.

"Yes, and makes the case even more bizarre. Vale and I recognized one of the other two bodies. She was a drug lord we had been chasing for a good decade at the start of our time as partners. They called her Crony."

"I actually remember you talking about her," Madelyn said.

"She consumed us for years... especially Vale. So that's probably why. She was never caught, though, and she was one of the few who retired from the game and got out alive. She disappeared from the Northeast Quadrant."

"How do you know it was her?"

"The tattoos on her body. She had an X over each part of her body for where she had shot or stabbed a gang member. She always aimed at the torso and thighs, wanting them to bleed out. Then she would have her underlings use the blood and wipe "X"-marks over each eye after they died. That was her signature. It had been so long, I even forgot her full name until I saw the tattoos in the coroner's office."

"Are you positive it was her?"

I shook my head.

"Do you think Elara's death was gang-related?"

"Not one bit. I have no idea what to make of her association yet."

"Anything else?"

"Nothing. But I need to ask you something, Maddie— did you know Dean Dalton?"

"I knew of him. He never worked for me, though. The mother was actually a psychiatrist for a while at Dougray. I knew her briefly before she left; always thought she was a bit out there."

"Interesting," I said, wishing she had shared this fact last evening.

But once again, Madelyn detected my reservation and said, "Jesus, Liam, I'm not hiding anything. If it was anything important, I would have told you."

"I guess it wasn't a big story?"

"Of course not—no one cares about Pinelands. Most people forget it is technically part of Haddon." She scowled. "Stop doing that. You always fiddle with your eyebrows when you're surprised."

"Because I care! It's just what I do."

"Well stop it, sheesh!"

"I'll add it to my list of things to do." I instead scratched my chin and stared at Madelyn, deciding how to word my next inquiry. "I have a concern about Vale."

"Go on," Madelyn said, understanding that was the real reason why I was here.

"Overnight, I had a PATC journalist I trust investigate his health." I left out the specific details as to whom I called and why I suspected he would know because I purposely distanced Madelyn from this reality for years.

"You did," she said with a cold stare.

"For Christ's sake, Maddie, the boy's like a son."

"If you'd just put a tenth of the effort in our granddaughter."

"Of course I do with Novah. I always have! No matter what she says."

"No, no, you do not! Are you still building those damn spaceships?"

"Sarina loved them."

"Liam, our daughter is dead." Madelyn lost her breath on the last word. "She's been dead for eleven years, and *her* daughter has been waiting for you to reappear. You're nowhere."

I stayed quiet, unintentionally furrowing my brow.

"You know what?" Madelyn took a deep breath and closed her eyes. "I'm not going any further... I brought our granddaughter up. That was my own doing. What the hell do you want?"

"He takes medicine for anxiety."

"What's the big deal?" Madelyn asked.

"I'm just surprised, that's all," I said.

"Anxiety is a common problem. And I doubt whatever he is doing to you now is in no way tied to it."

"It doesn't fit his personality."

"Maybe you don't know him as well as you thought you did."

"That's not it. There's a reason why he has never told me. I knew I should have checked sooner. I could have at least made sure he was taking his medication."

"What's wrong with you? As much as you try, you two are very different people. It's not your right to know."

"He's had it for ten years. He was diagnosed when we were in the Northeast, and he never told me."

"I am not his doctor, but if you didn't know, I am sure the medication has helped for a long time. So don't bring it up."

I placed my hands on the armrests and stared at her. "No one from the Board's mentioned this case yet?"

"No one."

"That's not good."

"Exactly, come by later; I'll call you."

My phone rang, and I jumped, caught off-guard. "Excuse me," I said, in effort to suppress a wave of heat from a blush.

"You should excuse yourself when you enter."

I disappeared from the office, not wanting to respond.

The unexpected call was Vale, requesting to pick him up immediately. He sounded nervous.

After I picked Vale up, he kept studying his surroundings with the jitters, similar to how I kept checking the back seat for Marie Dalton.

"I finally have my list, old man," Vale said, waving an open page from his maroon notepad.

It was only a matter of time, I thought. I had never seen a man so obsessed with going through a checklist, but what was paradoxical—and most frustrating—was the constant change of its content.

There were some cases, in a moment's notice, Vale would add a dozen obscure items keeping us until late in the evening, while other times, I'd book off my entire day in anticipation of his peculiar tasks, only for him to scribble them off and toss it in the garbage at the last minute.

"Did interviewing Marie make the cut?" I asked, knowing he would give his usual response.

"We'll see."

"I have you know, Darwinn took Marie from the station," I said.

Vale rested his pointer finger on his chin for a moment, and his irises intensified. "Is that so?"

"Not just that, I think he followed me out."

Vale tapped his fingers on his maroon notepad. "It will be accounted for."

"I'd expect nothing less," I said, grinning. I knew Vale would not budge on his plan. Over time, I somehow developed an odd trait: I had fun working under the context of Vale's unknown agenda. It kept my life interesting in a time when I desperately needed to avoid monotony. Plus, I gave up trying to keep track of this list. How we solved the case had little to do with the actual tasks, but why he took items on and off. And keeping track was easiest by just witnessing those changes rather than digging into his rationale.

A short while later, Vale and I went to his next spot—not interviewing Marie, but standing outside the psychiatric wing by the locked entrance at Dubruis Mental Hospital.

"Are you sure he belongs here?" Vale asked Dr. Morbus, the attending psychiatrist who admitted Carl Moreno. He was a large tan bald man with a strong chin and a dark goatee. He stood with his hands behind his back, looking down at us.

"Have you not seen him since he was admitted to the hospital?" Dr. Morbus asked with a heavy French-Canadian accent.

"No, we didn't," I said, "but I believed he was fine before we searched."

"Was he? Did you notice anything off with him?" Dr. Morbus asked.

"He wouldn't shut up when we were investigating the property," Vale said.

"In what way?"

"I guess he sounded more flat than normal. At the same time, he was usually like that. He says very inappropriate things with a straight face. But I had not seen him for a year."

"I heard he was your old partner."

"He was." Vale's eyes went to the floor. "But we had an argument, and he fired a gunshot in my direction in frustration."

"I'm not surprised. In fact, I think there's more off with Carl Moreno than you were picking up."

"What do you think is wrong?" I asked.

"I diagnosed him with schizophrenia," Dr. Morbus said.

In unison, our jaws dropped. I was stunned.

"Better yet, I think he has developed it for a long while. Especially since he lived alone—these people can break away from communicating with the outside world and slowly get lost in their own voices."

"How does this happen?" I asked.

"Lieutenant, we all have glitches in our bodies. Some people just have them in the unfortunate areas. One percent of us have schizophrenia."

"We really need to talk to him," Vale said.

"I'm afraid he's not making any sense today. Everything he says goes on wild tangents," Dr. Morbus said, stopping the thought in its tracks.

Vale thought for a moment, appearing to be debating an issue. I gave him a few seconds to get it out of him. He opened his mouth, and nothing came out at first. Finally, as if he pushed himself forward, he said, "Doc, I'm going to ask you a funny question, but the answer you give I will take very seriously."

"That's nothing out of the ordinary for you, my friend."

"Did Moreno ever say this sound?" Vale hissed a cluster of syllables.

The room chilled. Dr. Morbus raised his brow. "Somehow, you still manage to surprise me. I can't say I have heard that odd sound come from him. And no one else has brought it up in conversation since my staff only talks in English." Dr. Morbus smiled. "Care to shed any light?"

"We just need to talk to him when he's available," Vale said.

Dr. Morbus peered down at us curiously.

"You know we can't say," I said, just as captivated as I was anxious.

"Of course. I'll give your number to my nursing staff."

"Thank you, and please let us know ASAP."

"Will do, but now I need to ask you a question. Carl Moreno keeps telling the staff about demons. I tie this into his hallucinations, but I wanted to ask if he mentioned anything like that when you were at the crime scene?"

Vale's face sunk.

"He did not," I said, rubbing my forehead, "But he was not the first to mention demons. There was another officer by the name of Martin Brezniack who was at the crime scene with Vale and me.

Shortly after the rest of the events happened, Officer Brezniack quit on the spot and said we were not welcomed here and that he could not be there 'with the air this thin.' And that 'demons weigh you down in these parts.'"

"Do you think Officer Brezniack was a bit traumatized?"

"Yes, but he is basically not a cop," Vale said.

"I have missed that brashness of yours, Vale. When I want a real answer, I know who to depend on."

"I search for the truth like you."

"Still, it does not help too much."

"I personally think it's more creepy than interesting," I said.

"Our differences, old friend. Would you like to come into the triage for a quick cup of coffee?" Dr. Morbus asked.

"No, thank you," I said, knowing Vale would have no interest in coffee. "Plus, we need to keep on the case."

"Oh?"

"We're the entire team. Everyone's focused on the aftermath of this storm in the Northeast."

"I would have thought Haddon would want a man like you out in the city at this time."

"It was at the Board's request."

"The Board could be in for an extreme shake-up," Dr. Morbus said.

"About time," Vale said.

"How's Madelyn handling it?" Dr. Morbus asked.

"You know, she hasn't mentioned it," I said, lying.

"I heard about her Ted. Just terrible."

"Ted Billars is a stand-up guy," I said, feeling a pull in my stomach. He was the other suspect of mine from the start of the case, who also identified Elara's body to Dr. Sarkis. The man worked on the statistics behind Elara's research. But I never even interviewed him. I didn't have the chance.

I also fucking hated him.

I could hear the name ring in Vale's ear from our drive to Dalton Manor. He looked at me, confused. But at once, his puzzlement transformed into a glare. For the moment, I ignored him. I might have conveniently forgotten to mention Ted Billars's relationship with my ex-wife.

And it did not help I was especially vocal about him the moment Vale stepped into the car from the train station yesterday. At the time, I did not even greet him before rambling on about Ted Billars. He was a close friend to Elara Vale.

"The stats guy," Dr. Morbus said, "I used to listen to his news segment when he had it a few years back. They go to my church. It is pancreatic cancer, right?"

"I didn't actually know he had cancer."

"Ah, I'm sorry to be the one to tell you, another unfortunate glitch in this world. Seems Madelyn is taking it as well as anyone could; at least, you would never know by her quotes in the *Haddon Herald*. How long have they been together?"

"A year," I said. Most of the hospital knew we had been married for twenty-five years, but it still caught me when people would bring her up. She was unavoidable sometimes. Regardless, I exhaled a small sigh of relief knowing the cancer rehab books were not for her. I changed the subject. "When is Moreno's mental health court hearing?"

"Tomorrow." Dr. Morbus smiled. "I'll let you know the time of it once I find out."

"Appreciate it."

"And thanks for stopping by. It's been too long."

"I was driving near Dubruis, so I thought I'd say hello to my childhood friend."

"And it was nice to see you again, Vale. Hopefully, there won't be as long of a gap next time."

"We'll see."

"You guys are in a strange case. I wish you luck."

"What makes you say that?" Vale asked.

"It was in the *Haddon Herald* today. It was some little blurb in the middle of the paper—twenty stories about the flood before yours."

"Who was the author?" I asked, already knowing the answer.

"Arch Slayter."

He was the rogue PATC journalist I had contacted. Since I told him Vale was back in town, I also shared my knowledge of why he was back. I wasn't going to lie to him. I figured he would write about Dalton Manor, especially if Vale was involved. The article explained the deaths and was used to question the Board's ethical responsibilities to control the PATC better. It might just open the case for anyone to investigate. But I doubted it.

No one cared about Pinelands, especially with my quadrant flooding from the storm and the Board's paranoia about losing positive public perception from Washington. It was a trade-off worth taking—I needed that info on Vale to make sure he was okay, if anything, for my own sanity.

"Arch, huh?" Vale said.

"Yeah, I can't stand the articles that man produces. Hope he doesn't make your life too difficult."

"Appreciate the thought," I said.

"Until next time, old friend," Dr. Morbus said and brought out his hand.

We shook.

"Why did you make Ted Billars a suspect?" Vale asked as soon as we entered the Crown Victoria.

I started the car and backed out of my space, acting busy to buy time for a response. "I believe he was the one to tip off Maddie about Dalton Manor," I said. "I don't know how or when your twin revealed the location to him. But now aware of his health, I have a hunch he lied to me about what he knew of your sister's situation."

"That's not what I asked."

"What do you mean?"

"What you just told me sounds like he was protecting Elara. So why does that make you suspect he killed her? Do you have a motive?"

"Not exactly—"

"Did you conveniently forget to mention he was dating Madelyn?"

"He's suspicious. And I just don't like to bring her up unless I have to."

"Price, you have the tendency to bury some issues deep within yourself and forget the hiding spots—that has always been a dangerous game you play."

"And what's that supposed to mean?"

"Clearly, your suspicion of Ted Billars is not because of the case but because of Madelyn."

"I don't think you mean that."

"If he was not sleeping with her, he would not have been a suspect. And you would not have wasted my time."

"Shut the hell up."

For once, Vale listened. Although I wasn't sure if I wanted him to, I was ready to talk back. Yet my mind wandered, and I processed the number of times I reached Ted Billars's voice mail since the case started. It was well over a dozen. But then I buried the thought, constructed not by the man but by the emotions he created. It was a hatred that blurred my vision, boiled my blood, making me punch holes through walls in my townhome that I'd cover up with Dougray posters... pure destruction.

Of course, I would never actually see Ted Billars in person on this case, or ever again.

The only major role the man played was in my subconscious, revealing the cracks of my own psyche between the lines of this story.

So I buried the evil behind Ted Billars until I could not feel his aura anymore. Or at least I attempted to without repercussions.

The moment of clarity from burying him actually turned my mind's eye to another crevice in my foundation I hid from my conscious this morning: my usual three shots of whiskey to start the day. At least I'm fairly certain I had those. Because hell, that's what I always did.

I drank in the shadows. And in my drunkest states, I wandered through that darkness more openly, sliding through all those cracks except one while Vale was around. One so dark, I hid it from him.

I shook my head. In luck, other demons of mine bit me, taking me away from hell's gate.

After I had resurfaced, Vale murmured, "I will stay quiet as long as you don't lie to me about this case anymore. You're the only person I can trust right now, even beyond myself."

"Did you find out what you wanted from Dr. Morbus?"

"I suppose." His voice faded out until the silence dragged me to the edge of my seat.

"Would you like to elaborate?" I finally asked, shaking my head.

"We'll see," Vale said once again, drawing a line through words in his notepad that I imagined signaled this interview for the case was done.

I nodded, unsure how else to respond. I thought to ask him about the strange word he asked Dr. Morbus. It had not left my mind since it slithered off his tongue. But I was unsure how sensitive he was about talking about his childhood cult after my outburst. I decided to wait for the right time.

"Onto the next item," Vale said, a trip through the Pinelands later.

I drove the car down a single-lane road. A dark sheet of trees covered both our sides. Now that I have taken the path in the daytime, I was more impressed with my ability to locate Dalton Manor in the dark that terrible evening. Basically, no one lived out here. There were only a few houses off the main road. We knocked on each door for a second time, having done so the night during my mental fog. Again we heard the same information: no one had talked to the Daltons in over six years; no one was aware the manor was a private mental hospital; no one had even met Marie Dalton, for that matter.

There was one interesting detail we uncovered.

"Come to think of it, a nanny was with them for a while," an older woman said. "Never talked to her, just saw her once in a blue moon walking these roads in the summers." She sat in a wheelchair and wore a teal sweater. I remember not being able to look away from the warts on her nose.

Vale questioned the older woman for a few long, awkward minutes. They were polite for a while, but eventually, her visiting family appeared frustrated with us. However, I was happy he did because the more he questioned the old woman, the more clouded her judgment sounded.

"This is her home! There's nothing wrong with her!" a daughter growled as we were pointed to the door.

We walked back to our car, unsure how to handle the news about a potential nanny at Dalton Manor. After a few miles, we decided to let it sit. A short drive onward, we turned onto a narrow dirt road and idled. A car drove toward us from the other way.

Again, we were onto the next item. But this one was unique because I took the rare initiative to arrange this one.

We met with the rogue PATC journalist—Arch Slayter.

I pulled to the right side of the road and rolled down my window.

A man with pale skin and a narrow face studied us with cold eyes. His features hardened at the sight of Vale. He had severe acne scars on both cheeks and stubble around his jaw. He rolled down his driver's window, and a yellow tulip petal pinned on his arm sleeve bobbed with the motion.

I nodded a hello, hiding the fact he had just conversed with me about Vale only hours ago. Arch knew a lot about Vale.

No one is here. We're safe, I thought.

"You were holding a lot back in that article," Vale said. He read through Arch's article about our investigation for what felt like a hundred times on the drive over.

Arch scanned the trees, appearing to have an unsettling feeling about the area like us. Yet his collectedness brought a welcomed breath of fresh air, and I noticed Vale's shoulders loosening. The focus Arch brought to each conversation we had over time made his intense nature endearing. Each interaction had made me feel important, and he cared about that—it was great to see Arch again. He said, "Holding back like the lieutenant in his police report."

"I just write down what I see," I said.

"Then I must be a modern-day detective."

"Definitely not a journalist; you're missing all the hot stories from the storm," I said.

"I guess you are onto something there," Arch said. "The Board is facing the repercussions after all for stalling. Which members will be relegated and why? Here are forty articles of regurgitation. The Northeast's flooding from poor infrastructure symbolizes a failure to protect the other quadrants: another forty right there."

"A gripping read. Sounds substantial for your reviewers," Vale said.

"Readability is a huge factor, but after a while, a little more substance is needed."

"The blood room?" I asked, raising my brow. He gave the title to the room with the terrifying drawings of Vale.

"A little overdramatic but accurate..." Arch dropped the small talk. "Crony was one of the victims, any thoughts?"

"I was hoping you knew," I said. "She was retired but still had connections with my Northeast Quadrant."

"Needed more cash?" Vale asked.

"The last thing she needed was more cash, I can assure you," Arch said.

"You keeping tabs?" I asked.

"On all my targets," Arch said.

"I've heard stories of your detailed bookkeeping," Vale said with a smirk. Of course, he was well aware of that.

"Part of my love," Arch said, staring into the depths of Vale's eyes.

"I think there was a larger picture, though," Vale said. "Whatever research Elara did had a greater impact than just cash."

"It's not a weapon."

"What makes you say that?"

"Crony's mother was shot in the chest instead of her. That's when she quit. Any time I interviewed her afterward, she had turned a corner, and plus, she was looking after her father. I have no idea what her research could be for, though."

"Last night, I budgeted the funding based on her PATC proposal," Vale said. "The items she suggested have been absent from what I've seen in the manor."

"And her lab was completely empty," I said.

"Could you even understand what was on her budget? I can't pronounce half the items," Arch said.

"That makes three of us," Vale said, speaking for me. "And I'm sure it was watered down to reveal little of what she was actually doing. I've seen this before with the Board. It gives PATC members more anonymity with their research."

"Maybe," Arch said.

"And the little bit of information in the manor has been disappointing," I said.

"The funding for Dalton Manor came from somewhere," Arch said.

Vale nodded, implying his Society.

"But why?" Arch asked.

"That is the trillion-dollar question," Vale said.

"You asking around?" I asked.

"A great journalist never stops asking. Stay tuned. Any word on who the other body is?" Arch asked me.

"I'm waiting on the ID, but it could easily take another week. Anything about Elara?"

"Nothing. Not a word."

"How about Martin Brezniack?" I asked.

"Nothing there either, a lot of quiet people. I've got some of my other people to keep an eye out. They'll find him."

"They always do. It's impressive." Vale nodded in approval.

"Where's Marie Dalton?" Arch asked.

"She's not downtown anymore," I said.

"That much I know."

"Good question," I lied.

Arch cracked a small smile, probably catching my fib. We weren't always completely honest with each other and respected the space. Personally, I didn't want to risk Arch to Marie Dalton, especially after all this time protecting him.

Vale shook his head, and he said, "After seeing those bloody drawings of me, no wait, I'm sorry, *the blood room*, I don't think she's going anywhere far until she finds me."

"And if you're wrong?"

"Wouldn't be the first time, won't be the last."

"We're missing something with this case," Arch said. "For the moment, I will try to link a connection between funding to Dalton Manor as a mental hospital."

"Works for me," Vale said.

"Did you read that old journal article?"

"Many times."

"Few are aware of its existence. Pine Barrens articles never draw interest."

"No love for the Pineys," I said. "Keep us posted. Meet tomorrow, same time?"

"No, in two days, early morning. This process will take some time. And we should not meet here—too close to the crime scene. Let's say three miles south, two intersections over.

"You're the boss," Vale said.

"Ever hear there was a nanny?" I thought of the old woman's remarks at the last moment.

"You mean the owner of the building?"

I furrowed my brow.

"The mental hospital was first owned by the father, Dean Dalton, before he disappeared," Arch said. "All the Daltons' money—which was quite a bit—was given to Marie, but the property and Marie's guardianship was willed to the nanny."

"Does she have a name?" I kicked myself for almost forgetting.

"Donna Mugsby. She would be sixty-eight this year. And I think she has vanished with this case."

"Why?" I was unsure how to handle the news.

"Because she has to."

"Sounds like an enticing article," Vale said. "Tell Martin Brezniack I send my regards."

"We'll find him. My rule of journalism: blend into the background, and the sword won't know where to swing."

"A game well played," Vale said.

"Just a game?" Arch asked, now staring solely at him.

"If we're not players, then we're either part of the Board or dead, not like there's a difference."

Shortly after that thought, we said our goodbyes and drove away from Arch. Miles later, Vale said, "Thank you."

"I just thought it was important," I said. "Are you okay?"

Vale's eyes watered. He brought out a handkerchief from his vest and pressed it to his eyes. "I'm fine."

"Do you want to talk?"

"Nowhere near Haddon."

"That's never stopped you before," I said, thinking I was cognizant of the real issue. But in fact, I buried Vale's secret so deep I could outwardly speak about it with such obliviousness.

"Accomplishment partners with opportunity," Vale said. "Right now, it's time to work, old man."

I anticipated the last item on Vale's list.

We researched the entire Dalton Manor, and I was an anxious mess. To start, I never searched my crime scenes a second time, but with Vale's insistence, we visited. He was convinced there was more than we found to this manor.

It greeted us with the same chill. And reemerging into its darkness made me sweat. I could only recall near the end of our search. It was where Vale, Marie, and I originally found Moreno in the library. Parts of the little pieces of glass from when Moreno had flipped over a table covered the floor.

Vale looked invigorated, so I gave him space. He took out a tape measurer from one of the many pockets inside his green flowered vest and measured the distance between different slash marks Moreno had made during his psychotic breakdown. He brought out a notepad and frivolously noted dimensions.

"What are you doing?"

"Uncovering history. It looks like the powder that Moreno fell onto is also gone." Vale traced his finger from slash mark to slash mark, making a giant circle around the room.

"What does that mean?"

"It means nothing. Not one thing… But what does it symbolize? That's another story." Vale jotted more in his notepad, then placed it back in his vest. He brought out a camera and took photos.

After a few minutes, I lost my patience. "Just tell me what's going on."

"Price, to the untrained eye, all Moreno did was tear up the room with a shard of glass. But there's much more here." Vale adjusted his glasses as he took a deep breath. "I'm afraid it's time I bring you further into my childhood. My Society can be best explained by its symbol." Vale stood overtop a single slash that was one of the many carved onto the ground. "This line represents a connection between our soul and body. The one end represents the soul, the other the body." Vale brought out a small jar of salt from his vest. "If there is one thing you remember about my Society, it must be that it believes our most complicated feelings, such as love and hate amongst others, are actually energies. These energies are explained in religious scriptures, like the Bible or the Quran, as having ties to a higher power, such as a God loving you… But in my Society, it was believed these energies are instead nameless, and we still know little about them. Our religions tried to explain them. Can you remember that for me?"

I nodded. I wanted him to be comfortable digging into this world he had no desire to revisit.

Vale twisted open the lid, sprinkling some of its contents to the left end of a line carved into the ground. "That marking is our soul. My Society believes the soul is our gateway to communicating within the spiritual realm. You see, it believes these energies like love are interconnected between everyone's souls, some more than others." Vale sprinkled salt onto the right end of the line. "And this side represents our body. My Society believes we are only able to process a minute fraction of these energies, only a sliver of the feelings we could potentially sense. And those few we do detect physically change us in a way we interpret as 'feelings,' we release certain hormones, particular neurons fire, we make decisions off of these energies each day. That is how we experience love, Price. My Society is supposed to explain the connection between our body and our soul, using members' experiences from many different religions."

I placed my hand on my cheek, pondering Vale's remark. It was a lot to process.

Vale turned his head to the window, his eyes studying the trees.

"I just don't understand how this turned so dark," I said. "Everything you're saying has a real sense of beauty I've never heard of before."

"People mistook extreme emotions in our body as a stronger connection to our soul."

"Why—?"

"Someone's watching us," Vale said, cutting me off.

I dashed to the edge of the window and peered. A shadow dashed in the pine trees. We brought out our guns and crept up the stairs out of the library through the double doors. We glanced down the hall. No one was there in either direction.

"It looked human."

"What else would it be?"

"A demon," Vale whispered as we darted through the hallway and past the foyer. "The lines around the library made a particular shape we call a portal. My Society uses them to contact energies our bodies can't normally detect. That particular shape we saw in the library is supposed to connect with an energy you and I would refer to in our world as a demon—a specific one."

I was concerned for Vale's sanity. But I hid it.

"Don't worry," Vale said. "Someone closed the portal since yesterday: there was white chalk by Moreno's feet that has now been wiped away."

"Any idea who?" I asked.

"A Mad Morte."

"Does the demon at least have a name?"

Vale dashed outside without an answer. I followed.

We hopped onto the sand. The birds chirped as we scanned the pine trees. They went for endless miles in all directions. And with dusk approaching, the darkness took over only a few feet past the edge of the forest.

We darted by a rusted swingset to where we thought we saw the shadow at the edge of the pine trees.

A bush rustled, and Vale fired his pistol.

"Have you gone mad?"

"I just make sense of madness," Vale said in a calm voice.

"Let's go to the car and reset."

Vale studied the pine trees more. "Why not go in?"

"If you are so confident your Society is as fucked up as you say, strategize an attack instead of this blind ambush."

I heard the gears turning in Vale's mind. "Mad Mortes have definitely been here. I'm sure they were trying to open it our first night. I could kick myself for not catching it sooner. I did not piece the portal together last night. I needed to read the scriptures. And to think, Moreno had his breakdown right in it."

"Listen, Vale, I'm sorry you had to go through all this fucked-up shit. But I thought you tried to rule this bullshit out."

"That's exactly what I'm doing, Price," Vale said.

"They're waiting for us, probably watching right now."

"Those monsters. I hate them." Vale darted into the pine trees. I jumped in and followed him.

It was then my mental fog reemerged. At the time, I was terrified. The bristle of each branch against my body jolted me. All I could say with certainty was that no one came out, and on occasion, Vale signaled me to be quiet. We listened to the wind knocking the pinecones onto the sand. I was nervous for our lives. We were too exposed out here; someone had to be watching us, wherever they were. I had no idea what was happening. I was not ready to submerge my consciousness into the pine trees.

At last, I convinced Vale to leave. We made our way out and back through the sand into the car. I slammed on the acceleration.

The tree trunks banged against the floor of my car as I tried to speed through the narrow dirt road leaving Dalton Manor.

"It is a bunch of lies," Vale said with a sudden hardening in his tone. "They tricked people into joining and brainwashed them, promising a stronger connection to their God. They just wanted more bodies to help perform for anything extreme, torture, drugs, orgies—any rush that heightens their body's sensitivities, in their mind, enhanced their connection to the soul."

"And you're saying that connected to this spiritual realm?"

"Precisely. An ascent to the Deus."

"Okay. What the hell's that?"

And naturally, that was the first response to the Deus.

"A reoccurring word in my Society's language we've found so far in this case. It was in the library a few times, Crony's rancher, all over the blood room. I'm afraid the best I can offer on its purpose is that it means 'God' in Latin."

"Surely, you have your conspiracies for this 'Deus.'"

"What free man wouldn't?" Vale asked with a smirk. "But let's just say it's the afterlife, the spiritual realm our souls are connected with."

"Deal."

"Everyone wanted more connection to the Deus, and it destroyed my life in many irreversible ways, Price."

"But you got out," I said, trying to point out anything positive.

"I lost my innocence young. I was addicted to opium as a teenager. It killed my parents in the process and now my sister. Everything I had told you was what they used to brainwash them, to rationalize their actions when I was a boy. At least we recovered Elara's body. My parents will never be found."

Several seconds of silence dragged on for what felt like an eternity. Vale took a deep breath, and he closed his eyes. His shoulders unwound.

"I'm so sorry," I said helplessly.

"Moreno didn't sketch the portal."

"Don't talk about that now."

"He could barely function in his surroundings. I believe it was Brezniack who turned the library over and made the carvings."

"You don't know that, though. Just take a break."

"He is a member of the Society, I am sure of it. In fact, I think this was all planned. He beat us to Dalton Manor. He kept quiet, but he was not the best actor. He appeared to know where everything was, and when he grabbed my wrist at the foyer, I saw at least a dozen scars, and I noticed the edges of several others ended at the edge of his neck. They were faint."

"Are you sure?" I felt Vale was making several jumps.

"I'm certain."

I debated to myself if allowing him to guide the investigation had been wise. I drove for several minutes without talking, but then a question appeared I had thought about all afternoon. "Why did you ask Dr. Morbus about that word?"

"I heard Mad Mortes say that word when they were possessed, in the same demonic language my Society used. But demonic entities are an area I'm not too familiar with. It's time I get acquainted."

"Vale, for the ride home, just turn that mind of yours off. You're worrying me. You're not supposed to get lost in it."

"I'll admit, Price, I have been waiting for a moment like this."

"A moment like what?"

"Where they test me."

"Who?"

"The monsters of our world—do you think a 'diagnosis' like Moreno's is any different from your prime suspect Ted Billars? Disease is a birthright—we are just exploring the definition of a 'god' to expose the inhumanity of the human privilege."

"Vale, please just keep away from those fucking thoughts for now."

"It's not like I made them. Just observation of the terrain we crawl."

I kept quiet. It was my protest that he needed to unwind, as did I. But minutes later, I noticed Vale's fist hanging in the air over the center aisle. "What's this?" I asked.

"For setting up our meet with Arch, what else would it be?"

We fist-bumped, then snapped our fingers.

"I missed you, old man," Vale said.

"Missed you too, driving me fucking crazy…"

I turned on my acoustic synth to drown out Vale's mumbling the rest of the ride home.

With Vale's list completed for the moment, I drove us back to my home, where I officially unwound and slept. I learned later that as I slumbered, Vale once more wrote another diary entry, this time based on a key finding from today's search.

CONTROL

Diary entry written by Max Vale

SHYLA DALTON SAT on the side of the kitchen table tucked away in her nook. She grabbed the teapot and poured it into the cup of her interviewee.

The woman looked like she had just been on vacation at the beach, covered in a dark tan. She wore a bright blue sunflower dress over a skinny, fit body and flip-flops on her feet. She had dull shoulder-length dark brown hair and hazel eyes pinching her nose. She had several little plastic flower bracelets and a gold chained necklace with a dangling cross. The woman's outfit surprised Shyla. She expected one more professional, but on the other hand, the woman was interviewing to be Marie's nanny. Anything fun and colorful was desired.

"Why, thank you very much, dear," the woman said. Her voice was as lively as it was dry. Shyla was not sure if she was sick, if allergies were having an effect, or if that's how she normally spoke.

"You're welcome, Donna."

"Please, call me Ms. Mugsby. That's what I always had my patients call me."

Shyla had Ms. Mugsby's resume on the table and glanced at the first page. "Education at Jefferson College of Nursing… Fifteen years at Dubruis Mental Hospital… Experience with kids… I guess I only have one big question for you."

"Why am I here, dear?"

"You are by far the most qualified applicant and ideal for this nanny job in many ways. I could have made some phone calls since I work at Dougray, but I thought it would be more insightful to hear your answer in person."

Ms. Mugsby sipped her tea quietly for a moment, then said, "Well, I certainly enjoyed my time at Dubruis. Of course, some days, as you'd imagine, can be tough. I cared for a lot of my patients, and they cared for me. Criminals—some murderers, some thieves, others… just out of their minds—respected me. I'm not sure how. Some, in particular, hated everyone, but not me. Never. I had all the respect of my fellow nurses; the doctors would regularly ask me for my opinion; you can call Dubruis, and they will verify—but they will also warn you with what I'm going to tell you, dear." Ms. Mugsby took a sip of her tea again and closed her eyes, like she was meditating in a safe haven to protect herself from what she was about to say. "I am loyal to a fault. And it bit me."

Shyla poured more tea into her cup and was about to offer Ms. Mugsby before she brought out her hand and refused. Shyla took a sip and swirled the teacup in a circle with her spoon. "What exactly happened?"

"It wasn't one thing. It was a sum of many little events, many times during parole hearings, they would like to hear the staff's opinion about the patient, and once I rose through the ranks, they started to value mine. And as it turns out, I liked most of my patients; I thought they were good people deep inside. That's not what the parole officers or doctors like to have on record. All it took was one patient with rich parents to send a lawyer sniffing around. I'm not going to back down if I think they're a good person."

"But they're not," Shyla said.

Ms. Mugsby sunk and shook her head. "They are. They just need another chance to prove it."

"Ms. Mugsby, I don't mean to offend your beliefs, but most of those patients at Dubruis are qualified to be there. They can't take care of themselves."

Ms. Mugsby tucked her chin down. "I know who you are, dear. But have you ever met any of these patients?"

"Many like them."

"I'm not saying they should all be released, in fact, most shouldn't. But some should be free, and our system lets them slip through the cracks. As far as the others go, if there's no encouragement, how will they ever stand a chance?"

"The people that get released have a high probability of going back in. We are talking about risking innocent lives outside of Dubruis. And there are others that are just evil and manipulative."

"Respectfully, I'll have to agree to disagree, Ms. Dalton."

"Please." Shyla shook her head. "Call me Shyla. Always call me Shyla." She gave the resume back to Ms. Mugsby without looking at the rest of the pages. Ms. Mugsby looked surprised and took the paper, trying to hide her disappointment.

"How did you hear about me again?" Ms. Mugsby asked.

"I know who to ask at Dubruis. Listen, the only way I can offer you this job is if you do one thing."

"Yes?"

"Be loyal to a fault."

Ms. Mugsby sat back in her chair, perplexed. She sipped the last drops of her tea, then placed the cup to the side. "Now *I* have to ask... why are you here?"

"Why am I *here*?" Shyla Dalton leaned her head against the wall and held her tongue.

"Why are you looking to hire someone?"

"I need someone to be a constant figure in my daughter's life that's not just me."

"That's a job description. I didn't ask for that. I asked why are you here?" Ms. Mugsby sipped her tea. "It's Marie, right?"

"Correct."

"I have a feeling that my nursing license isn't the reason why I'm qualified."

"Also correct."

"Do go on."

"My daughter goes through psychological episodes where she shuts down, she becomes this… dead weight, she just sits and stares, sometimes for hours at a time. And there's nothing I've been able to do."

"So… she does nothing?"

"No, she believes she is nothing. And that we are nothing."

"It's not just her imagination?"

"She's intelligent. But how does a ten-year-old think that way?"

"Is there a diagnosis for her?"

"Many. Which might as well be none."

Ms. Mugsby shifted in her chair. "You're her psychiatrist, too, aren't you?"

"I'm her mother, her stay-at-home psychiatrist, her teacher… her only friend…"

"I can't even imagine."

"And that's why you're here. You would be a little bit of everything."

"If you don't mind me asking, where's the father?"

"Right down the hall." Shyla gestured behind her through the wall. "And he's not here a lot. He's a medical lawyer at Dougray."

"Really? Then why live out here? Why in the Pinelands? Wouldn't it be better for everyone to live in Haddon? I'm sure you can afford to live in the Northwest."

"We could. We've been fortunate that money hasn't been an issue in a long time, as you'll see by your paycheck—"

"If you decide to offer?"

"And if you decide to accept. This awkward-looking house has been in Dean's family for five generations. There used to be a time that the Daltons were prominent around here. They had own endless acres of pines and cultivated its water—some of the purest in the world."

"I had no idea."

"Few do, even though there has been a long history of entrepreneurs back to the 1800s trying to make pipelines from the pines to Philadelphia and New York City. But laws were passed to keep the water as a reserve instate. Once Haddon began to grow, even a generation before the Board, Dean's ancestors took advantage of the growth to be the main supplier for Haddon. But his father sold the business as Haddon pressured him to turn the company public. We reaped the benefits. This house was home base for the Daltons' operations for well over a century. But sometimes, with families, there's a saturation level… especially after the business was sold. Too many people, too many problems, and everyone was close but not nearly close enough, so there was more inclination to move to different areas of the pines after money was divided. Dean's the only one left here. He has a lot of pride for the pines and would do anything to maintain this house."

"Do you like it here?"

Shyla hesitated. "I do most of the time. I grew up on the border of the pines in a town that's more or less vanished, that doesn't necessarily mean I want to live here my whole life, but I lived in Haddon a majority of my schooling and was there most days when I practiced at Dougray, so that is enough for now. I'm sure you know people at Dubruis I was in contact with. What did you hear about my daughter?"

"That I would be qualified for the job, that I would like you, and as you alluded to, the pay would be nice. Otherwise, I know nothing about your daughter."

Shyla shook her head. "I have her charts in my office for you to look at."

"Wouldn't I be breaking the law by looking, dear? Aren't you technically still part of Dougray?"

Shyla shrugged. "Technically."

"So I would need to accept."

"And I would need to offer."

They looked at each other, waiting for the other to speak. Ms. Mugsby tucked in her chin, and Shyla fiddled with her necklace. Shyla didn't realize how afraid she would be to let someone else into their world. Could Marie handle such a change?

"Would you like to meet Marie?" Shyla finally asked.

"That would be great, dear."

They rose from their chairs, and Shyla walked into the main part of the kitchen. "Right this way, Ms. Mugsby, into the main hall."

They walked out of the kitchen and into the grand room. Two tables stretched across the room. The ceiling opened up to a high beam where light poured in from the many roof windows. At the far corner, there was a grand piano, two bagpipes hung up, and an acoustic guitar on a wall stand. A few mannequins were tucked away behind a shelf on the back wall. The rest of the room was filled with pictures hung on the walls and on bookshelves from what Ms. Mugsby imagined to be different family members of the Daltons over the years. The floor was open, and some dolls were spread on the ground.

"I was wondering what this room was from the outside."

"It was a great room at some point. I wished I could have witnessed it, to know what I'm preserving for Dean."

"We all do funny things for our loved ones."

"And what about you, Ms. Mugsby? Do you have a family?"

"Never could."

"Sorry, I didn't mean—"

"No, no, we all have our chosen paths. You asked, and I answered."
Shyla smiled then her face dropped.

"What is it, dear?"

She was looking over Ms. Mugsby's shoulder back into the kitchen. She darted in. A chill shot down her spine. Ms. Mugsby followed her.

Shyla gasped. "Agnes—" The doll sat in Shyla's chair in the nook. Her body had taken a beating over the past two years. Her brown hair was frayed, and her tan and white gown was covered in dirty spots. She sat with her mouth slightly open, attempting a smile and exposing a few teeth. On the table in front of Agnes was a pile of Marie's prescribed pills, roughly the amount for the past week.

"These stupid dolls," Shyla muttered.

"What?"

"Marie! Where are you?"

"Shyla, what's wrong with these dolls?"

Shyla turned to Ms. Mugsby. She would like to tell her. She would like to tell her that Agnes, Clarabelle, and Ragg were frequent guests at their therapy sessions, and for the past six months, Agnes had been missing. Clarabelle grew more worried about her sister, but Ragg insisted that she was on vacation visiting their family in Florida and that she would be back. They had become people to Shyla.

Agnes's right arm was sewn together.

"Dean!" Shyla yelled. "Ms. Mugsby, I suggest you leave."

Ms. Mugsby did not move.

"Behind you!"

Ms. Mugsby shot around. In the main hall, Marie sat on the bench and stared lifelessly at them. For a moment, Shyla watched Ms. Mugsby studying her daughter, taking in her petite frame, and long dark hair dangling in a similar way to Shyla. Marie's pale skin matched the tone of the other Daltons, on the pictures on the wall. Her lips sucked into her mouth, and her eyes froze the air.

Footsteps appeared from the other side of the Dalton Main Hall. They loudened until Dean entered through the other doorframe. His hands shook until he pushed them through his gelled back hair, resting them on the sides of his head.

"She's turning off," Shyla said. She tried to conceal her emotions, but she always lost the battle when it came to her daughter.

Dean sprinted towards Marie and kissed her on the forehead. He looked over to Shyla and realized someone was blocking her. "Oh, hello," he said clumsily. "Welcome to our world."

"She's been hiding her pills."

"Again? How long?"

"There's at least a week's worth here, but I don't know if that's been in a row or if she's collecting them."

"Dammit, Shyla. I thought you were on this."

"Dean, don't curse!"

"Don't belittle me. Can she have them now?"

"We'll wait till dinner."

"Are you sure?"

"Yes, I'm sure!"

"I thought you knew better!" Dean said, then stopped in shock.

Ms. Mugsby had walked to Marie and grabbed her hand. The light in the main hall lit up her eyes. "Is that what this is all about? You just want a little control?"

Marie did not move.

"Ms. Mugsby, I'm sorry," Shyla said, "she gets into strange fits right before she shuts off."

"Well, I think you can be a big girl and talk," she said to Marie. Her dry voice was obtuse and, oddly enough, had a powerful calming effect that livened the room like a spring day.

Shyla took a deep breath. "As I said, she'll go through hours sitting still, by sometimes days without talking."

"That's fine, dear. She can talk when she's feeling ready for it."

Dean looked at Shyla, confused. At that moment, the tension in the house had suddenly settled, and for the first time during one of Marie's episodes, in a weird way, they felt a little in control.

Ms. Mugsby kissed Marie on the forehead and spun back to Shyla.

"We can work out the logistics later, but I see her, and I sense I should be here. I'll accept if you offer—"

"Name your price."

Months later...

Ms. Mugsby drew X- and Y-dimensions to create a Cartesian plane. She labeled the X-axis with time and Y-axis with the average salary per family. She explained, "Poverty decreased dramatically during the first ten years of the Board. After that, a large middle class developed from the housing projects."

Marie sat at her desk in the Dalton Library and copied the graph into her notebook.

"And then, crime dropped shortly after."

Marie raised her hand.

"Yes, dear."

"I just don't understand," she said quietly. Her voice was soft yet low for her size. Her waves of silence had become infrequent since Ms. Mugsby had arrived. Dean and Shyla were starting to fight less, and Marie began to speak for herself. That was all Ms. Mugsby could hope for at the moment.

"What don't you understand, dear?" Ms. Mugsby asked. After nine months of tutoring, she voiced her thoughts more. Within the last few weeks, she began to open up to her. She did almost all the tutoring now. Everyone benefited.

"How does a poor class suddenly become a middle class?"

Ms. Mugsby put her finger on her mouth for a moment and pondered. She then put her chalk on the blackboard ledge. "Haddon had more money to work with."

"For jobs?" Marie asked.

"Yes."

"But where did these jobs come from?"

"The Board allowed more jobs to be made. I wouldn't worry about going any further at the moment. I honestly don't know enough."

"I understand that they allowed more jobs, but was it due to the tax cut for large and medium businesses that attracted entrepreneurs from out of the city? Or was it the requirements put in place to make a citizen eligible to be a voter for the American Law that increased public awareness? I realize the common theory is in the science boom in the latter decades. But I just don't think it adds up. Maybe it was—"

Ms. Mugsby stuck out her hand, and Marie stopped. Marie's response puzzled her. "Do you mind me asking where you thought of those ideas?" she asked.

"Well, those suggestions were in Dougray's Encyclopedia. The experts always seem to debate why there was such initial success, but I'm just wondering how I can believe these people's arguments when a large majority were born into these beliefs."

Ms. Mugsby blinked and shook her head in a trance. "Well, that certainly gives us a lot to think about… and I'll tell you what? How about as you do your math and writing homework tonight, I will… reflect on what you are suggesting."

"The analysis is in chapter twelve of the encyclopedia."

"Okay," Ms. Mugsby said, nodding her head, bewildered. She looked at Marie and smiled. The girl was clearly brilliant. She could be in a genius school somewhere when these issues finally subsided. Some geniuses have a bit of social compromise.

She wanted to point out to Marie how provocative her remarks were, especially for an eleven-year-old. She probably should not have stuck out her hand and let her keep going. She didn't want to be negative yet. Marie had just started talking. She did not want to comment on her ideas yet in case Marie got embarrassed after months of splitting hairs. After all, she was just starting to share her thoughts. She needed to wait and see what happened.

What Ms. Mugsby found most surprising was Marie's vocabulary. She sounded like a scholar and was unsure how she picked up the grammar especially considering her many silent stages between third and fifth grade.

"Can I ask you something, Ms. Mugsby?" Marie asked.

"Anything."

"Are you going home again tonight?"

Ms. Mugsby looked down at Marie and smiled. "I am, sweetie. Can I ask you why you want to know?"

"I miss having you around at night."

"Well, dear, I miss having you too. But sometimes everyone needs some personal space."

"You used to be here more when I was sick."

"I'm your nanny. Wouldn't you want me to?"

"Ideally, you'd be better here all the time."

"Don't you want some space? Maybe sometimes to play with your dolls?"

"I'm trying to grow out of dolls."

"That's wonderful!" Ms. Mugsby said, smiling. "Maybe you could find other hobbies to replace your dolls."

"And do something different?"

"Yes, sweetie, because it's fun to play with your imagination. You can find many other ways to express it besides playing with dolls."

"It's all your imagination, right?"

Ms. Mugsby stopped and curiously looked at Marie. "It is."

"Can I ask you another question, Ms. Mugsby?"

"Anything."

"What do you do when you're at home?"

Ms. Mugsby hesitated, tipping her head back and forth for a few seconds, and said, "First thing I do is shower and throw on PJs. I don't function well at home without them. Then if I have any bills or coupons to look through, I do that. Then I enjoy snacking on fruit and watching TV."

"Do you ever feel bad about yourself?"

"That's a peculiar question. I think we all do at some points in our life."

"But do you every day?"

"No, in fact, I rarely do. Can I ask why such a personal question?"

"I've lived the past four years thinking I was a miserable mess. Mommy and Papa never told me that, but I felt they thought so every time they looked at me. Especially Papa."

"Dear, don't say such things. Your parents never thought that. They love you!"

Marie rose from her desk and walked to the window on her left, surrounded by books. She placed her hands behind her back and looked out into her backyard like she was a CEO looking over the assembly floor.

"The last few months, I have been exploring more. Mommy and Papa have allowed me to see many characters in Haddon. What I did not expect was when I'd walk around with Mommy in stores or ride on the bus, I could see sadness. I could see it everywhere. I look at someone, and the first thing I do is imagine them in their house alone—what do they do? A lot of them are miserable. They live in remorse over the day's events, some cry, but most repress their feelings with some success."

Marie paused and turned around, glaring at her nanny.

"Then I look at you, Ms. Mugsby."

Ms. Mugsby took a step back. Marie's eyes were teary. She had never seen tears from her before.

"You could not bear children, and you were perfect for it. You can't get a job anywhere because you cared too much about patients, and now you're stuck here…" Marie sniffed. "With me…"

As soon as a tear dropped from Marie's eyes, Ms. Mugsby ran over and embraced her. She kissed her on the forehead and held Marie's head against her chest. Marie cried into her shirt. Ms. Mugsby rocked her gently, kissed her forehead, and rubbed her thin jet-black hair.

"I'm worse than anyone I saw. I know what sadness is. I see it."

Ms. Mugsby stared into her dark brown eyes.

"Marie, Marie, now you listen closely." She sniffed. "I think you are brilliant."

Marie hugged her tighter. Ms. Mugsby felt a wave of relief. After all this time, she had finally cracked her eggshell. "You can do whatever you want in this world—you really can! You just need to love yourself and love yourself for who you are."

Marie cried into her chest and took a deep breath.

Ms. Mugsby grabbed her by the shoulders and held her at arms' length. "Can you do that for me? Can you try?"

"It takes a long time to appreciate oneself fully," Ragg said in a bass growl.

Marie looked over her shoulder at her bed. Ragg was propped up on her pillow. "It's about time I start practicing."

"You can't practice. It comes over your life if you're lucky. Everyone has challenges that allow them to find a purpose to love themself and control their emotions."

"But it's so systematic."

"Why do you think that? Tell me what you saw."

Her palms started to sweat. "I saw the colors all over Haddon… everywhere. All different types. They are looking externally when the changes I see are all within. A lot of times, I'm noticing the more they look externally, the more their colors change in a bad way… to red."

"What you are seeing is everyone looking for balance. And what are those colors representing?"

"Emotions, hardships…"

"True, but at its core."

"What?"

"Control, you know that. It's always about control. Even if it's accepting what you can't control."

Marie stared into Ragg's dead black button eyes. "Ms. Mugsby is always blue, but after talking to her today, I saw tinges of green."

"That's because you are starting to win her over."

"With what?"

"Energy or… hardships. She's starting to think that she's gaining control over her life, but really she's forgetting how to accept you can't control everything. She will slowly turn to red. Many follow this path, most earlier than her. This path happens a lot with aging."

"I like Ms. Mugsby."

"So do I. We want her in on this."

"Will you always have control over me?"

"Marie, I am you. All I am doing in this doll is compartmentalizing who you are. And since you feel uncomfortable expressing it on your own, I just act as a placeholder. And that's fine for now. I'm not going anywhere. I've always been here."

"I hate you."

"Then you hate yourself. Remember what Ms. Mugsby told you, love yourself for who you are. And I know you love it deep down. I know how much you love playing with those birds. I know where you hide them."

"Not so loud," Marie said.

"I know where they all are. I could tell them."

"You would never."

"Just like Agnes and Clarabelle?"

"You made me!"

"I only watched you rip off Agnes's arm to practice. I told you she was already tortured enough."

"I wanted to stop controlling her! She needed to turn red. I was helping her!"

"I saw your face. I know how natural it felt. And whenever we want more practice, you can go out and stitch them back up."

Marie walked to her bed and grabbed Ragg. "I told Ms. Mugsby I'm growing out of playing with dolls."

"Then you've graduated to birds."

She walked over to her toy chest and threw Ragg inside.

"Dear, I'm ready."

Shyla put down her *American Journal of Psychiatry* and removed her reading glasses in the kitchen. "You are?"

"She's never mentioned her voices to me. I need to know more."

"This makes me so happy. She could use you in there. I could use you in there. You've been *the* difference in her life, and I don't think you can have your full effect on her until you take part."

"How do they... work?"

"She has voices in her head throughout each day. They are loud when she is in her silent stage but are loudest when she's transitioning into it. And it's that transition when the weirdest things happen around the house, like the day we hired you when her doll appeared on the chair."

"What do you think about the dolls, dear?"

"She has a few she cycles through, but the one she made called Ragg she keeps close."

"Did you ever think about getting rid of the doll?" Ms. Mugsby asked.

"Oh, I did. I hid Ragg from her once in my dresser for a week. But her silent stages oscillated much more frequently."

"Really?"

"This was shortly before we hired you. I think she uses them to funnel her voices just like any child would," Shyla said

"And what are you doing?"

"It's not what I'm doing, but what I'm planning to do."

"What do you mean?"

"I've hit the end of the line with medications. They have not worked."

"Oh, dear."

"There's not nearly enough research to give any other scientific options. I'm going to provide experimental psychoanalysis. I have an intervention I want to try. I think it will take time, maybe even a few years, if her voices don't go away as she ages…"

"What is it?"

"I want to get inside her head, learn about these voices, and make her realize that it is okay to have voices come and go and to let them just *drift* away."

"I don't know, Shyla. That's very dangerous. Have you ever dealt with her voices that head-on? You can't predict them."

"I don't want to predict them. I want her to control them. I want them to leave. I would need your help throughout. And any ideas you have, feel free to add. I want you to be there at every session for your insight and support. Ms. Mugsby, all of my energy has been placed into those voices. They've become their own entities in my head, too, like members of the family. I need other voices than those, especially one I trust. Can you do this?"

Ms. Mugsby felt a chill prick her nerves. "I will. But what happens if this doesn't work?"

"I have a friend who can help her."

"Shyla, you're turning white as a ghost."

"I hope I never have to do that."

"Who is this friend?"

"An old flame I had before I met Dean."

"I suspected something."

"He has an interest in her. And he is obsessed with my stories of her. Maybe even more than me."

Ms. Mugsby placed her hands on Shyla's shoulders. "We won't have to do that. She has too big of a heart. She's improving. This will make everyone stronger."

"I'm so glad you came to us," Shyla said.

"Me too. But can you do me a favor? Don't call it a silent stage anymore. I don't think it accurately represents what's going on. And if I want to jump all the way in here, I need to call it like I see it. Just be honest: she acts lifeless like she's *dead*. Call it a deadspell."

The wind blew against the window, and a shiver hit Shyla. "You love her, don't you?" Shyla asked.

"I do."

"Then we must realize we don't know where this will take her."

"I'm ready to try all means necessary."

End of diary entry

*   *   *

In the middle of the night, my phone woke me. For the first time in over a year, I had expected the text. "A-wing, stat," the message said.

Since our divorce, that text was the code. And for reasons I never fathomed, I followed the order. I always did. I tried to avoid Madelyn when I could because I could not control certain feelings I had for her. I'm not the most emotional human, but our love reminded me of a withered flower in the snow. It already had a slow chilling death, but nevertheless, the root still existed somewhere within my landscape.

A short time later, I arrived at Dougray. I took the elevator to Madelyn's office. She could not stomach revealing any need of want, any need of lust. She hated me deep down. I heard it many times. So I took my time getting there. I knew she would wait.

She always did.

After all of these years, I could never figure her out, or any woman for that matter. They had as many exceptions as the English language. But there were a few times, in the heat of the moment, when I suddenly understood Madelyn, why she felt the way she did.

I could feel her emotions and even understood some of them. Then the affection left, and I hid her love under a rock, and only a few triggers, like Sarina, brought them to the surface.

I walked down the half-lit A-wing, loosening my shoulders. At the end of the hall, I cracked open the door and slipped in. I did not feel like saying hi. I knew she did not want me to anyway.

Madelyn sat at her desk. Her exquisite autumn hazel eyes swallowed me like I was prey.

She opened her mouth, and words shot across the room, pounding my eardrum. "I have ten minutes."

Always so demanding, I thought.

I walked back into my townhouse to the smell of fresh tulips.

Vale lay on the couch, unmoved from my reentrance. He stared at the ceiling.

The wall over his desk was almost filled with equally spaced photographs. Lines connected to different pictures, and his illegible scribbles surrounded certain ones on my wallpaper. The red paint can was open. On the intersecting wall above his beat-up computer, red lines were painted in a variety of shapes, as well as several of those portals. I thought about what the portals could mean and shivered.

It was then I noticed, in small font, *"Ascend to the Deus"* painted throughout the symbols.

"A late night out around town?" Vale asked, his eyes still fixed on the ceiling.

"I was just out for a drive."

Vale threw his body off the couch and stretched his arms. "It's not my business to poke around in your world. But since it involves our inside connection, just be mindful."

"I know what I'm doing."

"Don't we all. I'm happy you are at least with someone, even with her hurdles."

"I'm not with her!" I was startled by his response. I wanted Vale to be angry at me, not accepting. "You just harassed me earlier because Madelyn is dating Ted Billars. We have nothing."

"You're right. You both perceive nothing. Yet here we are at some odd hour, and you're drooling the energy called love for nothing about no one."

"I'll be careful."

"That's all I request. And be honest. Those feelings are in your soul and thereby enter the Deus. It knows all," Vale chuckled. I could not tell if he was serious or not.

But in the end, years down the line, I learned he was right.

It was then I noticed how tired Vale's eyes looked and how much effort he spent with each word.

"Have you slept?"

"Very little." Vale looked away. He walked over to the drawings of the portals in red paint. "My rest has been troubling the last two nights. I have had a lot on my plate with this case. And to think, I believed our next get-together would be a little vacation to catch up."

"What the hell's going on?"

"Perhaps I had never been quite myself to you because I could not face my own personality. For that, I am sorry."

Vale studied a photograph behind his desk. It was of Haddon. He placed his finger on the corner and turned to me. "Do you see the difference between this one and the exquisite map you have by your bed?"

I glanced over and said, "Yours is zoomed out more."

"It would appear that way to the average brainwashed citizen… but I'm afraid to inform you that my picture is a more accurate depiction of our great city. Your little poster is just what they want you to remember."

"Where are you going with this?"

"The Pinelands, Price. Even with all the urban expansion, those pine trees still cover two-thirds of the county."

"But that's not really Haddon."

"Wrong, old man. It's the true Haddon. An appearance of civilization…" Vale pointed to the wealthier three quadrants, then slid his paint-stained finger to Pinelands. "Met with the reality that most of our state of being still hides in the shadows… primitive."

I stared blankly at Vale, unsure how to respond to his remark. Eventually, my greatest concern came out, and I asked, "Have you been okay since you left the police?"

Vale's lips curled, and he said, "Why I've never been better. In fact, I wish I had made the transition long ago. But that is only what I do during the day. At night, sleep has been a battle with me. You know my dreams are vivid and, at times, horrifying. As a child in my Society, they said it was a sign that I was more sensitive to the gateway, that I could let spirits contact me.

"Of course, it never happened because I don't think they were processing the Deus the right way. And all that has come of it is many tiring days. These nightmares are a fun way to keep me awake, but for some reason, they have been to another level the last two evenings." Vale sighed and contemplated for a few moments. "Price, I have something I need to share. I just ask for now that you are accepting."

"It's okay, Vale, I already know."

"But how?"

"You're having anxiety attacks. I understand. And I imagine witnessing your twin sister's suicide has only made it worse."

Vale's face fell, and he mumbled, "I don't think I follow."

"I know you were diagnosed and medicated for anxiety."

"So you've been busy?" he asked with a snap.

"Listen, I didn't want to go into your world. But since you've been acting a bit crazy around me, I was concerned you were okay. I've never seen you at this level. So I talked to Arch. You're anxious. I get it. I probably should have done that years ago."

Vale closed his eyes for a moment, clearly agitated. "Of course he told you. He has been worried about me since I left. Price, I am not anxious about this case. I am petrified. But anxiety is not feeling anxious." Vale straightened his glasses.

His words pressed on my chest like a heavy weight. It was only then realized how foolish I sounded. I knew he wanted to yell at me for my insensitivity and vulgarity. But to my surprise, Vale took a calming breath and lowered his shoulders. He sat on the ledge of the couch. "I only have it in me to do this once. I can explain as long as you listen."

"I'm sorry," I said quickly.

He ignored me. "Time heals my worries, but anxiety remains tangled in my psyche. Every ray of sunshine mangled in a storm; every flat surface feels like a point, every action I take I have lived in my mind ten times over before I do it. They are magnified and ridiculed by each person I have ever known in my head. Some days I fear waking up in the morning because I don't want to remember being strangled down the evening prior. That is not feeling nervous. To be nervous is human nature. We all get nervous—at least I hope…

"Since Arch took the time to say I have anxiety, I hope he explained further. Because it would have shown I have conquered that world as much as one can. I know when I am heading south, and I know how to respond. The medication has done wonders. I was hoping to be comfortable enough to share this part of me with you one day—but not tonight. Not now."

My heart ripped out of my chest. I stood, unable to speak, unable to move. My words cut deeper than I could have ever imagined.

"I have a fair number of odd habits, Price. I assure you my anxiety is not one of those and is not relevant to our case. That is all I will say. And I would prefer it if you did not apologize. It is in the past."

"I saw you lying on the bathroom floor."

"I told you then I was fine!" A deafening silence covered the room. "Now, I need our minds to shift to a different gear. We need to dig a little more into that question you asked about my sleep. Can you do that? Or should I wait?"

I shook my head.

"I am having a hard time explaining what is happening to me these last two nights and feel the need to share."

"Please, by all means." I was willing to agree to just about anything he'd request right now.

Vale grabbed a maroon notebook off his desk and paced for a minute, smacking the cover with his free hand. I waited, unsure what he was contemplating.

"I don't think I've ever inquired this… but do you have nightmares?" Vale asked.

"I rarely dream."

"Give yourself more credit; we all do. You must let them leave you as you wake. Good for you." Vale tucked in his lips. "I've always had nightmares, Price. Terrible ones. And to cope, I document them in my diary. But I must write down the dreams quickly because most dreams leave my consciousness by the end of each day, or at the very least become blurry."

Vale opened his diary halfway through and turned to a page filled with his scribbles. "But I have always had this one particular nightmare for years about a little girl and her kitten… *Marie Dalton*. And since we met her, I have had more nightmares about her childhood. Even by my standards, these dreams are extreme. I feel their anger; I taste their tea; I hear their inner thoughts…a trip without drugs. And when I awoke, I found the details did not leave my consciousness over time. In fact, they did quite the opposite and engraved into my mind. These dreams became memories. In such a profound manner, it makes me feel like I have lived in Dalton Manor at one point in my life."

Vale explained the content of the dreams and read through parts of his diary. I was disturbed by the detail in his notes, but at the time, I thought they were Vale's terrifying imagination. A detail caught my attention.

"Marie's doll said the exact words Moreno did when he choked me," I said, reliving his clammy hands on my neck.

"You're right, Price. I wish I knew why."

"That makes no sense."

"And I have no explanation. I can only tell you what happened. That newspaper clipping of Dalton Manor... I recognized Dean and Shyla Dalton because I have seen them for years. Still, I placed it as a coincidence. Maybe it was stretching the truth, so I tried to sleep, but it made me very suspicious to the point it haunted me. I then dreamt about Shyla Dalton acting as a therapist to her daughter. I woke up terrified. It was so real to me."

"That's why you had an anxiety attack?"

Vale nodded.

"I hope you at least got some sleep." But I felt sleep was the least of Vale's issues.

"I finally did while you... gallivanted. And wouldn't you know it, I had similar styled dreams. This time involving the nanny we're searching."

"That's fucking insane. You think these dreams are real memories of Marie and her family?"

"Price, our reality is failing us. I have no logical explanation for what is happening, just illogical thoughts."

"I would stay away from the illogical."

"We've been trying our best, haven't we?"

I felt sick. It was as if Vale's hand squeezed my brain, and its juices sweated down my face. "I thought you ruled this shit out."

"I provide explanations—nothing more... nothing less."

"This is a dark side of you I've never seen. I'm worried sick about you."

"Much appreciated, Price. But you see, some people prefer the dark. I look at you and suggest you get some rest."

"You're only up this late because you believe you have to."

"I wish it were so simple. The Deus becomes more intriguing with each passing hour as I've interpreted the blood room." Vale took off his glasses and wiped them with a cloth from his vest. "But that's enough for now, though, I'll see you in the morning. We have a busy day tomorrow. My list is shaping up in the most peculiar way. Someone important is consulting us in the morning, and we must interview Marie Dalton beforehand."

"Who?"

"I need to sleep on it before I decide for sure."

I left the thought alone. I took several steps out of my living room, and then a question popped into my head. "What was the demon called from the portal in the library?" I was afraid to hear the answer but felt I must know.

"Why, Price, 'demon' is just a word. The emotion behind its meaning is what you fear. The one we are ruling out my Society called a 'White Eye,' and they believed it was summoned from the Deus. I strongly suspect it because it was the only demon painted in the blood room. Sleep well." Vale smirked.

I would not sleep that night. And the entire time, I laid with an active imagination. I knew that was Vale's way of getting back at my anxiety remark.

I hurt him in ways few could.

*   *   *

Diary entry written by Max Vale

Darkness covered Dalton Manor.

Marie was fast asleep, peaceful, and vibrant.

A hiss came from the toy chest underneath the window.

She opened her eyes, nervous, and sat up in her bed. A chill crawled down her spine.

She turned to the toy chest. Nothing was there, but it watched her. "What do you want?" Marie asked.

It did not respond.

"Go away, Ragg."

"I am Ragg," Marie said in a grungy low voice.

She shook her head and felt nauseous. Tears formed.

"I said go away! I'm maturing. I don't want you here."

"But I'm you," Marie growled to herself. "I know how much you must love me."

Marie panted, looking at her arms and belly as if she was a time bomb about to explode.

"I love myself," Marie said in a bass voice.

She lay back down. Her eyes opened, and her frame sunk into the bed.

Seconds became hours as she stayed still, empty of life, hardly breathing. Dalton Manor became quiet once more in the darkness.

Marie did not move until near dawn.

Her eyelids flickered, and she began to cry.

"Mommy…" Marie said.

No one responded.

"Mommy!" Marie sobbed. She stared at the door, begging for help. *Mommy… where are you?*

At last, it swung open.

"It's okay, sweetie, I'm here," Ms. Mugsby said. Her gentle smile lightened the room, and she walked over to her side.

Marie sobbed. Tears poured down her face.

"Another nightmare?" Ms. Mugsby asked.

Marie shook her head.

"It's all over… it's just us." Ms. Mugsby hugged Marie. "How would you like an early breakfast, and we'll watch the sun rise over the pine trees?"

Marie once more moved her head up and down.

"There, there… it'll be okay. I love you, sweetie." She picked up Marie's frail body and kissed her on the cheek.

And I love you, Ragg said.

End of diary entry

PART II

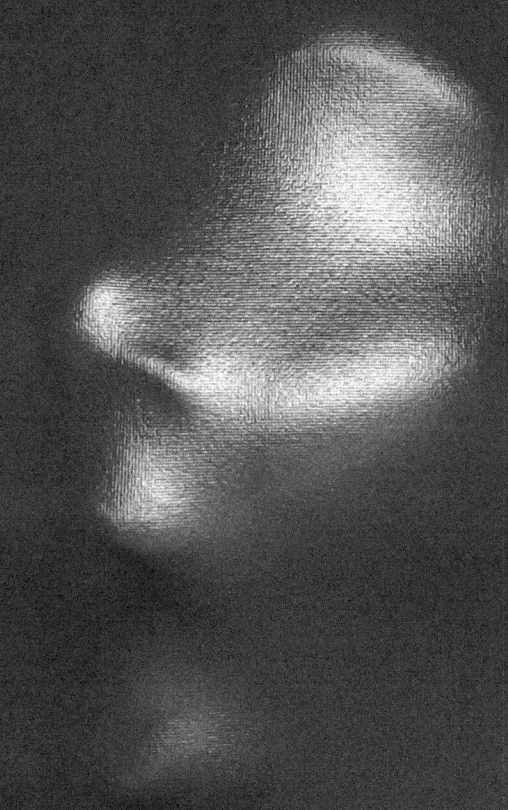

*"It is paradoxical, yet true, to say that the more
we know, the more ignorant we become in the
absolute sense, for it is only through enlightenment
that we become conscious of our limitations."
~ Nikola Tesla*

THE MAN FROM SPACE

IN A FOG, pine trees surrounded me. I spun around, bare feet on the sand.

I had no recollection of where the Crown Victoria was or even how I got here. In the distance, a bird chirped. I furrowed my brow, and I walked towards the sound, bewildered, weaving between the tree stems. Pine needles poked my heel.

The bird gasped for air, and the clouds became thicker.

My heart pounded. I reached for my gun, only to notice I was weaponless.

Within the fog, a pine tree appeared inches from my face, and I zipped around it. Several more pines flew by. One, the bark scratched my cheek. I froze.

A groan spread through the fog. It surrounded me, chilling my bones. I grew nauseous.

"Marie?" I yelled. My voice echoed into the pines.

The groan amplified. I could not distinguish a direction. Straight ahead, the bird chirped in agony. I sprinted towards it.

Out of nowhere, I smacked into a pine tree, losing my balance, and I fell to the sand.

I gazed upward. A shadow stood over me. I jumped up. It had a husky contour with a large head of wild hair. "Professor?" I asked, thinking back to Dr. Arnold Darwinn at the police station.

The fog thinned.

I screamed.

Dr. Arnold Darwinn's body rested against a pine tree. Face carved off, stabs marks in the neck—just like the victims at Dalton Manor.

A tongue slithered behind me.

"Marie?"

A clammy hand grabbed my face.

I gasped, and my body froze.

Marie growled.

The neck. The neck. The neck. The neck.

I awoke, sweating. My shoulders tightened, and I stared at my bedroom ceiling. I could not remember the last time I recalled a dream and concluded my argument with Vale had gotten the best of me. *I need to get out of my own head,* I thought, though the suggestion did not help.

I sank further into the abyss, reliving the murders at Dalton Manor, then Elara's suicide. After several times through, my stomach squeezed, and I fell out of bed and rushed to the bathroom in a stupor to throw up in the toilet bowl. I hugged the base.

After some time, I lifted my body in front of the bathroom mirror. My glossy eyes stared at my reflection as my mind rushed to Vale. I worried about what his response would be in the morning, to the extent I thought, *I need whiskey.*

Minutes later, I lay in bed with a new bottle.

To my surprise, after I arose in the early morning, Vale appeared more relaxed than ever.

When we were partners, I found his steady demeanor to be a masterful tool that became my crutch, and that was partially why I found his diagnosis so surprising. The Northeast Quadrant was not safe. And the job rightfully stressed most officers, but rarely did Vale worry.

In the depths of our most challenging cases, he had a way of slowing down time and analyzing every angle to the minutest details. I appreciated his craft. One I knew he spent endless hours on when he was alone at night, constantly breaking down his thought processes as he cleaned his office space over and over.

However, this case was different.

He brought to the forefront an unhinged calmness I had never seen.

At Vale's request, I left him alone, waiting for his list. But I made sure to check up on him occasionally. He dissected the blood room drawings into symbols, a few I recognized from our investigation. He muttered demonic words similar sounding to what he mentioned to Dr. Morbus as he jotted notes and dabbed streaks of paint on the walls, occasionally looking at the white tragedy mask on his desk. At times he would just stare at the pictures he hung of tortured animals and human paintings filled with television static, as if they were inspiration, then once again back to the tragedy mask. He worried me. On the other hand, I reviewed my notes in the kitchen and ordered my next spaceship model.

Once the transaction was complete, a realization perturbed me.

I had not polished the spaceships Vale checked out two evenings prior. I shuddered. It had been over a week, far too long if I expect to keep its paint pristine—especially for the older models Sarina had made with me.

I dropped everything and walked into my bedroom. The spaceships and robots covered most of my bedroom since they normally had more space in the living room. I grabbed the saucer with several tubes branching out into little pods and studied the detail. I smiled. *I can't wait for the next set to come out in the summer.* I drooled thinking of the possibilities of what the new pieces could contain: I bet they had to at least have more engine stations around the docking bay.

Then my mind drifted off into hyper-drive. *Where would be the most appropriate place to install the technology?* I stared at some of the robotic models, similar to the ones I had on my dashboard. They became lighter, sleeker, and thinner with every new edition, the human contour more apparent and smoother in their motion.

At least Sarina once explained it to me that way before she went to Princeton. She had such a beautiful brain... These projects were her idea as a kid and were by far the best way we bonded as she grew up. In fact, it made her teenage years not just tolerable but magical.

I flinched, then recomposed, shifting my mind to study a poster on my wall that said "ODYSE" in gold and blue paint. They were the premier company in Haddon, and it was where all the models were manufactured.

Their success under the Board's grant symbolized what Washington hoped their jurisdiction would accomplish: jobs, international respect, and above all, rejuvenation in American pride as they dominated the most lucrative field. ODYSE was the leader in space technology on both Earth and Mars, founded by my greatest inspiration—Os.

After countless years of therapy, I can fully appreciate my obsession with him.

It was now one day closer until he sat on the Board. He was deemed the chosen one to get a seat from a young age. His grandfather was the Dean of Dougray who founded the Board so long ago. He had a lone son, who died young leaving behind a child of his own.

Os.

For years, Os rejected his nominations from eligible voters in Haddon, promising he would eventually take a seat after he felt his credentials were deserving of the honor. I admired the man's respect for the Board. But above all, he created a lifelong connection to my daughter the day she made me promise we would always build his newest models. The sound of her voice normally crumples me, but at that moment and whenever I'm near those models, I hear her voice without pain. *"You promise we're making these no matter what?"* Her sweet, soft voice rang in my head for eternity.

"I promise, no matter what," I had said.

It was beautiful; she was beautiful. But I could not look at her. Her sound came from the shadows... the very same I drank in.

My goal was to learn everything about these crafts—for Sarina and me. And I swore I felt her presence when I constructed each plastic piece.

I jolted. It dawned on me...

Having beaten my alarm clock, I found my radio and spent the next while listening to this day's *The Os Daily Science Blast* as I polished my models. Os's deep smooth voice brought a calmness as my mind drifted into the wonderments of black hole photography and theorized if they could ever be man-made. Then near the end, Os switched topics.

"My loyal followers, I too am disappointed by the failed infrastructure of the Northeast Quadrant. Haddon is the preeminent city of our age, and all areas should reflect its prestige. However, as you are aware... Madelyn Katz's Board seat will be in relegation, and with that comes my destiny to fulfill what our worlds have envisioned for years.

"And tonight, I'm pleased to announce that ODYSE will be presenting a new discovery to the world. One we have been researching for years, and I will share it with the listeners early. It is called the Deus."

My ears perked to the word. And I thought of Vale in the other room writing with red paint.

"Our technology has grown at paces beyond our wildest dreams... and our 'bots have been at the forefront."

'Bots were the term ODYSE used for robots. Why would they, of all things, be able to detect it?

"They have detected a new substance, one we are calling imperium at the headquarters. It is unlike anything we've ever documented. It is not energy, and it is certainly not matter, but it exists with us in our civilizations on this world and Mars."

I stopped polishing and leaned into the radio speaker, mystified.

"We believe the Deus is a dimension, and its material imperium, one we hypothesize that matter and energy have evolved from. And since we are built from those pieces, little parts of that imperium still remain in our bodies, allowing us to connect to the Deus—this original dimension. And more fascinating is that our data, here at ODYSE, have documented that once we die, the imperium leaves our body and the universe, completely crossing over into the Deus. We think it strongly suggests that our imperium has the potential to be what we define as our soul. But what is this imperium made of?"

I sat on the edge of my chair.

"We will find out once I obtain a seat on the Board."

I sighed and sat in bewilderment, studying a shiny silver 'bot model in my hand. For a few minutes, my mind explored the concept… occasionally shifting back to Sarina's death.

I recomposed.

I wanted to call for Vale, but I was too worried about what his reaction would be after our scuffle last night. He needed more space. But I had to tell him soon.

After Os's segment ended—or "blasted off," as I liked to call it—I was still in search of another outlet and decided to listen again to some of his older episodes, diving into issues of quantum consciousness. I meticulously scrubbed away to the sound of his provoking points and his occasional side references about the Board of Governor's successes. But time after time, my mind would take me back in wonderment about the Deus and what an "original dimension" could possibly mean. And how did it tie into this case? Vale mentioned it, and that was not by accident.

I wondered what he was doing, too. Every so often, the floor creaked to his casual stroll around my home. At one point, he took a break to join me in the bedroom. I noticed the time was quarter after eight. He sat on a windowsill and stretched his arms.

I was about to mention the Deus, but he spoke first. "I'm sorry I kept my distance this year." He had a lighthearted tone I had not heard from him since we drove to Crony's rancher.

"Please, don't be," I said, and to my surprise, I dropped every thought about the case for a moment. I was afraid he would not want to speak to me, and I hoped the Deus would have been a way to knock down that wall.

"I'll be damned if I let this work get in the way," Vale said with calmness.

Instead, we chatted more about old cases, caught him up with how our old police team had been the past year, and dug into some whispers about what was going to happen to the Board. His warmth blinded me. It both blanketed my heart and gave me the sad realization that happiness had left my life. Sure, the spaceships were wonderful. But I understood what I felt. I lived alone, my only friends were those I worked with, and I never had the guts to reconnect with anyone from my past. I guess I was just not the same person I used to be. Yet, for those moments, Vale's genuine baritone laugh rekindled that magic.

Ten minutes later, on the dot, an alarm went off on Vale's phone. Paradoxically, his shoulders slumped, but his eyes shined with vibrant energy. Vale darted back into his temporary office and continued going through his investigative rituals.

I had not mentioned the Deus. But regardless, I kept a close ear to him.

Then, at quarter-past nine, Vale reappeared in my bedroom as I continued my never-ending quest to polish my models. He picked up our conversation exactly where it left off as if no time had gone by, but this time I noticed the excitement in his voice had faded some, and his mannerisms were not as exuberant. Eventually, his alarm went off again, and he jumped straight back to work.

But once more, I did not mention the Deus.

At a quarter-past every hour, like clockwork, Vale came in. Each time he sounded bitterer, and his paranoia filled the air just a little more. He was agitated, turning into a dark cloud. The positivity he had injected into my body was now withering, and I started to worry again about how much my anxiety comment had hurt him.

"You should take a break," I said in the late morning after I finished polishing my last starship set.

Vale took his eyes away from a magnifying glass that was pressed against a photo, one of many that had now covered the entire wall. "Perhaps on the way over to Dr. Darwinn. It's time we chat with Marie… actually now item one on my list."

About time, I thought. But I held out my hands and finally said, "Os mentioned the Deus on his show today."

Vale paused, then chuckled. "That sounds just… lovely. Did you learn anything?"

"You're not surprised?"

"I'm perhaps tired of being surprised. He means nothing to me, Price."

"But he knows about the Deus—"

"So he's the evil man behind this?"

I made a guttural yelp. I had not made any connection to Os being the culprit. I said, "Of course not."

"Excellent. Well, you're in luck; I don't believe anything Os says anyway."

"Just your own barbaric news shows?"

"Precisely, old man." Vale became silent. He continued to trace his fingers over a static human painting of a beefy man with shades of green around his chest. The side of a car stuck out of his left side.

"What do you make of those?" I asked. The question had been on my mind since our initial search of Dalton Manor.

"The Society believes apparitions appear as static…"

"Like television static?"

"Correct, rather than those white pillowcases for Halloween."

"But you've never seen a ghost?"

"Would you believe me if I said yes?"

"No."

"Then you're in luck once more, I haven't. And I don't think there are enough unexplainable cases to fill up the room we saw. So I don't think these paintings are of ghosts either. No, I believe these were interpretations of how a human in our world would perceive a spirit in the Deus."

"How is that any different than seeing a ghost?"

"A human's mind would have to cross over into the Deus, a path normally made just for the soul once you die. But the painter's body, for some reason, is so connected to their soul, they can physically sense the Deus. And spirits, the very souls who have crossed, live there. Static would be the anticipated vision—or physical sensation. At least that's what my books say."

"Do you think Marie made them in the manor?" I asked.

"We'll see."

"What about the colors?" I asked.

"That is an interesting finding, one I'm still working on… but while we anticipate, could you please do me a favor and straighten that mess of *Haddon Heralds* in your room before we go?"

"I'll do it when we get back."

"You know, it would be quickest if you tossed that filth."

I didn't answer, signaling I was done.

We got ready for the day, and minutes later, I sped the Crown Victoria down the main drag. I turned the car onto Dougray's Campus, a neighborhood in the Northwest Quadrant. The area had little effect from the storm and no flooding despite being closest to the river. In fact, I could not even tell tens of thousands had lost their homes only a half-mile away in the Northeast Quadrant I patrolled.

Vale and I attempted to talk about the flooding and the Board's missteps, but he was deliriously tired, and the conversation kept drifting, to the point I could not recall consistent sentences where he made sense. The energy in his voice drained by the moment. In response, I braced myself and turned on his radio show, hoping that it would wake him up.

But to my surprise, the topic gripped me. I jolted up, listening in a trance.

"God Bless Os Edevane's heart! For all these years tolerating the nonsense Madelyn Katz has thrown at him… I mean, really? This whole Board fiasco was supposed to be a compromise of that one fundamental question: do you want every eligible voter to have a voice in the government or only those with an appropriate educated background? The Board was not supposed to divide our community further!

"Os Edevane is the one man who will be on the Board who we can agree will do all he can to actually try and make this applicable to the Constitution. The endless journal entries he has written have been well-awarded by many on both sides of the aisle… yet here we are with all those ideas in a stalwart by Madelyn Katz. The Board was supposed to avoid these conflicts."

I couldn't believe even Vale's radio outlet was in favor of Os. I chuckled. Once more, the thought of him on the Board gave me a rush, despite their bashing of Madelyn. I felt bad for her, but perhaps it just wasn't the right time. I needed to hear more. So I disconnected from Dougray's luxurious laboratories that surrounded the road and wrapped myself in the station.

"What does Madelyn Katz even do? I get it, she has a lovely story, but you can't just be a prize possession on the Board of Governors. You need to implement real ideas!"

"Or at the very least, don't stop real ideas," a deep voice said.

"Madelyn Katz was adored for years. She voiced early on never to let 'a man like Os' gain this power. And what does she do? Nothing… ever. As much of a nightmare as this infrastructure failure has been for our poor citizens in the Northeast Quadrant, the one shining benefit is that Madelyn Katz will finally be relegated—the perfect one of the seven—

and Os Edevane will get that loser out of his way, and he'll finally get his shot after all this time."

"And I bet he's salivating to the idea of not being around Madelyn Katz…"

Vale started to close his eyes. I couldn't believe it. I cared more about his radio show.

"Just take a quick nap," I said, half-begging. I needed him to be sharp when we interviewed Marie Dalton.

"It's not so simple."

"You're thinking too much." I turned the radio off against my desire.

Vale blankly stared at the windshield. He looked like he was unraveling.

"I wonder what Os is going to do with the Board?" I asked, priming him to rant. I knew that would wake him up.

"Hopefully he just dies."

"You don't mean that, do you?"

"Don't worry, it will never happen. Life has trends. Nothing keeps a man more alive than a black hole in his chest, just as well as a good heart is sure to bury one underground. The key to life is to know when to hop from side to side—that is how you cheat death. Os does that better than anyone."

I stayed silent the rest of the drive, bothered by Vale, hoping he would doze off. But he did not. And he continued to rant on very strange irrational thoughts. Part of me took what he said for a grain of salt: he was without nights of sleep, and clearly, the trauma of the night in Dalton Manor was finally catching up to him. But I also thought he remained agitated about my comments about his anxiety, and he knew how to take swipes at me. He could be passive-aggressive in his weakest moments.

Nonetheless, I kept quiet and let him rabble on. His attitude brought bad luck throughout our morning. To start off, we got lost finding Dr. Darwinn's lab.

Unlike the rest of the university, his lab was in an old broken building tucked away behind several pristine new ones. And I could not fathom why the building still existed and why he decided that location, but it reminded me of Dougray before the Board. I had only seen photos but was told by older relatives they were never allowed to venture around campus alone at night.

No one answered Dr. Darwinn's lab door. He had not responded to my countless phone calls since he took Marie Dalton, and just like Elara, no one I contacted in Dougray knew him close.

I replayed my dream and shivered.

I worried for the professor, even though he was a prime suspect. Marie Dalton could have killed Dr. Darwinn in a similarly terrifying way as Crony and the mystery body. I imagined he was just lying in his laboratory dead, and we were locked out from the outside, unable to know. The labs were impossible to break into, even in the oldest buildings. The greatest locksmith would take days to crack.

And with that dependence on a clock still prevalent, madness had not distilled in my conscious yet to see Dr. Arnold Darwinn.

In a crazier state, we would return.

"How could we lose Marie Dalton this fast?" I asked.

"Maybe you have, but she seems to be with me every night." Vale knocked on Darwinn's door for a third time, appearing to awaken a bit.

I hesitated. I still did not know how to process his remarks about his dreams with Marie Dalton. "How about you don't focus on those thoughts right now? I'm sure if you sleep enough, they'll stop."

"They are memories. They don't leave."

I kept quiet.

"Price, I promise you."

I did not answer.

For good measure, we went through the school directory and located Darwinn's university apartment close to the lab.

Once we arrived at his apartment on a beautiful brownstone staircase, he did not answer that door there either, as expected, with our sanity set by society somewhat intact.

Darwinn's appearance at this juncture would be best for the flow of the case. His insight would be timely. But Vale was taking us down a path carved by the Deus, removed from societal expectations. And he looked frustrated.

It was the first time on the case I saw him this way. I did not mention to Vale about texting Madelyn to expedite a warrant for the professor's apartment. I could not confront her after last night. But he still asked. "Could she?"

"Not under our time constraint." I did not actually know the answer.

"I could message her."

"Don't be childish. Maybe we can talk to some of our old sources in the Northeast."

"The whole quadrant is flooded. Why would we go in there?"

"Come on, you know Crocket and Splench are hiding away. They've been holding their own there."

Vale looked unmoved.

"At least for old times' sake," I said, nudging his elbow. I was craving to go back there and rekindle some of our glory days.

"Price, no."

"Let's just give it a shot."

"I said no, dammit!" Vale snapped.

I stepped back, alarmed by his tone. But Vale followed me and said, "Price, I thought you wanted to find evil. It lurks outside those walls. Do you really think it's a coincidence the case hasn't taken us there?"

My phone rang loudly, and we jumped. I raised my brow. "It's from the commissioner... finally," I said, turning to Vale. I had requested to speak with him since the start of the case. "He'll meet us near the side gate of the Northeast."

We made our way across downtown to our quadrant. The large gray stonewall I grew up admiring covered the backdrop, towering a dozen feet in the air with barbed wire as the icing. I felt safe with it in view. I knew the real crimes lurked within those walls, and everything in my world was better for it.

I couldn't see any of the ghettos behind the wall—or how serious the flood damage was.

I sighed.

I recalled the first rush I had stepping inside as a boy. The pride I had to protect those in the other three quadrants, but then I remembered Vale's first day with me, giving him the grand tour. Of course, he was disgusted by the place. And I was floored why he could be. It served a clear purpose to protect the world, but Vale said, if anything, the walls symbolized Haddon's failure to protect.

Commissioner Jarek Brezniack met us in his car underneath bridge pillars by the river. The wall and side gate were no more than a few hundred feet away. All the news reporters for the flood were around the main entrance of the quadrant.

The commissioner was stocky, but built like an ox with no visible facial hair. His features looked like they were squished against a window, and he wore a yellow puffy rain jacket. No one was around. "Look who's wasting my time," the commissioner said.

"A rough few days?" I asked.

"Your quadrant drowns in its own shit, and the Wheeze King is nowhere to be found. We have volunteers from places in this city I've never heard of to protect the real quadrants, but not the lieutenant of the goddamn Northeast."

"A mystery," Vale said, ignoring my nickname.

"Go to hell, *Private Investigator*. Thought I'd never have to deal with your scum ever again. But you always found a way to fuck with my time at the worst possible moments."

"That's odd. I never thought you actually cared about the North-east." A fire in Vale's eyes awakened him.

"We've been busy," I said, sidestepping Vale's slap.

"Then you haven't even been there… pathetic. Your absence has caused me so much bullshit from the press. It's a good thing Madelyn is like a sister to me; it's the only reason why I'm keeping whatever you're doing away from the PATC. I had to throw a sergeant on your job."

"Ever wondered what actually happened to Officer Moreno?" Vale asked.

"You drove him crazy. Mad Morte strikes again. Listen, if you don't want to do real police work, then go back to the coastline before you screw up another person's career. That kid hasn't been the same since you messed him up—twice now."

My stomach sunk at his words. Vale looked ready to unleash havoc, but I heard his mind recalculating like a computer.

"Perfect. Then let's cut right into that real police work. Why did you assign your nephew when Price called for backup?" Vale asked.

"Leave the kid out of it," the commissioner said. "Is that why you're here?"

"I need him to fill out a witness report," I said as calmly as possible to lower the tension.

"I haven't heard from him. As far as I'm concerned, he still has all those stupid dinky toys on his desk at the station, so he's around somewhere."

"The boy told me he quit."

"Don't listen to that. He's still toughening up."

"Did you want him out of your way?" Vale asked.

"I would have never wanted him to work with your sensitive ass."

Vale's nostrils flared, but he kept quiet.

"After you called for backup, the Board called me and ordered to put him on the case with you."

"The Board called you?" I furrowed my brow. "After I called the station for backup, the Board specifically called you to assign your not-well-known nephew to my case?"

"You heard correct."

"The Board doesn't just call people. And they usually do not dive into my work. Who called you?"

"Jane Snelton."

"The secretary of the Board called you, and she did not say who the message was from?" Vale asked.

"There's only one Board, Vale. If they call for input or instruction, I listen and act accordingly. I don't ask if this is the same damn Board who called a half-hour ago."

"The tight knot works almost as well as the straight yarn, commissioner."

"Do I ever miss those beautiful little quips of yours, Vale, a perfect reason why your mentor and I are different ranks after our years of training together—I like to solve projects, while he has a habit of taking them on."

"Charming," I said, completely unaffected by what sounded like backslap to someone out of our loop. Vale was affected by his talk—he always hated the commissioner, but I knew him well, and this was a normal, productive conversation for us. We trained together and learned everything about the other, especially our flaws. In our early years in the force, they spilled out over whiskey time and time again.

We also were assigned to the same team in the Northeast Quadrant in our early years. And I once saved his life early in our careers—outdrew a man who was about to shoot him in the back.

He took a risk against the rulebook during that brief moment and almost paid the price. He played by the book to an annoying detail from then on, and in effect, he rose through the ranks fast.

I, on the other hand, had a harder time doing so.

When I crashed my car, killing my daughter, it was he—in the exact same rank I am now—who had responded to the scene first.

In my hysteria, he put me through a breathalyzer test only to say, "You're sober enough," and not show me the number.

The other officers who came after Brezniack all knew me just as well, were aware of the shit I was going through with Madelyn, and understood my drinking habits because most of them were already sucked in a similar black hole.

They liked me, and I was well respected, so no one ever asked for more information, or at least they could assess I was in a mild state for that time of the evening to be comfortable with ignoring it.

I got away with murder.

And when Madelyn asked, I lied.

She knew the answer. And even though we hated each other by then, it was at that precise moment I watched her glare morph into disdain, stabbing me. She has looked at me that way ever since, and I swear the more her beautiful irises glisten, the deeper her blade pierces me.

In a flash, my mind drifted away from Madelyn to relive Sarina's crash, then get dragged around Dalton Manor to relive the deaths and suicide. After torturing myself, my feet landed back on the ground, and my mind to the present. I heard my brain burying my feelings when I studied the commissioner and asked, "Can you explain why your nephew's nowhere to be found?"

"Try his batshit mother," the commissioner said, tired and groggy. "She's a little bit into the Pine Barren. She's into some weird stuff and has Martin under her thumb... the big reason why my brother—God rest his soul—could never toughen him up. I'll message you the address."

"Thank you, Jarek," I said, back to being numb.

"Otherwise, follow up with Jane."

"Is that an order?" Vale asked with a smirk.

I grinned at what I knew was clearly Vale's sarcasm and thought about our days trying to get information out of the infamous Board secretary. The commissioner said, "No, Vale. As much as you like to have wet dreams about your own opinions of people, I am a man of sympathy. I don't order death sentences."

"What? Jane loves me."

I wished Vale good luck on our drive backtracking to Dougray.

Fifteen minutes later, we walked through a several-acre garden towards my favorite building on campus, the Bureau of Vale's beloved Dougray Board of Governors. Pillars bordered a giant marble dome where the Lady Justice stood at the top. It was a hike to reach. After walking up several dozen stairs, the bronze entrance doors glimmered in the sunlight. Outside, a statue of George Washington posed from the portrait, *Washington Crossing the Delaware.*

I always marveled at the statue. It was a gift Haddon received after Dougray completed its first new building once the Board was created.

"You'd think they own the place." Vale stuck his hands in his pockets.

"You have to admit it's a beautiful building," I said.

"Certainly captures the imagination…"

We made our way through the Bureau's bronze doors. A tall bald man who was a guard gave us a suspicious look. We casually nodded and walked past them. I glanced at Vale to ask if they were in the Society, but he looked preoccupied. I didn't blame him. I would rather redo my searches of Dalton Manor than attempt the task Vale was up against, even if he chose this fate.

Once through security, we walked down several halls until we reached a temple of a desk. A furious glare swallowed us, one I had not missed.

"Vale, I had hoped never to see you again," Jane Snelton said in a screechy voice. The wrinkles on her face sagged so low I wondered how she could see. On the back of her head, gray hair was wrapped in a bun. She smelled like mothballs. And as long as the world kept turning, I felt she would always wear the same pearl necklace and navy-blue suit jacket.

"My dear Jane," Vale said.

"Put a sock in it! That smolder of yours goes nowhere with me!" Jane Snelton gripped the edge of her desk to pull closer.

"Why, I had no intention to lead you astray. I am only here for your guidance."

"And like I said. That's to leave my desk at once and accept the fact I will never release Board information to you without their authorization."

"Heavens, no. You know I would never put you in such a pickle of a predicament."

"That's what you're saying, but that's not what I'm hearing... After all these years, I can't understand why you insist on hearing my rejections firsthand."

"I admit your rejections are hurtful, but as I alluded, I came to only ask for help as to where to look for an answer..." Vale said, tucking in his lips and raising his brow.

"You want guidance, is that all?"

"You would never hear from me again."

"Well, in that case, you can start by going back down the hall. Then I want you never to come back here."

"An interesting tactic..."

"Or I can talk to the Board directly so whoever you're asking about will know you've been here. If they don't know already..." She shot fire through her eyes.

Vale smiled and took a step back. "Now that you mentioned the security, on the way in, I noticed a delightful aroma of coffee in the staff lounge that I feel obligated to seek out. Today's the day I could enjoy the taste. An urgent matter, really. In fact, I'm afraid this just might be our goodbye."

Jane Snelton shook her head and pressed the wrinkles further down her face to cover her eyes.

"Thank you, Jane," I said.

"Don't push your luck, Lieutenant," Jane said in a growl.

We swiftly walked back down the hall.

"Madelyn didn't put Brezniack on the case," Vale said in the Crown Victoria. "Jane hates Madelyn and would never be that defensive if she made that call, even towards me. I'm sure of it."

"Of course, Madelyn didn't. Please don't tell me you suspected it was her."

"I didn't until I saw you reenter the house in the middle of the night. It would make a lot of sense for her to use us if she was involved in this mess. She would have pretty good control over what we can find."

"Why would she be involved?"

"Why would anyone be involved on the Board? One of them is a Mad Morte. Probably even more."

"I swear you've gone crazy the past few days. You really think you can have this theory linger in your head? And that you can get a cold read out of Jane Snelton?"

"If you have something better, don't be shy."

"Talk to me. Why are you so angry?"

"I'm fine, Price."

"Are you just so sleep-deprived you can't think straight?"

"Of course not. I hardly sleep certain weeks. You know this is no different."

"Then what in God's name is it?"

"I need you to trust me!" Silence blanketed the car. Vale's shoulders loosened, and tears filled his eyes.

I shuddered.

"You're all I have to lean on, Price. I'm terrified to do this alone." He wiped the tear off his cheek.

"Vale, of course, I trust you. We're sort of stuck together. But it's my job to keep your thoughts in order."

Vale nodded.

"Let me do my job, okay?" I asked.

"The crime scene matches exactly to my family's old scriptures."

"*What?*"

"A White Eye feeds off a people's souls and leaves them just how we found Crony and the Jane Doe. Only special, powerful types of demons can kill like that."

My heart pushed to my throat.

"But it needs to possess a body. Whoever that person is must have an incredibly strong connection to their soul to take dark energy that powerful from the Deus."

My eyes bugged, and I took a deep breath. "How about you just give that thought some rest, Vale. Let it sit for a few hours and see if that makes sense. Okay?"

"Let's just go to the next item." Vale waved his list.

"And where are we going?"

"To a very strange place."

We drove into the Waterfront neighborhood in the Northwest Quadrant, amongst the skyscrapers that bordered the river downtown.

The parking was terrible.

After what felt like a lifetime finding a spot, we paced our way to a coffee shop through the crowds of people, dodging all the vehicles zipping by our heads. Vale and I walked down an alleyway that looked abandoned. But to my surprise, at the end was a door covered in metallic with a large glass window. The sign on the front door indicated it was called Orwell's Coffee and Cakes.

We entered. I had heard of the place. Many metallic paintings hung all around the room; occasionally, they moved on the walls and hopped to the adjacent one. To my right, a holographic hand reached out of the painting and grabbed a person's coffee mug. "I'll get your refill right away!" the picture said.

At the time, I could not grasp life in the Waterfront neighborhood—it was almost a different world. Endless cash poured into this section of the town since the Board was created. It paid for Waterfront's extraordinary growth in technology, beyond what I can comprehend or encounter in my days in the Northeast.

"Max Vale!" a pale man said with a dark mustache from behind the counter.

"Crocket?" Vale's eyes flared. His lips curled into an endearing smile.

"Is that really you?" the man said. He walked into the counter. The moment his body made contact, the wood of the counter sputtered with broken pixels as he walked through, and returned to its normal matter after he crossed.

"What are you doing out of the Northeast?" Vale asked.

They embraced and then grabbed each other's shoulders.

"Dodged it for now. Dougray has us working abroad during the flood."

"Did your daughter ever get my necklace?"

"I heard word from the Southeast Quadrant that she wears it every day. Hey, Splench! Look who decided to show his face!" Crocket yelled in the direction of the kitchen.

A stout man with a dirty backward cap and a grease-stained shirt entered from the kitchen. They embraced. Then I watched Vale shake hands and say his hellos to at least a half dozen people like he was a celebrity. The families in the Northeast had always loved him. He worked so hard to connect with them and be an active presence in their lives.

Until that point in the case, we kept ourselves in hiding. I forgot just how popular Vale was. He always seemed to know someone when we were in public, and he tended to talk people's ears off. For as difficult as he could be at times, he never judged a stranger by their flaws and instead made a strong effort to understand their pain.

It was one of my favorite qualities about him.

After he received his hellos, and I got a few subtle nods from Crocket and Splench's crew—they were always suspicious of me—Vale suddenly looked distraught.

"What is it?" I said in a whisper.

"Nothing…" He guided me to a table in the corner.

I gasped.

A man raised his eyebrow and smiled, revealing dimples around his cheeks and pearly white teeth. He had short brown hair, dressed in an impeccable suit, and those kind green eyes on all my books at home.

Os! I had been so focused on Vale's friends I did not notice the man had been watching us. My heart sputtered. *How on Earth did he consult Vale?* I thought. I could not believe what I was seeing. I couldn't speak.

"Private Investigator Max Vale. Had to do a little digging to find you," Os said, shaking Vale's hand.

"Os Edevane. And please, Vale is fine."

"I do prefer your full name, if that's okay."

"If you must."

"Thank you for taking my request." Os bent his lips. "And Lieutenant Price, a pleasure to meet you."

"The—the—the pleasure… well, it's all mine," I managed.

We awkwardly stood.

"Will you fine gentlemen have a seat?" Os said in his booming presidential voice.

We listened.

"I'm sorry to read about your sister in the *Haddon Herald*, Max Vale. I had to meet with you as soon as the right time came."

"Appreciate the condolences, Os. I understand you are interested in my services?"

"Actually, ODYSE is."

"And what exactly is ODYSE?" Vale asked.

"Vale, you can't be serious?" I asked, head over heels in a trance with my idol. "Os, I can assure you Vale is aware of ODYSE's significance."

"I know it involves space travel, Price… I get that much, but I never grasped the details. I'm afraid your models of ODYSE's robots and ships don't quite do justice," Vale said.

"Ah, you collect the models, loyal listener?" Os asked.

"I am such a huge fan of your work!" I blurted out. "Everything ODYSE does I follow closely and can't believe you mastered the gravitational forces to—"

Vale placed his hand on my shoulder to cut me off.

"Right. Sorry." I recomposed.

"I am certainly a fan of your passion and curiosity for space travel, Lieutenant Price, and am flattered by your dedication. You know, it was I who actually started the model project, hoping to connect to some avid space enthusiasts like yourself. Thank you for being here."

My cheeks burned for the first time in forty years because of someone other than Madelyn.

"To answer Max Vale's question, at ODYSE, our mission statement focuses on the utilization and transport of cybernetics for the growing inhabitants on Mars. But to be direct, we focus on robotics and spaceships. The new skyscraper almost completed a few blocks down is ours and will be our home base on Earth. We plan to open it to the public at the start of the new year."

I expected the answer. Only the elites space traveled, and residency on Mars was the ultimate sign of luxury.

"This is where you live?" Vale studied Os's features.

"I would call Haddon my childhood home. Keep in mind, I must journey back and forth to our country on Mars. But make no mistake, I am American born and raised—just like ODYSE. In fact, it started right here at this table, centuries ago by my family, and it has grown beyond our wildest projections with the Board's guidance."

I can't believe this is happening. I'm sitting with history.

"Then how can I be of service?" Vale asked.

Os took a sharp breath. "It is about our 'bots, Max Vale. In our newest updates, we wanted their code to provide the most accurate sensory known to man on either Earth or Mars. Our intention was to let the 'bots guide a new project to detect energy consumption on other planets from our home base here in Haddon. In particular, we hoped they could be a vital tool to study Mars's atmosphere as we update the ozone and be in constant communication with the 'bots on our sister planet."

"Sounds impressive. But I know little science," Vale said.

"Science is not about understanding; it's about being unable to falsify an observation. Perhaps you are just uncomfortable with science."

"I call it like I see it. If you don't mind me being upfront, why am I of such importance?"

"You intrigue the 'bots…" Os said with a sly smile, but then his face dropped.

We looked around the room. Vale jumped out of his seat and brought out his gun.

All five people in the front part of the coffee shop, including the people Vale knew, became sleek white 'bots mimicking a human contour. Bolts stuck out of their faceless heads, and at its center, a single circle with shades of light green shined, similar to Os's iris. The 'bots were slender, smooth, and unnervingly still. All of their hands pointed at Vale and me, shaping their fingers like pistols as if they were playing in a park.

Os looked ready to speak but then twitched.

To my alarm, the right side of his face sparked and flashed a chrome color several times, revealing a carefully crafted mask over his right half. That iris turned silver for several seconds before flipping like a switch back to bright green.

Os rasped and stared in terror at Vale.

My heart pounded, and I was about to put every ounce of energy I had into helping my hero. But Os stuck out his head before I could commit.

He stood square and heaved. "My apologies that you gentlemen had to witness such a personal matter…" Os turned to the 'bots and, with hesitation, said, "At ease, boys."

They lowered their fingers, and Os sighed.

Vale looked out the window.

"No one can see inside here, Max Vale. And the sign is already gone. The real coffee chain that I own is three blocks down."

"Why are we here?" Vale asked shortly.

"Because this table was where it all started…" Os said for a second time, searching for words.

"That was so cool," I said obliviously, waving my hands in the air. "I can't believe it. Real 42XC models—they're not coming out for another year. And they've taken their molecular imaging application to a whole new level. Unbelievable! I mean, they looked just like our real friends!"

"How is *this*… all possible?" Vale asked, waving his hand at the 'bots.

"An excellent reason why I brought you here, Max Vale. You see, the 'bots… well, I'm concerned their last updates are taking their capabilities to new *dimensions*," Os said, starting to sound more confident in his answers.

"The Deus," I said, still blinded by his aura.

"Excellent, Lieutenant Price. I was hoping you listened to my radio show this morning. You see, a byproduct of this coding led the 'bots to not only detect more detailed types of energy—but a whole different substance."

"Imperium."

"Correct again. We've developed equations and theories at ODYSE for this dimension for a long time; we have even constructed satellites for the past decade in an attempt to detect it. Never in my wildest predictions would I have suspected the 'bots be the first to sense it. But make no mistake, what they're detecting matches exactly to our equations."

"What did you do in the coding to sense the imperium?" I asked.

"A great question. I'm afraid we can't narrow it down to a single line or variable change. Simply as a whole, these 'bots can detect it."

"Why is this such a big deal?" Vale asked.

"The 'bots are collecting an insurmountable amount of data from the imperium of the Deus. I don't know what it is exactly... because it's merely the 'bots' interpretation of it. But I assure you my men are working around the clock to find out why. And that is where you come in, Max Vale."

I glimpsed at Vale, unmoved. I didn't know what Os was referring to.

"We can identify you, and you alone, in the 'bots' coding from the imperium. Would you care to share any light?"

"Me?" Vale pointed at his chest.

Os nodded.

"That's rather interesting... nothing I'm aware of, sadly," Vale said, emotionless.

"The 'bots have an interest in you, and I'd like to know why."

"Well, to their misfortune, I'm afraid I'm boring."

"I wouldn't talk so negatively, Max Vale. You are a fascinating fellow. A Type B Citizen, yet the ability to share our footsteps... May I see your identification, out of curiosity?"

Vale's face hardened. I nodded at him, reassuring him that Os was just being patriotic and meant no harm. Vale reached into his flowered vest and placed a blue aluminum circle on the table. "Exempted Type B Citizen" was engraved on the circle, no bigger than my palm. Vale nodded.

Os grabbed the badge and lifted it in the air. "Don't often see these. So few of you outside the Northeast…"

"A rarity."

"Just enough in you to escape the Northeast Quadrant." Os placed the badge back on the table and slid it to Vale. "But no potential to connect with the rest of the world. Must be a lonely existence."

"Less than you would think. Though I always said Elara got the better genes."

"My 'bots find you fascinating."

"No, Os, I believe your 'bots are the fascinating ones of the group, any idea why they could transform into my acquaintances from the Northeast?"

"I can only wonder, Max Vale. ODYSE's technology is outgrowing me, taking all new forms. And in case you haven't noticed with my face, it's affecting me in ways through the Deus I don't understand just yet." Os tapped the flesh-colored metallic on the side of his face that had sparked.

"What do you want?" Vale asked, cutting to the point.

"I want you to figure out how the 'bots chose you."

"And how do we do that?"

"The only help I can be is where the 'bots detected strange activity—Dalton Manor. I believe the *Haddon Herald* said you've investigated there?"

"We have," I said.

"Did you find anything suspicious?"

"Not in this dimension," Vale said.

Os and Vale studied each other. I had no idea what was going on but was too enamored with our guest.

"Not to be short, but I'm afraid we're out of time," Os said, his gentle green eyes softer than ever. "In case you haven't heard, ODYSE has a big announcement to make this evening. But of course, all of this technology is on public record. You could find out for yourself. My company does not keep secrets well, it's Haddon, after all."

"I see."

"Relax, Max Vale. You're an anxious man," Os said, sounding unnerved himself. He stuck out his hand.

Vale, begrudgingly, did the same, and they shook.

"You're hired. The 'bots already have your information."

"Much darker things could have appeared in this room."

"Then good thing your head was in the right place," Os said.

Vale smiled and said calmly, "Congratulations on your nomination."

"I thank you, and my apologies to Lieutenant Price's ex."

"I'm ready for your service, sir," I said, completely unaware of the world around me—in this dimension and the Deus.

"Excellent, then please contact me if you gentlemen stumble across anything strange and would like to seek an explanation. That's what we do here, after all." Os placed a business card on the table. The back had the ODYSE name in gold font and a blue border like the poster in my room.

We rose from our seats. The 'bots had turned off, looking limp. Hands extended from the paintings on the wall, picking up the 'bots and placing them against the wall of what was now an empty room covered in metallic chrome.

"Oh, and gentlemen…" We turned around. "As a token of my appreciation for your time touching basis, and in honor of Max Vale's new partnership, I'd like to personally invite you both to the grand opening of our new skyscraper at the end of the year."

I nodded, almost uncontrollably. Vale didn't budge.

"It will be a lovely party for the new year. See you at the start of the next century." Os flashed a blinding smile.

A holographic hand came out of a metallic painting next to Os to take his empty cup away from his hand. Vale jumped, not seeing it coming.

"Boys, you need to relax!" the painting said.

Minutes later, we hopped back into the car.

"What the hell was that?" Vale asked.

"Awesome. I can't believe you were in the 'bots coding of the imperium. You're so lucky."

"You can't be serious. Price. His robots literally threatened me."

"They're technically called 'bots."

"You're unbelievable."

"We're in the Waterfront. What'd you expect?" I asked.

"Are you this thick?"

"What?" I asked but couldn't help to think "thick" was the same word Madelyn had used on me over the years.

"Os tried to have the 'bots kill me."

"No, he didn't. He would never do that," I said quickly.

"I watched him do it while you were fawning over him."

"Then why didn't he?"

"The metal on his face sparked."

"That makes no sense."

"And why did *your 'bots* turn into Crocket and Splench? Are you not worried about this coding involving me?"

"It comforts me that Os is on our side."

"Get that fanboy crap out of your head, Price. ODYSE's clearly involved with this. You know it. He wanted to kill me and ask for your loyalty."

"No, you're just adding to your list. Tell me, Vale, is it ODYSE, is it the Mad Mortes, is it a demon? You have something new for me every hour."

"All I know is we can't trust him."

"Why would his face spark if he tried to kill you?"

"I think the 'bots did it," Vale asked.

"Why?"

"He doesn't know…"

"I'm sure Os can figure it out. I know he can."

"No, that is what he wants. We're missing something, Price."

"And where did you find out about his face?"

"My research spreads throughout the city. As a child, Os's face was burned in a fire while his father committed a hate crime. He developed that metallic material we saw to replace skin grafts."

"You almost sound like you know what you're talking about."

"I'm not the science wizard of the two of us, but I read some of those chemicals were part of the groundwork he used to enhance the durability of his spacecrafts."

"So you do know about ODYSE?"

"Of course I do, but I like to hear a man talk. I believe only a fraction of the words is meant for the listeners; the rest just satisfy the speaker. It's revealing."

"And what do you think?"

"Os has his priorities… I'm not sure what they are, but our case is at the top of the list, and for some curious reason, so is my death."

"Then why would he let us walk out of there unharmed?"

"He's scared of me and should be," Vale said.

"What the hell could you do to him?"

Vale didn't answer. I let him be, and I started to digest all the peculiar directions the case was going according to Vale:

'Bots… demons… his Society… ODYSE… the Deus… Crony… how could this possibly all connect?

The next item on his list he did not have to say. It had been set in stone since yesterday.

I drove down the Waterfront and cut through the Southern Quadrants to reach the edge of the Pinelands, letting Vale ramble about his own conspiracies. I received a text on my phone from Dr. Morbus, the man we were going to see.

"Shit," I said, "Moreno's hearing just got moved up. It starts in twenty minutes."

"We're not too far to feel ashamed." Vale flinched. I never encountered a man who hated being late more. He'd show up hours early if that was the ultimatum.

However, the Crown Victoria voiced a differing opinion and made a popping sound. The left side of the car sank.

We glanced at each other, and I pulled to the side of the one-lane road. Pine trees surrounded us. I studied the shriveled trees, expecting Marie Dalton to appear from behind one and stare.

"What the heck did you run over?"

"Nothing in the mirror. Dammit, Vale, I finally got new tires donated to this car."

"Were they from the Indian Ocean countries?"

"Not this time, somewhere in the Pacific Islands, I think."

"Never liked their texture."

We hopped out of the car. Vale brought out his gun, watching the pine trees as I changed my front tire. The several minutes felt like an eternity. The back of my palms sweated. Vale strolled around the car. Occasionally, he was quiet, and my imagination crawled into a dark place, picturing a scenario where Marie Dalton comes out of the trees and stabs him in the neck with scissors, leaving me on my knees, helpless and afraid to face the imminent death behind me.

But I battled my dark stories, and I finished. We dove back into the car and sighed. I slammed on the pedal, speeding to Dubruis Mental Hospital. Once we arrived, Vale insisted that he remain in the Crown Victoria. I did not have time to argue. I left him, and I sprinted across Dubruis's Asylum grounds to reach a tall brick building with four pillars.

The metal sign read "Dubruis Mental Health Courtroom."

I entered a hallway. Through the doorframe on my left were rows of chairs occupied by several adults in street clothing. In the back sat a handful of patients, a few of whom were blocked off by guards.

The door on the right opened. A gargantuan bald man in a black and gray suit stuck his head out and said, "This way, Lieutenant."

I walked past an open door where I saw bodyguards block several patients in tee shirts and sweatpants. A lone woman with short straight hair and a muscular frame sat in the front, looking like she was praying. I recognized the woman to be Moreno's mother from his graduation day at the police academy. My gears reset and turned into the waiting room.

Once again, I dove into a "big life project" of mine, the same one involving Arch.

"Ms. Moreno?"

"Is it my turn?" she asked, standing up. She was just as much a towering presence as her son, and her hair just as luscious.

"I'm afraid not yet. Lieutenant Price," I said, bringing out my hand and smiling. "I'm one of Carl's bosses."

"Oh... hello."

"I'm sorry to bother you at this stressful time, but I just wanted to ask a few questions."

"Yes... well, let me just say, I'm sorry if he's given you any trouble."

"Excuse me?" I asked, furrowing my brow.

"He's had issues since he was a boy. I tried so hard to hide it from the world. But after all that's happened to my son, I just want him to be safe."

"What issues may that be, Ms. Moreno?" I asked, scratching my chin, already aware of the answer.

"He always had these voices telling him evil thoughts. I had people-of-interest try to get them out of him for years..." Ms. Moreno said. Tears formed in her eyes.

"I'm sorry, ma'am. I didn't mean to make you cry." I searched around the room for a tissue, only for Ms. Moreno to bring out the damp one she had been using.

I gave her space. When she was ready, I readdressed the issue. "Ms. Moreno, Carl worked directly under me for a year, and I never noticed anything. I feel hearing voices is an extreme quality to miss. Let alone go through a hiring process unnoticed."

"My family kept them secret," Ms. Moreno said.

"Can you keep voices secret?" I asked.

"You can repress whatever you'd like," Ms. Moreno said, her eyes glassy. "Lieutenant, the voices told him feelings that went against the laws of our morals. The Board would have sent him... here."

"What were they?" I placed my hand on Ms. Moreno's shoulder and gently stared into her faded eyes. She cried more. With great caution, I sat next to her and gave a single sympathy rub on her back.

I knew it, I thought. My hand felt scars in a similar pattern to the three bodies. *She is in the Society—I bet Vale had always suspected.* When Vale mentioned he had seen Moreno before, I still thought it was a cult.

I feigned surprise at what Ms. Moreno told me next. I had known for years.

VII
A WITCH'S WARNING

"CARL... SOUGHT A relationship with..." Ms. Moreno could not finish. She whimpered. "I didn't want him to go to Dubruis. I gave up. It made him crazy... these voices won't leave him. And that Officer Vale... If I ever see that—"

"He's gone," I said with a sympathetic nod before she could complete her thought.

I didn't want to hear slander I had become sensitive to.

Vale was gay. When I met him, let's just say I assumed.

From the start, I knew there was something different about his habits, and he showed no interest in changing himself. For the first few months, our dialogue was mostly job-oriented, especially over whiskey. We worked well together, and I grew a fondness for his craft. It was not until a year in that I found out. I went to his apartment to pick him up on a late-night tip, and I unintentionally caught him with his partner—Arch Slayter.

Vale had missed my call.

At first, I was outraged. There was jail time for covering Undesirable Relationships. I yelled at him for putting my life in danger for his criminal actions. Those were the words I used, "criminal actions." And I'd never forget Vale's response.

"You're a miserable son of a bitch, and a shitty, alcoholic husband Madelyn was lucky to divorce—all crimes of nature. And you know what, old man? I'd still take a bullet for you."

His words stopped me cold. I left his apartment immediately, and the following day we did not speak of what happened. But as time passed, I learned about Vale's journey to self-discovery. He was once married to a woman of his class. And even though he had cared for that woman, in his heart, he grew to accept his love was for men. It didn't happen over one day but over years. At first, he was terrified; it haunted him in his sleep. I concluded it was the start of his insomnia. But once he came to terms, he did every possible opportunity to express himself in the most secretive ways.

He feared for his life. The penalty for the wrong selection was Dubruis. There was a whole hospital wing for those caught in Undesirable Relationships. But over time, Vale found the worst crime would be to repress your love.

I think Madelyn had suspected Vale's relationship long before I did. So she never asked, in fear of my answer and her career. I think she kept quiet because she was secretly against any sort of penalty for Undesirable Relationships—one of the few.

And I made every effort to keep it from her. But the more I obsessed over Vale's life, and the longer I spent hiding from my granddaughter, the more agitated she became with him. I can see why. After Sarina's death, Vale became the sole person I trusted more than anyone—including Madelyn.

But even though I loved Vale like a son, it was what he taught me about love that brought us closer. It all ties back to a day, months after I caught Arch and him. I remember I said, "Vale, you're a young, handsome man. I'm sure most men or women would be happy to be with you."

Vale stayed quiet and rested his mouth on his fingers. Then he simply asked, "Why Madelyn?"

"What?"

"There was a time before your divorce when you chose her. Why was that?"

I had paused, unsure how to answer, so I thought for a long minute. "I mean... when first met, the way she smiled at me... and she had this wit that made me laugh, especially when she was sarcastic." I chuckled and shook my head. "It always struck me as smart. I love smart humor. And I knew she had my back, always... parts of me still feel that way." I swallowed the lump in my throat, thinking of the boy who fell in love. My words thawed into a raw mess on the dashboard. "Hell, she's a beautiful person, you know? Time froze every moment she spoke, and when her hand rested, that was merely the Earth in her palm. I never saw someone so in control of their beliefs, so empathetic for mankind. Vale, I couldn't breathe around her because she took it away with every smile and gave it back with every laugh."

I would never sound more poetic. A tear trailed down my face. It was the first since Sarina died and one I should have used to mourn with Madelyn over our daughter. I did not see those emotions coming.

Vale placed his hand on my shoulder. "Why would there be a restriction on that opportunity?"

I could not answer.

The taboo of their relationship was rooted in why the wall surrounded the Northeast Quadrant. At the time, I would do anything to protect the cause of the wall, and any opposition boiled my blood. Vale knew, and over the years, he poked at my rationale. I think he enjoyed flustering me, but it solidified why I was right about my beliefs.

I took faith for fact. But for the first time, Vale cracked my foundation. Ironically, the one time he was not trying to. In hindsight, I was not crazy enough to explore my demons... madness was not yet my compass. However, I could already feel it nibbling my fingers. I was diving into the abyss.

I gradually did everything to protect Vale and Arch against their wishes. I felt I at least could still save a real relationship. Madelyn's love and Vale's love are each unique but still an entity for my soul. And I feel that makes sense. Because to me, love has no eyes and, if anything, is as blind as I am.

I reentered my mind to the investigation.

"I'm sorry… I shouldn't have said anything…" Ms. Moreno said, "Please don't tell. I can't go to jail. My boy will at least be safe in the intensive ward instead of th-that one…"

"Come again?" I asked as the bald man guided me away from her and to the court entrance. I turned away, not wanting to see Ms. Moreno's reaction. I turned to the guard. "May I ask who the physician for this hearing is?"

"Dr. Morbus."

I followed the security guard into the mental health court. I disliked being in the room—an austere and compact extension of the main building of Dubruis. Two wooden tables faced each other, one for the patient and the other for the state. In the back, Dr. Morbus sat at a comically small desk for his frame. And in the front, the judge sat at a large wooden oak desk. He was a balding lanky English male.

A digital clock hung at the edge of the desk, only turned on when a case was underway. In the background, the flag and large windows surrounded the judge's desk.

The state lawyer, who wore a navy dress jacket and a short pixie cut, nudged her head to the empty chair.

I sat down. My stomach knotted.

Carl Moreno stared at me. His eyes were bloodshot, his face was pale, and his thick hair lost all sheen. His cheeks were hollow, making his face look nearly as lifeless as Marie Dalton. He wore a white t-shirt and teal scrub pants, with handcuffs around his wrists and ankles.

The transformation disturbed me. I nodded hello to Moreno, but he did not respond. I decided then if you tell a man enough times that he's crazy… he will eventually believe it.

The clock turned on.

"Lieutenant Price, I'd like you to raise your hand," the judge said. I took my oath.

"I would like to hear your account of the events that occurred," the state lawyer said.

I explained the details of the horrible night in Dalton Manor, from when Vale and I heard a scream in the blood room until we found Moreno stuck, holding a shard of glass, then dropped to the floor.

The state and defense lawyers took notes. "I understand that both Officer Moreno and Officer Vale were partners in your quadrant," the state lawyer said. "How would you describe their relationship?"

"Appropriate."

"Could you elaborate more?"

"They were professional; they had each other's back. They could go out for some drinks… Listen, I get where you're going with this—"

"Then why did Officer Vale file a restraining order against Officer Moreno on April 5th of last year?"

"Officer Vale did not feel safe around Officer Moreno."

"I have the statement here. He said, and I quote, 'Carl Moreno fired a shot in my direction that I believe was intentional due to his recent episodes of instability.' Could you elaborate further?"

"From what I had heard from Officer Vale, during their last few months working together, Officer Moreno had isolated himself. I don't know much else."

"Do you believe Officer Moreno shot in Officer Vale's direction on purpose?"

"Yes. I don't see why this is relevant."

"Did Officer Moreno treat him differently?"

"*She told me how,*" Moreno said, flat-toned. Everyone turned to him, shocked he spoke.

The defense lawyer put his sausage fingers on Moreno's wrist. In response, Moreno banged the table. "No! He must know she brought me in!" Moreno said.

"Guards hold him down," the judge said with a bark.

"Wait!" I stood up and held my hands out. "I actually would like to hear this. This case has hit a wall, and Officer Moreno has not been able to speak to me."

"Objection, Your Honor," the defense lawyer said.

"Sorry, Lieutenant, this is not your interrogation room."

"It stared at me with that fucking eye." Moreno blankly stared. Silence took over the court. "All I wanted to do was get those feelings to go away. Make them go away! But it dragged me into a hole. I could not see anything."

I clenched my jaw.

He said "eye"... He couldn't possibly mean White Eye, could he?

Vale's demonic White Eye plagued my imagination.

"I advise you to stop speaking," the defense lawyer said to Moreno, sounding defeated and already indifferent to his client's behavior.

"I didn't want to go," Moreno said, "but darkness surrounded me, and I sunk in. It opened my head. My little fucking head. I needed to leave it. I need it to go away. It kept licking my fingers, wanting to get more of a *taste*. But I killed it. It was a powerful moth-erfucker. I was so happy I could *screeeaaammmmmm...*"

A chill shot down my spine.

What the hell have they done to him here? I thought. *This couldn't actually be real? If it was... how could this tie into everything?*

Then I caught myself. Was I actually starting to enter Vale's train of thought?

The guards restrained Moreno. The defense lawyer shook his head, and his toupee tipped over. The judge's eyes flared.

"Carl Moreno, since you have shown signs of being a threat to others and yourself, you will be required to stay for a maximum of sixty days before being reevaluated again." The judge slammed the gavel on the desk. "Bring in the next case."

The guards lifted Moreno, and he attempted to resist. Three more bodies tackled him. "Code Blue!" a voice yelled.

A hand dropped on my shoulder. It belonged to Dr. Morbus. His towering presence and baldhead stood over me. "You best leave, my friend," he said, guiding me through the lone door.

I quickly traveled back across Dubruis's Campus, wondering about what exactly Moreno had said. I was baffled. The way Moreno said "that fucking eye" in a trance replayed in my head. The case was making less sense by the minute.

But the White Eye isn't real, I thought.

I walked into the parking lot. From across the way, Vale lay unconscious in the passenger seat. My heart galloped. I sprinted over, hopping into the car and shaking him.

Vale's eyes flared open, and he pulled his gun to my cheek.

"It's just me," I said, nerves firing.

Vale breathed heavily, and his eyes darted everywhere around the Crown Victoria. I noticed a jar of rubbing alcohol and gauze on the car mat.

"Tell me everything Moreno told you." Vale lowered his gun, sweating.

"Jesus, what the hell happened?"

"I knocked myself out."

My eyes widened. "What in God's name is wrong with you?"

"I acquired another memory of Marie Dalton while you were in the courtroom with Moreno. Tell me exactly what he said."

"This shit is getting out of hand."

I sat down in the driver's seat and closed the door. I studied the parking lot and saw no one.

"Start driving," Vale said.

I drove the car out of the parking lot, past several dormitory-style buildings, and onto a one-lane road in the Pinelands. Once Dubruis was out of sight in my rear-view mirror, I told Vale the entire court hearing and the exact words from Moreno.

Vale tucked his lips and stared at the windshield. "Of course, the Morenos are in the Society."

"I thought you didn't know."

"I always suspected. But it is hard to see a beast behind its mask."

"Moreno never brought it up?"

"Not once. And I never noticed any prominent scars. He was probably shunned due to his history."

"Jesus."

"Thankfully, he did not repeat anything I dreamt from Marie's memory."

"Please, just call it a dream."

"You must believe me."

"I don't, Vale. Think about what you are saying. It sounds fucking crazy."

"I'm just following scriptures. There is a chance he was infected with the White Eye by standing in the portal at Dalton Manor. If that was the case, my dreams of Marie's memory might have been able to tap into his possessed state. But thankfully, you heard nothing like that in court. Though, it has been a few days. He could have returned to normalcy by now."

"Dammit, none of what you're saying makes any fucking sense. And I suppose all that Os said was bullshit?"

"What does he know?" Vale asked defiantly.

"A lot more than us. Look at what we're stuck with, the little we have! We're in the Stone Age out here, Vale. He has resources beyond our comprehension. The Waterfront is one of the few places that's on track with the rest of the world. He's someone we've been looking for as an ally this whole time."

"You don't honestly trust him? Who needs that stuff? I deal with people; there's nothing more real."

"That is just the thing, Vale. You set up your own limitations."

"Price, when I was on the coast for the first time, I saw some real magic trickle down from the black markets that have opened my eyes to what we've missed in our lives."

"You sure it's magic? I thought you ruled out the unexplainable."

"I do. But I've still seen things I can't explain."

"Did you not go to the coastline to escape from the life you could not face here?"

"Are you serious, Price?"

"Damn right, I am."

"I left this fucking place so that court case you just waltzed into would not be for Arch."

"And what about you?"

"I would have killed myself long before then."

"You don't mean that do you?" I asked, my tone suddenly soft.

Vale did not respond for several minutes. Once more, I wished he would say something.

"Vale?"

"Have you ever seen someone leave the Undesirable ward?"

I didn't answer.

"That's because no one has ever. You'd be better off a *lesser* in the Northeast Quadrant."

Silence took over the car.

Lesser. The vile slur for Type B citizens not exempted from the Northeast, the most damning word anyone could be called. My eyelid twitched, and my darkest demon smelled blood anytime the word was spoken. I could feel the demon poke its nose into my consciousness and sniff, salivating.

"Did you tell the lawyers what really happened with Moreno?" he asked.

"Of course not! You know I would never. Let's just take it easy for a moment," I said, after fully processing Vale was the source of that word, the slur lesser. I repressed my demon back into the dark abyss of my subconscious.

Vale did not respond once more and turned away for a long while as we drove deep into the Pinelands. Several county roads later, Vale said, "I'm just being human. No less than you."

"And what's that supposed to mean?" I asked, already knowing where the conversation was steering.

"Do you really feel you're more similar to Os than me?"

"Genetically, yes."

"I need a better explanation."

Vale didn't budge. I gave in and said, "Os and I still have the same genes to connect to robotics as last year."

"It's just funny," Vale said, "you don't have any robotics installed."

"With my pay grade? Of course not. Who can outside the Waterfront?"

"Yet, you really think Os identifies with you."

"Just as much as with you."

"I am not a cyborg."

"And here we go."

"Just observation. The Waterfront strolls around with their cybernetics and spaceships to Mars."

"First off, they're human, not cyborgs," I said. "This isn't some fantasy bullshit."

"And I'm less human? A lesser?"

"No, Vale. For the hundredth time, if either of us were, we would be in Northeast."

"More likely dead. Do you know what the life expectancy is Northeast?"

I raised my brow. "Just watch where you say 'cyborg.'"

"I called Arch a cyborg many times. He laughs."

"Because Arch has patience that I'll never understand. Look, maybe you'll be able to reconnect to robotics one day…"

"And maybe you'll reconnect with humans…"

"Do you listen to yourself talk?"

"ODYSE's robotics might connect to your brain. But your drives, emotions—you know, that really make us human—don't care. Why do you think the penalty is so severe for cyborg intimacy with humans?"

"To protect our gene pool for survival," I said sternly. "The rest of the world is more connected with cybernetics."

"Price, whether you want to believe it or not, humans are more attracted to humans! Not cyborgs. The Waterfront is getting less human."

"America needs every genetic chance to catch up," I said, rolling my eyes.

"The American Dream," Vale scoffed, taking out his maroon notebook from inside a pocket of his flowered vest. He jotted notes, signaling he was done.

I didn't bother asking what he was doing.

I drove in silence.

At some point, Vale turned on the radio to bug me successfully.

"*—in Board member Clifton Bagwell's words, he 'wanted to check on the spirit' of the Waterfront citizens at a town hall and be more hands-on to better address the needs of the Northeast's infrastructure during the flooding.*

"*Of course, many of the Northeast Quadrant's homes have been flooded for over two days and for the next foreseeable future.*

"*The confrontation with several Waterfront citizens started as soon as Clifton Bagwell entered with several of our news cameras. He had interrupted a large prayer circle organized by St. Mary's Protestant Church's pastor and fellow Board member, John Radnor. Pastor Radnor came unannounced to the town hall each night since the ordeal began to discuss with the citizens their beliefs about why this happened and learn how to address the Board's shortcomings.*

"Some of the outraged citizens assaulted Bagwell. Two were arrested.

"Of note, Pastor Radnor has no strikes under the American Rule, and recent polls have indicated he will be spared from the Northeast infrastructure failure. Clifton Bagwell, on the other hand, already has one strike and will almost definitely be getting a second, whereas Madelyn Katz will be relegated at the end of this month with her third after their monthly votes of approval are counted..."

I zoned out to Vale's radio show as the drive became frustrating. We got lost twice. I rarely ventured this deep into the Pinelands. The roads turned to sand, and signs were sparsely used. I drove the Crown Victoria several miles off the nearest paved road and parked beside a sandy lawn. Through the pine trees, a split-level house with blue shutters and mossy siding hid against the shadows.

Vale and I stepped out of the car and took in the surroundings. The density of the pine trees darkened the background, and the stillness spiked my neck hairs. We walked along a stone driveway.

To my surprise, the closer I came to the house, the more put-together it became. A vibrant red radiated underneath the moss and vines that grew up a layer of trellis that bordered the house. The window frames looked new. And a plethora of orbs of various colors hung off branches of the pine trees. The driveway met a fork, leading to either a garage tucked off in the distance or a small porch that fit only two lawn chairs on either side.

We walked to the entrance, and I pressed the doorbell.

Halfway through the chime, the door opened to reveal a stocky woman with brown hair towering to the sky, held up by what smelled like a healthy dose of spray. She wore thick oval frames that magnified her heavy black eyeliner and over her wrinkly eyelids. Colorful earrings of different shapes hung from her earlobes, and locks of red hair dangled from a single chain necklace. She wore a loose black cloak over black dress pants.

She looked at us, alarmed.

"Good afternoon, ma'am. I'm looking for Marseille Brezniack," I said.

"This is her," she said in a heavy French accent.

"I'm Lieutenant Price of the Haddon Police." I brought out my badge. "And this is Private Investigator Max Vale."

Vale brought out his badge with the blue circle and nodded.

Concern pulled her brows together over her eyes. She asked, "Is everything okay?" She widened her eyes and puffed her cheeks.

"Your son Martin was on a case with me two days ago. Since then, I can't seem to contact him. I was wondering if you had heard from him."

"No, I have not," she said.

"May we ask a few questions about your son?"

"Sure, would you like to come inside?"

"If you don't mind."

Marseille opened the door, and we walked in. My heart pushed through my chest at how dim the room was. In the center, four candles were lit.

I scanned the room, having difficulty making out details. A sharp fragrance I had never come across smacked my nostrils.

"Excuse me, let me open up some windows." She stepped into the darkness. One by one, light appeared from five windows.

I furrowed my brow. Four candles stood on an altar that surrounded a carving of a star within a circle. A large textbook was to the left of the candles, and steam wafted from a cauldron to the right that I believed to be the source of the fragrance. Over curtains, fangs of all different shapes and sizes hung, tied together by strings. Two knives wedged into the ends of the altar.

I jumped. A shadow of a person was in the far corner. I then realized it was a life-size carving of a woman wearing a curly red wig.

"You have to excuse me, sir. I was in the middle of meditation."

"No need to excuse. I apologize for interrupting," I said.

Marseille guided us into the kitchen. The room had a similar feel. The wallpaper was black, and crystals rested along shelves against the back wall. Several potion vials and a tower of animal skin next to the kitchen sink rested on the countertops.

"Please, gentlemen, have a seat," Marseille said as she opened a cabinet and pulled out two candles.

"Thank you, Ms. Brezniack."

"Please, call me Marseille."

We sat down. I scanned the other side of the kitchen and noticed from this angle, through a different doorframe, several more knives hung on the wall over a couch.

"Tea?" she asked.

"No, thank you," we both said.

Marseille sat down on a small wooden chair across from Vale. "What would you like to know about my son?"

"When was the last time you talked to him?" Vale asked.

"Last week. We usually start to prepare for Samhain around this time."

"You'll have to forgive me. I don't encounter Wiccans much," I said.

"You probably have. Most of us practice in private within our families. Our craft rarely leaves our lips in public. Samhain is on Halloween to celebrate the change to the 'more spiritual' side of the calendar."

I scratched my chin.

"The darker side, officer! We believe it enhances our mediation. At least, that's how I was raised. Wicca is a lot more—how should I say—*diverse* than other religions. You ask ten families, you will get ten different answers. For example, my rodent skin on the kitchen countertop is an essential part of my mother and her mother's practice. But I know most other Wiccans don't use them."

I sat back in the chair and nodded. "Do you talk to Martin much?" I asked.

"I do, but not as much as I used to."

"What makes you say that?" Vale asked.

"Since he came back from the college a few years ago, I can sense he has been straying away from me by getting involved in darker arts."

"What do you mean by darker?"

"Evil," Marseille said, chilling the room.

"Is he not involved with your meditations as much?"

"No, that is the same amount. In fact, if anything, he has become more spiritual."

"I don't think I understand," I said.

"He's hung around a new group of friends since he came back from college. I don't know what exactly he has been up to, but I feel it's a different world than what I do. And for whatever reason, when we meditate together on the holidays, it gets more intense than I'm used to."

"In what way?" Vale asked.

Marseille leaned back in her seat and wrinkled her nose. "He seeks suffering," she said. "That's not what we do. See, when I grew up, I was taught the differences between the light goddesses and dark goddesses. What good is that? The goal has always been to find light in the darkest places. That is when we feel most in touch with our light goddesses because that's how we can fully appreciate the importance of light within our spiritual awareness, hmm? But with Martin lately, I can sense when we are in meditation, more and more, he has shifted his energy to seek the darkest places possible without questioning if the light goddesses can go there. Officer, these are places that no one should enter."

"Any physical changes?" Vale asked.

"None that I've seen."

"Does he have any other family members?" I asked.

"That deadbeat uncle of his! But that's it."

"I don't feel like you are too concerned with his absence..." I said.

"No! Why should I? He's done this the past few years. I guess never with his job… But still, he will just run off with his friends for days at a time. Why is this no different?"

"I was the last person from the police to see him two days ago. We were on a case together, and he became spooked, quitting on the spot."

Marseille grew tense. "Now there's one word you said there that concerns me, sir… *spooked*. Because my son might not be built to handle a gun, but he does not get spooked."

"He was from the moment I saw him that night. In fact, I've rarely bumped into him in the station before then. So I can't even picture him any other way," I said.

"Then I don't know what he is up to."

"You think the way he was acting could be related to this change in spirit with him?" Vale asked.

"It has to be!"

"When he left our crime scene, he told us, 'We are not welcomed here,'" Vale said.

"Then you should probably listen."

"He also said, 'Not with the air this thin. Demons weigh you down in these parts.' Then he repeated a few times, 'I can't be seen.'"

"Officer, I can't tell you what my son was thinking. Because it has no ties to me, and I want no part of it."

"Right. Sorry again for disrupting your meditation for this," I said.

"Nonsense, you are always welcomed here. But if there is actual meaning behind his words that is associated with whatever darkness he keeps searching for… well, you should be on your guard. Because he might have found it."

Arch finished his daily search through Dalton Manor. He stepped outside. The light scurried through the pine trees onto the sandy yard.

A tulip petal was pinned to his sleeve, and on the same side, a sleek gray cloth covered his thumb and pointer finger. He pressed them together. Red dots appeared on his knuckles. He spread his fingers to the shape of an "L," and a light blue screen grew to the size of a piece of paper in space. He gripped the screen as it turned solid.

On the screen, he typed the evening's details from his search of the manor. He had found a whole new section that Vale and Price did not discover. Once he finished, he pressed the cloth on his thumb and pointer finger again, and the screen faded.

Arch scanned the pine trees. Within the weeds, there was a rusty swing set attached to a broken-down wooden tree house and slide. It looked ready to disintegrate with the next gust of wind.

His head perked. From the ground, a baby robin chirp near the edge of the forest. Arch's eyes caught the robin lying in the sand in agony. With caution, he walked over. The bird had a broken wing. He studied the wing as his mind rushed back into the horrors of the blood room. After a moment, he decided he didn't have the heart to take the bird out of its misery. He gently picked up the bird. "I'll fix you."

Across the lawn, behind the swing set, something had been watching him.

He took out a flashlight and shined it in that direction. The light caught nothing. He softly placed the bird in his coat pocket. He sprinted over and brought out his pistol to the edge of the pine trees.

A knock came from straight ahead. His flashlight could not capture the source.

For a minute, his heart pounded through his chest as he studied the trees and found nothing significant.

Then the knock spread through the forest again.

Arch fired a warning shot back. "Get out here!"

From the pine trees, a shadow of a creature appeared with several spikes on its back.

Arch grew pale. He fired a second a shot at it, but it disappeared into the dense darkness of the pines. *I need to get to my fucking car.*

He stepped backward, keeping his gun pointed into the darkness.

Through the weeds, the creature growled and grabbed onto his legs and face. A massive force pushed him onto the ground. He tasted sand. It dragged his body into the pine trees.

Arch, half-dazed, gripped onto a root that flew by his vision.

The creature effortlessly yanked him. Arch lost his grip and was tossed into another row of pine trees, knocking his pistol out of his hand.

Arch cursed. He reached for where he heard his gun bang on the ground. But before he could find it, a cold chill spread onto his cheeks and ripped into his skull. His fingers were bitten off, all at once. He screamed in agonizing pain.

The last sensation he felt was the prickle of pine needles against the roof of his mouth.

VIII

STATIC CREATURES

Diary entry written by Max Vale

MARIE SAT ON the left seat. She had grown a few inches over the past couple of years and let her dark hair dangle like her mother.

Ragg sat on the other chair.

"Let's end today's session with some arts and crafts!" Ms. Mugsby said. She placed the box down at the corner of the desk and blew the dust off the cardboard box and into her wavy dark hair that recently sprouted some grays.

"Where did you find all that?" Shyla asked.

"Your boxes have been piling up here and there, sweetie. They were throughout the library. So I thought it be fun to get creative with a project today."

"Doesn't that sound fun, Marie?" Shyla asked.

"Yes, Mommy."

Ms. Mugsby dug in her hands and pulled out an array of items—a bottle of glue, cardboard, scissors—and a dozen pieces of black silk.

Shyla's eyes widened at the sight of the black silk scraps. They had belonged to Marie. She tried to remain composed, but she felt herself shrivel.

"What is it?" Ms. Mugsby asked.

"I guess… I didn't realize I had all of that," Shyla said in a daze. "What were you thinking of making today?"

"I thought since we've spent so much time in the recent months birdwatching, it could be fun to make a few cutouts. Would you like to do that, Marie?"

"Yes, please."

"What would those be for?" Shyla pointed to the black silk.

"Feathers… Darling, are you okay?"

"Of course I am," Shyla said, grabbing an extra pair of scissors from the box. "Marie, is there any type of bird you'd like to make?"

"A small one."

At the front of Shyla's desk, Ms. Mugsby's hands guided Marie to cut a shape of a bird from the cardboard. Shyla watched Marie cut pieces out with the black silk, and she crinkled her nose as the scissor blade sliced. Then Marie glued the silk on, plus other knick-knacks from the box—little eyeballs and orange paper used for a beak and legs—to complete a bird.

She made more and chopped into the cloth. In the end, four flat small black birds lay on the desk.

"Great job, sweetie!" Ms. Mugsby said.

"They're cute but sort of funny looking. I think that's why I like them," Marie said.

"That's wonderful, dear," Shyla said. "How do they make you feel?"

"Relaxed, because I made them. I know what they will do."

"Not all things you make are in your control, though," Shyla said, mind still fixed on the silk feathers.

"That's true, Mommy."

"And you don't want to be in control of all these birds, right?"

"No, Mommy, I only want to do what feels right, showing them my love. Just how you love me." Marie held a bird in the air, flaunting its black cloth.

Shyla jotted a few notes onto a loose-leaf sheet of paper. She asked, "When you get to the point when the bird no longer listens to you, what will you do with it?"

"I'd put the bird somewhere out of sight."

"Would you ever see it again?"

"No."

"Would it be inside or outside?"

"Outside."

"Could you show us where you would put the bird outside?"

"I don't know where," Marie said with a bite. Her face started to empty of emotion.

"Well, what would you do first?"

"I'd stand up."

All three stood up. Ms. Mugsby bumped the box off the table, and an assortment of knick-knacks fell all over the room. "Oh, dear! I'm so sorry. Are you okay, sweetie?" Ms. Mugsby said to Marie, who did not budge from the items falling on her.

A piece of black silk covered Marie's face. Her arms lowered. "Nothing you could control," Marie said in a raspy bass voice.

Shyla dove across the desk and ripped the silk off. Her daughter appeared lifeless. "Marie?"

No response. A heavy energy sunk the room. Ms. Mugsby and Shyla started to shake. "Did she ever shut off this fast?" Ms. Mugsby asked.

"Never." Shyla stared at Marie's empty face. "Do it again." She handed Ms. Mugsby the silk.

"Why would we ever?"

"Just try."

Ms. Mugsby hesitated, then placed the silk over her face.

"Can you hear me?" Shyla asked.

No response.

"Cover her entire face," Shyla said. "And press it into her so she cannot see the light."

"Shyla, she needs to breathe."

"Do it," Shyla snapped.

Ms. Mugsby glared.

"She'll be fine," Shyla said.

Ms. Mugsby expanded the silk as far as she could and positioned it exactly how she had it before. The edges of Marie's features pressed through the cloth. Her nose and brow protruded.

"Can you hear me, Marie?" Shyla asked again.

"I can always hear you," Marie said in the low voice. Her jaw moved against the black silk.

Ms. Mugsby's hands began to tremor.

Shyla tensed. She sat in front of Marie, staring at the black silk as if there was a deeper image. She tried to calm herself. "Where are we?"

"In the dark."

Shyla smeared her hands on her thighs. "Am I talking to Ragg?"

"Yes, my dear mother."

"How?"

"You brought my change to the surface."

"What do you see?"

"I don't see, Mother, I *feel*."

"Then what do you feel, Ragg?"

"Everything. Your world is only a fraction of mine."

"How can you do that?"

"Mother, I live it. Everyone feels and creates a powerful substance we have yet to detect. You… Father… Ms. Mugsby… the people we see in Haddon. The birds. Everyone who has and will ever exist creates these feelings, and they connect with the Deus."

Shyla and Ms. Mugsby looked alarmed by the word. Shyla said, "How did you know about—?"

"The Deus? Of course I know. I feel our souls before and after we cross over."

Shyla paused and paced around the room. Ms. Mugsby looked dumbfounded, unable to speak.

"What do the dead feel like?" Shyla asked.

"*Colors intertwined with static*—a mix of my existence in both the spiritual and physical world. The colors are what they really feel like in the Deus, and the static is the physical world's interpretation that I must also see since I am bound to this world."

"Where do they exist?"

"In the darkness."

"If you're in the dark, how do you feel colors?"

"Mother, I am the darkness," Ragg growled. "Spirits, amongst many other entities, enter my labyrinth in the afterlife."

"Why are you in my daughter?"

Ragg laughed.

"What's so funny, you monster?"

"I love you, Mother, that's all."

"God dammit! Get out of her!"

"I am Marie Dalton."

"You're not my daughter!"

"I am Marie Dalton. I am Marie Dalton. I am Marie Dalton. I am Marie Dalton. I am Marie Dalton."

"Stop! Stop!" Shyla said while waving her hand at Ms. Mugsby to keep the mask on.

Ragg's laugh deepened, then tumbled into a low hiss that left Shyla shivering.

"Why Marie?" Shyla asked.

"She was the bright star in my darkness. I must fill the space, especially when she shines the brightest." The silk wrinkled around Ragg's jaw and turned into a gloomy smile.

"But how? Why not me? Why not anyone else?"

"I don't care to know all answers, Mother."

"How did we summon you now?"

"Because humans might only give a fraction of what's in the Deus... but make no mistake, love and hate are the two strongest contributions."

Ragg's smile widened, stretching the silk to indent Marie's lips. "When I look through this cloth, this poor excuse of a mask, I feel the love you felt from Nana when she wrapped your frail body and sang to you every night as you battled your cancer... and how you tried to do the same to your daughter. Love is so powerful... I know you feel it. But let me assure you, it is nothing compared to what I *sense*. I feel an endless amount more of this love in the Deus. It spreads beyond your physical laws. So much so it presses into your world. I enjoy watching it haunt you... Can't you feel the weight of the room drag you down?"

"What the hell is wrong with you?" Shyla yelled.

"Mother, do you know what I offer only for your cooperation? An entry into the spiritual world..."

"Why would I want that?"

"Because I can make your daughter well."

"How?"

"She is not alone. There is another I sense in this physical world who can help... oh, but he does not shine nearly as bright. And his light has faded for years..."

"Who?" Shyla asked. Ragg only laughed. She grabbed Ragg's shoulders. "Fucking tell me what is happening to my daughter!"

Shyla's voice echoed in the office. A chill swarmed her as she realized how tight of a grip she had on her daughter's shoulder bones, stunned she could have hurt Marie.

Shyla released her daughter and trembled.

Ragg's laugh deepened.

"Your path is written in the Deus. If you really love your daughter, I am sure the dead could help show you how to help her."

Shyla stood shocked, now as frozen as Ms. Mugsby.

"Do you want to talk to a spirit? Like your mother?" Ragg asked.

End of diary entry

*   *   *

Vale told me the details of his dream on the ride home to my town-house. I was distraught by the level of detail he went into and his enthusiasm. "You're saying this shit won't leave you?" I asked.

"Do you even care about the details? You're just going to brush off all that's going on? That person is me! This is what the Society had planned for me!"

"You're getting too caught up in this case. How the hell are we going to get to the bottom of this if you keep getting this lost in your past?"

"It's not like I wanted to be in this mess," Vale said.

"Your twin sister died. As much as you can outthink emotions, I knew you would do anything if there was a chance to save her, even with Moreno there."

Vale did not respond.

"How can you follow the evidence when you're too worried about every person coming after you?" I asked.

"We don't know who we are investigating," Vale said. "This isn't some corner bust in the Northeast. We're entering a world where people have died in horrifying ways on a regular basis. The coastline morphed bodies into deformities I could never imagine."

"You've seen it?" I asked.

Vale shook his head.

"Then I'm sure there's some explanation like every other case we've been on."

"The world's full of hate, Price. That's your answer."

"That's some depressing fucking shit, Vale."

"It's not us, Price. We didn't look for it. The way this world is set up has evil planted in our minds. You and I chose to hunt in it, searching for some sort of endgame, just like simpletons before us."

"Dammit, Vale. We're out to get one evil son of a bitch, not the entire world."

"Why are you not worried about this more?" Vale asked.

"What do you mean? Of course I am. I've been terrified ten times already."

"Looks like nothing more than any other old Northeast case?"

"The rest is all bullshit. I'm worried about you more than anything."

"Fine. What would you prefer we do tonight then, Lieutenant?"

"Stay away from the scriptures, don't dive into that weird fucking language of yours. Let's just drink some whiskey."

Vale's face hardened. "You want me to drink whiskey at a time like this?"

I glared.

"That is the stupidest thing we could do. I have a night's worth of reading to tackle, and I'm finally making headway about the Deus and the blood room. You have all your fieldwork reports that you haven't even started. We're just going sit back and do nothing?"

"No, Vale. We're going to screw our heads back on our shoulders."

"That's doing nothing."

"Exactly."

"Nothing comes of nothing."

"No, everything comes from nothing. If you just turned your mind off sometimes, maybe you'd see that." My stare pierced him. And for once, Vale folded.

A short time later, we arrived at my townhouse and went into the kitchen. I poured my favorite bottle into two glasses before he could object.

"Cheers. To our sanity," I said.

Vale grunted but played along.

The clock in my kitchen ticked by the hours of the night as one drink unintentionally became a few.

For a long time, we talked about nothing, absolutely nothing. I thought the case would have clouded Vale's mind, but the moment we pushed it aside, I felt he never wanted to think about it ever again. It was beautiful. Even the Board or PATC did not even come up.

"Your tolerance has gone down," I said, pouring my fifth glass.

"Of course, when I'm competing with the marathon drinker." Vale placed his hand over the cup.

I shook the bottle.

"Oh hell, fine," Vale said.

I poured him a healthy helping. I didn't want the fun to stop. But with the fourth glass, Vale slipped back into his anxious state. He morphed. His words became less slurred and more cryptic and deranged. He kept staring at the clock. And with each passing minute, the conversation shifted to a topic I would have never brought up again sober—Vale's anxiety.

"The medication did wonders for the longest time, and you did not even suspect me," he said.

"Why would I? You were always so calm."

"On the surface, sure. You have to realize no matter how much you know me, all you see is what's on my surface. The medication digs."

"How does it work?"

"It makes certain switches of mine harder to turn on, and when they, do it's not as potent. I'm still me."

"You know you don't have to hide the meds from me while you're here. You can just take it in front of me."

"What do you mean?"

"You have everything else out in the living room labeled and organized... You don't have to hide your pills."

"I don't take pills anymore."

"But you just admitted it to me last night."

"I told you I have anxiety, and I have my own medication; that's what you forced from me. I haven't taken a pill since I moved to the coastline. This is my medication now." Vale brought out the small maroon notebook he had been writing his dreams into.

"Writing is your medication?"

"Of course, Price, and arts and crafts."

Vale pointed behind me to the counter. I was so focused on drinking I had not even noticed Vale's mask. It was the Greek tragedy mask he had from his desk. Only now, red paint, like blood, outlined every crevice with little straight lines. And there was an "X" over each eye.

"The mask was mine as a teenager in the Society. It was from when I was the conduit to connect to the Deus. You see, we would trace these markings in bird's blood over our masks before a ritual and wash them away with our sins. The Society abolished them some time after me. I decided to repaint it as I relived that life, the one item I never tossed."

"This is madness."

"It's exploration. I need to search for darkness on my own."

"You stopped taking pills for your fucking job?"

"I sacrificed my body to try and abolish my Society, whether I'm their prodigy or not."

"And you lost your sanity on the way."

"You think I'm crazy?"

"I've never met a man so afraid of people looking at his shadow."

"Because I actually know what I am." Vale leaned back on the kitchen counter, flaring his eyes. "I don't hide it like you."

"I do what's best."

"That's getting you real far, Price."

"Like you're any better? You ran away to the coastline to try and hide."

"I did what's best for Arch. I didn't settle."

"I have a granddaughter; I'm not leaving her."

"Funny, I don't recall you running off to visit Novah this entire visit."

"Why would I?"

Vale did not respond for a minute. I took a large swig of whiskey and felt it burn the back of my throat.

"Price, we need to discuss everything," Vale slurred.

"Not now."

"Then when?"

"There's nothing I can say to change what I did."

"At least know it's not your fault."

"No, it's all my fucking fault Sarina died, Vale."

"You have to face it."

"I'm going to bed."

"Wait, Price…"

I rose from my seat, and Vale hopped off the counter to block the kitchen entrance. "Then we at least need a fucking plan. I think they're onto us."

"No, they're not. And I'm starting to think no one cares about this case besides Os, and good for us! Marie Dalton should just be our focus." I stumbled down the hallway.

"You can't hide in here forever, Price!" Vale yelled. "I've seen a whole different world on the coastline. You don't know the half of it."

"Oh, for God's sake." I turned back around. "The real world is *here*, Vale."

"You've said that for decades. And yet we're still stuck with the same old technology. There are other ways to evolve. I've seen it."

"I thought you wanted to rule that crap out."

"Don't you get it, Price? I was that 'other star' Ragg was talking about. I was told during my whole childhood I was a god connecting to the Deus. I'm supposed to do something more. Maybe that's why the 'bots detect me."

"And you haven't done shit. Live in the real world, Vale. I need you on this case."

"Not everything can be explained, Price. Facts tend to twist in ways fiction can't imagine."

"I believe in what we're trying to do in Haddon. We're trying to save ourselves."

"You need a therapist," Vale said. "I've told you that since Sarina died."

"Don't say her name."

"Then sleep on it."

"Fuck you. Enjoy the dark alone."

I marched into my bedroom in a whirl of rage. My hands shook, and my jaw clenched. I wanted to scream. But I underestimated the whiskey's effects, and within minutes the alcohol got the better of me.

I passed out into a deep slumber.

*   *   *

Diary entry written by Max Vale

Canvases covered the room.

Some were hung up, and others were propped against the walls over top of each other. The content of each painting focused on two themes: *static* and *colors*. The shapes varied; some were lobular, while others were complicated enough to reveal parts of the human frame. The patterns varied in each picture; some were darker while others had a greater frequency of white. They were decorated with physical items such as cars, hats, and wedding rings. But the paintings also portrayed intangible concepts like feelings, aromas, and sensations through swirls. Each was labeled by a piece of paper and thumbtack.

Cutouts of newspaper articles from the obituary section of the *Haddon Herald* and surrounding newspapers were stapled below some of the static shapes. Their names, ages, dates of death, and certain phrases were highlighted.

Shyla's black wavy hair mixed with gray. Her frail hands and bony wrists rested on her desk, covered with scattered scribbled papers.

Marie sat on the usual chair to the left. The black silk covered her face tightly, with a small hole for breathing. Her dark brown hair dangled down her faded pink dress.

Ragg sat in the other chair with its blonde hair, two buttoned eyes, and a hint of a smile.

"Now it's time to go over your last session's painting, Ragg…"

"Thank you, Mother," Marie said in a bass voice.

Ms. Mugsby brought over a canvas. Two static creatures were painted like deformed humans. A third creature was a small lobe with little static.

"Of the three spirits you painted, we so far identified one."

The static shape on the left side of the canvas had an arm and a detailed hand. Its contour was of a pointy face. A blue rocking chair and hedge saw were embedded with streaks of orange.

"Nathan Lloyd. He was sixty-eight, passed four days ago. A carpenter, a loving father of three… He was known to be serious about his craft."

Shyla pinned the obituary below the static with the remarks highlighted and wrote the date of his death.

"The less static lobe was of a stillborn."

Shyla stiffened. "How do you know?"

"Her spirit was not fully developed. The colors can barely be felt in the Deus."

"Are you sure?"

"I've done this enough times."

"Why would the stillborn have less static and color?"

"I can't answer that, Mother."

"What are you sensing now?"

The time ticked by for ten minutes as the room stayed still. Shyla and Ms. Mugsby did not move, almost as lifeless as Marie.

"Nothing exists around me," Ragg finally said.

"Nothing…" Shyla exhaled like she had been holding her breath. "But… that's never happened."

Ragg kept silent.

"Give it time, Shyla!" Ms. Mugsby said in a dried-out voice. "Let her sink into the world a bit more."

"Thank you, Ms. Mugsby," Ragg said. "Your words keep you in great standing."

"Last session, you said you felt Nana close by," Shyla said.

"I'm having doubts, Mother. Her spirit is far away now."

"Why, after all this time? She needed to guide us from the other side. I needed to talk to her. You promised me we would talk."

"Mother, I promised you no such thing. You only felt you two would talk. Perhaps, you feel her all around you because she has been here the whole time."

"She couldn't do that, could she?" Shyla asked.

"Spirits can take many different forms in the Deus and stay with people and items for generations in our universe."

"So she's been here?"

"The whole time."

"Why didn't you tell me?"

"You felt it. Your love for Nana is so strong you can still feel her love from your soul on Earth to hers in the Deus. But her love wasn't enough. You wanted more questions answered… and I aim to serve." Ragg laughed.

"Then you failed. Nana hasn't helped me."

"Nana followed her path in the Deus, as we all do."

"I need to talk to your grandmother."

"And your souls will eventually do so one day… After all, we leave this place at our own pace."

"But why did she feel close to you in the Deus?"

"Because I'm her granddaughter. Every spirit has its own feeling of colors. Nana is one you recognize immediately, as have I with the taste of this cloth sucking into my mouth. Now, I cannot feel her colors anymore. She left you. It was her time to ascend higher."

"From our world?"

"Further in the Deus, Shyla! Listen to your daughter."

"Thank you again, Ms. Mugsby—"

"No, she couldn't have!" Shyla said. "She needed to help us from the other side!"

"And yet, you have her bloodline staring at you in the face," Ragg said. The black silk stretched into a possessed smile. "I'm everything in your world now."

"No, you're not."

"Shall I keep reminding you? I am your only daughter, your spawn, a product of your love. Why, what else would you like to imply?"

"Can we contact anyone from our family?"

"You mean your family?" Ragg asked.

"I thought you were my daughter, Ragg."

"I suggest you quiet your voice," Ms. Mugsby growled.

Shyla ignored her.

"I am your daughter on this planet. Yet, family is more a general term for the collective souls in the Deus. Colors are not as nuclear as you would like. Nana could still follow us in our universe from the Deus because the spiritual world and physical world exist together."

"Can we contact anyone else?" Shyla asked again, this time louder.

"Why would we?"

"They're your family. They love you."

"Like your husband?"

"What did you just say?"

"Do they treat you like your husband? Always talking down, patronizing…"

"Can you talk to anyone in the family?"

"I don't like your tone. I think you need a greater sense of my power in both universes. Would you like my influence?"

"What do you mean?"

"We've done this enough. You know the gist, right?"

"I hate you," Shyla said.

"Maybe if you come near me, I can let you in a little bit more."

"I would love to be part of your world, sweetie!" Ms. Mugsby said.

"Wait your turn. This question is directed at my mother."

Shyla stood up from her chair and walked around her desk. She ripped the homemade mask off of her daughter. Marie stared pale, cachectic, drained of life. "You're toying with us," Shyla said.

"She wouldn't do that," Ms. Mugsby said. "Put the mask back on."

"Fuck her."

"She was about to let you find the rest of your family!"

"She's been promising this for months!"

Shyla paced, huffing, then stood over her daughter. "Do you know what I can do to you? Do you think you can just sit here and pretend like nothing is going on?"

Shyla smacked her daughter on the cheek.

"You're killing us."

She smacked her again.

"Little by little."

"What are you doing?" Ms. Mugsby yelled.

Shyla punched Marie in the nose. She yelled from the pain in her arm and shook it off. She raised her arm and smashed her fist into her daughter's face again. But before she could swing a third time, she froze.

Ms. Mugsby had sprinted over and grabbed her arm, stopping it mid-swing.

Marie remained unmoved as blood dripped from her nostrils. Her nose was now bent.

Shyla's arm dropped.

"You won't hurt her anymore," Ms. Mugsby said.

Shyla walked back to her desk and sat down. "She's hurting us. She knew we couldn't contact them directly and has been dragging us further into her darkness."

"Shyla, she's too precious to be treated this way. The way she can grab your soul and bring you to another place! We need to keep exploring."

"Oh, we will. This is just the beginning, but we need help."

"You mean..." Ms. Mugsby's eyes flared.

"Yes, it is time. Our family chase was my last attempt to reach her with just us."

"What do we do?"

The office door opened. Ms. Mugsby turned and gasped, but Shyla remained unmoved, studying her daughter in a trance. A shadow stood at the doorway.

"Ms. Mugsby, I want you to meet an old childhood friend of mine. You've probably seen his face around Haddon..." She hinted a smile. "Os."

Ms. Mugsby was slaw-jacked by his presence. After several guttural pushes, words finally broke through. "I didn't know *he* was the man you saw."

"Shyla," Os said. His deep, smooth presidential voice filled the room. "I watched your session, and I am more convinced than ever she's everything the Deus's scriptures have prophesized."

"We need to keep her safe," Shyla said.

"You, Ms. Mugsby, and she will always be worshiped. And your theories... they can be explored in ways no has ever attempted."

"Anything to keep her safe," Ms. Mugsby said.

"The Deus chose her, Shyla," Os said. "She can connect her mind to her soul in ways no one has ever. It is the blessing of my life to take care of her." Os's shadow bent down on one knee. He hissed in a low demonic voice.

"What must we do next?" Shyla asked, watching the blood drip from Marie's nose.

"Perish the non-believer," Os said.

"I can do it tonight." Shyla hinted a smile.

"Soon. Last session, Ragg said he still held purpose. And I only advise through words from the Deus," Os said.

"I hate him!" Ms. Mugsby yelled before Shyla could echo the same sentiment.

"I'm afraid the Deus decides our significance," Os said. "When the time is apparent, *we* strike."

I'm coming for you, Dean thought. He opened the door and automatically reached his hand to the right. His hand punched a box. Dean shook. He felt around for the light switch, then turned it on. "You have to be fucking kidding me."

Containers flooded the foyer. It seemed like every day for the past six years, the number of boxes in the Manor grew. He had yelled at Shyla and Ms. Mugsby a million times to get rid of them. He even tossed some, but they would always get replaced with more. He had no idea what was in the containers, nor did he care. It was all junk. What the hell was the point of having all this stuff if you can't use it?

He grumbled and followed a path through the foyer to the living room, which he gave up maintaining. Boxes covered the floors and left only paths from the foyer to the kitchen and the couch to the TV. The only parts of the walls he could see were paintings Marie had made as part of her therapy of weird gray mutated humans. He never understood it.

Dean walked into the kitchen. The wall of appliances was by far the least occupied area on the first floor. But the kitchen nook was full of containers underneath the table.

"Hello, Dean."

He jolted and turned on the lights. Shyla sat at the table. "What are you doing in the dark?"

"Why did you jump? Didn't you recognize my voice?"

"You know how I hate getting startled!"

Shyla menacingly smiled and sipped her tea.

"Why are you drinking tea so late?"

"I'm waiting for you."

"Don't disrespect your husband. Why were you waiting in the dark?"

"You were supposed to be here at seven."

"For what?"

Shyla sunk her eyebrows inward.

Dean jolted again. He had forgotten.

"Happy twenty years... darling," she said.

Her voice stung the back of Dean's throat. He couldn't speak. "I'll make it up."

"I don't want to hear it."

Dean looked for any excuse, but there was no way around it. He had just been sitting in the office until late because he hated being home.

"I'm in real deep shit."

"Don't play with me, Dean Dalton. Or so help me God."

"Where's Marie?"

"Asleep."

"Can we talk in the library?"

"Here's fine."

"If I didn't want to talk in the library, I wouldn't ask you to."

Shyla sipped her tea and gave Dean the stink eye. Eventually, she stood up. They walked into a hallway where the library connected. They walked down the front aisle into the backspace. There were two rows filled with computers; three shelves in the back were stocked with vials and jars full of things he would never look at. He hated science and got queasy easily. He had no idea what Shyla was doing in here.

"Anywhere I can sit?" Dean asked.

"By the window."

Dean looked over to the windowsill. There was a ledge; he went over and leaned against it. Shyla sat down on her black lab chair and looked back at him. Dean stared at Shyla's brilliant green eyes.

"Have you looked at this place?" he asked.

"What about it?"

"Do you not see this mess?"

"We have a lot of things we need for Marie. I'm getting around to cleaning it."

"No, you're not."

"I'm not having this discussion again."

"What's happened to you, Shyla? Ten years ago, you would never have allowed this. Has she made you that mental?"

"I'm tired of you not calling Marie what she is, our daughter!"

"Fuck her. Can't you see the daughter we loved is gone?"

"We're getting through to her. Her bouts are getting less frequent."

"Shut up. They always come and go. She's playing games with you. You haven't gotten anywhere with her after eight years. Hell, she's *doubled* in age."

"I've gotten to know my daughter. I've gotten to know how self-conscious she is, how much she hates herself. All that I'm trying to do is—"

"All you've been is her psychiatrist. Once Ms. Mugsby came here, you passed the nurturing roles onto her. She has no real mother now! You're always down here otherwise!"

"I am her mother."

"You're as much her mother as she is our daughter."

"This is exactly why she hates you."

"She hates me because she knows I'm not falling for her traps. She knows I won't tolerate it. She knows that—"

"What, Dean? What does she know?"

"She knows she's crazy and can't be trusted. She knows what her future is if you give up on her. And she knows how to manipulate you from all of these damn books you've left lying around. Look at Ms. Mugsby. She's poisoned her too!"

"Ms. Mugsby sees the best in Marie!"

"There's nothing wrong that can be fixed!" Dean yelled. "That's the problem. You keep looking for a magic button—there's nothing! That's the fucking point. For five years I thought like you! She is my only child, Shyla. I've accepted that. Especially after your two abortions."

"Oh! Screw you! Screw you, Dean! You haven't been around for one kid; I can't even imagine three!"

"Shut up, woman."

"You gave up on her too early! You helped fuel her hate. You were never around to show her love."

"You used to be like Nana. As much as we did not get along, I respected her. She had all the confidence in the world, and I honestly thought you had that. But once she passed, it just zipped out of you, didn't it?"

"I hate you."

"And I fucking hate you too."

"When was the last time you even saw Marie?"

"Two months. And I hope I don't see her for another two."

"How can you do that to our daughter?"

"Because you can only do so much with her, Shyla. Her inability to have an ounce of good in her is not your fault or mine! Some people are just evil. That doesn't make you a bad mother! That doesn't make you a failure! Dammit, you did all you could do, and judging by the state of the manor, it clearly took the life out of you! You're mentally and physically breaking down. You won't even tell me how you got those scars on your back!"

Shyla started to tear up.

"You were once an excellent mother, one any child would be lucky to have."

"So it just didn't work out! I dropped... a lemon!"

Dean's eyes started to well with tears.

"Our daughter has locked you up for the last eight years while she runs around in the pine trees torturing animals. She is not made for the outside world. Do you not see the danger, Shyla? That could be a person soon! You know how creeps just hang out in the woods. We've been lucky nothing has happened!"

"She would never harm a person."

"Do you know that?"

"Of course I do!"

"No, you don't! That's the thing! You do not see what she is capable of! She has distorted your world. But okay, I'll play your game. Let's say she never harms anyone. Off the top of my head: what if she kills a deer in the off-season—or even in-season—and, you know, doesn't register her kill. Anyone comes sniffing around here, she could get arrested for that. That sounds crazy, but you know it's plausible."

"What's your point?"

"The moment she gets in trouble with the police, it's over. She's going to Dubruis. Don't you see? We can't hide that fact."

Dean stepped away and walked back to the window. "I hide in my office, Shyla. I'm the top lawyer at Dougray because I have nothing to come home to. I'm scared to come home half the time. The longer I'm here, even in just a day, I can feel the life being sucked out of me. Look at Ms. Mugsby! She's looking more like a skeleton every day. And your mind! You're forgetting things all the time, left and right."

"Not our anniversary."

"Hey! My office has saved me, do you understand? All I do now is watch everything in here slide away from reality. It's killing me inside! Don't you see? You can't avoid Marie going to a mental hospital."

"What! Do you want my permission? Why don't you just report our filthy little daughter! You could have any time!"

"Because she is still a Dalton!" Dean's face froze as he struggled to find breath.

Shyla tilted her head.

"I didn't plan to take you out tonight for our anniversary. I forgot about it; you never mentioned it...whatever. I'm a bad husband. You deserve better than me. I was planning to ask you if you wanted to go out to dinner tomorrow, not tonight, and not for our anniversary. I'm sorry." Dean put his hands behind his back and stared out the window. "I was too busy thinking about the future the past few months. Someone has to."

"Oh, and I'm not? What the hell have you done in the past ten years for our future?"

"Shyla, I meant to take you out to dinner tomorrow to tell you that I have filed a report behind your back."

"What could you have possibly filed?"

"I'm a lawyer; it's in my blood. I squeeze words until all the possible interpretations come out, and I create a logical argument that no one had thought of. If you ever wanted to ask me how my day was—well, that's what I do. And you know what I was able to find? A loophole, and a tricky one at that."

"What did you do, Dean?"

"What if I told you due to Haddon's more ambiguous political structure, I found a way to register with the right requirements for a mental hospital to privatize under the Dalton name."

"What!"

"We can choose how many patients we will have without a minimum. I think one would be perfect."

"What the hell are you doing? I thought you hated her."

"I hate her with every ounce in my blood. I don't have to love her, but she is a Dalton! And I will preserve my family name at all costs!

I have already filed the request. It was accepted for the beginning of next year. A PATC journalist already picked up the story and is writing a publication on it tonight. Once the Board reads about it, the law will be fixed by tomorrow morning. I've dealt with cases like this over and over. Businesses do this all the time; the only difference in Haddon is that it gets fixed."

"How? How the hell did you do this?"

"A few words here, a few more there, sometimes too many unambiguous words make the whole paragraph ambiguous. And when I did that over seventeen pages, I was able to piece together a logical argument that I could within the law. But time is of the essence. Contractors are coming in two weeks."

"Dean!" Shyla's face turned from scarlet to pink. Tears formed again. "Why didn't you tell me sooner?"

"Because Marie would have known, she can't have any say in this."

"I wouldn't have said anything—"

"Of course, you would have. That's the problem."

Shyla went silent.

"No one is going to know about this place. An article might be published, but the *Haddon Herald* doesn't care about the pines. Hell, most national pundits don't even realize we're under the Board's jurisdiction to sample rural areas."

"Sometimes, I hate you."

"Think about it, Shyla, just think! Everything continues as is: you and Ms. Mugsby can continue to try and treat her, Marie can live her life as a Dalton, and we can protect our name. It's not perfect, but putting her in Dubruis isn't any better."

"I can't believe you are doing this."

Dean grabbed Shyla's shoulders and lifted her up with force. "*We* are doing this." She stared at him, terrified. "I don't know what the hell you're doing to my daughter. But you can do more." Dean dropped her and walked back to the window. Shyla's mouth tightened.

"Just keep her here and out of my sight when I'm around. This whole deadspell bullshit."

"Deadspells was just a starting point. What she is doing is beyond a single name—"

"Well, whatever. Now you will have all the time in the world to make up more words for her."

"What are you going to do to this place?"

"First, it will be hidden below the pine trees. We are knocking off the second floor and lowering the ceilings for the main hall and the library; I'll have the architect design something extraordinary to blend the exterior into the pine trees. Second, in Haddon, it needs to be a minimum of five thousand square feet for buildings. Since we cannot build up, we are building lower. He seems confident he can design a drainage system with the Dalton money."

"The basement would be flooded in the pines."

"Two basements." Dean smiled. "They'll be two floors underground, and there will be no flooding. The next thing, well, we would have to prepare the place as if it were to hold fifteen patients."

"Why fifteen?"

"In order for me to make a legal argument, fifteen rooms had to be the minimum. We'll squeeze the other fourteen patient rooms in the second basement out of sight."

"This is insane."

"No, Dalton Manor as is, is a place of insanity that you and Ms. Mugsby built. All I'm doing is legalizing it. And to show off our accomplishment, in the main hall, you will find our portraits hung once the construction is complete. I hope you'll marvel at them as I will."

Shyla pinched her necklace.

"The staff… well, that's Ms. Mugsby and us. There was no number we had to meet there since there's only one patient."

"Do we have to offer jobs?" she asked. "Aren't you endangering the workers by bringing them here?"

"Now you're concerned? I don't know what all your therapy sessions have told you, but she does not kill for fun. She wants people to suffer as long as they can. I would never risk anyone coming in here. Dalton Manor is a private asylum. And security? We will have fences and security cameras installed through the house and property—always the top of the line. I've been telling you to install that in her bedroom for years, but you insisted on giving her freedom."

"Where will we live when the construction's being done?"

"The building process will be in steps. Marie's bedroom will remain unchanged until near the end."

"What about everyone in the pines?"

"There are no kids around her age. No one knows she is sick. No one cares! And if they did, doesn't that sound like a silly rumor that some Pineys thought of."

"You are insane!"

"I am a lawyer. I dream up scenarios every day. This was no different."

"It won't go this smoothly."

"Of course not. Nothing does."

"You're giving her what she wants, you know."

"We all get part of what we want."

"Is anyone inspecting us?"

"Not with this rule. And if that gets changed, I can work my way with a close friend or two in the system."

"This is so wrong."

"It is wrong."

"But what about the boxes?" Shyla looked around the library, and piles of boxes towered over them.

"They're coming in two weeks. Better clean it up or toss it because the last time I checked, this mess would not be legally tolerated in the contract I constructed. Of course, I can hire people to throw whatever you want out." Dean got up and walked toward the front aisle.

"Where are you going?"

He turned to her. "I've decided to go back to work. Happy anniversary—" Dean paused and walked passed Shyla to a painting. "What the hell's this?"

Shyla rose and walked around Dean, who had blocked her vision. She gasped. "She must have completed the painting from our session yesterday."

Dean stood in television static in excruciating detail on the canvas, revealing wrinkles under his eyes, locks of hair that gelled back, broadened shoulders, and his hands placed on his hips. Colors of red tied around the static, and pieces of paper stuck out of his body contour. His eyes shot a look of fire, one he had not given in years. In the bottom right corner, in red paint, said "Father."

"She thinks she can play with me?" Dean yelled.

"Dean, don't."

"Like I'm some fucking joke."

"Dean, stop. Please. Don't hurt her."

"I'm not going to hurt her. I'm just going to make this place a living hell for you both."

End of diary entry

*　　　*　　　*

I opened my eyes to the sound of gagging.

Vale? I thought.

I pushed my body off the bed, and the room spun. I leaned against my dresser and wobbled into the hallway. From the bathroom, I heard puking. I hobbled over, pressing my body against the wall. The door was ajar, and I tapped it open.

Vale's head was half immersed in the toilet. He did not respond.

"Let me help you," I said in a slur. I attempted to step into the bathroom but tripped over absolutely nothing and smashed my face onto the counter. Blood dripped down my face. I was too drunk to process the source.

"You don't drink like you used to," I said.

"Why would I with you not around?" Vale said, voice echoing from the toilet bowl.

I wiped the blood off my face with my shirt and sat up against the sink. In this precise position, the room did not spin. I slowly lifted myself off the ground. The change in movement was enough for my body to reject me. I vomited in the sink.

"Sarina wouldn't have wanted you to be this way."

"I'm fine, Vale. Leave it alone." My shoulders sunk hearing her name again.

"What do you even do when you're done working?"

"Prepare for the next day, learn about intergalactic travel, construct models."

"Don't let her die in vain."

"Vale, shut the fuck up. Never bring her up to me again."

"You're making me face my past. Why can't I do the honors with you?"

Fire shot through my veins.

"Price?"

I didn't answer.

"I'm getting colder these past few days... Ever since we entered Dalton Manor, I can feel the world becoming darker..." His voice became softer. "Colors swarming around me..."

I sat back down and found an exact position where my head did not spin. To diffuse him, I simply said, "Goodnight, Vale."

"I can't do it. I won't do it. I don't want to go back there."

"You'll black out and forget this ever happened."

Vale rested his head on the side of the bowl.

"It'll be okay; it's just a dream."

"I'll remember it more than this right now."

For an unknown time, Vale and I mumbled back and forth to each other until we passed out in the bathroom.

*   *   *

Diary entry written by Max Vale

Dean sped his car through the pine trees.

"Shouldn't you make a reservation?" Shyla asked, sitting in the passenger's seat. She wore a black dress, with pearl earrings and a silver necklace. Her stomach was nauseous.

"The Dalton name does the trick in this place," Dean said.

"Funny, you've never taken me there before."

"I would if you had asked. What's your point?" Dean curled his lips.

"I'm just surprised you asked."

"Good. I'm happy." Dean forced the words through his teeth.

The car drove in the darkness for miles. Shyla kept quiet, studying her husband, who had become more possessed, in particular about Dalton Manor since its construction was completed.

She could never rest comfortably with him in the room.

She knew the glove compartment was empty. And she embraced him before they entered the car and felt nothing in his pockets. Just in case, she was ready… and *they* were ready.

The moment of truth was about to come up.

Dean pulled up to a stop sign. Turning left went into Haddon, and turning right led deeper into the woods. Shyla held her breath and internally recited several demonic phrases.

"Before we get into town, I wanted to show you something," Dean said. "A cranberry bog I would walk by as a boy. It was a beautiful little area to contemplate."

"I'd rather go when it's light out," Shyla said, hiding the excitement that it was time.

"It's not like Marie's out here." Dean turned the car right.

Shyla did not answer and gripped the door.

The road went on for miles without anywhere to turn off. All Shyla could see was the endless layers of trees through the peripherals of the headlights.

"This bog has had a lasting effect on me. It's never left my mind, watching the cranberries change from white to purple as the summers turned into autumn… My head escapes there when I'm stressed, especially as I work through what we have. I thought it would be nice to show where I've run to after all these years. Isn't that nice?"

Shyla stared out the windshield, stiffening.

"I think it'll be a treat. In fact, I'd like to take you here many times and see what memories and fantasies the Dalton name can experience."

"Someone's lying on the side of the road!" Shyla said.

"What? It can't be," Dean snapped.

"Face down into the sand."

A body, half-covered in a dark tarp, lay at the edge of the pine trees.

"It's none of our business."

"Dean, please, I beg of you."

The car zipped past the body, and Dean clenched his teeth. "Fine." He pulled the car to the side of the road. "Don't you dare move a muscle. I'll know." Dean grabbed a pistol that he had wedged between the center console and his car seat.

He got out of the car. Silence swarmed around the pine trees. The back of his neck hairs spiked.

He walked over to the body, and with each step, the body became less lifelike.

"What the fuck?"

A mannequin—one that had belonged to Nana—lay with a black outfit under the tarp.

Dean ripped away the tarp and stood up. "Shyla!"

But then he froze.

From across the road, a black hooded cloak studied him. Its shoulders protruded and exposed the center parts of its pale chest.

"What the hell do you want?" Dean yelled.

It slurred a string of low groans.

Sweat plummeted down Dean's face. He pulled out the pistol from under his coat. But a slimy hand from behind him grabbed his arm. It belonged to another black cloak, groaning in a strange demonic voice. It twisted his arm. Dean grabbed the hood and fell down, dropping the gun and uncovering its face.

It was a man, pale as a ghost and bald. Blood marks in the shape of an "X" dripped over its eyes and within each crevice of its face.

Dean screamed.

The man licked his lips.

Dean threw his body up and dodged the man's attempt to grab him. Another hiss came from his side. The previous cloak was only a few feet away, its hood down. Blood covered its eyes in the same pattern.

Dean darted to the car.

From the darkness of the pine trees, a dozen more cloaks emerge. They dashed to block off his path.

He was surrounded.

"Shyla!"

Dean looked at the car. She was not in there.

They closed in. Several hands grabbed his body. He punched one, and they all hissed.

A swarm of black hands grabbed his arms and pressed them behind his back. Spindly fingers brushed through his hair, licked his body, violated him. He screamed in terror.

He was tossed into the sand on the side of the road, then dragged across the ground, stripping layers of clothes off of him like he was a doll.

Dean's face eventually pressed against a pine tree. Hisses swarmed, and something sharp dug into his lower back. He screamed as the piercing sensation scraped up to his neck.

Then the sharp pain released, and silence ensued. A breeze blew against his naked body.

Dean panted. He tried to move and realized he was tied. He could not budge. "Stop… please…" Dean sobbed.

From behind, two hands surfaced on his cheeks. The nails dug in.

Dean screamed in agony. The nails pressed further. He could taste the iron from the blood dripping into his mouth.

Hisses swirled around him.

Dean blacked out.

"Finish the job," Ragg said, devouring Marie's attention with its beady button eyes and stitched smile.

Marie sat on her parents' bed, her feet off the side. The air was thin.

"You've cradled me long enough," Ragg said. Marie gripped Ragg by the neck and pressed the doll against the wall. "Kill me."

"I can't."

"Your father wanted a son. And your mother wanted a friend."

Tears formed in Marie's dead dark eyes.

"But you were neither. All you could be was a freak, and they never wanted to love a freak, now did they? All they ever wanted to do was control you. You were an even bigger freak than they realized, so they gave up, and you became a lab rat—that's right, your father made you a wheel, and your mother studied your every move."

Her hand shook as she tried to suffocate Ragg.

"Still, you ran for them. For years. Hoping they could appreciate the freak you are. Now you're dead inside, just like them."

Marie pulled scissors out of her jean pockets and opened them, placing the blade against Ragg's neck.

"There's nothing left inside of you… except me…"

Tears flowed down Marie's cheeks.

"Your days with dolls are finished…"

"I can't do it," Marie panted. Her arm was locked in place.

"Nothing's left to say you can't…"

"I hate you."

"And there's nothing left for you to hate."

Marie screeched.

The roar echoed through Dalton Manor. Then, like a curtain, darkness asphyxiated the sound.

Footsteps rushed down the hall.

"Just hold your breath," Ragg said. "Like we practiced."

The room collapsed onto her.

Marie cut Ragg's neck. The doll's head and body fell to the floor, separated.

The freak is gone, Ragg thought.

Silence ensued for minutes as Marie stood motionless.

Then a knock came from the door. After no response, it gently swung open.

"Ragg?" a high-pitched voice said. A light turned on in the room, and soft footsteps creaked around her parent's bed.

A gaunt, pale police officer stood no more than five feet high. A few stubbles of hair were on his chin. "It's an honor, Ragg…" His gray eyes sparkled in marvel at what he was witnessing, but there was great rigidity to his movements and worry in his voice. "Martin Brezniack, at your service." He bowed.

"I must inform you that your father died in a terrible car accident." Suddenly, Brezniack unclipped the black tinker toy from his pants and let it rest in the palm of his hand. Four small rods were connected to the point of a pyramid. For a minute, he spoke in a demonic hiss. As if it was awakened, the toy unraveled into a straight line from his fingertips to his wrist. It turned into a silver centipede.

At the one end, a holographic laser shined a light on the ground where the doll was split into two. He placed the bug onto his shoulder, and it gripped him, keeping the light locked on the decapitated doll. His grimace turned to a possessed smile. "I've heard there are many special things about you, Ragg. It's a privilege to finally meet."

Ragg stared into the light, unmoved.

Brezniack hissed a prayer. Minutes went by, then he said, "And with us, you will be able to understand why you have this remarkable ability. You, Ms. Mugsby, and your mother can live here just as happy as you were."

Brezniack leaned over, grabbing the doll's head and body. His mouth curled. "I have something for you to replace it…" He brought out of his coat pocket a small green and yellow bird with one broken wing, barely alive, chirping and gasping for air.

"They're hard to find this time of year… Thought you could use a break from Ms. Mugsby. I'm sure it is tough to get through these winter months…" Martin placed the bird in the exact spot the decapitated doll had been.

He waited for a response, and as each second grew, his back tensed more. "Right, well. I'll be going…"

But Ragg did not speak. Ragg did not move.

Brezniack's body shook, and after several minutes of debating, he stepped around the bed.

Ragg's face slowly turned, following his every move, contorting Marie's neck.

With great hesitation, he left the room.

Hours onward, the bird stopped chirping.

Some time later…

Dean awoke.

He picked his body off the ground. It was nighttime. Pine trees surrounded him. He was naked. His chest had indentations revealing his rib cage. He had lost all fat in his body and all muscle in his limbs. Scars covered his entire back.

He looked around the pine trees. No one was there.

He hobbled.

Did they release me? Dean thought. He walked with a limp. How much time had passed since he was freed?

He missed Dalton Manor. He missed his job. He missed Haddon.

"I want to go home. Please, take me home. I'll do anything," Dean said to the pine trees. He stumbled onward for a long while, losing traction with each step. Eventually, the wind tossed his body backward onto the ground.

He could not get up. He cried, pressing his head into his elbow, exhausted. It had been days since he last ate. He was parched and would do anything for a glass of clean water.

Dean glanced up. "No…"

Hisses came from the trees. Goosebumps covered his body.

"Please… no…"

The dark cloaks stepped out from the pine trees.

"I'll give you anything."

One by one, they took off their hoods, each ghastly white with blood in the shape of an "X" over their eyes.

Dean was too weak to scream. They circled him and froze. Dean watched them, his heart beating out of his chest.

They did not move. It felt like forever.

Dean cracked. "Please don't hurt me."

They took a step inward.

"Shyla…"

The black cloaks marched inward one step at a time until they were shoulder to shoulder. They raised their hands and sprinkled white chalk onto the ground. It created a circle.

Metal chains clipped onto his limbs and neck. The chains were pulled until he was sprawled in the air, held up by tension.

Hisses erupted. Whips broke into his back, and he screamed hysterically.

The hisses deepened and became rhythmic. Lines of chalk were tossed onto his body.

Then there was silence.

Two black cloaks stepped aside, cracking a hole in the circle to reveal a person staring lifelessly.

"Marie," Dean said in disbelief.

She did not move. The hisses grew louder.

Hands placed a white sheet onto her scalp, and one by one, they attached electrodes to different parts of her skull, shooting wires off to dangle behind her head. A black cloth was placed over her face and tied around her head.

The black cloaks screamed in ecstasy.

Marie became less rigid, more moveable, injected with life. She raised her arms in the air, and the voices grew louder, rippling through the pine trees. The black cloaks roared, whipping at Dean's back with more vigor and frequency. He screamed with each crack.

Then she placed her arms to her side, and a deadening quiet took over.

She stared at Dean for an eternity.

"Please, help me... my daughter... my dear sweet daughter..." Dean whimpered.

"Your daughter is dead," Ragg said.

Dean's screams traveled through the pine trees until he took his last breath in this world.

End of diary entry

THE MASTER OF THE DARK ROAST

I OPENED MY eyes and felt my bed sheets over me. I must have stumbled back to my room in a stupor at some point in the night. I sat up. My head felt like I had run straight into a brick wall. Slowly, I rose and walked into the hallway.

A snore came from the bathroom. I followed the sound and found Vale passed out on a bathmat.

It was then I noticed the time on my watch. "Holy shit, it's three in the afternoon."

Vale's eyes popped open at the news; they were bloodshot, and he was pale. He lifted his body off the floor and leaned against the sink.

"We've missed our meeting with Arch," I said.

Vale stared into space for a minute, then he turned on the faucet and wiped water onto his face. He looked indifferent to my news. "The Society had been worshipping Marie as a god," he mumbled. "They think she can feel spirits and understand a language used in the Deus. It's all making sense. She was the next in line to be a prodigy."

"Just focus on waking up for now."

"I swear to you, these memories won't stop forming. And they are getting crazier with each night."

"Vale, you had a lot to drink, and the last few days have been scarring for anyone. Why wouldn't your dreams be more exaggerated than normal?"

"Exaggerated? Really, Price, that's all you think this is?"

"I just want to think about the facts for now." After Vale brought my daughter up twice, I was not in the mood to be accepting of his ridiculous theories anymore. I needed to talk back and hope he'd wake up.

I walked back to my bedroom and found my phone. To my surprise, I had several missed phone calls, not from Arch but from Dr. Arnold Darwinn.

"We have to talk to Marie Dalton," Vale said.

"You're in luck."

We got ready for the day, and Vale told me his dream sequence in extreme detail as he jotted in his maroon notebook with abandon. I was disturbed by his story, but what concerned me the most was how positive he felt each detail actually happened.

"Marie is mostly dead, Price. Don't you see? 'Ragg' has taken over a majority of the imperium in her soul, and Marie becomes partially alive when she wears an item that could channel something with a lot of love or hate into her body—like that silk cloth. Only then, Ragg can then move around in her body. That's why you couldn't get an answer out of her."

For the moment, I just agreed. We had more important things to take care of. Unfortunately, on the drive over, the Crown Victoria thought differently. The car stopped. "Shit." I banged my fist on the steering wheel.

"This hunk of junk," Vale said. "What do you expect with reused engine parts from decades ago?"

No matter what wish or curse I uttered, the Crown Victoria would not start up. "What do I do with all my models?" I asked.

"Leave them unless you have a better idea. I'm sure they won't play with them at the shop."

"You wouldn't have room in your vest?"

"I would crush them," Vale said. I couldn't tell if it would be on purpose or not.

I placed my finger on my cheek and paced around the side of the road. I decided to take each one out and dug a little hole to bury each.

"You're not serious…"

"Give me some cloth. I know you have some." I stuck my hand out.

Vale rolled his eyes and whipped out several pieces of tissue. I rolled the robot up and buried each into the ground.

"I need to come back here," I said.

Vale did not answer and began to mumble to himself. After a tow truck came, I had the sinking realization I needed to say goodbye to the Crown Victoria. I hoped it wasn't my last. I wasn't ready for that.

I wanted to call the station for a ride. But Vale thought calling would be a trap to reveal our whereabouts, so we bickered about it. And reluctantly, I called a driver to pick us up, using an alias and feeling ridiculous the entire time.

Dr. Darwinn did not leave a voicemail, and his most recent call was about two hours ago. I called back many times without response while the cab sped across town to Dougray and dropped us off at his old broken-down building.

We made our way back to the entrance of the professor's lab, just like the morning prior. Still feeling hungover, I had a hard time keeping up with Vale, who seemed energized despite last night.

Vale banged his fist against the professor's lab door. We waited for a long minute, and at last, it cracked open. "Your lateness is punctual," a nasal, eerie voice said. It was ironic. Because I've since appreciated this genius has no schedule. Time is created and destroyed in waves, regardless of rhythm, no matter how many clocks tick, never to be early or tardy, only at the right moment.

"Sorry we couldn't fit in your schedule," Vale said.

"Ah, another Vale, I hear." Dr. Arnold Darwinn appeared.

He was short and obese with a balding scalp whose remaining hairs shot backward, and a bushy gray beard trailed down his chest. Flakes dangled off his tan skin, and strangest of all, he wore a white coat, suspenders, and a blue t-shirt that read, *YOU, SIR, ARE A NAKED CASSOWARY.*

"At last, the infamous Dr. Darwinn," Vale said.

"The pleasure is mine, and I'm sure you're happy to be here too. Strangers call me Dr. Darwinn. But I only deem you as strange, so please... Darwinn will suffice." He revealed an uncanny smile.

We each shook his hand.

"Come in. We will talk. But I must ask you to remember this is my lab, and I need to keep the juices flowing. You see, today's actually a big day. A really big day. Several years in the making, in fact..."

"I didn't realize we were interrupting your career," Vale said cheekily.

"Oh no!" Darwinn raised in hands. "It's all out of your control. Please use whatever you want, except, by all means, stay absolutely away from the center aisle. Hmm? Otherwise, make yourself at home for however long you need. Elara is partly why I'm here, so I'll do anything to help outside of compromising my experiments."

Darwinn turned around.

Vale and I glanced at each other and entered his lab. I gaped.

Two black lab benches stretched across the room, and metal shelves stretched to the high ceiling. The configuration divided the room into three aisles. The shelves were filled with different vials, beakers, and flasks. Sinks were frequent, and refrigerators plenty. Notebooks and marker boards were consumed by scientific jargon. But above all, the constant activity from Darwinn's apparatuses in his forsaken middle aisle baffled me—I could hear the active chemical reactions, the motors from little machines. Outlines from towers of clamps and glass tubes created experiments I could never fathom.

The only item whose purpose I understood was a dual computer screen connected to a giant generator by the experiments. One monitor displayed a large loading bar that said, "97% complete," and the other made several different buzzes that sounded like a lawnmower failing to start as different colors appeared on and off the screen.

I had entered a new world and wondered why it took us this long to arrive here.

In fact, Darwinn's viewpoint had been present this entire case, just as much as Vale's and mine, with the same minute detail. I was just never aware of it. It strikes such a beautiful chord into my psyche to encounter Darwinn's mind this far into our tale. For it is this sonder, this awakening that every human encounter is constructed from many minds... those thousands of previous feelings, the endless collage of past situations, the infinite details of our lives blended.

The world cannot be seen with two eyes, only with a gullible mind. It takes more men.

Before this point in the case, I went through most of the events in my own head, with even my sincerest worries about Vale still being just my own. There was one moment that broke the trend, and a world that was not my own meshed with mine.

Yet this emersion into Darwinn's world was different, for he was all but a stranger to me.

However, I found few things crazier than his back wall dedicated to over a dozen grandfather clocks. I noticed each one's hands stuck at a different time, every moment bulging in an attempt to move the second hand, only to return. They all clicked in unison, amplifying the sound.

"Pardon my collection," Darwinn said as he hopped into the middle aisle. "But as a student of time, it's a practical hobby. This is how we dissect our puny problems in here. It all likes to connect in one way or another—every little piece in its own time." Darwinn jumped back out of the middle aisle and rested his hand on a grandfather clock. "See this guy in the center? The split pediment—one of my favorites! And who couldn't adore the swan's neck?" Darwinn rubbed his hand on the clock's side.

"You'll have to forgive me, Darwinn; my knowledge on clocks isn't up to par," Vale said.

"Surely you can appreciate the time put into each."

"What about that one?" I nudged my head to a wooden coo-coo clock overtop the door we just walked through. It had several engravings and chains dangling and was the only clock that appeared to be working properly.

"Ah yes… that one is a family heirloom. Ignore that one."

We stared at him for a few seconds in silence.

"Where's the girl, Darwinn?" Vale asked with a cold stare.

"Why, Marie is in the other corner of the lab."

"You going to follow us, like you followed me out of the police station?" I asked.

Darwinn raised his brow and said, "Please… elaborate."

"Cut the crap. I saw you dart down the back alley."

"Mr. Price, I took Marie and left. Right now, I am too busy with my experiments to be lollygagging."

I studied Darwinn's brilliant blue irises. Not an ounce of truth in them.

"Then explain what's going on," I said.

"I'm working on that, you… Marie doesn't have to stay here. She can leave whenever she wants."

"Would you like her to leave?" Vale asked.

"What are you implying?"

"I'm sure you're a busy man, and I can't imagine why a boring woman like Marie would be of that much interest to you."

Darwinn's smile flat-lined, and he scratched the bald spot on the back of his head. "I'm hoping to continue what your twin sister could not accomplish, Mr. Vale."

"Taking a suspect of a double homicide into the public... The journalists will devour you."

"Just like they did to Elara?"

Vale's face turned red.

"Mr. Vale, I am your average PATC member. In theory, I can do whatever I want. But if you really sit and think about it, I can't, nor can anyone else at Dougray. If you have made it this far in the selection process, you're not going to waltz around with this privilege. You're going to spend every waking moment towards gaining your tenure. I got approval from the PATC journalists before I took Marie. In fact, they even questioned why she was held in jail without the proper evidence."

"She could leave whenever she wants," I said.

"She did with me. I'm working with all the right people, Mr. Price. If any journalist pounces on me in a negative light with the proper facts—good luck getting past my review swimmingly! We in the PATC are governed by a much more powerful force—fear of failure."

"Failure?" Vale asked shortly.

"Why, Mr. Vale!" Darwinn exclaimed, suddenly perky. He shot his head backward, and he gripped his suspender straps. "We certainly do fail!"

"You're saying my sister's failures were governed by her desire... not to fail?"

"Now Elara... she was different. Let me tell you, she had her own formula, her own way of doing things. Is it good? Is it bad? The thing with lab is you need to find what works for you, your identity. And Elara, she was a thinker. She certainly liked to let ideas sit and blossom in solitude."

"The Elara I knew was high-strung and an over-analyzer. Unless that all changed..."

"If only I knew her when you did." Darwinn tightened his smile. "Have you ever seen your twin work through thoughts? It's quite beautiful. She would let those ideas sit in the back of her head and watch them brew just on their own. She's added many theories to my project—and I mean groundbreaking, insane theories—some of the craziest I've ever heard in my life. But you know what? That's how you know she was onto something." Darwinn kicked out a stool and stepped to our eye level. I could smell his coffee breath. "Because they're crazy thoughts, Mr. Vale! And my project deals with time. So in my mind, time just needs to allow those ideas to succeed. Then they'll be *brilliant*." He scrunched his face so tightly that the end of his lips and eyebrows nearly touched.

"Did she ever mention me?" Vale asked.

I was surprised by the question.

"A couple of times, in fact, but never anything with substance. Yes, I'm afraid you're pretty much a stranger to me, outside of your recent struggles. But don't worry, I already granted you '*strange*' as your status quo in my official introduction. And because of that honor, I need to know. So perhaps I will inquire one more item… who is the real Max Vale?"

"Take me out to dinner first."

Darwinn roared with laughter. "Oh, you are too hilarious! Just floating along in this little world of yours… Listen, this conversation—it's been a pleasure. And in many ways brings me back to my dear conversations with your sister."

"I'll have to take your word."

"You see it, Mr. Vale! I know you do! Elara disregarded any law of life, and it didn't stop her until she committed suicide." He looked into the back of Vale's head possessed. "You just need to embrace it."

"What's it?"

"How little you truly know."

Vale stayed quiet as they each studied each other. Finally, Darwinn broke the silence. "Thanks for the intrigue, kiddo. That will have to replace my confidence in you for now."

"Why do you have such an interest in this case?" Vale asked sharply as if he grabbed Darwinn by the cheeks to keep their eyes locked.

"Because I think your sister's results will benefit my project."

"Your concerns are all about your research—"

"That's what the PATC is for, am I wrong? Now, please entertain Marie, since she has been such a polite guest waiting for you. I hope you treat her nicely."

"What do you want from this?"

"Time." Darwinn patted the grandfather clock, then pointed to Vale's right. "Straight ahead, down the back aisle. She likes to hide in my old incubator room."

A timer went off. And without another word spoken, Darwinn turned around and sprinted off.

We glared in frustration at each other.

"He told us nothing," I said under my breath.

Vale didn't respond, looking preoccupied.

We walked across the lab and turned to the back aisle. At its end, a gray door stood with a square window. My chest tightened.

Marie Dalton stared into our souls. Dark dead eyes stood out over her pale complexion, with oily hair falling to her shoulders, clipped behind the ears. Her lips were hidden, and her cheekbones prominent. She wore an old, dampened one-piece blue dress covered in green and purple flowers, with worn holes gashed throughout the cloth. Her shoulders slouched, making her look forever lost in purgatory. She stood in the middle of the cold room in front of a wooden chair. A hospital bed was pushed against the back wall.

"She feels like a childhood friend," Vale said.

I shivered.

"Now we're creating memories," Vale said.

"Focus. Don't waste your energy with that shit. We got one shot at this."

I jumped. Darwinn's coo-coo clock struck. It rang loudly, coo-cooing the number of hours. Off in the distance, Darwinn counted gleefully, "One… two… three… and four."

"The PATC at its finest." Vale turned to me.

"Keep your cool."

"I've never been more calm."

"And what cult did you come from?" Darwinn's voice echoed from down the middle aisle.

Vale's eyes widened. "I'd be careful how you use that word."

Darwinn stood in the front aisle so fast as if he magically appeared there. "I imagine it runs in the family."

"It sounds like you know the answer."

"You're not denying your sister's involvement?"

"Why would I? We grew up in it together. It's part of who I am."

"Then you could imagine my curiosity."

"What? Elara didn't trust you enough to tell you anything after three years?"

"Perhaps I knew when not to ask questions."

"That worked out nicely for you."

"Mr. Vale, you're killing me. Have some coffee, good sir." Darwinn disappeared into his office, sounding preoccupied. "I just hope you like my dark roast."

As much as I was ready to tell Darwinn to shut up and go interview Marie, Vale's agitation surprised me. I had never seen someone get under his skin this well and this fast.

Darwinn reappeared, holding two coffee mugs. I would have refused the offer if Darwinn had not stuffed a mug into my hands. My mug was white and had a row of rooster heads—the last one wore a monocle. The scent from the coffee trickled into my brain. I took a sip and felt a rush of energy. Layers snuck into my mouth. It had a rich flavor: first, a dab of dark chocolate, then a tinge of smokiness… "A decent cup you have here," I said.

"Why, thank you, Mr. Price. In my lab, life's too short for crappy coffee. The mind deserves better treatment."

"Now, either talk to Marie with us or get out of my sight," I said.

"While there's still time, I need to hear Mr. Vale's thoughts…"

Vale held a mug with a picture of two tin cans. He had not sipped the coffee.

"No!" Darwinn shrieked.

"Oh yes."

"But you're exactly the kind of man who could use a caffeinated beverage!"

"The world's a mysterious place."

Darwinn started to sweat.

"You okay?" I asked.

Darwinn sprinted across the lab without replying—dumping buffers from one tube to the next, turning knobs on and off, whistling as loud as a kettle.

"He's never been okay," Vale said.

Darwinn froze and cemented his eyes at two computer monitors. The screen read "99%" and showed a near-filled loading bar. He was possessed.

"So soon?" He asked to the screen.

The computer beeped. The screen turned to 100% and blasted an array of sounds. Lines and numbers appeared on the screen. Darwinn scanned it, and a grin twisted across his face. He screamed and jumped in the air for what felt like an eternity.

"I don't believe it! Theory after theory, correct! All of this rabble has meaning!" Darwinn heel-clicked then engulfed Vale in a big bear hug, whose eyes popped open. "I was not expecting results until this evening. It's just so simple! That's what's so amazing!"

"What happened?"

"Oh, Mr. Vale. Ha! Its dependency on energy!"

"English, Darwinn," I said.

"A link! An *energy-time* dependency! This will revolutionize how we view life! Don't you see? Energy and time are categories of change, not parallel independencies!"

"Normal English Darwinn," Vale said.

Darwinn regained his composure and placed his hands together by the beginning of his suspender straps. He stared through his frames upward at Vale and me.

"I'll have you know I spent years developing controls to prove this hypothesis! And even more important, I needed to perform another eleven tests to eliminate other possibilities of what time-energy dependency might be. But as a consequence of my project's set-up, I could not see the results until they were all done. And with the right tweaks here and there, wouldn't you know!"

Darwinn froze. He fixed his eyes back on the computer screen. It continued to spew out more data. "What?" he whispered. He crept back to the monitor carefully, like it was some kind of monster.

"What is it, Darwinn?" I asked.

"Impossible… There's another dimension… in addition to time and energy…"

"The Deus," Vale said.

Darwinn glanced at him. He asked, "Elara?"

The lights flickered. We studied the room. There were no windows.

"No, not now…" Darwinn said. "This broken-down building."

The lights shot on and off every few seconds.

Vale sprinted down the forsaken middle aisle and grabbed Darwinn by the suspender straps. "What the hell is going on?"

"I don't know! This doesn't make any sense!"

My heart pushed to my throat.

Marie appeared next to me, lifeless.

The lights went out. Darkness swallowed the lab. The only sound came from the ticking grandfather clocks.

I swung my arms to tackle her and whiffed.

Silence.

A jolt of electricity shot to my fingertips. I pulled out my gun and brought out my flashlight. No one was there. The air around me turned frigid. "Marie?"

Darwinn broke away from the computer, and his footsteps traveled somewhere to my left. A door opened and closed.

"Interesting strategy, Darwinn." Vale scanned around the middle aisle with his flashlight.

I walked through the middle aisle on alert. I passed different beakers, test tubes, and towers constructed in complicated contraptions.

We scanned the lab.

A shadow darted by the clocks.

Vale and I each sprinted to the opposite ends of the middle aisle and over to the front of the lab by the clocks, hoping to surround her.

A wave of nausea smacked my stomach.

Our flashlights caught each other. She wasn't there.

"Marie Dalton, it's nice to see you again," Vale said.

My hands shook.

"Is your aim to kill us?"

Silence persisted. We needed a plan.

"No, I doubt that—you wouldn't kill, right?"

"Vale, shut up."

"How did Ragg kill them?" Vale asked, ignoring me. He darted across the lab; I assumed to check the back area where she stayed.

Coolness swarmed my body, and my heart stopped. I could feel Marie staring at me, but I wasn't sure from where. "Marie, we're here to help," I said. I turned my body around and shined my flashlight. Nothing. "I need your help."

The lab lights turned on, and I looked around.

Marie stood six inches behind me. I jumped backward, gun pointed at her.

Marie's eyes flickered, and she returned to her still self. She held a scalpel. I felt like an ice pick prodded me.

Vale rejoined the front of the lab.

Darwinn emerged from a door with some wires wrapped in his hands and a phone peeking out of his jean pocket. His brilliant blue eyes revealed how lost in thought he was from whatever was on that computer screen.

"We need to leave... *now*," Darwinn said.

"What the hell are you doing in this place?"

"Mr. Vale, I better be able to trust you and the lieutenant like I trusted Elara."

"Put your luck to the test."

Darwinn sprinted to a cabinet in the corner and swung the door open. He stuck his body in there and pulled out a champagne blazer, a thermos, and a .44 magnum.

"Mr. Vale, we have fifteen more minutes of backup power with my old generator, and I don't intend to let it simmer out! Now, who would like some coffee?"

"Tell us what is going on," I said.

"There's not enough time!"

"What about all of these contraptions?" I waved my right hand at the apparatuses Darwinn had constructed in the middle aisle.

"Never mind those!" He held a sheet of paper up as his eyes bugged. "That's my perpetual quest to design the perfect dark roast."

"What?" I asked.

"You were the first to sample it!"

"What the hell is wrong with you?"

"Everything else is backed up!" Darwinn sprinted around the lab a bit more, moving several tubes around, and unplugging different machines. Darwinn paused and glanced at us. "Well, come on, guys! Where's your urgency?"

"You tell me what the hell is going on," I said.

"No, Price. He doesn't have to say a damn thing, and he knows it. He's going to take Marie as a hostage from us, so we will be forced to follow him."

Darwinn sprinted into his office as he awkwardly threw on his blazer. I could hear a coffee machine brewing.

"At least tell us where you are planning to go?" I said.

Darwinn sprinted back into the lab with steam oozing out of his thermos and grabbed Marie by the wrist. She made no reaction. "Marie wants to go home, Mr. Price, can't you feel it? I'd certainly suggest we go there then."

Darwinn dragged her effortlessly through a door that brought them into a dimly lit hallway. "Meet us down by the utility entrance. Please don't tell anyone you're with me! They are already furious with me for short-circuiting the floor. Take the elevators to the basement floor. And when I pick you both up in my truck, you'll need to tell me all about the dark roast, Mr. Price!" Darwinn and Marie broke out of our vision before we could answer.

"What the hell just happened?" I asked.

"Marie is taking us to her world."

"Vale, I'm not going anywhere until you start thinking straight. I thought a night off would have done that to you."

"Price, I'm completely focused on this case. Especially since we are trying to solve a double homicide." We stepped out into the hallway.

From behind, Darwinn's lab door beeped, slammed shut, then locked.

Vale and I paced the length of the hallway. No one was around. The lights were out through every lab door window. Most rooms had no nametag and looked like they had been unoccupied for a while. This Dougray was the one I heard stories about as a boy.

We reached the elevator and pressed the down button. I watched the numbers light up on top. When "3" appeared, the door slid open.

The elevator looked just as outdated, with parts of the ceiling tiles broken off and wires dangling. Dougray's science buildings were known for their architectural mastery bent in shapes I had never encountered elsewhere. This building was not that. Darwinn's lab didn't even have a window.

"Price, why don't you believe me?"

"All I'm saying is prove it to me."

"What's left to prove? I've predicted what's happened throughout this case."

The elevator stopped and opened onto the ground floor. We entered a utility hallway. The walls were white cinder blocks, and the floor was cement. Several drains guided the path down the center of the hallway. The lights were attached around pipes that hung from the ceiling. They were connected by a few wires that dangled throughout.

"Every detail you mentioned I can justify," I said.

"You really think I'm crazy? What I'm doing is not possible. Even Darwinn knew about the Deus."

"Of course he did. He drank coffee with Elara for years."

"We were partners for decades, and you never knew."

"He looked as unconvinced as me. I'm just asking you to put that aside for the next few hours."

"Open your mind, Price."

"Use yours, Vale. We have no idea what Darwinn's motive is…"

"To be a smartass," Vale said.

"You dreamt that?"

We darted towards an exit sign at the end of the hallway and reached a faded teal door. I cracked it open, peering outside.

I didn't know where we were, but in front of us was a parking lot. Only a few vehicles were parked.

Headlights appeared in the distance. They shined on us and grew. To my surprise, an old red pickup truck came into vision and stopped. Through the window, Marie stared at the windshield. A chill shot down my spine. The passenger window rolled down.

"How are *things*?" Darwinn reached over Marie and opened the door.

I wondered what kind of vehicle a man like Darwinn would drive, and an ancient pickup truck would have been one of my last guesses. But there we were—Darwinn, Marie, and me—cramped in the front row. Vale took the back. The truck sped down the near-empty main drag. A badge of the Dougray Crest that said "Professorial Act for Tenured Candidates" rested on the dashboard.

In the center of the dashboard, in between two air vents, a dusty red button stared at me. It had a picture of an orange bird with feathers that shot out like a Mohawk, two black holes for eyes, and a thin beak. Cobwebs covered it.

"You wouldn't pet a wild bird, right, Mr. Price?"

I furrowed my brow.

"Exactly. That there is a Hoopoe. One of my favorites to admire." Darwinn rested his thermos in a cup holder in front of the radio. "Don't touch it, or else we might just become extinct as well."

Heaviness filled the truck.

"What do you want from us?" I asked.

"Mr. Price, I believe there's more to Dalton Manor than you discovered. We need to find it."

"How do you know that?"

"A childhood friend of mine… Ted Billars. Name sound familiar?"

"What about him?" I asked.

"He's gotten calls from a number with a Haddon area code, one I recognized from my phone. Stop calling him. He's getting chemotherapy at John Hopkins. He has no purpose to this case."

"How many calls?" Vale asked in a stern tone.

"At least twenty. How do you get anything else done in the day, Mr. Price? Ted Billars is a wonderful man, who at the moment has more important problems to deal with than Elara's brouhaha."

"So I heard," I said, disregarding Vale's glare.

"But that hasn't stopped you? You are relentless, Mr. Price. He is the only person left I can trust now that Elara's gone. And even he only has six months to live. Knock those shenanigans off."

"Why didn't you answer *our* phone calls?" I asked, dodging the points of my morning I had conveniently left out in my recollection.

"You work on a single project for three and a half years, and I'll see how you are in the days leading up to your results. I called you as soon as I completed the final touches."

"Looks like we're witnessing history," Vale said.

"Tell me, are you not the least bit saddened your twin sister died?"

"I did not love her like you."

Darwinn flinched.

I raised my brow, surprised by the remark.

"Maybe I'm reading in too much," Vale said, "but you remind me of a fool."

For several minutes, the car stayed quiet. Darwinn drove head down in a trance. And from where Vale sat, I heard a whisper. "*Silence is deafening.*"

Time dragged. And I stared at my phone, wondering why I had not heard a response from Arch. It was very unlike him not to respond to my text. Then I unintentionally slipped into darkness. I thought of all the hours I spent calling Ted Billars. For an instant, it triggered an anger that poured from the depths of my mind into my body. I felt a heaviness weigh me to the floor as my mind drifted to all the arguments I had with Madelyn over the years. And with each passing one, I had less hope of being happy.

Why is Ted Billars any better than me? What the fuck could he have?

Then my mind explored all the key times I downplayed my alcoholism to Madelyn, and for a moment, such evil uncovered the darkest pit of my soul, where my worst demon hid. It always lurked inside, out of my view, but its presence was always felt.

Its bony claw appeared and gripped my consciousness. I panicked. That beast could not come out now… I didn't want to bring it out around Vale. Then without my input, the claw slipped back into the shadows, and I swiftly buried my darkest feelings deeper.

"Why, you seemed concerned, Mr. Price," Darwinn said.

I was silent, then under my breath, I said, "I'm losing my mind."

Darwinn sighed, and whatever arrogance he had in his demeanor vaporized. "Mr. Price, I doubt it. We're all crazy. It's just those that are ignorant about it who tend to be the craziest."

I was taken off-guard by the humility in his voice, even for a statement with such a sting towards the world. But that was Darwinn—zany one minute, then a straight shooter out of nowhere. To this day, I have yet to master when that switch turns.

"You see, we've been stuck on belief this whole time. The most twisted form of reasoning…" Darwinn swirled the truck down an exit ramp, making my driving resemble one of a cautious new mother. I could hear Vale holding his breath until the truck straightened out. We entered the Pinelands.

"Mr. Vale, remember how I told you Elara was a thinker? Can you remember that?"

"Perhaps," Vale said.

The trees whistled against the car door.

"Well, let me tell you a little secret of mine. I'm a progessor—I let things *progress*. Stick and unstick… Admire the complexities we face and let them soak all around me. Isn't that something, Mr. Vale? Isn't that something…"

I noticed Darwinn's face, and my heart sank to the ground. For how strange the professor had sounded today, at this moment, he looked equally as possessed. His eyes glared into another world, wrinkles gripping his eyes, cheeks, and chin. A realization gripped me. Vale and I had only been on this case for three days, and our minds were already playing tricks. Whatever Elara's research was had plagued Darwinn for years.

"We're up to here with clues, Mr. Vale, and I mean *really* up to here. We will talk them out, oh we will. But we need to do it piece by piece as we're solving Elara's suicide and these two murders. Otherwise, if we do it all at once—we'll lose our minds!" Darwinn slipped into a shadow once more. "Wouldn't want that to happen? Am I right, Marie?"

Darwinn patted Marie's shoulder. I repressed the urge to shiver.

"So the first thing," Darwinn said, "I see you holding onto that gun. Remember who else has one. I don't doubt some negative impulses aimed at me will fly by those minds of yours, but allies like me are nice."

"We don't need your help."

"You're too funny, Mr. Vale. Is that what you believe?"

"That's what I know."

"And what are you basing that inkling off of?"

"Your shady appearance, your mannerisms, no wonder you live alone."

"We all live alone in our own rights. What's your real source? Why do you think I'm untrustworthy? Is it what you see with those eyes of yours? Or is there a reliable source to your claim?"

"My intuition, dammit."

"A statistically insignificant finding, Mr. Vale. Not enough of a sample size."

"There's nothing more dangerous than a man calling something fact."

"Facts are not loud opinions, Mr. Vale. It takes years of repeated observations to get to that point. A lot more thought out than those beliefs of yours."

"If I don't believe, why am I alive? Why am I even here?"

"Belief will always let you down. True facts never change."

"There's no such thing as a true fact."

"I mean, looks like I won't change your mind."

"What do you know about the Deus?" Vale asked.

"The Deus? Mr. Vale, I would categorize that into a belief, one Elara would prefer to preach over almond croissants."

"Sounds like you guys kept yourselves busy."

"Make no mistake, curiosity might drive my attention, but in the end, I strive to be unbiased." Darwinn spun the truck right onto a dark one-lane road.

My body slid against Marie, and by mistake, my hand pressed into a gash on her blue dress, skimming her clammy skin. I felt like I had swallowed an ice cube.

"And you think whatever you found in your research ties into the Deus?" Vale asked.

"I simply do not understand what my research just revealed. But have no fear, Mr. Vale; everything has a probability. Though if you want a fact, I can promise you with the utmost certainty whatever your belief is with this Deus of yours is probably wrong. Or else Elara would be alive to correct me."

"So, you think her research was about the Deus?"

"It was. That's all I ever knew of it."

"Why didn't you tell me?" I asked.

"I didn't trust you. Now I do. Congratulations."

For the next while, no one spoke.

The truck drove through the endless miles of pine trees. Even after three days of exploring the area, I still had no idea where we were. At some point, we reached the small series of houses off the main road. On the edge of the trees was the one-lane road covered in tree trunks. Even staring at it in broad daylight, the road blended well into the shadows from the density of the pine trees.

"I don't know. What do you think, Marie?" Darwinn turned onto the abandoned road, bouncing over the tree trunks. The headlights revealed several tire tracks guiding the way. He drove with caution past the "DAL-TON MANOR" stone gate decorated with a stone lion in mid-roar on either side. Minutes later, a small field opened up to our left.

Darwinn slammed on the brakes. "This can't be it." He sipped his thermos.

"It's right in front of us," Vale said.

"Is that a fact?"

"You're staring at it, past the first layer," I said.

Even in broad daylight and knowing its exact location, it was hard to see Dalton Manor. But after a few seconds, Darwinn's face turned pale. He looked defeated, and he glanced at Marie. She curled her lips ever so slightly at him. He hopped out of the truck with her, and Vale and I hopped out of the passenger's side. We studied Marie over the hood. She was as rigid as she had been all day.

"Don't worry about her," Darwinn said.

"You don't know what you're dealing with," I said.

Darwinn stopped in his tracks. A shadow appeared through a window. We all brought out our guns. "Someone is there," Darwinn said.

"Someone or something?" Vale asked in a solemn tone.

I furrowed my brow.

It moved to the right. Vale followed it to the last window. The contour of a face appeared in the darkness.

"Some*one* is going towards the entrance," I said.

We crept to the side of the manor. The lone door creaked open to reveal a figure standing in the shadows.

"Marie?" a feeble voice stuttered from the darkness.

"Hello there, stranger," Darwinn said with hesitation.

We brought out our flashlights on the right side of the house. A woman emerged.

"Marie, I missed you so much, sweetie… and to bring guests."

I froze. *Ms. Mugsby?*

The woman looked like a skeleton. Her long gray hair frizzed down to her stomach. Her neck was shriveled and veiny, permanently bent left, and her mouth was locked open, creating white patches at the corner of her mouth. She wore a patchy black fleece jacket with several holes over many other layers. She leaned against the wall with her bony hands and long fingernails, then shuffled her feet forward.

"Vale?" Ms. Mugsby asked.

"Donna Mugsby, we need to bring you downtown for—" Vale nudged me.

"It is you..." Ms. Mugsby said with a stutter. Her smile never stopped. "You have finally come back... I wanted to give you a tour when you first came, but I was away... This is wonderful, sweetie..." She looked at Darwinn and me. "And who are you both?"

"We're friends," Darwinn said.

Vale and I glared at Darwinn. He made no reaction.

"Vale... and friends, what you are about to witness is a manor of wealth, a manor of class, but most of all, a manor connecting life to death... I am fortunate enough to watch over this plexus... Occupancy of two for the last while, Marie and myself... But of course, there are always guests who come and go... Please, come inside and join the spirits..."

PART III

THE NECK

MS. MUGSBY HOBBLED into the darkness of Dalton Manor. Marie stared at the back of her nanny, unmoved from reuniting.

"Any of you gents know why one Donna Mugsby is here?" Darwinn studied the three of us.

"I was expecting her," Vale said.

"Please, flaunt that fine reasoning of yours."

"I thought I saw her in the pine trees two days ago."

"Why didn't you tell me?" I asked.

"We didn't find her, and I thought you would want some evidence."

"That's never stopped you before from speaking your mind."

Vale grinned.

"But you never actually saw her, Mr. Vale."

"She's lived here for at least a decade, Darwinn. I'm sure she knows how to disappear in the pine trees."

"I wish I could sleep well with your logic."

Vale stepped into Dalton Manor. Darwinn walked behind him, holding Marie's wrist, his features tense. I stood outside for a moment, formulating a plan.

My top priority was getting Vale out of his world—I needed to depend upon his sanity to solve the case—then interview Marie and Ms. Mugsby while ensuring Marie did not try to attack me again. I sighed. I hated the plan, and nothing about our approach made me feel safe or made sense to me, but I was at the bottom of the command order right now, a feeling I was not used to. Where was Ms. Mugsby during these murders? And how did Darwinn's experiments tie into Dalton Manor?

I entered. Little sunlight touched the foyer. Ms. Mugsby watched us, never losing her deranged smile. I panted like the air could not satisfy my lungs. I kept my hand close to my gun and watched the stillness of Marie's grimy hair.

"Before I give you young men the official tour of the top floor… there is one warning I must give… In Dalton Manor, you are never alone… Spirits crawl around these parts freely… Doors will open and close on occasion, and items will move if you look close enough… You might just feel a hand or a breeze… I assure you it is all part of life here…"

Once more, I found myself deciding to either go left into the Artistry Room or to the hallway straight back with several doors, one of which led to the bedroom where Vale witnessed his sister's suicide.

"Let's bring ourselves into the Artistry Room… shall we?" Ms. Mugsby hobbled to the room on the left. We trailed.

"My dear trusted comrades, what is your professional opinion of her?"

"She's a suspect, and we need to question her," I said under my breath as Ms. Mugsby began to mumble about the static paintings, which now took a creepier meaning after hearing Vale's dreams.

"I wouldn't trust anything she says," Vale said. "She has all the classic symptoms of the post-possession syndrome."

"Post-possession syndrome?"

"From a White Eye."

"That's out there even for you, Vale," I said.

"I read it in the scriptures—glazed eyes, ghostly pale, recovering mental state probably, which would explain her wandering in the pine trees, motor function rigid. I had seen several people in this recovery state for days in my teenage years, but I never believed them."

"Why would she even be that way?" I asked, hopeful to talk down Vale's irrational reasoning.

"I bet she was possessed by the portal Brezniack opened our first night in the library. He could have done it before we arrived. And we saw it had been closed by someone brushing off the white chalk our last visit. She probably will need at least another twenty-four hours before she can answer with any sense. White Eyes infect the soul more deeply than most demons."

"Then why didn't we see her our first night if she was possessed?"

"Takes longer time as a consequence. She was probably in the pine trees—silent."

"She's a suspect for a double homicide, dammit."

Vale did not respond.

Darwinn studied Ms. Mugsby, dumbfounded.

I had no idea why she desired to give Vale a tour of the manor. It made no sense to me. And beyond that, Marie stayed quiet and continued to act like a fly on the wall. My chest tightened more as I accepted that I had no read on her.

"Next we enter the kitchen..." Ms. Mugsby shuffled onto the black and white tile. I could see the closet door open from where we found Crony.

"Donna Mugsby, would you please have a seat? I need to ask you a few questions."

"Mr. Price, we should really let her go through parts of the tour," Darwinn said. "She probably knows places in Dalton Manor neither of you has searched."

"A person died right in that pantry, had her face carved and each finger bitten off."

"And yet I have the PATC."

I glared, and my face burned.

"Ms. Mugsby, could you be so kind as to take me to the bottom floor of the manor?"

She did not respond to Darwinn and kept mumbling about the appliances in the kitchen.

"You're doing a bad job of trusting us," Vale said.

"There's more to this manor than what you've searched in that police report by Mr. Price. I'm sure of it," Darwinn said.

"How would you know?" I asked.

"Darwinn lied to us. Elara told him before she went missing."

"Wrong again, Mr. Vale. Your twin sister told Ted, who told me. There's a second basement. It sounds like you had no clue existed. I bet you my research is being used there."

"What for?" I asked.

"And here we have the main hall…" Ms. Mugsby lifted her shaky arms into the air.

"I'm working on it, you…" Darwinn said.

I glanced at Marie, who had nothing to add.

We walked past the pantry. Dried blood still covered the floor from Crony's murder. I shivered and followed Ms. Mugsby. The main hall looked untouched from our two previous searches. Two giant wooden tables stretched out to the back of the room by a piano. Like the Artistry Room, the walls were also covered in paintings, except these were portraits of various men and women, dressed professionally behind a backdrop of pine trees, all with the Dalton last name. The two closest portraits were of Dean and Shyla Dalton. Dean had slicked-back brown hair with a gray and black suit jacket. He smiled with sternness. Shyla, on the other hand, looked more mystical with piercing emerald eyes, wavy black hair, and a dazzling black dress, revealing an hourglass figure.

There was no frame of Marie.

Against the right wall, a row of six old papier-mâché mannequins stood. On each head, a black silk cloth was tied with two strings. I had not known what to make of the masks in the previous two searches. But the more I heard Vale's dreams, I felt less comfortable.

"Let's at least question Marie before she tries to stab me again."

"I assure you, she is not the place to start."

"You're not scared of her?" Vale asked.

"Why would I be? She is an innocent young woman who's been nothing but a victim in your little case," Darwinn said.

"She tried to stab me in the dark with a scalpel in your own damn lab," I said.

"Have appearances really worked out for you this far, Mr. Price?"

"Explanations are better."

"And again, I'm working on it, but ruffling the feathers will do us no good. We need to look at the bigger picture."

Vale's eyes flared.

"What is it?" I asked.

"I've seen this moment, Price." His tone calmed, and he closed his eyes as if he was in meditation.

My stomach dropped. I looked around the main hall. "Where'd she fucking go?"

Marie was gone.

Darwinn and I swung my gun around to the sound of Ms. Mugsby's ramblings, oblivious to our actions. One of the silk masks had left a mannequin. Vale stood still, calculating his next move.

"Ms. Mugsby, did you see her?" Vale asked.

"My daughter… has the tendency to come and go… like the rest of the spirits…"

"Your daughter?" I asked.

"Ragg," Vale said.

Darwinn and I turned to him.

"You keep things interesting, Mr. Vale."

"The mask is on. Ragg is out and ready to kill. It's okay, Price. Let Ms. Mugsby be. The White Eye brings out the shells of our deepest demons because it penetrates so far into the soul."

"Then why the hell did we come here?" I asked.

"She can't talk without the mask."

"What good is it if we're dead like those bodies?"

"A White Eye killed those bodies, Price. They have all the signs," Vale said.

I rolled my eyes.

"I don't understand, Mr. Vale, why would Marie disappear?" Darwinn's features hardened.

"Maybe if we asked her in your lab."

Darwinn did not listen to me and scanned the main hall.

"We need to find her fast," I said. "She already has the upper leg in here."

"No, it will be a waste of our precious time. We need to get to the bottom of this... manor," Darwinn said. He sprinted from the main hall and into the hallway, the very one that wrapped around to the foyer.

"She'll kill us if we don't find her," I said, following him.

We walked to the corner with two glass double doors. I heard Vale pace around the hallway, mumbling to himself.

"My research takes priority."

"More people will die if we don't figure out what's going on."

"Did you ever stop to ask yourself why those three women were in Dalton Manor in the first place?"

"Of course I have."

"Apparently not enough."

"Are you saying your research killed them?"

"No, Mr. Price, but we certainly would not be here without my fun-packed theories. It would be to our benefit to stick together."

"Exactly. We need to find Ragg together," I said.

"Already ingrained Vale's little nickname into your head? Interesting. Marie's not dangerous," Darwinn said.

"Ragg is," Vale said.

"Ragg or Marie or whatever the fuck we call her," I said, "how is someone who stalks me in the dark with a scalpel anything but dangerous?"

"Why didn't she stab you?" Darwinn asked.

"I don't know! Why was she there in the first place?"

"Something is terribly off, Price, and Ms. Mugsby… she's still in that room going on to herself," Vale said.

"We need a plan of attack."

"Ragg is there," Vale said calmly. He had passed us and stared into the lone open door on the left, the one where we watched Elara commit suicide.

Darwinn and I dropped our argument and sprinted over.

"I interpreted this image in the blood room," Vale said. "She was amongst the pine trees on her swing."

Draperies dangled from the bedpost in the center of the room. Through it was a lone window, and my heart pushed to my throat. Outside, Marie sat on an old metal swing set along the tree line in her black silk mask, watching us.

But it was Darwinn who stepped into the room and as if in a trance, walked across the bed frame and stared lifelessly at the closet, where Elara killed herself. Blood stains were still splattered on the walls. Tears formed and trailed down his beard.

I followed him. I placed my hand on his shoulder.

"Elara was a special woman," Darwinn said and turned away from the closet. He wiped his tears.

"Let's find who did this," I said.

Darwinn exhaled a soft chuckle. "You really think that will take me away from my research?"

"You'll end up just like her if you don't start thinking straight."

"You might want to watch your friend."

A demonic groan came from outside. I turned my head to the window. On the sandy lawn, Vale fired his pistol. Marie was now at the edge of the pine trees, staring at him.

Then her body disappeared into the shadows. Vale darted in after her.

"Fuck."

"You have some fight in you, Mr. Price."

"I'm trying to save our damn lives." I ran out into the hallway.

A shadow was there. I screamed.

"And now… we have Dalton's master bedroom…" Ms. Mugsby smiled at me in a daze.

I darted away from her down the hallway, through the foyer, then outside onto the sandy lawn. A rusted swing set was to my left, connecting to a playhouse. I sprinted behind it to the forest's edge and saw Vale's footsteps. Even though the sky was a beautiful clear day, without a single cloud, the density of the pine trees dimmed the sand and fogged my mind. I felt a heaviness for a third time at the border of the pine trees. But this instance, the feeling brought me to my knees. Sweat dripped down my forehead. I panicked. *I must find Vale…*

It pushed me forward. I submerged into the pine trees, tracking Vale's footsteps. Weeds and bushes scratched my pants. I weaved back and forth, dodging the pine needles from the branches. For several minutes, the tracks went straight in. I scanned my eyes around the shriveled trees with every step. I heard only nature. I lost sight of Dalton Manor and accepted I was alone in the middle of a forest whose soul had been sucked out.

A chill shot down my spine.

My foot kicked a dead sparrow that lay on the sand.

No one was around me.

I sprinted onward, constantly checking the footprints. But the further in I went, the denser the forest became, and layers of dead pine needles covered the tracks, making it hard to see.

A bush rustled to my left. My heart pounded. I pointed my gun at the sound and crept over. No one was there. In the distance, a shadow appeared between the pine trees, then vanished. Since every tree was scrawny, I ducked into a bush and studied the area in silence.

For a minute, I studied my surroundings. All I heard were birds chirping.

I crept towards where I saw the shadow. I gaped. Nausea gripped my stomach and stuck its nails in. Within the trees, chalk was sprinkled on the ground in the shape of a circle. Clusters of dashed lines were at its center.

I stood perplexed. I stared at what Vale described to be a portal.

I scanned the trees and saw no one. I cautiously stepped into the circle and stared at the dashed lines. Then, remembering what Vale said about the portal in the library, I wiped off the lines in the center to, in theory, close it. I rolled my eyes and could not believe I did that without hesitation.

"Well, I'm a convert, Vale." I closed a portal to the Deus.

A scream came in the distance. I pointed my gun in that direction, a rush of adrenaline shaking me, and I sprinted towards it, sliding through the pine trees.

I reached where I thought the noise came from. But, again, no one was there.

In the distance, I saw another portal. I crept over to it and shuddered. This time, a dead creature was in the center of the portal with lines of chalk sprayed over it.

I pointed my pistol in all directions. I was alone, so I moved closer.

The creature became a fawn. Its limbs were detached, and it had bled out. I fell to my knees once more. *How the fuck could someone do this?*

This time against my better judgment, I placed my hand on the dead fawn and wiped off the chalk marks.

I forced myself to rise up and scan the trees, feeling the shadows were all watching me, studying my every move. I couldn't stay here. I needed to run, but I didn't know where to go. I had become so drawn to every sound and shadow I lost track of where I was. I needed to get back out onto the manor's lawn, rethink a plan of attack, and go from there. Maybe I could convince Darwinn to help.

I studied all directions and made my best guess as to the way back. I ran, giving up on dodging the branches, sprinting right through them, and letting the pine needles dig into my face.

The forest became denser. And occasionally, a bird carcass passed my feet.

I ran for what felt like an eternity. And with each passing second, hope drained from me. I didn't know what I was up against and had yet to find a good way to assess it.

I felt like prey. I had to change my position. I scouted the branches. I darted to the pine tree I deemed the least scrawny. I jumped up and gripped the first branch, then pulled myself up and reached for a second branch. It snapped, and I fell back down, cursing as I landed flat on the ground.

A shadow stared at me in between the pine trees. I wanted to scream, but my lungs turned to ice. It groaned a hiss that tensed my muscles.

"Ragg."

My nausea now tore holes in my stomach.

I arose and darted in Ragg's direction. It went further away. I was possessed. I needed to find it.

I needed to know if it did anything to Vale, if he was okay.

But Ragg disappeared.

A knife swiped at my shoulder, and I ducked.

Ragg jumped out to my right and swung the blade again. I slid to the side and pushed myself into a tree trunk, shaking needles off the branches.

Ragg darted into the shadows.

I had nowhere to go. I crouched onto the ground against the root.

A knife shot out from the dark from behind the tree. I rolled out onto the sand. Ragg lunged for me and swiped again, but I hopped back, just missing the blade. It quickly stepped forward and swiped three more slashes. I threw my body to the side to dodge them.

I grabbed Ragg's scrawny arm and rolled on top of it. Ragg spun me back on the ground, showing strength that took me off-guard.

My gun flew out of my hand. And with my free hand, I punched Ragg in the rib.

It fell off me onto the sand, hissed in pain, then slid behind a pine tree.

I stood up and looked around. In that split second, it was already gone. Ragg was so petite that it could easily hide behind the thin trees.

I grabbed my gun and sprinted as fast as I could in the opposite direction of where I thought I had been running. All I saw were pine trees and the odd dead bird, and just as I had begun to lose hope, I reached a clearing on the horizon.

The sight gave me a new wave of energy. I picked up speed, losing care of my surroundings. I was there… I was free… I made it!

I reached the end, and I turned to despair.

I was not at Dalton Manor.

I was at a marsh. The musty smell pinched my nostrils. Grass went right to its edge, and sandy islands popped up throughout the water where birds congregated. Dirty brown grass spiked through the water line, and the sun shined on my face. Bird carcasses lay around the edge. Beads of sweat rolled down my jaw.

I turned my head around, and, in the distance, I saw Ragg dart back in between the pine trees coming in my direction. It darted to my left, lightning-fast. I dropped to the ground and hid in the tall grass by the edge of the marsh. I looked around. *Where the fuck are you?*

I scanned the trees with my pistol. All I needed was one shot.

I lay in the tall grass, near the edge of the marsh, for several long minutes.

My neck hairs pricked. And for a strange reason, I felt constricted. I turned around.

Ragg stood behind me. Before I could move, it dove into me. But I knocked the knife out of its hand just before it swung. The blade just missed my head.

Ragg grabbed my wrists and pinned me to the ground with its left hand. I tried to separate my arms but failed.

Ragg's long oily black hair dangled limply over my face. Its features pressed through the silk, morphing into a menacing grin. Ragg pushed me to the edge of the marsh. The dirty water skimmed the back of my neck and chilled my spine.

I bit into its arm. Ragg screamed, which brought my right arm free. It grabbed the blade on the ground and swung at my neck. I gripped Ragg's wrist just in time with my free hand. The blade was inches away. But Ragg pushed it in, slightly nipping the skin. The cold metal shocked my body.

Ragg growled in a low hiss. "*The neck. The neck. The neck.*"

I screamed in horror. I spun my legs to the left, and it flailed, spinning its body sideways into the sand.

I then realized it was Vale who had thrown Ragg off.

"Price, don't shoot."

Ragg rose. Vale locked his arms around its shoulders.

It screamed.

"It's okay, Ragg."

"What the hell are you doing?" I demanded.

"We need to question Ragg about the Deus."

"Ragg's going to kill us."

Vale and Ragg fell to the ground and wrestled with their legs flailing back and forth to gain the dominant position. Ragg stomped on his right knee, pushing backward. Vale screamed, releasing Ragg. It jumped to his right and kicked itself off a pine tree back into him, swiping at his shoulder. Vale threw his body sideways.

I grabbed my pistol and fired at Ragg.

It disappeared. I heard footsteps run away.

"We're not going to get anywhere with you scaring off Ragg like that."

"Vale, you just saved my life."

"Ragg has answers. I need to get them out. I wish you stayed back with Darwinn."

"I'm not going to watch you die over this."

"You're right, Price." Vale's eyes widened. "The blood room said I'd come here to find…" Vale mumbled and walked to the edge of the marsh. He watched the birds, and I automatically kept guard. "We need to go back to the manor."

"Don't keep me out of the loop, Vale. What is going on with you and this blood room?"

"It's been correct about the entire case. And there are more symbols hiding in the room, I'm sure of it."

"Did it say who killed Crony and our Jane Doe? Because that would sure as hell save our damn time."

"A White Eye." Vale's features hardened.

"Yes, you've said that before. That's not the answer we need."

"I can take us back. The marsh was a half-mile southeast of the manor. I've studied maps of the property ten times over in the late hours."

"We should hunt Ragg down and take off that mask. Bring Marie in for questioning, we can always put the mask back on." I looked around the marsh. In this area, the pine trees were so dense a layer of dead pine needles covered the floor, hiding any footprints. We had lost Ragg.

"We'll find Ragg soon… but I need to see if there's more to the symbols in the blood room."

"I found two portals; one had a dead baby deer in it."

"Did you close them?"

"I did."

"You Mad Morte." Vale grinned. "I closed five, all guided by the blood room. Two had rodents."

My jaw dropped.

"Some demons require more than one portal to break into our world from the Deus. This White Eye must be powerful."

"It's still in the manor?" I caught my tongue and kicked myself for asking the question with such conviction.

"I think so. It can hide in people well, usually those more sensitive."

"Like who?"

"Ms. Mugsby."

"Isn't she supposed to be in a post-possessed state?"

"It just makes it unlikely. Records have shown several instances where people with post-possession symptoms can still be possessed. Especially when some demons are buried deep in the soul."

I kept quiet. I accepted I wasn't going to convince him right now, and if anything, I'd get him more lost in his world.

"Come this way." Vale reentered the pine trees. I followed him, on constant alert for Ragg. Vale was fast. I followed him as best as I could, but he had always been quicker than me. A few minutes went by, and there was no sight of Ragg, but I became anxious the longer I was blanketed in the forest, and the scenery did not change.

Vale would occasionally look back and slow down some to stay in my vision.

I followed what was now my ritual: take four steps and check my left, take four steps and check my right. I wasn't sure if I had lost feeling in my legs or if I was still in shock from Ragg's blade nipping my skin.

At last, the pine trees finally became less dense, and my hope to survive became a possibility. My mind went numb. And at some point in the distance, the pine trees stopped. I was almost there. I could feel the darkness leaving, the creature hiding back in its hole. I pushed forward into the light.

I made it.

I threw my body out of the trees and onto the sand. I rolled on the ground for a moment, keeping my ears pinned to the pine trees. The sweat poured down my face, and I took a long, deep breath.

"Ragg or not, Marie seems to like you," Vale said. He offered a hand and pulled me up.

"I would have thought she favor the infamous Max Vale."

"So did I, no offense."

"I don't know how you do it." I felt my nerves cool down. I took another deep breath. "What do you make of all the dead birds?"

"Blood for rituals."

"Fucking great."

I looked at Dalton Manor. Even ten feet away, it blended in with the thin layer of trees. We trudged across the sand, past the swing and playhouse.

"You didn't see Ragg in the pine trees?"

"Not until I saw you... I'm sorry I tried to push you away. I should've asked for your help. I'm just terrified, Price..." Vale's face sunk.

"So am I, Vale."

"I'm losing myself like the first night."

"You've been getting worse each day."

"No, not in that way, but my... anxiety."

"Will you be okay?" My heart sputtered.

"I'm fine."

I raised my brow.

"I'll let you know if things start to go south."

I nodded, unsure what to add that could relax him. We walked through the entrance into the foyer. From the library down the hallway, Darwinn's voice grabbed our ears. "Elara, please come back..."

We darted across the manor, through the double glass doors, down the stairwell, and into the library.

Darwinn leaned against a shelf, his eyes glazed over. He opened his mouth but could not put together any syllables.

"Have a seat." I pulled up a chair that had been turned over during Moreno's breakdown during our first search.

"I just can't rationalize my sensorium." Darwinn plopped onto the cushion.

"Tell us what you saw," I said, keeping my eyes on my surroundings. I had no idea where Ms. Mugsby or Ragg could be.

"Mr. Price, it makes no sense. And the mere observation is lunacy."

"Then please enlighten us," Vale said.

"She was television static. Like those paintings." Darwinn's shoulders tensed.

"Or a ghost?" Vale's hands shook.

"They'll be an explanation."

"Darwinn, we found open portals in the pine trees. I'm sure there's more."

"Not quite the rationale I'm hypothesizing."

"Elara never told you about portals?"

"Why, of course, Mr. Vale, they're from that cult of yours."

"It's not a cult, Darwinn. It's a Society." Vale's tone sharpened.

"Sure, kiddo."

"You realize if enough are open, it's documented in scriptures that you can detect other entities in our world that we normally could not because they usually stay in the Deus."

"Such as…"

"Ghost, spirits, however you want to call them. They have already crossed over, and they are made of imperium."

"Mr. Vale, my scientific theory supports imperium and allows the potential of the Deus to exist. So please, keep entertaining me."

"I'd love to," Vale said, scanning the library as I had been for shadows. "If there was ever a place you could sense a spirit, it would be here because the three of us are surrounded by portals in the pine trees."

"But why Elara?"

"The spirits you'd sense would most commonly be ones you had a strong relationship with and who most recently passed… We closed seven."

"That's what you hooligans were doing?"

"I don't believe it," Vale said.

"Why Mr. Vale, I thought you were all about beliefs."

"You talk to a ghost, literally stared at one, and you can't open your mind to even the idea."

"You weren't even there."

"I'm not here to convince you. If you simply provide a better explanation to me, I'm completely on board with you."

"Settling for an explanation is not the same as not having one."

"Don't worry, she tried to kill me again," I said to cut off Vale. "We'll figure this out, Darwinn. Just tell me what happened for a start."

The floor creaked from the hallway. We all stopped and looked at each other. We stayed silent for a minute, unsure where to move. We were trapped.

But the sound did not repeat itself, and Darwinn softly said, "Mr. Price, I came to the library, and she was there—right there!" Darwinn pointed to the corner by the bookshelves. "She told me about how much she enjoyed our days discussing theories over coffee, how much she missed me, and was sorry she left me the way she did... I demanded an explanation as to what was going on. But she would not explain what she had been up to... just like old times."

"How long did you talk to her?"

"Time loses all relativity when I'm with her."

Vale rolled his eyes.

"And where did she go?" I asked.

"Right down that hallway through those bookshelves."

Vale and I looked at each other, perplexed. I walked down the aisle and found nothing but rows of books on psychiatry and physics I couldn't comprehend. I had no reasonable explanation for what Darwinn saw and why he thought it was Elara. But with the list of strange encounters growing by the hour, I decided just to take what he saw at face value and work through an explanation during the rest of the search.

"What do you think is going on?" I placed my hands in my pockets and studied Darwinn.

"I'm still working on it… but I fear we're short on time," Darwinn said, staring at where we had heard the sound.

"He's right, Price. A White Eye could be around here somewhere. We need to go to the blood room to find out the next step."

"I suppose you didn't have your luck with Marie?"

I pointed to the cut mark on my neck.

"What? But that's preposterous." Darwinn's eyes widened, once again at a loss for words.

"Why are you so surprised?"

"I can't rationalize a motive to target you, Mr. Price."

"Feel free to let me know when you do. Did you see Ms. Mugsby?"

"She was still going on with her own tour of the manor upstairs before I had a visit from Elara."

I furrowed my brow.

"I don't know what to make of Ms. Mugsby either, Mr. Price."

"So you're not coming with us, Darwinn?"

"If you officers feel the need for an awakening in this blood room of yours, who am I to stop you?"

I was torn on what to do.

The floor creaked again.

My mind sped up. Should I find and interview Ms. Mugsby? And was any information I get from her trustworthy? Marie was out of the picture for the moment, and Darwinn had his own agenda that clearly differed from Vale's. I decided to work with perhaps the one constant I knew for certain in Dalton Manor—wait for Marie. She would find me. And I would be ready to arrest her or, at worst, shoot her in self-defense. She talked to me with the mask on, something I could not get her to do at the station on the first night without the mask.

My next concern focused on Darwinn. Could I trust him?

At the time, my gut answer was a resounding "no." I could not rule him out as a suspect, and his research was a strong motive to tie him into this case, but the gruesome details of the crime seemed out of his façade. But what did I really know about Dr. Arnold Darwinn? I couldn't even tell if Ms. Mugsby was okay. He could have killed her as far as I knew.

I took a deep breath. I had no rationale for Darwinn's story. But at the top of my list, I needed to wait for my killer, and I would do so beside the man I have always trusted, no matter how frustrated I could be with him at times.

We finished our last words with Darwinn, then Vale and I darted out of the library back into the hallway where the creaking sound had been. Nothing. We froze and listened. *Silence.* There was no trace of Ragg or Ms. Mugsby.

We crept back to the basement door, down the stairwell, and reentered at its bottom to where we initially found Marie on the first night.

"Did you catch Darwinn's shadow?" Vale asked.

"No. Should I have?"

"Hard to tell with the lighting in that room. When a White Eye completely possesses a soul, it becomes the person's shadow."

"What does it look like?" My eyes widened.

"You'll know it when you see it." Sweat dripped down Vale's face.

"Are you sure you're okay?"

"Depends which scene I play out." Vale wiped his face with a handkerchief he pulled from his teal flower-covered vest.

"Let's sit down for a minute."

"We can't afford it."

We surveyed the basement room where we initially found Marie on our first night. A crack in the corner, the one opposite the cement hallway that led to the blood room, grabbed our attention.

We pointed our guns at the crack. Vale pushed against the wall, and it opened and swung backward. We shined our flashlights into the gap. It led to a wooden, dusty stairwell going back up to the top floor.

"There's more to this place," I said. "I think Darwinn's onto something."

"Maybe someone's watching us," Vale said.

We cleared the room. The couch was empty. And the closet door was open that still had bloodstains from the Jane Doe.

We walked through the musty, stripped-down hallway covered in cement and cinder blocks to reach the blood room. Bird carcasses were still wedged against the wall. The painting was just as gut-wrenching as I remembered.

Vale stared at the blood. He brought out a small flashlight from his vest and shined it against certain areas of the painting. I guarded the lone entrance. There was no sight of Ragg.

"And right here, Price, the drawing said I would find you." Vale pointed to the edge of the painting.

After Vale's breakdown of symbols earlier in the case, I appreciated how much detail went into the painting. But it seemed every time I could piece together parts of his deformed face, all the minuscule details became overwhelming, and the image shattered. Wrinkles revealed stick figures of creatures, his anatomy constructed strokes of smaller pictures, and every other space was occupied by the tiniest of markings.

"Remember, Price, there's no curvature, so the drawings can look primitive in some areas."

"How do I read it?"

"In layers, you read it inward to outward, then…" Vale turned away without talking and mumbled to himself.

I stepped away and guarded the door to give him space.

"It's so simple." Vale brought out a small jar of black paint and a brush from his vest. He unscrewed the lid, dabbed the brush in the jar, painted a giant rectangle around the edges of the blood painting, then made boxes around his faces. "I understand it now. I need to connect the portals to find the center of them all."

I felt we were being watched. I shined my flashlight into the hallway. "Vale…"

Ms. Mugsby stood at the far entrance of the cement hallway with her demented smile. She stumbled forward, swaying side to side.

"Ms. Mugsby, freeze." I pointed my gun.

She didn't listen and hobbled forward.

"Ms. Mugsby, I will shoot."

"Don't. We don't know how to handle darkness this evil." Vale breathed heavily, and his hands shook.

"But we can't tell what she's capable of," I said.

Ms. Mugsby reached the entrance. She looked paler and more veins surfaced on her skin.

My heart stopped.

Her shadow emerged on the wall.

What the fuck am I staring at? I thought.

In the shadow, spikes shot out of a human body. Two sets of conjoined legs gripped the floor, connected to Ms. Mugsby's feet, and a pair of horns shot out of its head, where the shadow somehow became even darker. A bright hole was in the center of the head. It watched us.

"White Eye." Vale's voice was the calmest I had ever heard it.

XI
THE DEUS

THIS ISN'T REAL. This can't be real, I thought. I didn't believe my eyes. There was no possible way Vale could be spot on about this. There had to be some mistake.

But then it screamed. And my skepticism vaporized. Several octaves smacked my face, but a low, dark tone crawled into my ear and rung in my head, trying to fry my mind. Then it seeped into my bones. I lost all sense of existence. And terror dug into every inch of my body.

A chill swarmed my face, and tongues licked all my fingers at once.

I screamed.

Vale had stepped in front of me and shined his flashlight into its eye.

Ms. Mugsby's shadow roared in agonizing pain.

Vale's flashlight bulb exploded. Smoke rose from it.

"Run! Now! We only have a few moments," Vale said.

"How—what—"

"Now, Price!"

The White Eye stuck to the ceiling, and its tongues dangled by our heads, hissing in a low demonic grown I had heard Vale use around my townhouse. We ducked down.

I'm dreaming… this is all a nightmare…

Vale's face started to morph into pure horror. We ran through the cement hallway back into the basement room, where we first met Marie on our initial search.

"What the hell did you do?"

"Stun it."

"You read that in your scriptures?"

"It was from a children's rhyme we used to sing in my Society. *White Eye, White Eye, Stun it where the sun shines.*" A hiss came from the blood room, and Vale's eyes bugged.

"You okay?" I asked.

"I've been better."

We ran to the steps to take us back upstairs.

At the bottom, Ragg swung its knife.

I threw my body backward, and Vale kicked its side onto the ground. He tried to grab the back straps of Ragg's mask, but it jumped away, back onto the stairs, hissing.

I brought out my pistol and fired.

Ragg had already jumped to the ceiling and wedged its body in a corner.

"No! Don't shoot, Price."

"Let me slow Ragg down!"

"It knows what's going on here," Vale said.

"Then we need a fucking plan. I can't just wait. Ragg will kill me."

Without answering, Vale darted to the newly discovered wooden stairwell in the opposite corner. I tried to keep my gun on it, but Ragg somehow disappeared, as if it had melted into the darkness.

I entered behind him and closed the wall just as Ms. Mugsby's soft footsteps entered the room. I shined my flashlight onto Vale, who listened in suspense.

Ragg stood two feet from him. It swung its hair back, revealing its face's contour through the silk mask.

I screamed; I tried not to, but my world was crashing.

Ragg threw its body into me, swiping its blade at my shoulder. But Vale grabbed its arm just in time. Ragg hissed.

"Marie?" Ms. Mugsby said from across the wall.

From the basement, the White Eye screamed from all different pitches and shook into the stairwell. This time I heard distinct voices. People begging for mercy… others screaming in ecstasy…

I kicked Ragg off, and Vale threw it against the wall, pressing into its back.

"Freeze!" My gun dug into Ragg's back. I reached for the mask, but Vale's hands shook so much from the White Eye screeching that Ragg slipped right out and pushed into the wall. It opened, revealing the start of a small square passage. Ragg slid right in before I could fire.

Vale and I stood in disbelief. I shined my flashlight in.

It was no bigger than a pipe and bent out of view fast. Ragg was gone.

What the fuck is this place? I thought. My mind couldn't wrap around the White Eye or make any rationale as to why Ragg focused on me, of all people.

The White Eye's screams faded.

We darted up the stairwell. It leads us to a narrow hallway up against a wall. I kicked it open, and we found ourselves in the main hall. I went to the mannequins and took the other five silk masks.

"Price, we don't have time." Sweat dripped from Vale's face.

"All I need to do is rip off that one damn mask, and we have her. Let's go to the library and find Darwinn. He shouldn't be there alone."

We ran down the hallway to the double glass doors. Vale cursed.

On the other side of the hallway, The White Eye stood at the door of the basement stairs as Ms. Mugsby shuffled her way up.

I was more surprised by Vale's reaction, reminding me of the loud screech I once heard when we chased Crony into a dumpster. His body shook, and as if all at once, he broke down.

"Focus, Vale!" I nudged him to the double glass door. My touch appeared to snap him back.

The White Eye swayed back and forth, its eye bending in our direction.

We sprinted through the double glass doors. I locked the doors behind us, and Vale closed the blinders at the entrance. We sprinted down the stairs and together lifted a bookshelf that had been tossed on the ground from Moreno. We carried it up the stairs and wedged it against the glass double doors.

The door handle jiggled.

We proceeded to toss a pile of furniture and shelves to block the entrance. The door shook louder.

Vale leaned against the wall by the closed portal in the back. He panted and curled his legs towards his chest.

"It's okay." I placed my hand on his back.

I looked around the library. Darwinn was not there.

Vale did not answer and stared into space like he was in a different world. I could not bring him back. "Vale?"

"We're dead."

The knocking grew louder with each strike. I scanned the room. There was only a single ceiling window, smaller than our body circumference.

"Sorry I brought you away from the coastline," I said.

"Don't be. The coastline was not what I had hoped it be."

My heart sunk.

"Price, I still felt the same."

"But I thought it was different there?"

"In the end, I suppose human flaws are the one constant you'll find at all corners of the Earth." Vale lowered his head onto his knees.

It killed me watching him. But I felt just as helpless. The preceding minutes had come in such a whirl that the White Eye still didn't appear real to me. It was like a figment of my imagination, and the real explanation would show. But its scream doesn't leave you.

Vale turned to his side on the floor, in the exact position I saw him in my bathroom.

The door shook louder.

What could I possibly do that would make him feel better? I thought. I gave up trying to think of a way out. I wouldn't leave Vale, and I'd be damned if he died here in this agony. But I had never been one to say the right words.

He was motionless. And for a moment, I closed my eyes and tried to feel like him, caught in his own thoughts, stuck to every possible action he could do or has done, bent up over any word anyone has ever told him—the idea felt like needles pricking my entire body and processing each one for its own pain.

How could I do this? I thought.

Then a realization smacked me in the face.

"You are not alone," I said without thinking. "I can promise you that. You might be in your own head. But so am I. I can't escape myself, and I guess I'm in a cage right next to you… We can always talk when we feel like it and reach our hands out through the bars."

I took a deep breath and closed my eyes. The White Eye screamed through the door, and I heard Sarina's voice in the noise.

Then her scream stopped.

Vale was hugging me.

I stayed still, too hardened to reciprocate.

"You and I will never be alone," Vale said, shaken.

At once, the last pockets of love I saved for Sarina, hoarded while I begged the universe for one more chance, poured into Vale.

He balanced me in ways I had never imagined. For a second, harmony took over Dalton Manor, and the horrors of the world became quiet.

I couldn't say how I felt. We just existed—the love of a father and son, created by two lost souls.

Ms. Mugsby broke through the glass.

"Can you get up?" I asked.

"I will always try for you."

She knocked a chair off the stairwell that we had wedged against the door. Then several pieces tumbled behind it. Ms. Mugsby crawled in through the glass. The room was hardly lit, but I knew the White Eye was there. Even in the darkness, it somehow looked darker. I could not believe it.

"How should I stun it?"

"Like anything else, with a clean shot."

Ms. Mugsby crawled into the center space where we stood.

The White Eye appeared.

It screamed in several different octaves at once and bent vertically in half. Through the shadow, a giant mouth emerged in crisp detail in shades of black and gray, unveiling endless rows of teeth stacked on top of each other and the source of the tongues. They slithered, and it made a guttural sound.

The eye tucked out of sight from my flashlight.

I stood, broadening my shoulders, ready to strike.

"Ragg…" Vale said.

A hand appeared from behind Ms. Mugsby and wrapped around her head. Another hand popped out and grabbed her waist. Frizzed black hair rose over Ms. Mugsby's back and draped over her chest. She shrieked in terror. The White Eye left us and hid in the bookshelves.

"Sweetie, please… Have mercy…" Ms. Mugsby screamed. Her body bent backward, and she desperately tried to flail her legs.

"Don't kill her, Ragg," Vale said.

The White Eye roared as it slid away with her, dragging her up the stairs of the library. Ms. Mugsby's deafening scream traveled down the hall.

Vale darted across the library, but I grabbed him.

"What are we defending if we don't save her?" Vale asked.

"We can't, that's the thing! We're lucky to be alive. We need to get the hell out of here and get ODYSE on board to figure out whatever the hell was behind that thing."

Vale bit his tongue.

The front door slammed shut, and Ms. Mugsby's screams diminished.

"What the hell just happened?" I asked, still digesting the last few moments.

"I-I don't know… A White Eye, I guess…" Vale said.

"You guess?"

"You have a better answer?"

"Fuck."

Before Vale could speak, in the back corner, a bookshelf pushed backward and opened sideways. We glanced at each other, then paced towards it.

I shined my flashlight, revealing a downward stairwell. No one was there. "Darwinn?" I called.

"I don't believe in coincidence," Vale said.

Without hesitation, we entered, guns in hand.

The further we went down the stairs, the sleeker the walls and steps. We arrived at a door on our left. It was silver and had no handle. There were square lights on top blinking various colors.

Vale's eyes flashed blue. I jumped.

He had the same reaction as me.

"*Scan complete. Welcome, Liam Price,*" a gentle female voice said from the lights.

The door slid open. We entered, and my jaw dropped.

The lowest basement looked nothing like the rest of Dalton Manor. The entire room was metallic. Rows of clear screens floated around a clean circular table, each displaying charts, computer code, and images I had never seen. Holograms of humans moved around the room and tapped on different hovering screens. On the walls, lights and knobs covered every square inch. Some of the images looked identical to the symbols used in Vale's childhood Society. Except instead of using blood, they were in distinct dark lines, with calculations surrounding every detail, as if the symbols were now geometry.

Vale squinted, studying an image of several lines that reminded me of our search in Crony's rancher. He jolted. A hologram walked right through him.

"Never mind those maintenance 'grams." Darwinn appeared from the far corner of the room. "They don't like to be bothered with the *sapiens* of their world."

Vale and I pointed our guns at him.

Darwinn's lips curled into a possessed smile. "But by the looks of you gents, I suppose neither of you has ever encountered a 'gram. Shame, they're interesting creations to work with. Most of them can perform tasks rather well, and their ability to harden certain limbs has further optimized productivity in our world. However, I'm afraid there's not much intellect… Perfect for many roles, but quite the contrast from our 'bots." Darwinn brought out a flask from his golden blazer and unscrewed the cap. Steam rose into his nostrils and his face relaxed. He took a sip and shook the flask at each of us. "Coffee, anyone?"

We didn't budge. And after a dragged-out moment, Darwinn continued. "Well then, my strange gentlemen… Welcome to Elara's real lab in the depths of Dalton Manor." He looked at the barrels of our guns. "I appreciate the respect, but I'm afraid time is not on our side."

"How did you find the entrance?" I asked.

"It's a bit of a whirlwind. The shelf opened when I grabbed a book Elara had recommended me to read."

"I checked that shelf on our last search."

"I believe you, Mr. Price. But perhaps there's more to this manor than you know. At least the manor seems to know you both more than you realize."

"Stop playing games, dammit."

"Why, I'm only a piece trying to fit into this puzzle. I mean, look around you! Does this place not scream Waterfront technology to you? Do you even know what you're staring at?"

Darwinn walked to the circular table. I followed him.

At once, lines of formulas floated in the air as if they were part of a screen. No matter where I stood, they continued to face me.

"This afternoon, you witnessed a hypothesis become a theory that was neither mine or what I'm suspecting to be Elara's... but rather a fusion of the two."

Darwinn petted the variables hovering in the air and glared at us. We were about to get the full blast of Darwinn's switch from kooky to serious—with an occasional shift of the toggle back.

His transitions used to feel sharp, but the more I've experienced Darwinn's quirks, I discovered that most humans obsessed with a craft are crazy by nature. And if I'm around one at the right times, I experience the full spectrum of their thought process, the emotional range of their insight.

"Gentlemen, my gun is away," Darwinn said. "I hope for your support."

After internally debating, I slowly lowered mine, but Vale kept his up. "It's okay, Vale," I said.

He ignored me. "Keep talking, Darwinn."

"Fine, be that way..." Darwinn sipped his flask. "I had an idea, one I've dreamt about for ages, that energy and time are dependent on each other. Do you know what that means? Without progress, the universe can't function, and without the universe and us releasing energy and doing those things we do... time can't exist. And for the longest span, I thought my experiments would be unable to falsify that theory, the greatest form of success in the scientific community... Years of work slaving into this world that for a moment I swore made sense to me. But to my shock, there was a whole different variable to the equation." Darwinn pointed at the series of letters floating in the air. "A completely different *substance*, a third component to time and energy, creating its own dimension that this software in my lab—and apparently Dalton Manor—can detect."

"Imperium?" Vale said, lowering his gun. His eyes became concerned.

"Correct, Mr. Vale. Imperium. At least that's the title this lab has given this material. The results from my research explain the scientific reasoning behind it. And here, Mr. Vale's Society has been developing a way to quantify it in our physical realm... through the guidance of their religious textbooks."

"*But how?*" I asked, unsure how to phrase a more constructive thought.

"According to the documents in this lab, which belong to Elara and Mr. Vale's Society, it was like any great idea. There was the funding and the inspiration. First, the funding—ODYSE, it has to be. I partnered up with them to use their technology through my PATC years for tenure. And wouldn't you know, I met Elara shortly afterward, and I now don't think it was by chance." Darwinn's brilliant blue eyes unveiled shades of gray.

"Os reported it on TV last night."

"I saw that peculiar show, and I've read their problems in this lab. What is it... their 'bots have detected imperium? I bet you their new updates contained my coding. I shared snippets with Elara. Ones I developed to verify my own theories. And now, they don't know how to handle it!"

"Os told us his company's 'bots detected the imperium first by accident."

"Wait, *you* talked to Os?" Darwinn asked.

"What's wrong?" I asked.

"I've never even seen him in person."

"He contacted me for a consult," Vale said.

"How?"

"Through my private investigator number I have on the coastline."

"He used a phone to talk to you? Oh, this is not good... What did he say about me?"

"Nothing about you in particular," I said. "Just that they had been working on studying the theory of the Deus for a decade, and the 'bot updates detected it by mistake."

"And my theory was the key cog, I bet. Oh boy. He kept that fact from you."

"Os also mentioned they were getting sort of a 'strange reading' on Dalton Manor property," Vale said. "You didn't help them?"

"My plaid trousers, I did! I might be using their software and machines in my lab, but that's to help my theories—I had no access to their 'bots or satellites. In fact, all I knew about imperium before I saw you detectives this afternoon was the mere pie-in-the-sky beliefs about this Deus dimension. Elara had referred to it in the past over coffee in reference to Mr. Vale's Society."

"They don't know what's going on, Darwinn. That's why we were consulted," Vale said.

"Why would they contact you?"

"Because I'm Elara's emergency contact."

"Who assigned you this case first? Your ex?" Darwinn turned to me. I shook my head.

Darwinn paced around the table, stroking his beard.

"It's okay, Darwinn," I said, "ODYSE detected this substance and saw we were on the case because it's in the *Haddon Herald.* And then they contacted Vale."

"They detected a White Eye," Vale said. Darwinn and I stared at him. "All the portals are open, leading to the spiritual realm, and a White Eye somehow came through. Os is sharp, and he knows my past. Someone with experience who could find an explanation to the unexplainable phenomenon."

"Mr. Vale, a great segue into the second part... the inspiration. From what I have read from Elara, this project was started because Marie can sense imperium without any machines." Darwinn waved his hands around the basement.

"That's why the Society worships her like a god," Vale said.

"They ran her genomics. She has a single mutation within the DNA of her neurons that reconstructed the quantity and pathways of her wiring."

"And she's able to talk to spirits."

"Mr. Vale, she can connect to this imperium in the Deus."

"Phrase it how you want, Darwinn. I bet you there are different consistencies of imperium, just like how there are different types of spirits in the afterlife, and we're only getting started."

"And how would you know that? In a scripture of yours based off nothing?"

"I dreamt a memory of Marie that showed me."

"Now that... is interesting." Darwinn's eyes flared with an inquisitive glow. He scratched his beard again.

"How can a dream intrigue you," I said, "when Marie Dalton, or whatever this White Eye creature is, does not bother you? What's wrong with you?"

Vale closed his eyes and began to mumble to himself.

"Because Mr. Vale apparently has this same mutation, but his DNA expression level is only altered slightly. You and Marie are the only two documented—or at least sensed—by the 'bots..."

"The 'bots detected Marie too?" I asked.

"Oh, Mr. Price, did your friend forget to mention that as well? What am I missing here?" Darwinn turned to Vale.

"Elara's Society thought I was the prodigy to communicate to God... or the Deus, and once I was unable to, they shifted their search for another... apparently Marie."

"How interesting... this Deus. According to my lab work, this imperium has always existed. It is currently not only a continuum with time and energy, but it binds all three together. Time and energy actually *evolved* from imperium, and just like that, it creates an entirely new universe— our universe—that we live in, though still embedded in the Deus."

"The spiritual realm," Vale said.

"The Deus is the platform... and imperium is the material."

"What the hell are you guys talking about?" I asked.

"Price, the Deus is the first universe. And it exists throughout our universe because that's where we came from originally," Vale said, opening his eyes. "God does not exist *on* this planet. He exists *with* this planet. He lives in and is the spiritual realm—a place where our souls enter, but our bodies cannot."

"View it as you must," Darwinn said. "But Mr. Vale brings up the key problem: we can't physically enter the Deus, nor do we have the biological sensation or capability to detect it like we do with other things in our life, such as temperature or pressure. As a result, the three of us, and the rest of the civilization, live on worlds where we can't detect the imperium, just energy and time."

"How do you know that?" I asked.

"Marie Dalton," Darwinn said. "By biological anomaly, she happens to be that one person with the exact mutation, in the right century to show that she can detect this imperium, this Deus dimension. Even the great Mr. Vale could not show that."

"Impressive, Darwinn," Vale said, pushing his browline glasses up the bridge of his nose. He stared at the professor for a moment.

"What even is this imperium?" I asked.

"A beautiful question I'll need years to investigate, Mr. Price. The best I can offer is it's a substance we don't have the capabilities to understand just yet. Mr. Vale's Society was originally studying Marie's detection of it by her clinical symptoms and EEG waves from her brain. The strongest readings they documented were from two very strong substances in the Deus, of which we sense only a sliver of in our universe and label as emotions—*love* and *hatred*. A lot of these tests tried to evoke those feelings out of Marie because the feelings we create actually make the imperium in our body that enters the Deus."

I turned to Vale, who said, "Our deepest loves and hatreds ingrain into our soul and cross with us to the afterlife, fulfilling the mind-soul connection that the line represents from the Society. Once it's in the soul, it can run rampant in the Deus."

"Not *everything* is so on par with that cult of yours, Mr. Vale." Darwinn shook his head and glanced behind me. "Mr. Vale?"

Vale had darted to the corner of the lab.

"Where the hell are you going?" I asked.

"Mr. Price, the software here is almost copied onto my mind-drive." Darwinn tapped the side of his temple, and a small gray square lit up. "In two more minutes, we need to leave this place if ODYSE isn't already here."

"Why would ODYSE be here?"

"That's what I'm reading... Turns out, they've been following us this whole time. I'm able to hack into their main database from here..."

"Why?"

"I'm working on it..." Darwinn scanned his eyes back and forth like he was reading a sheet directly in front of him. "This can't be true..."

"What is it, Darwinn?"

"Find Mr. Vale and run. I can't speak for my own awareness... but apparently, they know about him."

My heart dropped. "They know? But how?"

"Go! There's another way out down the back hallway at the end."

"Why would you help us?"

"Elara wants me to. Just go."

I darted after Vale down a corner, during which several 'grams glided through me. The room curled back into a hallway containing a long series of metallic doors, each labeled with a number.

Down the hall, a door slid upward with ferocity in front of Vale. He entered.

I darted over and raised my brow.

The room was small. On the side, rows of orange hologram whips were attached to their respective black cylinders on the wall. We swung our pistols around. Blindfolds, gags, and chains covered every inch on the other wall. Nothing else was there.

"The rituals of my childhood," Vale said calmly.

"Vale, they know everything about you. We need to leave."

"Of course they know. What do you think I'm doing? I saw a floor plan on one of those screens while Darwinn was babbling."

"It's this one." I pointed to the lone metallic door at the end of the hallway.

"There are several ways. That door takes us out, but a long way from where we need to be."

"Anything close will take us to them."

A mumble filled the hallway. I glanced at Vale; his features hardened. The mumble came again, this time clearly from the door across the hallway from us. "Let's just run," I said.

The metal door opened. We pointed our guns at it. I shined my flashlight into the dark room. There Ms. Mugsby stood, smiling, staggering between a bed and a toilet.

"Freeze!" I yelled.

I turned to Vale, who looked just as surprised.

She mumbled to herself.

"Donna Mugsby, put your hands in the air!" I ordered.

She dragged her feet into the center of the room, glaring at us.

"I will fire if I have to."

"Price, don't do it!" Vale said.

"She'll kill us."

"Something's not right."

"Now something's not right? There's all these trap doors in this hell hole. She could have come from anywhere."

"There's no White Eye in her shadow."

"You said it would still be in her. I won't fall for it," I said.

Ms. Mugsby grimaced in a dazed, oblivious to my gun. She mumbled nonsense. My hands shook.

"Ms. Mugsby, are you okay?" Vale asked.

"Marie… Where…"

She jumped at us. I shot her in the chest.

She stopped in her footing. Blood filled her crinkled fleece jacket. She stumbled back against a wall, and tears formed in her eyes.

Vale sprinted over and grabbed her. With gentleness, he placed her on the ground and stroked her hair. He took her hand in his. "It's okay, Donna."

My stomach sunk like a brick.

Her dark eyes scanned around the tiny room, mumbling. She breathed heavier as the blood poured out of her chest.

Tears filled my eyes. I didn't know how to think. I had no idea what I was doing anymore.

Vale brought a jar of white powder from his flowered vest and sprinkled a little on her forehead. He spoke in a demonic voice. Then he hummed a few lines of those slurred syllables I had never heard from that language.

It was then I saw at least a dozen scars that crept from the lower part of her back, around the side to her abdomen.

"Price… what did you do?" Vale asked.

"What do you mean? She was about to attack us—"

"She fell." Vale stood up and paced the tiny room.

From the main room of the lab, the female voice at the lab entrance said, "*Welcome, Martin Brezniack.*"

The Society, I thought. Vale had to be frightened.

"Forget the other way. We need to leave—now." Vale dashed to the metallic door at the end of the hallway.

I followed, running through the hallway door. It slammed shut behind me.

To my surprise, the next room was another hallway, as far as I could see. Vale wasn't kidding. The walls were metallic the entire way down, and water slid down each corner to moats.

Even though hearing Brezniack's voice gave me a rush of adrenaline, I could not keep up with Vale. He already appeared a hundred feet ahead of me, sprinting away. I followed him, my mind numb, my face frozen.

My body weakened as I realized that I had just killed a helpless woman. *But it was self-defense. She was going to kill me, right?*

In the distance, I saw the end of the hallway lead to a ladder that rose to ground level. Vale had already climbed up.

I glared back. At this point, the door I came from was a speck. I reached the ladder and shined my flashlight up to reveal a lid. Climbing up and cracking it open, I wedged the end of my pistol out and peeked through. No one was there.

"Marie!" Vale's voice was close.

I opened the lid as quietly as I could and jumped onto the sand. I saw no one. Pine trees surrounded me, and I heard birds chirping. In the near distance, I saw the start of the marsh.

Vale scampered by its edge.

I followed him, constantly scanning my surroundings for Ragg's shadow cutting through the trees. "Vale!" I reached the end of the pine tree line, and the sun smacked my face.

"Stay back." He swung his arm at me to get between him and the marsh.

"It's okay, Marie… I promise you it will be okay…" Vale looked at me, his eyes partially deranged. "Put your gun away. You shouldn't have come."

"Are you mad? After all this time?" I asked.

"I need to talk to her. Your weapon's not helping."

With reluctance, I placed my gun in my holster and glared at Vale. "I hope you know what you're doing."

"I don't. But I think she does."

"Some plan."

Ragg stood at the edge of the pine trees.

"Marie, do you know who I am?"

"Run…" Ragg growled, its voice higher than normal.

"I'm sorry about what everyone's done to you. I'm here for you. I can protect you. I know what you're going through. They chose me to be a god before turning to you, but I defected… If I had just stayed, this would have never happened to you. Let me help you in return." His face sunk.

A hiss filled the marshland, and the birds flew away. I scanned the pine trees.

A chill struck my bones.

Spikes appeared from the shadows, and a white light watched us in the distance.

"My daughter… my sweetie…"

I gasped.

Somehow, Ms. Mugsby stood at the edge of the forest, a walking corpse. Scratch marks covered her face. The White Eye hid in the pine trees, larger than I remembered it to be in Dalton Manor.

Vale's body stiffened at the sound of the White Eye's hiss.

"Hey, stay with me." I grabbed Vale's shoulders.

He became pale and locked in place, unable to move.

Ragg tackled Ms. Mugsby. They fell on the pine needles hissing at each other, swiping every opportunity they could, then rolled into the forest out of sight.

"Stay here." I jumped from behind Vale.

He grabbed my shoulder. I turned back. He couldn't speak, but he looked determined at all costs to help. We ran into the pine trees. I bought out my flashlight. In the distance, Ragg kicked off a pine tree and flew into the head of the White Eye. It roared, shaking my core.

We sprinted over to the White Eye.

Ragg swung a knife in every direction. But the White Eye swarmed while Ms. Mugsby hid in its shadow. Surrounded, Ragg tried to jump to a tree branch, but Ms. Mugsby's bone-dry hands shot out from the White Eye and grabbed its ankle, sending it to the ground.

"No!" Vale yelled, his body paralyzed.

Ms. Mugsby ripped Ragg's black silk mask off. Marie lay on the ground, frail and malnourished.

Lifted by the White Eye, Ms. Mugsby rose in the air. Then she dove into the sand and slid underneath Marie, locking her body. Her hands grabbed onto Marie's jaw.

For the first time, I heard Marie Dalton's voice, on her own, without a mask—it was an agonizing, horrifying scream. She wailed in hysteria, sounding no more like the creature Ragg and every bit the tormented young woman.

The White Eye's body split open, and endless rows of teeth jumped onto her, its tongues lifting her arms in the air as its mouth chomped at her fingers. Ms. Mugsby's growls grew louder and more rhythmic. The eye locked onto Marie's face, taking three big gulps. With each, one of its horns wedged into the right side of her neck.

Silence took over.

The White Eye released Marie Dalton, face carved off, fingers snapped off, and three neck stab marks—dead.

It roared, hungry for more.

But I was there. "Go to hell, motherfucker." I shined my flashlight into its eye, and it howled.

Ms. Mugsby slithered to me on the sand, and I shot her in the chest with my pistol three times. The White Eye tried to move its head, but I followed its every nudge for long enough to fade out of sight from Vale. It screeched and fell backward onto the pine needles.

My flashlight sparked, then burned out, like Vale's.

The White Eye hissed and froze in the shadows of the trees as Ms. Mugsby's body lay dead on the ground once more.

I darted in the exact opposite direction until the sounds of it faded and the bird chirps returned. I didn't know how much time we had.

Vale stood by the pine tree where I left him in complete disarray. I walked to him.

"Let's get the hell out of here."

Vale shook his head, then looked behind me, bewildered. I glanced in his direction.

In the distance, a single light green circle emerged that looked like an iris. A laugh huffed through the pine trees, and the dot blinked in sync with its vocal pattern. The voice shook Vale back into the present, and my heart sunk.

It couldn't be. I thought.

At least a dozen more light green dots appeared everywhere around us.

"What the fuck is going on?" I scanned the forest.

A single laugh echoed through the forest, and the dots blinked in unison. "Relax, Lieutenant Price," the voice said. "I'm not here for you."

GHOST MINING

I KNEW THE voice far too well.

It was Os, and I was the least bit star-struck. Even though he sounded the exact same as any other day, this time, his voice perturbed me. It chilled the air and sunk my feet into the sand. There was a nasty bite like every syllable nipped closer to my face.

He was everywhere, yet I couldn't locate a single source.

The brightest green dot shined straight ahead of us. It grew bigger. At first, the shadow of a human appeared, then it turned into a white 42XC 'bot, the very model that could detect the Deus, identical to the ones we encountered on our consult with Os. It was shaped like a male, though plated in white and silver. A green light flashed in the center of his faceless head to the rhythm of Os's laugh. The 'bot walked with fluidity and stopped only a few feet away.

The other green lights remained in the distance.

"Anything you would like to share?" Os asked.

"Show yourself, dammit," I said, enraged. No one, not even Os, causes this pain to Vale.

"Lieutenant, I'm specifically asking this question to Private Investigator Max Vale."

"We're not safe here," I said. "No one's safe here. Your men need to leave while there's still time."

"Of course my men aren't with the likes of *him* here. That's why I brought some friends."

The other 'bots came into view, surrounding us, all identical to the first one. They blinked the green light in the same patterns.

Vale had not moved, paralyzed by the turn of the events. I had no idea what we were up against, but my gut sank. I could not fathom what these 'bots were capable of or how he was controlling them.

"Max Vale... I can see why your charm is legendary in pockets of Haddon—your genetics are just *beloved*." Os's voice projected and thumped my eardrums as if he spoke from all the 'bots at once.

"I do keep busy."

Os laughed, then his tone darkened. "And you'll burn in hell for it..."

The center 'bot stepped closer to Vale, who remained rigid. We stared at the head plate of the 'bot's green light as if we expected it to scowl.

"All I needed to do was ask around," Os said. "I must say your fellow officers love you. They would do anything to watch you die. You're a traitor to them. They don't care your Type B Citizenship was exempted. They were more than happy to tell me every little whisper they heard about you. An *Undesirable Relationship*? A wild, disgusting story, going against the human race—"

"Show yourself, you fucking coward! I've had enough!" I said. "They tortured Marie Dalton in this hellhole for years—her body is right over there! And there's this monster who has been killing people."

Os's laugh echoed, and all the lights flickered in unison. "Your efforts are appreciated, Lieutenant, but I assure you they're no longer needed. We already identified and found the killer, who admitted to the crimes."

"Impossible. There's a monster around here called a White Eye. I wouldn't have believed it myself if I hadn't seen it."

"A monster? I suppose Max Vale has controlled your mind as well."

"Then who did it?" I asked.

"A young officer named Carl Moreno, who had been poisoned by Max Vale a year earlier."

"Bullshit," I said.

Os laughed again, the sound morphing into a grumble that made the air feel heavy. A thud smacked Vale in the side of the head. My gun followed the source to a 'bot sitting in a pine tree. Vale's maroon notebook lay on the sand, the very one he had written his dreams into. "Look a little familiar?"

Vale's eyes flared as he picked up the notebook. He appeared like he wanted to vomit. "I might have some accounts in there..." Vale said, in reference to Arch.

"You did..." I said, sullen.

"It's normally in my vest. Things got out of hand last night, so I must have left it on the desk..."

"You're the monster, Max Vale," Os said. "A relationship with someone not in your class, an Undesirable Relationship against humanity?"

"They're just stories," I said in a trance. After all this time, I could not bring Vale's relationship to the surface. My heart pounded.

"I'm sure a jury will feel comfortable with stories mixing our genes with yours. Funny, I can't seem to remember the courts making any exceptions," Os said. "But then again, I am talking to the man who just can't be defeated."

I glimpsed at Vale, who stood petrified.

"We've given you every opportunity to die these last few days. We even assigned a Morte each night to assassinate you at Lieutenant Price's home, but every time they went near the property... dead."

"I suspected that much," Vale said.

I furrowed my brow, unaware of the news.

"And strangely enough," Os said, "they all died the exact same way hundreds of Society members have this past month… Their faces were carved off, all fingertips were bitten off, and three stab marks to the neck with an odorous stench to them… The exact same way you found Crony and your mystery body, Shyla Dalton."

I stood in disbelief. *Marie's mother?* I thought back to Vale's diary entries and the news article from Madelyn.

"I heard word of these deaths on the coastline," Vale said. "Ragg is killing off your Society. I suppose ever since your 'bots entered the Deus."

"Ah yes, Ragg… This imperium that's reacting rather oddly in our universe. The 'bots can detect Ragg but don't know how to decipher it. But that's okay; since they are soulless, Ragg can't possess them, only humans who can sense it. And according to the 'bots' data, there are just two with the genome capable. Well, at least there were two…" Os laughed. "I was hoping to kill you off first, thinking you were the easier one. Even still, we made extensive plans for you, Max Vale. But before we could even *reach out*, you came waltzing into Dalton Manor with a tip from the patriot Dr. Madelyn Katz."

My head pounded. I couldn't believe what was going on.

"How that cunt found out… Well, no matter, because I should thank her. Since you took care of the *real* issue, Marie Dalton, I now have little worries. She was the one with the ability to manipulate the Deus in ways we could not understand. She even destroyed several of the 'bots' circuitries when they tried to detect her. So they stayed away, even against our orders. We had no reassuring plan for her… Now it's just you."

"They won't kill me," Vale said. "Just like when we met in Waterfront."

"If they don't, I'd be excited by that prospect as well. Thankfully, we have true loyalists in the Society who understand the bright future even through these onslaughts. The Morenos are an example, proud contributors to the Society, and they reached out, requested we let their son's psychiatric dilemmas be a scapegoat for Lieutenant Price's case if needed. Carl Moreno is waiting in the psych ward and can either be crazy for a jury… or possessed by Max Vale's grotesque nature."

"Oh, God. None of that is true!" I said.

"Doesn't matter, Price. Martin Brezniack set up the crime scene," Vale said. "And he'd be used as a witness."

"I'm afraid there is a path for law and a path for life. I have yet to find its intersection… such a beautiful freedom," Os said, laughing. "Die out here or go to jail and have a mishap. I don't care how many lives Ragg has to take before you get what you deserve."

"You think you can let Dalton Manor go unnoticed?"

"Lieutenant, what exactly am I getting away with? All this technology is on public record. Dalton Manor is in the *Haddon Herald* twice now; anyone can swing by and check it out."

"People are going to find out about this," I said.

"Price, no, they won't," Vale said.

"The PATC will never stand for this."

"They have, and they will," Vale said. "They'll believe anything in the *Haddon Herald*—just like you."

My heart flattened as the realization finally sunk that the man I had admired, whose models I spent years building, had targeted Vale this whole time. Was I any better for believing?

"I have to wonder, Max Vale," Os said. "You seem to be in touch with the city. You understood your… *choices*. Why did you accept my consult?"

"I have nothing to hide, Os," Vale said.

"Is that so? You put up walls very well at that little coffee shop experiment."

"I miss my friends in the Northeast, Os. Certainly, you would miss your friends?"

Os laughed, and the 'bots' green circular lights flicked around us. They stood still. "Don't sound so... normal. You are anything but that."

"You're behind this place. You're in the Society," I said.

"I have evolved a unique partnership with the Society. View me as their IT consultant."

"Bullshit," I said. My head pulsed; everything was falling out of control.

"Lieutenant, I assure anything we find here will be reported appropriately... speaking of that." Another 'bot walked into my peripheral, dragging Marie's torn-up corpse. "You told me a woman was dead? Who did that? Was it you? After all, I'm told you killed her nanny."

"She was possessed by the White Eye and became alive again," I said.

"Price, the real White Eye is Ragg," Vale said. "That wasn't Ms. Mugsby like we thought."

My mind exploded. Vale continued.

"The White Eye is made of imperium unique to Ragg. But my scriptures humanized its power and turned it into the creature we call today. That was the name we gave it."

"Who would have thought of that so accurately to put it in a scripture?"

"I did. When I was a boy."

My jaw dropped.

"To everyone's surprise, from a young age, I had dreams involving Ragg... I gave mine a different name, a White Eye... I see they've evolved it since then, but those dreams made me holy in the Society. They said I was connecting to the higher power in a context that blended all religions into one. And I would be the next great prophet. Once I lost my ability to connect to the Deus in my teenage years, they exiled me, only sparing my life, just in case I reconnected. In the end, they were not sure what they were dealing with, so I took it all as a farce. I spent years in the police monitoring the Northeast Quadrant, trying to uncover their sacrifices, only to grow in more despair as I got nowhere. I left for the coastline... amongst other reasons. It was all a lie to me until recently when I heard about the deaths. Even then, I didn't fully believe it until I saw the blood room. I'm sorry I kept this from you, Price."

"Who? The killer?" Os asked.

All the 42XC 'bots turned their heads to me. My stomach twisted.

"A lovely depiction, Max Vale. I assume you expect to die if you are this open to the killer right now... I think that's wise. Price won't be going anywhere for a while. You were caught on camera killing an innocent decrepit woman with severe dementia," Os said.

"It was self-defense. She had attacked us all night," I said.

"The only Donna Mugsby that existed you killed. The rest was Max Vale's terrifying imagination."

The first 'bot we saw turned back to Vale and walked within several feet of him.

I gasped.

It morphed into a shadow as tall as the pine trees.

Spikes shot out of its back, and it stared at us with a bright white light between two horns. Tongues slithered out of its chest and swarmed into Vale's direction, demonic hissing spitting from its mouth.

"I made the connection right before Os came," Vale said. "I'm too late."

"I'd like to reacquaint you to your monster, the White Eye... After all, it has been this interpretation of ODYSE's you've been chasing. You have a very dark mind, Max Vale. Can't say I'm surprised, given the choices you've made."

"There was never a real White Eye?" I asked, deflated.

"We've had molecular imaging for years," Os said. "But our updates allowed the 'bots to tap into the Deus and create these images based on the imperium they gather. At the moment, they can't decode what that imperium is in the Deus, only when it's gone through and landed back into our universe. The imperium in our soul is easier to decode. That makes you and Marie their test subjects. And since Marie could fight off the 'bots… that leaves the infamous Max Vale."

"You're mining our souls for data in the Deus," Vale said. "You don't know what you're dealing with."

"ODYSE needs to be at the forefront. Cybernetics might connect my company to our minds, but imperium has information about the meaning of why we exist. The potential value is immense," Os said. "Now, Max Vale, you must die so we can close the portal from Ragg. We can't have it any other way. Thank you for helping, Lieutenant Price. This turned out better than I could have hoped for."

"I don't believe it," I said.

"Why not let me help you?" Vale asked.

"You would never. And seeing that this creature is just a reflection of what's at the forefront of the creator's mind, I'm deeply disturbed by your presence."

"But how are you thinking like this?" I asked Vale.

"This is my anxiety, Price, my fear of the world, my hatred for mankind… that I can't be myself. It follows me most places."

"Max Vale, I don't know how you live with this beast inside of you, this White Eye…" Os laughed. "You really are a sick monster."

Vale couldn't respond, his body was rigid, and his eyes locked on the White Eye's mouth.

"You've been controlling it this whole time," I said to Os.

"Not quite, Lieutenant. Often, it's just your error-prone friend, Max Vale, controlling the White Eye, telling it how to move. How to kill you." The 'bots' lights flickered to his laugh.

"Fuck you," I said.

The 'bot who held Marie threw her lifeless body right in front of us. "Look at Marie Dalton," Os said. "She was stronger than Max Vale, and now she is dead." Half the 'bots surrounded Marie's body. "I want you to feel Marie." The 'bots pointed their fingers, and blades shot out like nails. At once, they each sliced a hand into her abdomen.

Their hands spread open and gripped inside her body. "Do you feel her insignificance?" Os said. "Rip her apart. Until she is out of your coding." The 'bots began to tear her into pieces. Others jumped in.

The White Eye grew wider, blocking the mutilation. It growled at us.

"Run, Vale," I said.

"I can't…"

"I would love to kill you, Max Vale," Os said. "But I'm busy. You'll just have to die out here without any real murderer. A suicide makes sense in that mind of yours," Os said. "By the way, this creature you created—your White Eye—it killed your friend, Arch Slayter… right around here."

Vale's jaw and shoulders dropped. He leaned forward, unable to speak, his hand on his heart.

"That means you killed Arch," Os said.

Tears formed in his eyes. "Impossible."

"You're a murderer just like your mentor."

"No…"

From a tree, a 'bot dropped a dried-out tulip petal on the ground near Vale. It was the very one Arch had pinned to his sleeve; they had met by a tulip tree at the city park. Vale dove onto the ground and picked it up. Tears welled in his eyes, but he kept looking at the White Eye.

"Now die out here with your friend," Os said.

Vale stood, his features darkened into a possessed glare. "I will kill you and all of your followers, in one form or another—Cyborg!"

"Will that filth really be your last words?" Os laughed.

"Run!" I screamed.

My voice finally hit Vale. As if I found the "on" switch, he sprinted away into the trees. The White Eye chased him.

Several 'bots started to follow, but Os yelled, "No! Only one can go! Not until the next update! We can't handle more than one connection to him!"

Their green lights flashed silver, and several sparks shot out of their heads. Os's raspy breaths filled the pine trees.

I tried to follow after Max, but several more 'bots appeared in front of me. I noticed more sat in tree branches, studying my every move. In the reflection of their faces, I could see the hands of their comrades digging into Marie's corpse.

Os's breathing returned to normal. He laughed, slow and heavy, and said, "Madelyn sends her regards, Lieutenant."

"I've barely talked to her in years," I said.

"I wouldn't disconnect from the one ally you sorely need. I'm still supposed to believe you're infected by Vale."

"Why are you doing this?"

"Not everyone here is my machine, Lieutenant."

"*What?*" I swung my head to the 'bots ripping into the organs of Marie. I gasped. Amongst the 'bots, in the shadows, several hooded cloaks tore into Marie, their shoulders protruding.

"Some are my 'bots. Others are Mortes in their ritual attire, wanting revenge, searching for the mind-soul connection… They wanted it so badly that they requested to be part of the sacrifice. My gift would have been Vale, but they are rewarded someone with even more evolved genetics…"

At the word *genetics*, my darkest demon swiped a bony claw out of the shadows somewhere in the depths of my subconscious. I flashbacked to my childhood, saluting the American flag inside the Northeast Quadrant… I repressed the thought.

Terror took over. My heart pounded more as I heard tears and snaps from Marie's body. Os continued.

"Lieutenant Price, I wonder… in complete darkness, can you tell which ones are human?"

An extra loud crunch of bone shook my body.

"You can't?" Os asked. "It's because they're all machines of the divine. And soon, they will get what they want. Thanks to the years of studying Marie, we now have a blueprint for creating medication to alter our genetic expression to match Marie. One injection, and suddenly you're sensing the Deus… Crony had been a wonderful help with the new age steps for synthesis due to her expertise. We'll miss her, but she lived a good life. They all do…"

"Why are you telling me this?"

"I'm just giving you what you want. You all want the same thing—*purpose*, a connection to the higher power, any bit of significance. And since you are a loyal follower, *Wheeze King*, I'm going to give that to you…"

I shuddered at the nickname. On a normal day, I would have been proud.

"*You* are the next step, not Max Vale. When you sit in your jail cell, let your thirst to protect the human race foster. And I will be watching soon enough once we figure out these updates."

"I'll never be like this," I said, gesturing to the Mortes.

"Lieutenant, you're a patriot," Os said. "I'm sure you were taught that man sits on top of the food chain… The phonetic suggests it is a collective effort, but I remind you the fine print gives the title to only one *man*. And soon I will be that one to control all purpose…"

I sprinted away. Os laughed and hissed something at me, but his voice softened as I ran past the 'bots after Vale. I could hear the demonic hissing of the White Eye in the distance.

My mind immediately shifted to Vale. I needed light for the White Eye, but both of our flashlights were fried. I could not tell if anyone followed me. I sprinted by one tree at a time, trying to think of a plan.

I wondered if we could hide on an island in the marsh furthest from the shadows if we'd be safe from the White Eye there. But I honestly had no idea what this creature was capable of. And if we stayed out on the marsh for too long, why wouldn't another 'bot come and turn into something else just as devastating. Could I use my phone or something else with a light? Would that do anything permanent? These were all products of Vale's mind...

I decided my best shot was to relax him somehow. I could not think of a better plan. But how? When I got him out of his anxiety attack in the library, the White Eye didn't go away.

I halted. There was a long steel fence with barbed wire. I noticed an area was torn open further down, so I ran over and climbed through. I was officially off Dalton Manor property.

In the distance, Vale screamed, and a rush of adrenaline kicked my body into overdrive, pushing through the branches, dashing through every bush. I couldn't bear to hear him this way. I would rather die than watch him go through this inner turmoil.

The shadow of the White Eye came into vision, but to my surprise, it was a lot smaller. It was around human size, huffing and stamping around the sand, turning its eye in all directions. It looked lost, and I swore I heard it whimper.

In the distance, I saw Vale on the ground in the weeds. He was in meditation.

How is he holding himself together? I thought.

It was this inner peace I became accustomed to over our years, but not on this case.

I sprinted over.

Vale heard me, and his eyes flared open. The White Eye expanded to the height of the pine trees. It roared in all different pitches, exposing all its teeth and slithering tongues.

I turned to Vale, who was submerging back into the abyss of his mind. "Arch..." Vale said.

I locked my eyes on him, wanting to say something inspiring to lift up his spirit, to make him stand up and fight the White Eye head-on, but I watched its mouth open from its body, exposing the layers of teeth.

For a moment, I lost hope. I thought he was about to die and that I would lose another child, this time hearing the screams right before my demise. But somehow, I reached deep within my mind, my soul, and found a light that shined from deep within. Its feeling took over my body and spoke what turned out to be the exact thing he needed to hear. "I love you, son."

The demonic hisses stopped.

Vale looked like he had melted into the sand. He sat up, at first confused by my remark. But then, all the anguish left his face.

I smiled, solidifying to myself I was not like Os.

The feeling, this love, brought me back to our usual bar, where I first shared it, right after we solved a case a year in our partnership. Vale was frazzled and worried about the world retaliating against him. It was then he first mentioned his childhood for the first time, though it was a mild tale compared to what actually happened. Still, I was floored. I decided to order a round of whiskey for us, which became two, then three, and finally, four drinks in which we toasted, and out of my plastered mouth came that.

Before Vale, I told Sarina those words every day of her life…

"I love you, old man," Vale said, accepting my hand. I lifted him.

The forest brightened. Over the 'bots' forms, television static appeared.

"Elara?" Vale asked. His feature dropped into disbelief.

I studied the static, just as baffled. To our side, the White Eye had become Elara Vale, identical to the static portrait of her in Dalton Manor, even down to the necklaces, except she appeared more alive, if that was possible. Her features were relaxed, eyes radiating calmness.

I just want my sister to know I love her, Vale had said at our bar that night after the topic of love sloppily arose over whiskey. Over the years, he referred to Elara as his rock. She was the voice to solidify his homosexuality, to try a new relationship. Then one day, she vanished from his world, ignoring all phone calls, avoiding pop-up visits to be with men from their Society… Vale feared she had submerged too far.

"Max…" Elara's ghost said, opening her arms.

In a trance, Vale stumbled to her and said, "It can't…"

"It is."

They embraced, sincerely, longingly. Vale immersed into her static.

I stood, mystified. I thought 'bots were just a projection of Vale's imagination. Why would he hug her?

"But how?" Vale asked, no doubt it was her.

"I had to be at the forefront of your mind."

"You were this whole case. You told me I would be special, and you were chosen to help. Why did you disappear after that?"

"It was time. And now it will be from the Deus."

"I thought you gave up."

"I was just getting started."

Vale smiled as his eyes watered. "Your theories were right, you know."

"Partly." Elara's static smiled. "Thanks for listening to my rabble all those years."

"My pleasure."

"Darwinn knows to help. I told him everything."

"How? Only Marie and I could sense the Deus."

"Max, we all sense the Deus in different ways, just as we all have variances in our genome, connecting our soul to something, whether God or gods or the world around us, but we oversimplify its role. Imperium has many beautiful properties to uncover, but while you see my ghost, this imperium is also data for ODYSE… They can collect data from our souls."

"We can't let that happen. We need to stop it."

"That is why I am here, brother, to warn you… Darwinn is on the back road waiting."

"Elara…" Vale's face sunk.

She spoke to him in a demonic voice for a long minute. Then, in English, she said, "And you must remember, your light will shine brightest in absolute darkness. I won't be too far."

Vale's eyes widened.

"Now go… this way." Elara pointed to her left.

"Wait. Please come. I'm sure you can control this 'bot."

"You must leave now," she insisted.

"But—"

I pulled on Vale's sleeve, to which he had now pinned Arch's dead tulip, and dragged him away. There was no time to process Elara's appearance or what she warned.

"Hurry!" she yelled.

"Focus, Vale."

He looked drained, pushing forward with the last bit of will he had.

We dashed through the pine trees. Time ticked by. Every moment dragged on as we stomped our feet in the sand and zipped past each trunk. I listened to our surroundings and heard only birds and rodents through the bushes.

Will these ever end? I thought, partway into our marathon.

"The back road is a mile still," Vale said and ran on.

I watched his eyes get colder with every minute, his face sweatier, his back more hunched. I didn't want to ask what was wrong—because everything was, and we were just lucky to be alive.

It was past our third marsh when Vale stuck out his shaky arm, and I stopped. In the distance, a cloak stood in the shadows. I could not make out more than his towering frame in the darkness and protruding shoulders. We turned around—another stood equal distance behind us. They were quiet.

"How many bullets do you have?" I asked.

"Five. But don't shoot," Vale said.

A third appeared to our side.

"Why not?"

"We won't have nearly enough. This way!" Vale darted to the opening, and I followed.

Several more cloaks came into view in the distance. They glided closer.

Adrenaline spread through my vessels, and I pushed my body into overdrive. Every few steps, our passage narrowed, walled by Mad Mortes. Vale picked up the pace, and his breathing deepened. Then something strange happened.

Our path somehow opened, and the Mad Mortes stopped, revealing the sand amongst pine trees. We darted through.

"I see him!" he yelled.

Headlights were in the distance, driving by on the road. I recognized it at once. I couldn't believe it: the static was really Elara. Darwinn's beat-up red truck sped by. We jumped onto the road and flapped our arms in the air enough to fly away.

The truck slowed and rolled down his window, revealing Darwinn's worried face. He asked, "Where's Marie?" Darwinn opened the truck door, and we dove in.

"What do you mean?" I asked.

"She's not here. What happened to Marie?" Darwinn asked, raising his voice. "There's no record of her in my mind-drive."

"She's dead," Vale said. "Os's 'bots got to her."

Darwinn sighed. He slammed on the accelerator in frustration. To my surprise, tears formed in his eyes. Sweat poured off his balding head. "I should have left her in my lab."

"We all should have stayed in your lab," I said.

"Mr. Price, if we didn't dig into their archives, we would be dead in days."

"If you kept her in the lab, someone would have taken her," Vale said. "Her soul was so drained, she needed the mask to function."

"Except with me for some reason," I said.

A tear trailed down Darwinn's face. He said, "I just let her go off in the woods. What's wrong with me?"

"And you would have stopped her?" I asked, surprised to hear Darwinn question his own intellect.

He sighed again. Holding the steering wheel with his knees, he unscrewed his flask. "Coffee, anyone?"

We shook our heads, declining. "Darwinn, what am I missing?" I asked.

"Marie is my niece."

My jaw dropped. Darwinn continued. "Crazy Uncle Darwinn, I guess… that is if Shyla had not shunned me from her family."

"Why were you shunned?"

"Because I hated Marie's father. Dean verbally abused my sister, and she isolated herself from the family. She barely even saw our Nana…" Darwinn shook his head. "I feared knowing what abuse was going on in the house. But this, I never imagined. As much as I discussed my theories with Elara for knowledge, I was prying into my poor niece's life. Shyla became a monster. I took Marie from the station the moment I found out, the first time we ever met."

"Darwinn, I'm sorry. I'm so sorry," I said, flabbergasted.

"I don't deserve an apology. I wasn't there for her."

"You couldn't."

"I don't care! The state she's been in—was there any life left? She said nothing to me."

"So you didn't grab Marie for your experiment?" Vale asked.

"Never. Only to protect her, for once. I wouldn't have guessed she was the subject. I hope she at least felt my love. Anything. But I don't think so. I still can't believe she attacked you."

"I don't think she did it on purpose," I said. "Why didn't you tell us?"

"I just met you whippersnappers. Why would I? And more importantly, why didn't you know? I'm sure you had their records."

"There's no mention of you."

"Exactly. Nothing would have changed. I'm only alive because ODYSE needed my coding to work. I didn't go into relativity to be a target... but my sister did with open arms, right, Mr. Vale?"

Vale exhaled.

"I could run, but it's not like I'm flying off to Mars. I'd rather change the cards I'm playing with," Darwinn said. "Nonetheless, I'm impressed to see you both again. I imagined you talked to Elara."

We nodded.

"Still working on an explanation for that one." Darwinn sipped his flask. "But even little me, with the right circumstance, can expand my horizons past infinity... Our imperium is at stake."

"You didn't see any of Vale's Society?" I asked.

"No, but let's not test our luck. I've already had a few fortunate breaks. You see, after you gents left, I hacked deeper into ODYSE's database because, as I said, we need the leverage."

"How could you just break in?" I asked.

"Why, you give me too much credit, Mr. Price. I got in due to conversations Elara had with me—she highlighted some key-words that ended up being passwords to several documents. Elara even verified them in person—or in ghost. They revealed the entire inner workings of ODYSE. I deleted their hard copy before anyone saw it. So now only I have that file in my mind-drive." Darwinn tapped the side of his head. A screen flickered in front of his eyes, then disappeared.

I had never seen anything like it before tonight. "Who would be interested?"

"The United Nations, of course, they've been suspicious of prison camps like the Northeast for years."

"It's not a prison camp," I said.

Darwinn raised his brow. "Sure, kiddo. Listen, not a single soul knows this besides you two. Consider that a token of my trust."

"And now you trust us?" I asked, aggravated at his Northeast comment.

"Mr. Price, all my family is dead now. And my one true friend… almost. I need to trust you both, and I think you need me. I don't have a—Great Beans of Ethiopia!" Darwinn slammed on the brakes.

Three bodies lay on the road, covering its span. They all wore black cloaks.

"Drive closer, scare them off," I said.

"I'm not going to risk everything to run over them. I'm still under PATC, you know," Darwinn said. He turned the truck into reverse and sped the truck backward.

"They want you dead."

"Not for now."

"Darwinn…" I said.

A dozen more cloaks emerged from both sides of the pine trees. They charged.

XIII
HAUNTING

DARWINN SPUN THE truck around with a horrible turn radius and sped the other way. The angle was wide enough for two of the cloaks near the edge of the pine trees to land on the bed of the truck. "Get those hooligans off!" Darwinn said.

It was then that I noticed Vale in my peripherals, meditating. "Vale!" I smacked his shoulder, but he did not budge. Confused but short on time, I left him alone and aimed my gun through the back window.

"Don't you dare fire, Mr. Price!"

"Can't you just cut a sharp turn?"

"I think you overestimate the capabilities of this truck."

I rolled my eyes and readjusted plans. I tried to lower the passenger window but couldn't find the button. To my surprise, my leg bumped into a lever, and I squeakily rolled it down.

With a thud, one cloak swiped at the back window. I couldn't make out his weapon. I shoved my body out the side and fired a warning shot.

Both cloaks jolted, extending their necks, and letting the window blow their hoods back. A tall bald Caucasian male stood closest, and at the end of the bed was none other than Martin Brezniack. His gray eyes looked possessed as the wind yanked his lips into a menacing smile. Red X's were painted over their eyes and on every crevice of their faces.

The bald Mad Morte held a black metal bar, and Brezniack took out the black tinker toy I had seen clipped to his pants on our first search of Dalton Manor. I now noticed it was made of four rods that joined in an apex, creating the shape of a pyramid.

Darwinn threw open the back window and shot at their feet with his .44 magnum.

In the bald Mad Morte's wrist, the black metal bar shot out an orange holographic whip, swatting the bullet onto the truck bed. Without moving, he stared at Darwinn's gun.

"Mr. Vale, what on Earth are you doing?" Darwinn yelled.

Vale did not answer, still like a stone.

The bald Mad Morte snapped the whip, smacking into the glass on the rear windows. It cracked, and pieces fell onto the bed. *Good God, this is what they used in rituals?* I thought.

Darwinn grabbed the end of the whip and dragged it inward before the bald Mad Morte could turn it off, flinging his body near the broken window. He dumped some of his precious hot dark roast on the bald Mad Morte's face, and the Mad Morte howled in pain.

I slid my body out of the window until I could place my feet on the ledge. I jumped onto the bed of the truck. The wind waved around my hair and pushed against my body, trying to throw me off.

Brezniack had the tinker toy in the palm of his hands. He had been reciting a demonic incantation. The toy unraveled, turned into a straight line, and then morphed into a silver centipede.

"Who are you?" I asked, in complete disillusion. This man could in no way be related to the commissioner who spared me life in jail or the introverted officer I heard rumors about from the station.

"Lieutenant, I am one of thousands."

From the centipede's eyes, a laser flashed a blinding white light. For a moment, I thought I went blind. I fell to the bed of the truck. The centipede crawled over his shoulder and shined a light again. I rolled over, dodging its glare.

A spiked ball grew from the other end of the centipede and spun in the air. It flew at me.

I panicked and threw my body to the other side of the truck bed. The spiked ball banged into the ground, just missing me.

Then the bug crawled onto the other side of Brezniack's back and flashed again from his shoulder. It blinded me. Brezniack leaned down and punched me twice in the rib.

I grimaced. But from the corner of my eye, I saw the spike ball from its other end swing toward my head. I threw my torso upright. It zipped under my back. On the way up, I grabbed Brezniack's fist as he tried to punch a third time and kicked him in the legs.

Brezniack stumbled and tried to balance himself before falling onto the ledge of the truck. I stood and grabbed his body, pushing him to the edge of the truck bed. His cloak flew off, and I gasped.

His entire right arm was robotic… sleek and silver until his hands returned to human texture. But the material was rusted and looked clunky, scraps compared to the biomaterial Os had on his face.

Despite my force, Brezniack pushed himself up with the robotic arm. The centipede snuck around his neck and flashed a blinding light again into my eyes. I accepted being blind for a second and swiped my hand in the tinker toys' direction. At first, I missed. But in my second attempt, I gripped the centipede, which was slimier than I expected, and tossed it off.

But as if Brezniack was a magnet, the bug flew right back on and continued to crawl.

"Hell of a friend you have," I said, quickly elbowing him in the side of the head.

Brezniack fell into the sidewall of the bed. On the floor, Brezniack swung his arms at my legs, but I stepped back. Behind me, the bald Mad Morte just started to rise from the burn wounds, and Darwinn, his body contorted, stuck his arm out, swinging it as he drove down the straight road. "Mr. Vale, I swear, I will wedge the contents of this flask down your throat if you don't participate!"

Vale did not answer.

"Freeze," Darwinn said, pointing his .44 magnum.

The bald man reluctantly listened, but the whip on its own waved back and forth, creating a wall separating himself from Darwinn. I dove into the bald man's back like a ram and plunged his body into the wall of his flailing whip. I didn't know what to expect, but the wall felt as dense as any brick I would pin a suspect to.

The bald Mad Morte swatted at me. I pressed my gun into his back, and he stiffened. I pushed him over the ledge onto the ground. The truck zoomed past him, and I turned around as Brezniack rose. The rods flashed blinding light after blinding light. The onslaught left me disoriented. It was all I could do to stay balanced. "Freeze!" I yelled, pointing my gun toward the light source.

"Don't kill the man!"

"For Christ's sake, Darwinn, what do you want me to do? Dance with him?" But for once, Brezniack followed my order as my vision came back.

"Marie has risen," Brezniack hissed. His gray eyes grabbed me. "And so must Vale. Bring me to the Deus if you must."

The truck slowed down. "Mr. Price, we might have another problem..." Darwinn's headlights caught another row of black cloaks lying on the ground, blocking the entire road.

"Shit," I said.

We were surrounded. More cloaks appeared from the pine trees.

"Hop in. I have him," Darwinn said, keeping his eye on Brezniack.

I jumped off the bed of the truck and slid through my open passenger window.

"I have a plan," Darwinn said.

The cloaks sprinted at us.

"Better do it fast," I said in a panic.

"It might shut off the truck. I haven't used it in ages... oh, I don't know about this—"

"Well, don't start being shy *now*!" I yelled, rolling up the window. The closest Mad Morte brought out a crowbar.

"What the heck! I give you the honors, Mr. Price." Darwinn looked at the button of the orange-colored bird he had mentioned on the drive to Dalton Manor.

Unsure what to expect, I slammed my fist into it.

The engine roared. Vale and I sank into our seats as the beat-up red truck rose to the height of the pine trees. Hands scraped the undercarriage, dragging its bed and yanking down the back end. Brezniack was flung off, screaming.

"Come on!" Darwinn slammed on the accelerator, and several screams came from the ground, letting go of the truck, and at once, it shot off into the sky.

I looked onto the ground and saw the Mad Mortes shrink, jumping, screaming at us.

"Technically, anti-gravitational laws are only for the Waterfront neighborhood, but while I have these last six months on the PATC, I guess I should start crossing things off my bucket list..."

"How does this even...?"

"The tires turn to the ground and thrust us up. You've never driven this high against gravitational forces?"

"Never."

Darwinn passed me his flask.

I accepted and let the smokiness of the dark roast wash over me as I looked at Pinelands in marvel. The treetops spread as far as I could see, with dozens of divots I imagined were for its marshes.

Darwinn, however, looked up, widening his eyes and studying the moon as if each crater was a code to crack.

Vale stared emptily, eyes still open.

What was he doing? I thought.

*   *   *

Diary entry written by Max Vale

The rain pattered against Dalton Manor. No lights were on. The air was thin. Hope was draining.

In the basement closet, Shyla stood, stuck against the wall, as if she was chained. Bags hung under her glazed eyes. She was pale, malnourished. Her dark hair fell onto her dark cloak.

Shyla whimpered. She didn't know how long she had been in the dark. But it felt like days. She was starving and parched. "I only wanted the best for you… to have a childhood…"

Marie had to be waiting outside. She knew it.

Shyla continued. "You deserve nothing but the best. And all I've ever done was to try and bring that to you. To try and be a loving mother… I gave my life to you, and I'd do it all over again. My daughter…"

In the basement, through the door, Ragg sat on a couch in silence. The black silk mask pressed against Marie's face, contouring her roman plug nose and cheekbones.

"Nothing beat watching you grow up," Shyla said, tears forming. "You are my sunshine, and… the greatest gift life has given me." She sobbed. "I need you, Marie, darling. I am nothing without you."

Tears dropped to the ground.

She had nothing left.

"Say something…"

No response.

"Say anything!" she bawled. "Say something to your mother, so help me, God!"

Her heart dropped.

The closet door swung open. From the couch, Ragg turned its head to Shyla. It stood, loosening the mask, then slowly walked over. Her daughter's face became more visible through the silk cloth with each step. Ragg's lips morphed into a wild smile.

Shyla couldn't speak.

Ragg stood inches from Shyla and placed its hand on her forehead. It slid its fingers under her chin as it said, "Say goodnight, and fall yourself to sleep, little child. Kiss goodbye, dream up in the clouds with your smile."

Shyla cried. Tears trailed down her face. Ragg continued.

"Cheek to cheek. Fly in the sky. No matter how far you—"

Shyla grabbed onto Ragg's silk cloth. Ragg snatched her wrist in self-defense, body shaken from the attack. A warmth attacked Ragg. The love Marie felt every night from her mother's singing as a child tightened its chest.

Ragg recomposed and squeezed Shyla's wrist.

Shyla's eyes now shot fire.

The imperium from Nana, Shyla, and Marie's love surfaced. Ragg felt a deep-rooted vulnerability, like a nail bed, crushing its aura. Ragg's grip lost firmness.

But only for a second.

Tears streamed down Shyla's face. Her jaw opened, and her arm shook. Shyla screamed, bloodthirsty.

Ragg roared back, in all different octaves, wrapping around Shyla's body, stabbing her brain.

"I... love—"

Not waiting for her to finish, Ragg ripped her arm out of her socket. Shyla screeched in agony. Ragg tried to dive into the closet, but Marie's body remained outside.

The door closed, and Ragg tore off her arm. In seconds, Shyla lay on the closet floor, face carved and fingertips bitten off. Stab marks sliced into the neck. Blood sprayed on the walls and pooled onto the bottom of the closet.

Ragg stepped back in Marie's body, hands on its knees, breathing heavily. Ragg caught its breath and stood up. The deep-rooted pain permeated through Marie's body. First in her chest, then to her limb.

Ragg stood alone in the basement—face burning, fingertips prickling.

Mom... a voice thought.

Marie ripped off the mask and sat down on the couch.

Minutes later, footsteps creaked down the stairwell. Ms. Mugsby stepped in with a limp, wearing a torn fleece. Her neck was bent, hair shooting in all directions. "Darling, your Max Vale will be arriving soon. Time to clean up. I'll catch us some birds for supper." Ms. Mugsby hobbled back up the stairwell. "Don't forget about Elara, sweetie..."

Vale broke away from the dream, and entered a different one.

Footsteps disappeared down the alleyway.

I chased, sliding around the dumpsters and climbing a fence. I hopped over onto the other side. I was in a junkyard.

Several piles away, atop a mountain of trash, a man in a balaclava jumped onto the flat rooftop of an office near a set of buildings.

I ran over and pulled myself up onto the top of the roof. The suspect looked at me on the other side and jumped across the alleyway onto the next one. I sprinted over. On the way, a lone door to my right opened. Moreno appeared just in time and followed me. A gunshot was fired.

The wind of the bullet skimmed the back of my suit jacket. My body shook uncontrollably. The gust from the bullet rippled waves in my coat. By the time I snapped back to the present, the suspect had already left the next rooftop. Moreno and I were alone.

My mind flashed back to the previous few weeks.

"Aim was a little off..." Moreno had said.

"I suppose you won't miss next time?"

"If I do, I'll be sure to strangle you in your sleep."

"Moreno, there's nothing to be afraid of. I've seen you grow in so many ways over the last year, understanding yourself more, loving you for who you are..."

"They said the voices were demons... telling me these thoughts." Moreno's eye twitched.

"You're wrong. They made those demons. Nothing more. You're you. And you need to live your life as that."

"I'm not like your fucking sick head, Vale."

"You were the one to try and hold my hand—that's not my role in your life. I'm sorry if I gave the wrong impression, but all is forgiven, and we can leave it at that."

"You tried to force me into it, you fucking pervert. You played with those demons, made them louder..."

"Moreno, that's just the world trying to control you—make you something you're not. I swear to you, nothing beats loving yourself. You need to love yourself for who you are."

Moreno shot at my feet, and I jumped.

"You think so, dickbag? If I don't get these voices out of my head, they'll think I'm crazy. You made them appear. You made them stick in my head."

"I'm more than willing to switch partners," I said, starting to feel less sure about my options to escape.

"So you can tell everyone?" Moreno asked. "Make me go to Dubruis because your brain is all fucked up?"

"You can't just kill me, Moreno."

He walked closer. "Who was your little fuck buddy before this? I bet it's the lieutenant."

"Price?" I laughed. "You picked the Northeast's most loyal hound."

"Fine. At least I'll get one fucker out of this world." Moreno spat on my face, then fired into my stomach.

I flew onto the ground.

Time stood still.

I lifted my head up. Marie Dalton stared at me across the rooftop.

I pushed my body up and regained my composure, placing my fingers on where the bullet entered my flowered, bulletproof vest. "Hello there," I said as nonchalantly as one could.

Marie stepped forward, and a chill swarmed my body.

She took another step, then another, building up momentum until she ran full speed at me. I panicked and looked around the roof for any way out of her grasp. But I was too late. She dove into me. I did not fall or die. I instead stood mystified.

Marie had embraced me; her petite frame thumped into my chest. "I'm so sorry," she said, crying hysterically.

She gripped my waist tighter. At a loss for words, I merely placed my hand on her shoulder with great hesitation. As the seconds went by, I gave in and patted her on the back.

"I couldn't help it, I swear." She pressed her bent nose into me.

I cautiously placed my other arm around her and squeezed. "It's okay, Marie. It's over."

"Ragg became too powerful in my soul, going on a killing spree in our universe and tearing holes into the Deus, ones only you could sense... They led right into my soul. At first, all I could share was my darkest memory... the day Ragg fully entered when I was a girl. And once you invested your soul into the case, our connection strengthened through the Deus, and more of my closest memories slowly came in as you guided them. I only shared my mother's death by accident, as we entered such a sensitive memory of yours. This dimension navigates differently."

She glanced up at me, and I was alarmed at how much life was in her eyes behind the tears. They looked like the sunrise. "You poor child," I said.

"I want to bring you into this world with me and show you what it means to be dead," Marie said in a dark growl. She shook her head and brightened. "Sorry, that was Ragg."

I jumped and let go of Marie. Then I smiled. "It's okay. You don't have to apologize."

Marie stared away, blushing in embarrassment.

"Do you mind if I ask you what Ragg is?"

"Ragg is a unique type of imperium."

"Is it a separate entity, or is it a part of your soul?"

"Both." Marie stepped back and placed her hands behind her back. "A trend I've noticed already in the Deus is that imperium comes in many forms, and the spiritual forms always ascend... To where? I can't say. But they all feel different—based on purity. The evilest imperium very slowly ascend and can fuse to slow the process even more. Ragg is made of pieces of imperium from the souls of the evilest humans, who were too monstrous on Earth to ascend far in the Deus."

"I see..." I rested my hand on my chin, digesting her thought. "Why did pieces of these dark spirits target you?"

"Because I think I was born to be a good person, Vale. My soul was most connected to the Deus on our planets because of the mutation in my genome. I was alive on Earth but perpetually bound with those who had crossed over... And being a child, my innocent nature brought light into the Deus in ways that had not been done before." Marie's eyes watered. "Darkness hates light. The fractions of those evilest souls wanted their darkness to invade my light... and it won."

"Marie, you were still a good person."

"No—I was an evil human being." Tears rolled down Marie's cheeks. "The darker souls in the Deus just had so much experience, they knew how to corrupt me, and all together, they were too powerful."

"Ragg—"

Marie shook her head. "I lost all control over who I was, and there was not a single thing I could do about it!"

I hugged Marie and stroked her hair for a few minutes to have her let it out. She slowly stopped panting and rested on my chest. "It'll be okay."

Marie nodded.

"If you were here to say you were sorry, consider yourself forgiven. I do have a few questions I need answers for, though... is it all right if I ask?"

"Ask me anything."

"Why were your mother and Crony killed in a closet?"

"I dragged their minds in to constrict their last thoughts before I ripped into their necks and drained their souls. It was only Elara who fought me enough to bring a pistol as her weapon to alleviate herself of my wrath." Marie shook her head until she appeared ready to be herself.

"Didn't mean to do that," I said, hesitant. "Does it bother you when that happens?"

"No. If anything, it gets me excited because I make it shut up. What Ragg could not anticipate was how different my soul was from others. This was important because although darkness possessed my soul, I had too many experiences of love as a young child instilled from my mother to get rid of the light in me permanently."

"Ragg couldn't darken the love your mother shared?"

"It could not. Love is that powerful. Ragg might have controlled my body, but in my soul, there were parts it was powerless to overcome. So it quarantined those spots of light, the pure love I felt as a daughter.

"When I was born, my genome stretched my soul from the physical world to the spiritual world, and when I died on Earth, I began crossing over into the Deus. A normal soul ascends quickly—milliseconds. But due to my mutations, it will take some uncertain time—months, years, or even decades—for my soul to completely cross. And what stays true regardless of gene expression is that pure good souls ascend much faster than dark souls."

"You're saying even though your soul is still stuck in both worlds for the foreseeable future, your physical death allowed the ascent to continue. Marie, the parts that are actually you will ascend much faster. Ragg has no chance."

"It's like you were chosen for this," Marie said with a smirk. "I had to ascend, so my spirit—the good parts—are in the Deus by default. This prevents Ragg from leaving the physical world for a while. Still, it can voice its opinion at times for reasons I'm not too sure. I'm concerned I don't have complete control over it."

"Ragg is in my soul, too," I said.

"I know. He haunts those with our genetics, our souls born partly into our universe and the Deus. It will only be worse now that he is stuck on your side and in the fraction of your soul in the Deus."

"It's been slowly possessing me since the deaths started in the Society, and I've spiraled out of control since the case started. Marie, I killed at least two dozen Mad Mortes on my escape through the pine trees."

Marie nodded knowingly, too saddened to speak.

"Innocent people. Families. Children… I needed a path so we could get to the road. I didn't try to kill them… it just happened. I don't think Price saw."

"It was just like how I died, but swifter," Marie said.

I nodded. "I can't live like this."

"He wants you to think that. Don't listen," Marie said. "As long as you are alive, the way your genetics are made, Ragg is bound to you."

"No, Marie, if I die, Ragg goes back into the Deus," I said, turning to Moreno, who I forgot remained frozen, close to me. I stepped aside.

"Vale, we're in the Deus. And we know nothing about it. Or what Ragg will do now that ODYSE can detect it."

"How can Ragg possess both of us?"

"I don't know. In fact, I don't think we have touched the surface of my Ragg and your childhood White Eye. That lone entity."

I studied the building tops in the distance, unsure how to respond. "How did we get here?"

"I brought more of your soul in from the physical universe. Without knowing, you chose a memory that's been imperium in your soul for a while, one that was lately near the surface, because your soul is looking for orientation as I made you cross over. Every soul does this…"

"This would have to be the one since I can't think of Arch in fear of the 'bots. My love will have to rest in peace for now… I'm too terrified not to relive some of the other ones. This day, in particular, has haunted me more with age, as less has changed in the world for the better…"

"So we're here."

"Just two friends catching up?"

"Our relationship has no words because there are none to describe the specific imperium that connects you and me through the Deus. In fact, our vocabulary only expresses a sliver of imperium our real emotions create in this place."

"But how are we here now? I thought I was wide awake in Darwinn's truck."

"I'm connecting to you, just how Ragg connected to me. It lived in my memories before it infected my soul deeper and came into the physical world. If I didn't do this, you would have killed many more lives around the truck."

"You could have stopped the other deaths?"

"And Price would have died."

"I'd kill every man alive for his safety."

"Exactly. I couldn't get in. It's harder to possess you when your will is strong. I'm not familiar enough with our souls' constructs."

I closed my eyes, processing the news. "Price is figuring out my genes are not like yours… or anyone's outside the Northeast for that matter."

"He loves you."

"It won't matter."

"I know."

We stood in silence, excepting the reality. Then a question appeared. "Why did Carl Moreno capture some of that memory with your cat?"

"I'm still understanding that one. Very little is black and white in here," Marie said.

"I wouldn't downplay your knowledge," I said.

"I know little of this dimension. It is vast and dangerous... There are fates worse than death in here, Vale."

I shivered.

"Carl Moreno's psychological state was fragile and shattered from the world he lived in. As a product, he's more susceptible for Ragg to enter just by proximity."

"Why him, though?"

"Even after all these deaths, I don't think ODYSE realizes that Ragg can enter souls if you are close enough spiritually to someone who's possessed. Darkness likes to spread and will enter any space without your ability to shut it off if the setting is right. Moreno loved you."

"I knew that. That's why it hurt me so much to watch him deteriorate."

"Ragg was part of me on the night we met in the physical world. Reading your soul—which I can do very well, by the way—Ragg probably tormented Moreno internally with his own memories. But on the surface, he was scared..."

"Scared?"

"Yes, around Price in particular. I noticed when Ragg gets scared, it likes to refer to my darkest memory when I killed my kitten... I think it feels comforted by that."

"That's rather human."

"Ragg is a product of the evilest humans, after all."

"But why was Ragg scared enough to attack Price?"

"Because you love Price like a father. The imperium we describe as 'love' is so powerful in the Deus, and I think we feel the indescribable effects as a product. But even though your love for Price is strong, its roots are built in the deep-seated pain you two have endured. As a result, they are significant parts of your love's imperium that has pain intertwined. Imperium is complex, to say the least. Your love can actually cause me a great deal of pain because I am so sensitive to it in the Deus. That is why Ragg had trouble killing my mother. Even though I can't predict Ragg, one trait I have noticed is it does not like pain. In fact, I've found the darkest souls are the ones most sensitive to pain."

"But Moreno's love was full of suffering—why Price?"

"I think the pain behind Price's love was too relatable to parts of Ragg—an evil person or two must have lost their own children. And this is unique to you because your connection with the Deus is stronger than others. Normally, Ragg can look past it—at least it did with many deaths in the Society. But anyone involving you… it feels too real."

"You're wise beyond your years," I said.

"Naturally."

"Were you implying Moreno was possessed by Ragg?"

"Yes, technically. I don't like that word, though. Possession implies an endpoint. My family proved there is no end. Ragg devoured Ms. Mugsby and my parents into the darkness. It dug into the depths of all their souls, and something had to come to the surface to make room— their own darkest demons. That takes a longer time in your universe, months to years.

"I watched each succumb to Ragg and lose to those demons. For Ms. Mugsby, it was her infertility; my father's was to be responsible for the end of his prominent family line, and my mother's was her inability to help her daughter…" Marie's eyes softened at the mention of her mother. I placed my hand on her shoulder for a moment.

"Every day, they darkened, changing into the demons they feared the most. Once they all entered the Deus, I entered their souls and took their perspectives from the memories I shared because I needed to know… It was horrible… I can't even relive the last years of my mother's life; the memories of her abuse hurt me so much. They are buried somewhere in the Deus I couldn't even share with you."

"And you never have to. Marie, I'm so sorry for your family."

"Don't be. They crossed over and are ascending in peace. And at least I got to meet my Uncle Darwinn after all these years. It is I who feel sorry for you, Max. I feel the anguish in your heart. I know your lover has crossed, but you want to protect Price as well."

"Marie, I want to, but I know I can't. Price is already in enough trouble. If I stay around, I will destroy whatever is left of his life if he follows me to the coastline. I need to give him every opportunity to reconnect with his granddaughter."

"Max, I need you to listen to me." She placed her petite hands on my chest, and her bright hazel eyes stared into mine. "You are with both now. Arch is with you in the Deus dimension, and Price is in the physical dimension—" Marie stopped mid-thought and looked around, her features alert.

"What is it?" I asked.

"It's coming from other places." She sounded terrified.

"How?"

At once, the world felt heavier, as if gravity tripled, pushing onto my shoulders.

"I don't know…" Marie said, "I was controlling Ragg…"

All the buildings dimmed to black, and Marie's body turned into colored lights that swirled around her. They joined other streams of colors that filled the sky on a red backdrop, blocking the view of the daytime, and taking me into another cosmos. The longer I stared at the colors, the more I felt like I was being pushed to the ground.

Marie disintegrated.

I wanted to run, but I felt paralyzed, and I knew it was useless. My heart pumped against my chest. I could not see or hear or touch Ragg. Much worse… I felt it by my side.

"I was told we'd come face to face," I said, thinking of my demonic conversation with Elara. She had warned me.

Ragg did not speak. Its body blended into the dark background of the buildings.

I turned to it. And no matter how I tried to study it, the sensorium I used in the physical universe failed. But feeling Ragg was enough. It spiked the hairs on the back of my neck and took the air out of my lungs.

"I see, you're one of those quiet types," I said.

For an eternity, Ragg remained still.

At first, I was just nervous, like someone was watching me from across the street. But gradually, I felt cold and frail. Like a hand reached into my soul and dragged the root of my anxiety attacks to the surface.

My mind broke down, and a whisper filled the darkness.

Take my life, Ragg said, except it was not speaking. It sent me that feeling, and that was how I interpreted it with my senses.

I shook my head, unsure if how I felt was correct, but my gut knew it was true. The feeling controlled me like a weight invaded the depths of my mind and froze there. Ragg continued as the feeling became hopeless. I was in despair.

Take my life. Take my life. Take my life. Take my life. Take my life. Take my life. Take my life. Take my life. Take my life. Take my life. Take my life. Take my life.

End of diary entry

XIV LESSER

UP IN THE sky, the red pickup truck soared over the pine trees with the birds. In the far distance, I saw the skyline of Haddon come into view, and the letters "ODYSE" lit up over the tallest building.

I looked back down onto the ground. We were flying high over the forest, and I brought my attention back to the truck, afraid to ask if he knew for sure it would hold up. It was then I first noticed Vale twitching—his first sign of movement since we entered the truck, coming back from a "deadspell." I continued to give him space.

Darwinn said, "Mr. Price, I believe my niece evolved in ways no one had expected. While we were fighting for fun back there, my mind-drive loaded dozens of reports where members had nightmares, and she would appear, in her 'Ragg' state of existence, as you folks call it, haunting them in ways personalized to the individual. One reported having to murder her kids every night because she couldn't take the burden of being a single mother anymore. Another pushed his wife in front of a train, or else he'd watch her slowly lose every limb… They started becoming insomniacs, and within weeks, were insane."

"Jesus."

"The moment these members appeared on Dalton Manor property to perform rituals, their bodies would morph into the position you gentlemen found Crony and Shyla Dalton. They were probably killed by this unique imperium Marie labeled as Ragg, and Mr. Vale called the White Eye… I think Elara saw the fate of the project a few steps ahead of the others. She was rather distant during our last few meetings, leaving me little tips to get into her lab, into their database… And of course, she gave the meat of the information to your favorite person, Ted Billars, who tipped your favorite ex-wife the exact details, and me, just some clues to compile with Elara's clues. And now you gents had a fun little case."

I shook my head, but couldn't help from deep within, a claw swiping from the shadows to the name Ted Billars.

But the red pickup truck shook, and I regrouped, grabbing onto the ledge of the passenger.

"Looks like we're coming back down to Earth…" Darwinn said, sipping his flask. "Pull yourselves together."

It started to lower.

"Is this on purpose?" I asked.

"I'm surprised we've made it this long."

The truck roared below us and halted every few seconds. Darwinn turned several knobs on the dashboard, but the truck picked up speed. "Oh, come on… must be one of these buttons…" The truck shot down, closer to the pine trees. He yanked the wheel, and we turned in line with a road. "Oh, fudge!" He banged the steering wheel, and the truck roared an obnoxious birdcall as its horn. The truck flopped onto the asphalt and sprung us off our seats, sliding forward and spinning a one-eighty.

Somehow, it stopped without turning over.

"We all okay?" Darwinn placed his hands up.

"What the hell is this thing?" I asked, observing Vale blink and shake his head, coming back down to Earth with the truck.

"I built it for kicks." Darwinn tapped the acceleration, and to our surprise, we nudged forward. "Been adding parts on and off to it over my lifetime. My father was a mechanic; I guess that's what you do."

I furrowed my brow, surprised by the remark. I wouldn't expect Darwinn and Shyla's father to be a blue-collar worker. But I was too busying scanning the edge of the forest to comment before Darwinn said, "Well, good to see there's no Society lingering... Let's keep moving."

The truck sped off as we continued to look out for Mad Mortes.

"This is all just too unbelievable." I paused and shook my head to offset my brain's rattle from the landing.

"Every century is just as unbelievable as the prior," Darwinn said.

Vale opened his eyes.

"Why, Mr. Vale," Darwinn said. He did not answer, so Darwinn continued. "Good evening, happy for you to join us... missed a little part back there."

Vale still didn't answer. He didn't even acknowledge us and instead scribbled furiously away in his maroon notebook.

"Give him some space," I said.

But to my surprise, Vale shot his head up, features crazed, and said, "Price, we need to go back to your townhouse."

"Are you mad?" Darwinn asked before I could articulate the same sentiment.

"I left my badge there," Vale said.

I cursed. The monster from within the darkest corners of my psyche stuck its claw out, only this time, it growled.

"It was with my notebook on the desk..."

"I wondered where that tidbit was when you both came to my lab," Darwinn said.

"But they don't have it," Vale said, taking out his phone. "They put trackers on all of the badges. It's in your townhouse."

"How?" I asked.

"I don't know... Price, I need it. I can't live on the coastline without it. Even though they had communities where I could live... there was just as much disgust for me when I didn't show my badge."

"We'll get it, I promise. I don't care what I have to do," I said, using Vale as a crutch to push my worst subconscious issues back into their hole.

I refused to bring it up to Vale. Especially after what we just went through. Though something felt off with Vale… My gut did not have an exact word—but his presence felt heavier.

"Mr. Vale, allow me simply to grab the badge for you," Darwinn said.

"You have a different battle to fight, Darwinn," Vale said, who jotted in his maroon notebook.

"It will be useless without my two best assets," Darwinn said. "Let my action be a warning to them that I will not stand pat."

"Darwinn, it's not just us. I have my friends on the coastline," Vale said. "Many of whom I consider family. I have already contacted them. They will hide us."

I was surprised Vale was so willing to have me go to the coastline. I expected resistance and insistence to serve time in jail, to at least be some presence in my granddaughter's life over time. However, at this point, I wanted to do everything to protect him. And I was no good to Novah behind bars.

But we needed to get there. Going to my townhouse, we were walking right into ODYSE's path. If they had Vale's maroon notepad, I'm sure they found his Type B Citizen Badge and left it as a trap.

Or maybe they were scared of Vale? After all, they attempted to isolate us around the 'bot, hoping Vale's anxiety would kill him through the White Eye. Once again, something was off.

"I wasn't planning on being so formulaic," Darwinn said.

"Have you ever been to the coastline?" Vale asked.

"Sadly, I don't venture into those parts."

"It's much easier to slide through the cracks there, good and bad. We need to meet with my people in the Northeast and leave for the coastline. It must be fast because we will be tracked while I am in Haddon's jurisdiction. The moment we leave, we are undetectable. I was able to get friends from the Northeast to reprogram it that much."

"I don't like this," I said.

"It's not like I do." Vale's face sunk.

"All right… fine," I said as the truck finally broke through the pine trees. I looked out west and watched the Haddon skyline in the dark.

"I'll be keeping a watchful eye on you, gentlemen," Darwinn said, "somehow."

The rest of the drive back, Vale and I ironed out the details of our escape as he wrote out more of his diary entries. He did not mention what they were about. And I figured right then was not the time to ask.

Eventually, Darwinn entered my neighborhood. "How should I drop you off?" he asked.

"Two blocks over." I pointed down the road.

"What if they're guarding the townhouse?" Vale asked.

"They're not, Mr. Vale. In fact, there's no conversation at all from ODYSE about either of you…" Darwinn tapped the side of his face, and a silver square flashed where his mind-drive was.

"Then now's our chance," I said.

I guided Darwinn to park on the street. We studied our surroundings. No one was watching.

"Shall I wait a bit for you, gentlemen?" Darwinn asked.

"It will only bring attention. It's best you leave," Vale said.

"Be smart," Darwinn said, studying Vale with his brilliant blue eyes.

We exited the truck onto the street, and Darwinn darted into the night. Vale and I hopped over a neighbor's fence. We stood in tall grass beside a pool, then crept over to the side of a shed. We hid in the dark.

I drew on my palm our exact location and how we were getting to my townhouse. Cautiously, we cut through another neighbor's property, dashed across another road, and walked down an alleyway before entering my yard.

Vale followed right behind me, but I could see other gears turning in his head. So much had happened the last few days that I felt it had caught up to him.

From the alleyway, I scouted my yard. The lights were off in my townhouse. No one was in the back, and I heard no sound. We hopped the fence and landed near my patio. I guided Vale to the side door as he swept his gun around the perimeter. I gently turned the doorknob—still locked. I brought out my key and unlocked it.

I softly tapped it open and slipped inside into the back hallway. Vale followed. I brought out my phone and turned on its light. Terror ripped into my soul and shot ice through my veins—I became numb. *This can't be real.*

My home was destroyed.

Words sprayed all along the hallway, blanketing every square inch. I turned to Vale. He was more horrified than I had ever seen him.

I stepped forward, panting, slowly distancing myself, as if the walls moved further away from me with each step. But gloom filled the spaces in between. And at once, all the words attacked me.

Burn in hell, the yellow letters said.

The further I went, the deeper I submerged into the darkness. Words surrounded me, attacking me at all angles.

Kill yourself, you fucking rapist.

And with each step, I suppressed my feelings, my thoughts, myself…

I ran to my bedroom.

All my models were ripped into little pieces… All the memories I created with Sarina, before and after she died… in smithereens.

I wanted to cry. But I had to keep going. Once more, I told myself not to feel. I ran through the house to get to Vale's temporary office. Windows were shattered, and a breeze blew onto my face, chilling my bones.

In the hallway, my whiskey cabinet was destroyed, bottles scattered and broken on the floor.

I ran—becoming less of a person and more of a robot with each step. Little by little, I took in more graffiti.

Don't fuck with my marriage, green letters snarled.

I darted past my kitchen, completely destroyed, at last reaching the living room.

Vale's entire workspace was in shreds. All of his neatly organized pictures were in pieces all over the floor. The furniture was knocked over. His laptop was cracked. Graffiti covered the walls.

I'll fucking kill you in your sleep.

I stood, hardened. I let the offensive slang wrap around me, and my body shut down. I felt nothing, just like I had for years. The worst words that were particular to Vale, I could not process. I stood in silence, unable to move, no will to think. I was lost in a world I couldn't understand. A world Vale had to live in every day.

The badge was not there.

Where the hell is it? I thought.

My darkest demon growled. For a brief moment, it targeted Vale.

I pushed my mind away and walked back into the hallway.

I will slit your fucking neck, sprayed on the ceiling.

The slandered pressed inward against my psyche. I felt like the floor would open below me. I focused on the far end of the hallway to see if Vale was around. He was nowhere.

I sprinted in that direction. Halfway down the hallway, I stopped by my smashed whiskey cabinet. I raised my brow. Underneath a broken shard, I saw a sliver of Vale's bright blue circular ID card. A whiskey label was blanketing it.

I grabbed the badge. "EXEMPTED TYPE B CITIZEN. MAXWELL VALE."

Of all places… I thought.

Next to the cabinet, a door was cracked open. Blood was smeared across the doorknob.

Get the fuck out of my country—if you make it.

I walked over and tapped the door open into my office. There were no windows. Even with my phone flashlight, I felt like I had walked into a cave. My eyes adjusted with each step. My office was not spared. Wooden shelves covered the walls, sliced. Outlines of a few guns, photos, and badges over my family's career were dismantled and torn over the floor.

I was devastated.

The room felt heavier, like gravity was more prominent.

I tried to dodge the items, tiptoeing, but there were so many I'd hear a crunch every other step.

Fuck you, Wheeze King, mocked the wall.

I could hardly breathe. My mind fell into an abyss, and fire shot out of my chest. My palms sweated.

I stared at the back of the room. My gas mask stared back, cracked, and I yelped. Three others wore on the ground, shattered. Each was a family heirloom, from my grandfather's to Sarina's. Cylinder filter cartridges protruded; all were black. The face shield was modernized with each generation, the material sleeker and straps optimized.

My eyelid twitched.

My demon stuck its scaly nose out and put me in a trance.

I studied my mask. The seal was torn, and pieces on the top chipped off. My fingers skimmed the lengthy filter cartridge. One word was engraved on each side. Together, it read *Wheeze King*.

My demon growled, and the office felt heavier.

Reality shook me.

I replayed what Os would yell at the end of each episode: *"There's only two types of us walking on Earth and Mars! Humans and those lesser! Lessers have no genetic purpose to America!"*

Suddenly, I heard my father yelling, "Kill the lessers! Spray 'em dead!"

Lesser. Haddon's slur for Type B Citizens left my family's tongue often. The connotation was crippling. The Price family weapon was a nerve agent—we thought the choice was symbolic since lessers' nerves were already functioning wrong, without the ability to connect to robotics. The legacy gave me a great reputation amongst my comrades.

Lesser covered my apartment in graffiti.

And worst, the word was used throughout the case by everyone we interviewed... Dr. Sarkis, Os, Crony's neighbor... in every derogative way. They all called Vale a lesser.

I couldn't process the word while Vale was around. So I didn't hear it.

And I didn't write it.

I chose not to because Vale was not one, though his exemption as a Type B Citizen brought no merit to Haddon's citizens.

The Wheeze King used "lesser" all the time in the Northeast, but never with Vale. I knew it drove my department crazy.

The only time I processed lesser was when Vale said the word, because I could not ignore his feelings, only my own.

I grabbed Sarina's gas mask off the ground. The lens was shattered, and a chunk of the bottom half was detached. My eyes watered; I had taught her well. Her ID badge clipped onto what was left of her gas mask. It was circular, metallic, similar to Vale's, though the color was red. In the center of her badge, bolded font said, "97%."

Ninety-seven percent of her cybernetic genes were compatible with ODYSE's biomaterials, just like her father. Every citizen had a percentage in adulthood. My breathing grew sharper.

I reached into my pocket and brought out Vale's Type B circular badge, blue. In bolded print, it read, "79%." The cutoff for the Northeast was human genetics less than 80 percent connected to robotics, with a rare exception like Vale. Elara's percentage was 80 percent.

I studied Vale's badge. For the first time in our years together, I was alone with it. Aside from being with Madelyn, I had never felt more vulnerable than in my annihilated office. *How* did that percentage matter?

I lost everything and killed so many people without an answer.

My demon's nose reached further into my consciousness, and several fangs emerged. I gasped for air.

An arm came from the shadows and wrapped around my neck. I tried to reach for my gun, but it was swatted away.

I flailed my limbs, kicking into a shelf and banging my hand against a wall. My body lowered. And my senses failed, the world became blurry, and I stumbled to the ground.

In the last moments, I saw Vale's browline glasses over me.

Why would you strangle me? I thought as my demon growled.

I passed out.

Some time later, I awoke on my office floor.

"Vale?" I asked immediately. No one answered, still unsure what exactly happened prior to passing out.

I stood up and walked on top of my scattered memorabilia to the hallway. "Vale?"

Footsteps broke into my foyer. Several police officers, some I knew closely, pinned me against the wall and arrested me. They said my rights, but I yelled through them. "Where's Vale?"

"Come on, Price," one said coldly.

"Where is he?"

They pushed me down the hallway.

"Dammit, will someone tell me where the fuck—" My breath was sucked out of my chest.

Blood smeared the living room—Vale's temporary office.

I screamed and tried to run towards it, but several officers grabbed me and dragged me out of the house before I could see it. "Let me go!"

They gripped tighter. A wave of rage took over my body, I tried to punch the officer, but several more tackled me. I was pinned onto the cement. An officer closed my front door, removing my view of the living room.

"Dammit, Price, don't make this harder on yourself." I looked up, and Commissioner Brezniack stared at me, enraged.

With several officers gripping me, I stood up and gave my stoic stare—one I was known for in the force after all these years. I walked to the police car without hostility.

I was taken to Dougray University Hospital to be evaluated because I couldn't leave as a free man. I was to be tried for murder and "inhumane sexuality by association" for aiding Vale and Arch—completely absurd—and normally five to ten years in Dubruis Mental Hospital. But over the next week in Haddon's court system, I learned that I was only to be sentenced to six months in regular prison... at the mercy of Madelyn. What convinced the jurors of my confused mind was her stand in my defense on the last day. When she appeared at the court, it was the first time I had seen her since our affair that one fateful evening.

I discovered her motive then. She had taped our intimacy. And she used it as evidence that I was not, in fact, attracted to "lessers," but I was merely a victim of Max Vale. My attack on Ms. Mugsby was intended to be self-defense due to my psychosis from being around him. And now, with him dead, all I needed was time to recover.

I could barely keep myself together in the courtroom.

Madelyn had sabotaged her entire career and publicly humiliated herself for me. I took the one successful piece left in her life. She would surely be relegated from the Board now. She had received enough bullshit from our divorce throughout her initial nomination and battled the stigma that women had less genetic similarity to robotics than men on average—which was disproved many times after a small study was first published generations ago.

Rumors against various groups came out over the years, like the Pineys.

And I always listened.

During the entire proceeding, I wondered why she did this all for me. I had done nothing but give her pain.

But it was only at the end, when she walked away from the stand and gave me a brief look, that I understood. It was a look I'd never forget—her beautiful autumn sky eyes pierced into me and said those complicated words—*I love you.*

I hadn't seen that look from her in years. Ever since Sarina died in the car crash, she couldn't even stomach to look at me long, let alone show any hint of affection unless our clothes were off.

I gave her the same look back, and I knew she felt satisfied.

We did love each other. There was a part of me that would always love Madelyn Katz.

My granddaughter felt the opposite. I left the courtroom handcuffed. In the distance, over all the press, Novah's voice echoed from down the hallway.

"I will never see him!" she yelled. "I hate him."

"Novah, you might now," Madelyn said, "but hate is not timeless, and these opportunities are ones you can't have back when you're older. He loves you unconditionally. That, over anything else, will never change."

"I will never see my mom's killer. Let him die with his *lesser* friend."

My mind shut down, and I was dragged away from the courthouse.

THE COTARD DELUSION

I ENTERED HADDON County Correctional Faculty alone. I blocked everyone I loved. Sarina... Novah... Madelyn...

Vale...

To help, I spent most of my time in my jail cell dissecting all the technology I encountered. Even after everything ODYSE had taken from me, my curiosity was unbreakable. The 'grams, the 'bots... they were experiences now, not just models. The Deus, above all else, captured my intrigue. My head could barely wrap around the idea, yet my imagination unleashed giddiness. I would daydream for hours, having my thoughts swim around, wondering what it felt like to be in the Deus, what it even was.

But as each day darkened, my mind returned to reliving those evenings in Dalton Manor and my home. The events still were just facts. I blocked any feelings away and transferred my energy to the prison's gym, building muscle and toning my body. Then every night, I dreamt. Oddly enough, I had never done so with this consistency in my life.

The dreams were all of Vale—at least I knew it was him.

Though I could not see my old partner, I felt his presence, as if he had his own scent—a warmth I knew instantaneously. At first, Vale kept his distance. I kept pressing him, and the more entangled we became, a strange sensation took over me. I felt his anxiety; it would wrap around me and tighten my body until icy hands came out of the darkness and gripped my skull. Its nails dug into my mind and froze my thoughts. I couldn't move. I couldn't do anything. I never knew this was how he felt; it was so painful to experience. The night I walked through my destroyed townhouse paled compared to these feelings. Afterwards, Vale kept trying to space himself, to not unleash that side of him to me. But in response, I opened myself to him even more to show him he was not alone.

Then my dreams took a strange turn as madness took over.

At first, I would see snippets of Arch's death in the Pinelands, then Elara's suicide. I do not think Vale intended to do that, as I would only see sporadic seconds of the sequence, oftentimes out of order. It felt like he was fine-tuning an exact memory to tell me, one he had a hard time bringing to the surface. Then one night, I dreamt of Vale as a young adult, and the elements felt *real*.

Vale was lanky, with dark hair several inches longer than I was used to gelled backward. He wore a navy zipped-up coat with several pockets and tan pants. Gold hoop earrings dangled off each lobe. On his oval face, his hazel eyes stood out, even over his pointed nose. His palms sweated.

Vale closed a steel door and turned around. The room was large; the other three walls and ceiling were made of glass. Outside, the skyscrapers covered Waterfront, bent into all different shapes. Advertisements blanketed the sky, floating by as if they were clouds, lighting Haddon like the sun. In the distance, a number of stories below, an endless stream of cars flew down highways.

A lone metallic desk was at the other end, and there sat Os. His buzz cut and presidential smile highlighted his prominent nose. He wore a white dress shirt with the sleeves rolled up. His green eyes lightened. "Earrings now?"

"How about that."

I raised my brow, confused by the interaction.

"Please, have a seat," Os said, pointing to the lone transparent chair, its border hard to define. "Don't be shy. It will turn metallic once you intend to sit."

"That's new." Vale walked over, feeling like he was hovering in the sky.

"Working on a prototype, the material is similar to the walls. Any cars or spaceships within a few hundred feet see the same color as your chair. Only this our minds can control."

The chair remained as glass once Vale came within several feet.

"You were really expecting my mind to connect to it?" Vale asked.

"Worth a shot."

"Keeping busy… good for you." Vale sat down on the glass chair carefully. At the right angles, he looked like he was levitating.

"How's your sister?"

"Off to Dougray. Of course, she's been the one interested in cybernetics."

"So I've heard. I think she could be of great value one day."

"My parents would've been happy," said Vale, hollow. I was surprised at how indifferent he sounded. "How's your grandfather?"

"Keeps acting like he's dying. He's only one hundred and twenty… just roaming around these hallways."

"Still a young man," Vale said, then sat in silence.

"You're rather calm."

Vale shrugged. Os continued.

"You know, I've been trending through your genetic tests over the years."

"I've seen better."

"But you don't seem to be bothered by your predicament."

"Not like I have a choice."

"You would be off to the Northeast tomorrow. The waiting list for gassing is two years."

"Pretty quick these days."

"Our Intimacy Policy has done wonders. Only 15% lessers for the first time ever... no thanks to you."

"Gave it my best effort."

"Your neurons have never once connected to cybernetics. How is that possible? Elara could since birth."

"So, what am I missing?"

Os smirked. "How's the White Eye, Max Vale?"

Vale rolled his eyes. "Haven't seen him... just like our last annual little get-together."

"I wrote a program that says you did."

"That's why I'm here," Vale said, raising his brow. "I thought last year was our goodbye."

"Likewise. Yet after years of our 'little get-togethers,' as you so graciously worded, my algorithms tell me you almost certainly have been in the White Eye's presence... even now in this room."

"It was just a childhood nightmare."

"I trust my programming more."

Vales studied Os's cold features. "I don't care. I haven't felt anything in years," he said.

"Not since my parents died."

"Max, I analyzed your boyhood genetic expression over the last decade with various versions of software I made. What I find interesting is that my software gives me back different answers to static equations. I should be able to control all elements of how your DNA functions in a lone cell with the right coding. At least, I can do that with any other person's cells. Yet when I run these tests with your cells, something else will alter your genetic response..."

"What's your point?"

"Your cells' response to my software is not due to your cybernetic genes but something else. And the more I become obsessed with the idea, I think what you visualized as the White Eye was part of it. What frightens me is I think the White Eye responds through the software."

"I don't understand."

"I will type a line of code in my program to have your genes make a specific protein, ones our cells need to survive. But while other people's cells will respond—it is a program—yours do not. In fact, your protein changes without any command on my end, *profound* changes that do not make sense. If I want a receptor for serotonin in a brain cell for our mood, it will do the opposite and make enzymes to break serotonin down, a completely different molecular structure. Too exact to be error… The odds of that happening by chance are near zero. The software makes the opposite genes of what I ask for, which could only be done with coding lines that are not present or a cellular intervention by a different creator outside of my software, playing twisted games back at me. Divine intervention."

"Divine intervention?"

"Like an intelligent creator making your genes express the exact opposite of my coding to send a message. I swear, since our first meeting, any cell you've donated has had a lasting aura."

"You're insane," Vale said.

"And you're a free man."

Vale sat silent, exhaling through his nostrils.

"You get to miss the Northeast," Os continued. "But you already knew that was coming. Type B Citizen with exemption. Grandfather got approval from the Board this morning."

"I was going to run to the coastline."

"Without the Board's exemption, you would have been sent back eventually."

"The moment someone finds out I can't connect to robotics—"

"I already changed your record. Your *status* is between the two of us—as long as you stay away from Waterfront technology."

"Whatever you're doing is made up. Just like the Society."

"Oh, you left the Society the moment you could, didn't you?"

"If they weren't so afraid of me, I'd be dead."

"They want a lot of people dead."

"So my genes are the future but morally wrong for the present?"

"You've only gotten bolder with age."

"Why are you studying me?"

"Max Vale, I always follow my curiosities. It has served me well. I'm looking for options evolved beyond cybernetics for the future…"

"Earth and Mars's values all tie to cybernetics."

"Society will have to change how to hate. Just like it always has. *Blindly.*"

Vale shook his head. "Then watch out for my White Eye. It just might kill you like every Lesser I sacrificed."

"There are warning signs, Max Vale, curiosity kills the cat first." Os leaned back in his chair. He said to the ceiling, "Dr. Dalton, do you mind walking down to get Max Vale? Sorry, I don't know where my secretary went off to; she's not listening to my mind-drive." His features softened, and he laughed.

"I saw them in the cafeteria," a bright young voice said throughout the walls. "I'll be right there."

A minute later, a door squeaked open from behind Vale, and shoes clomped on the floor.

"Have a nice life, kid," Os said. "I'll be watching."

"I hope you both burn in hell with my parents."

"The only goodbye I could have expected." Os smirked.

Vale's chair turned metallic. A soft hand rested on him, and he looked up. Dr. Shyla Dalton smiled, dimples emerging on her square head. Her green eyes popped out of her golden skin. She wore a dark suit jacket, and her belly stretched her teal shirt, visibly pregnant. Several charm necklaces dangled from her neck.

"My apologies for keeping you waiting, Shyla," Os said, his green eyes shimmered off the sunlight.

"No worries, Os, traffic from Dougray made me late anyway."

"I'm happy to say Mr. Max Vale is approved for Type B. After all your experiments."

"You connected to cybernetics?" Shyla asked. Her voice dropped, pinching her necklace.

Vale stood. He tucked his lips to a corner. "Much more than connect," Vale said. "You're painting sessions made all the difference."

I flew away from the scene.

I awoke in a cold sweat, breathing sharply and sweating.

I couldn't believe it.

I was there, I thought. *I felt it.* I had never dreamt like that. It was like a memory… everything Vale described about his diary entries of Marie. *What was happening to me? That couldn't be real, could it?*

Vale knew Os growing up! And Marie's mother! *Why didn't he tell me? How were they involved?*

If I was still a lieutenant, my mind would have wrapped around the news for hours. But as reality washed over me, a fire boiled in my chest. I stopped caring about the significance of Os and Shyla's presences or why Os allowed approval. The case meant nothing.

Vale lied to me! I always suspected it. He never had proof he connected to robotics… I was threatened this whole time!

In that moment, all the fondness I had for Vale did not matter.

I screamed every slur I knew for lessers. I used them every day in the Northeast.

My demon emerged. Front and center, it roared throughout my mind. Its gray hair blanketed its face as its fangs drooled slobber, horns pierced through the sides of its skull, and dark eyes swallowed energy like food.

But then the mask fell off, and I was the beast in the end.

At the time, I would have killed lessers all over again.

Born into a prejudiced city, with generations of genetically rooted hatred before me, I knew how to fear before I could eat.

I screamed for days, sometimes in my jail cell, other times in dreams... I couldn't distinguish when I was awake after a while. I stopped going to the gym, I hardly ate, and I was truly alone—even from Os. I couldn't process why he would exempt Vale knowing he was a lesser.

Then, certain nights took a turn. I felt physically ill from them.

At the time, I couldn't understand what they were, but now after my amnesia has worn off over the decades, I knew exactly what happened—I was taken for questioning. Officers grilled me about Vale. Who he was, what he was like, and what happened to him. I remember yelling, "I don't care about that *lesser!*" and adding more genetically-rooted slurs.

A needle would go into my neck, and then I'd wake up, most times in a rush to the toilet to vomit.

I thought I was losing my mind to my biggest fears. It gnawed on all my countless memories with Vale. I couldn't let them go; I needed them—they were all I had left of Vale.

I just sat in my bed, rocking back and forth, humming to myself to distract the demon.

How he communicated made sense to me, though. It was what Marie did to him and Ragg to Marie... through the Deus.

But what did happen to Vale?

The further I grew into delirium, the more he consoled my dreams, his energy telling me it would be okay, and we'd battle my beast together, somehow.

Then I'd wake up angrier than ever. I could hear my grandfather's yell, calling people out—he was the first Price to be an officer for the Northeast Quadrant. Then my father, who had an even more stringent tongue, brought me in as a child to make me "understand the threat to our world," showing how the different nerve toxins killed.

Every week, new lessers came. I realized then I didn't give two shits about why they showed up or the exact criteria—the Board had told me how to hate, and I happily gassed. They waited their turn, then off to the pits, a field with holes where other lessers lay dead.

I let them choose what hole. Because as the officers said in the Northeast...

The Wheeze King always wins.

And he did. The Wheeze King made me an alcoholic. My hatred for others collapsed onto myself. I could at least drink in the dark with the beast, not having to look at it in the eye.

That was how my prejudices and I got along. I could live a life with Vale as my son in the light, but in the dark...

In the bottom of my soul, I had always known Vale was a lesser, but I was too afraid to confront it. I hated myself for it because he kept me alive. Hell, I thought after I killed Sarina, I would have been dead in a year or two's time.

But instead, life brought me to Vale, and over time, I stopped hating myself as much. I thought he'd never understand the impact he had on my life.

I remember having that realization one day, rocking back and forth on my bed, because that night, I happened to feel my impact on him in my dreams.

I entered Vale's memory about the day we first met. The day after Vale graduated from the Haddon Police Academy for the Northeast. Years removed from seeing Os or Shyla Dalton.

Still lanky, Vale stood in a navy police shirt and tie, walkie-talkie clipped to his side. He wore a peaked cap. I never saw him wear the attire again.

It was odd, sensing Vale's insecurities as he watched me for the first time outside the police academy, finding it strange how burned-out I looked, my stubble prominent, hair fraying out of my cap. He was warned I was going through a "rough patch"—a fair assessment.

Reliving this moment through his shoes, I could feel his apprehension and reluctance. I didn't blame him: I looked horrible and probably smelled like last night's bender. Still, Vale stuck out his hand and said, "Lieutenant Price, pleasure to meet you, sir."

I studied it for a minute. Then, "Who the hell are you?"

"I am your new partner, Maxwell Vale."

"I'm just bullshitting. No formalities, rook."

"What?" Vale shook his head. I remember the confused look and how indifferent I was because of what happened next.

I stuck out my arm to back Vale off and stumbled into a bush nearby. I vomited. A few blown chunks later, I turned back to Vale, who stood aghast.

It was seven in the morning. I had not gone to sleep yet. As much as I missed drinking in prison, I didn't miss feeling the hangover.

"Sorry. I mean, welcome… to my bullshit," I said.

Vale's jaw lowered, unsure what to say. Which, as I later appreciated, was an accomplishment.

"But my bullshit is your bullshit. Feel free to return the favor."

Vale's features betrayed his confusion. "Um—"

"You mind driving? I could use a snooze. Masks are in the back." I tossed him the keys before he could answer. "And pardon the robots on my dashboard."

Vale fumbled the keys. After his pointer finger hooked into a key ring, he said, "I can do that…"

"You're sober; of course, you can. You drink whiskey?"

"Not really, Lieutenant—"

"Allow me to broaden your senses later. And please, rook, always call me Price."

"Then you call me Vale."

"Not yet, rook." I staggered into the Crown Victoria's passenger seat.

Vale opened the driver's door and sat down. He gripped the wheel but didn't start the car.

"Well, what is it?" I asked.

"Where are we going?"

"Take us somewhere productive."

Vale raised his brow and started to sweat, looking around as if the answer would fly by. Finally, he started the engine and remarked, "The gas light is on."

"That's the spirit."

As the Crown Victoria drove away from the police station, I realized I could be a piece of shit on my worst days. And as time went on, I got better at hiding it from almost everyone, especially myself. But never Vale, and oddly enough, it was exactly what he needed.

In years of reflection, my blind acceptance of his flaws opened our relationship. I was so fucked up with Sarina's death, I felt I had no right to judge Vale. The action would challenge us in ways I did not know possible.

For we first bonded in the dark corners of our psyche, where our pain, those demons, liked to lurk... Our love took root in the darkest parts of our souls.

I awoke in the middle of the night and sat on my bed. I was no longer sweating, and I felt a strange energy.

It was love.

I thought only hatred existed in the darkest pits of my soul where my demon roamed—but so did the strongest parts of my love for Vale.

The epiphany flushed the demon out. And I never felt the beast's presence ever again. Although I admit, there would be times in the future when I heard the beast knock, wanting to come back inside and retaliate.

I never let it enter, for what it's worth.

Around halfway through my imprisonment, I had a visitor—Dr. Arnold Darwinn. He showed up unannounced.

I remember studying him through the glass window. His gray hair was unkempt, and his beard brushed his stomach, making him look like the one who belonged in here, especially with his golden blazer.

"Pardon my stealth," Darwinn said. "But I need to ask you a favor. And I'm afraid it's the least bit about the dark roast."

I stared at him for a while, confused by his prompt introduction. Eventually, I said, "I'm doing well. Thank you for asking."

"No time, Mr. Price. And congrats on your sentence." Darwinn sipped from his flask. "I see you sitting there in silence, and I wonder maybe you're not interested in what I have to say. And whatever you do in here is plenty busy for your time."

"Just wanted to say hi first…"

"Oh well, hello there," Darwinn said, already switching gears. "How much would you like to learn about the technology of our world?"

"I used to," I said, having let the technology go once the dreams worsened.

"No, you still do. I know your interests will certainly come back, and I need you to challenge them."

"What are you talking about?"

"Mr. Price, curiosity is a rose with many thorns. I have never detected you in agony from it. And it's time I let you in on the suffering of scientists. Would you like to learn this pain?"

"I mean, I can give it a shot."

"But are you willing to be a slave to it?"

"I guess…" I said clumsily.

"That'll work. Welcome to research. In the library, you'll find a worker with a gray mustache. Tell him I sent you. He will have a dozen books about the theories on time and energy, the history of the Society, and my personal notes about the Deus. They're for your eyes. No one else."

"What am I supposed to do with it?"

"Learn, Mr. Price. You're a curious man above all else, right?"

"I can't learn your level of knowledge," I said, suddenly less concerned about my own issues.

"The material in there you can figure out... or at least the basic premise. My quirkiness you're referring to goes beyond the textbook. And I hate to break it to you, but you don't have as much of a choice as you would like. The day you get out, you will be targeted. So it's important we stick together. I will need you to go to the top floor of the ODYSE building that evening. There, you will walk into the New Year's Eve Party Os invited you when you were on the case. I'll be waiting in my office at eleven forty-five in the evening—I have guests to please prior—but by that date, I will have completed my time under the PATC, rejected Dougray's tenure, and begun working with ODYSE full-time to investigate the Deus."

"That's a terrible idea," I said.

"It is. But I don't have another option—I need their resources. And they can't touch me for the moment, Mr. Price. The instant they do, my mind-drive sends their files to every journalist on both planets."

"Why are you doing this?"

"There are bigger pieces here... and graver theories. Stuff you can read about. By the way, I need to hire you when you're out."

"Why me?"

"I trust your character. And above all, I trust our mutual love."

"For what?"

"The Deus. There is love in there anyway. And much darker entities..." Darwinn twisted a smile. He took out a business card and pressed it against the window. "And you'll need a tailor. Remember this name, and of course, make sure to say yours truly sent you."

"I need time to think this over."

"You will, Mr. Price," Darwinn said. "They'll be options. Not all the jackets come in gold."

Three months later...

In the elevator doors' reflection, my eyes were a shocking blue. The door opened to the top floor. I stepped into a marble hallway, wearing my new three-piece gray suit with a tulip petal pinned to its lapel.

"Welcome, Liam Price, to a night of wondrous festivities as we celebrate the turn of the century here at ODYSE Tower," a 'bot said. It looked similar to the ones Vale and I encountered on our case, but I could tell by a few changes in the design pattern that it was an older model—a 41XC.

I walked past it into a lobby. The floor was also made of marble, and a giant chandelier hung over the lone glass table on a maroon rug. A dozen or so guests talked in their own pockets, leaking out from the main sets of double doors. I walked to the entrance. On my way, I noticed several well-dressed guests.

A few of their eyes met mine for a brief moment, and they glared. A shiver shot down my spine. I hinted at a smile and walked into the main ballroom.

It was beautiful.

Pillars surrounded the main space and raised many stories into the air. The walls were sheets of glass that curved into a giant semisphere overlooking the stars, like a real-life planetarium. The blue and gold ODYSE logo occasionally flashed on the glass. In the center were exotic dancers with visible silver robotics nailed to their bodies. A crowd clapped along to the music, and several among them stared at me, their features morphing to disgust.

Looks like they handled my sentencing well. I thought.

Someone bumped my shoulder. I spun around.

I couldn't make out who it was.

I was on edge.

Along the sides of the room, hundreds of men and women ate hors d'oeuvres off plates held by 'grams. In the back, a waterfall of wine trickled down. I noticed guests placed their glasses close, and the stream magnetized to the cup.

I quickly scanned the ballroom for the hallway entrance to find Darwinn's office. Nothing obvious popped out. As inconspicuously as possible, I darted through the crowd of people, walking past several ex-Board members over the past decade. A particular scrawny one with slicked-back gray hair, one Vale could never stand, gave me an extra-long stare.

I gulped. By his side stood Martin Brezniack and the bald man who attacked me on Darwinn's truck. I felt like prey.

Cheery, I thought, sweating, wondering if I had made the right decision to come here.

I walked through a few of the pillars to a gold curtain that draped along the glass.

My heart stopped.

I saw the back of Madelyn's dark shoulder-length hair. She wore a beautiful red dress that revealed the curves of her frame. She did not notice me and walked by herself through a lone glass door to the outside balcony.

I grabbed a glass of champagne from a 'gram and swigged it down, then looked at my reflection on the glass wall, taming my messy hair.

I followed her, my heart fluttering. I needed to see her, thank her… tell her I still loved her. The moment I pushed open the glass door and stepped outside, the wind blew against my hair, undoing what I had just tried to fix.

The view was gorgeous, overlooking all the lights in the city and all the hover cars flying over Waterfront. I scanned the deck. A few couples stood in the corner leaning against the ledge—but no Madelyn.

I did a double-take.

On the other side, tucked away, I saw a flower petal. I walked towards it, furrowing my brow. The petal belonged a tulip. *Vale?* I thought. *But how?*

The corner led to an entirely different side of the deck, out of sight from the entrance.

On the far end, a shadow stood in a black cloak and hood. A chill swarmed my body. No one else was around. I walked over, but the cloak made no movement.

Do I say his name? Would that cause attention? I thought. I settled on being nonchalant.

"A beautiful view up here, isn't it?" I asked.

"It's nighttime. Everything beautiful has left you this day," the voice was deep and filled the air.

My heart pushed against my ribcage.

"Ragg?" I asked in disbelief. I chose that name over the White Eye because I immediately recognized the tone, reliving Marie's knife piercing my skin by the marsh. It was one I would never forget. "How are you here?"

"I am darkness. And the night is still young, Price."

"But Marie died. I watched her die."

"I've died a thousand times, but here I stand."

"Why are you here?"

The cloak slowly twisted its neck to me. "I never want you to feel alone."

Terror sucked the air out of me. I stared at Vale's white drama tragedy mask, covered in red markings over its crevices, X's over each eye, and tiny symbols covering every space, similar to the pattern of the blood room.

"It is you," I belted out. *But it couldn't be.* Yet it had to. I was sure of it. *How did he get up here?* I was both relieved and absolutely terrified. "Why are you wearing a mask?"

"True darkness has no face." Vale turned back to look over Haddon.

Was he possessed by Ragg? How? I had so many questions for him.

I joined for a moment to recollect myself. In the distance, I noticed the Northeast Quadrant and how dark it looked compared to the rest of the city.

"Are you alive?" I turned back to Vale.

No one was there.

I scanned the entire deck, but the shadowy cloak vanished. I was alone until two shadows appeared from the other end of the balcony. The bald man and Martin Brezniack stood in tuxedos.

"Gentlemen," I said calmly, discreetly scanning my end of the porch. There was no other exit, and I had no weapon.

The bald man brought out his black bar and swung it, flaunting the holographic whip that darted out and snapped within feet of me. Brezniack's tinker toy had already turned to a centipede and crawled to his shoulder. A shimmering spiked ball shot from one end, swinging behind him, gaining centripetal force.

They hissed.

"A little out of place for a ritual," I said, trying to buy time. I had no meaningful escape.

"Ascend to the Deus, where you belong," Brezniack said.

The bald man cracked the whip again.

"Let's not do that," I said.

Brezniack laughed, then stopped. The bald man looked at him bewildered. Brezniack levitated several feet in the air and froze, paralyzed. But his eyes revealed how terrified he was. He made a guttural sound, and then his body flew to the top of the ledge and flopped onto it like a doll. He fidgeted, trying to fight. Then his neck swung to the side, staring helplessly at the bald man and me.

A rib cracked.

At the same time, the bald man's face got punched in the cheek by the wind, knocking his head away.

Another of Brezniack's ribs cracked. And the bald man got punched on the other side of the cheek.

I stood helplessly, watching their eyes meet in complete despair.

Then in a rapid-fire, every rib cracked down Brezniack in exact timing to each punch in the face of the bald man, who fell on the ground, then got thrown back up to standing in a daze.

A wilted hand shot out from the bald man's chest, gripped his face, and whipped it inward. A loud crack from his neck echoed, and he fell to the floor dead.

Brezniack stared in immense terror, then his jaw dropped out, ripped from its socket, and blood dripped out of his eyes. His head then repeatedly banged up and down on the marble railing. Blood splattered further with each thump until Brezniack became limp, laying on the edge, lifeless.

I stood, staring at the two bodies, horrified at what I had just witnessed and what was to become of me. Surely, they would lock me away again. I was the only person out here. "Vale?" I asked to the air.

No one answered.

"Can you put your mask on?"

He appeared, the black cloak staring at me, wearing a blood-painted tragedy mask—at least, now I was convinced the markings were made by blood.

"Never do that again," I said.

The mask did not respond.

"How could you do that?" I was terrified. All the worst qualities of Vale had come to the surface.

And in the core of his soul, Ragg rested.

Slowly, the cloak brought out its fist, covered in a black glove. He let it hang in the air.

My heart sunk. I hesitated.

But as if a force nudged me forward, I pounded his fist, and we snapped our fingers.

Before I could ask anything else, Vale lifted his mask off and disappeared.

I stood, flabbergasted and petrified by Vale. *Did he die? Was he alive? Was Ragg involved?* I thought.

I had to find Darwinn. I needed a place to hide, somewhere to escape.

A bird crowed. I turned to the sound and noticed a black vulture flying in a circle above me. It looked down at the bodies… and me.

"Horo! Get back here this instance! You're going to tire yourself out!"

I turned my head up to the source of the sound.

Three stories higher on the other side, Darwinn stood on a porch, his arms flailing. "You've had a broken wing for three months, and you want to risk it all flying at the highest point of Haddon?"

"Darwinn?" I yelled, equally as relieved and bewildered.

"Ah yes, good evening Mr. Price. I see you've met my friend," Darwinn said, not even looking down at me.

"You didn't just hear all of this?"

"Of course! And I saw it too, terrifying… But I need to finish walking my vulture around the porch."

"Dammit, Darwinn, I need to escape," I said, my eyes widening. This was my first conversation with him as a free man, and we were talking about his pet vulture.

"Why you need to do no such thing! Mr. Price, I promise your safety."

"How?"

"We need to chat. The stairs to my office are on the other side of the ballroom."

"Darwinn, if I go in there, they will kill me."

"Mr. Price, if they could kill you, I wouldn't have invited you." The vulture finally flew back to Darwinn and landed on his shoulder. He lifted up his wing. "Anatomy is all in order… wonderful, Horo! Now you must come." Darwinn sprinted back inside.

In shock, I rubbed my hands on my face and then placed them on my thighs, processing how distorted the two dead bodies appeared. I gave in and sprinted back to the other side of the balcony. No one was outside.

"Just be quiet…" I slipped into the ballroom. I scanned the entire room and made no eye contact. My heart lifted. On the other side, I saw the entrance Darwinn instructed would lead to his office.

But slowly, everyone began to stare…

I tried my best to casually cut through the crowd, accidentally walking through a 'gram. I didn't allow time for a response. I picked up the pace, reached the other side, and dashed into the hallway. It led to stairs that brought me up several flights. I was to go to the third—the highest one.

I arrived. The hallway pressed against the glass wall, overlooking the ballroom and all the lights of Haddon. Rows of doors went against the opposite wall. Darwinn's office was the first door on the right. I brought up my fist to knock, but then I stopped. The door opened.

"Mr. Price, how you do wander. You're almost as bad as Horo," Darwinn said. His loony hair and beard popped out. And, of course, he wore his golden blazer over suspenders and a shirt of a bird's side profile that looked like a squished owl. It appeared very indifferent. The text under the side profile said, *No, you're the frogmouth.*

He petted the black vulture resting on his shoulder and seemed pleased with the attention. It crowed. "Aviation rehabilitation… always a project of mine, strictly business, of course. Now get in here."

I listened.

The office looked exactly how I imagined it would. Grandfather clocks covered the walls. Giant metallic machines for his dark roast project filled up the center space. A thin white desk was wedged in the front corner, surrounded by two chairs with a levitating screen at the table's end. In the back was an open door that led out to the porch.

"Great to see you back in the nuthouse, and as always, we're short on time."

"Darwinn, I need to get out of here *now.*"

"I can assure you, you're fine this very moment."

"Vale, he's alive. I just watched him brutally kill those two people. And I'm the only person who came out."

"Mr. Price, relax. Would you like some of my dark roast?" Darwinn waved his hands to his extensive coffee apparatus in the back.

I realized then just how much I was panting. *What was Darwinn hiding?* I thought. I played along, lowering my shoulders. "Fine. Who am I to say no?" I sat down in a chair, appreciating the walls were made of glass. "Some gig."

"A terrifying one."

"I'm sure I'm not helping."

Darwinn puttered around the coffee machines until he placed my old rooster monocle mug on the desk with his dark roast.

"How could you see me?" I asked.

"We're in ODYSE, Mr. Price. Why wouldn't I able to?" Darwinn walked to a tall oak grandfather clock and lifted his arm. The vulture hopped onto the top and nestled.

He then sat down and clapped his hands twice. At once, a handful of cameras came out through the walls and pointed at me. "Mr. Price, these bugaboos are in each room, watching our every movement, collecting data for the 42XC 'bots... except in here. I have hacked into their security and turned them off in this room. This room is the one place in Haddon I knew we could talk in privacy."

"I'm glad we've taken the path of least resistance."

"Then we are the least bit futile." Darwinn opened his fingers into an L-shape, and a blue screen the size of a paper formed. "I was afraid I'd never see either of you again."

"What's this?" I asked.

"Your contract." He placed the blue screen on the table and slid it across.

"You don't understand. I'm going to be wanted for murder... again. And unless you have another way out of here, I'm a dead man. There's no chance of me even getting to the elevator."

"I told you, don't worry about that. If anything, you gained more freedom for the moment."

"I don't understand."

"Mr. Price, they can't do anything about those deaths. They know Vale did them, but they don't have an inkling of what to do about him. In fact, they are petrified. You realize they were trying to isolate you and kill you?"

"I followed Madelyn to the porch…"

"So you did, but judging by the cameras, she had no clue you were even there."

"Impossible."

"Madelyn has her own motives… ones we currently overlap with. Don't worry, Mr. Price! The moment word spreads, you will be able to walk around this building freely."

"This is madness."

"Madness can be a high functioning level of sanity." Darwinn tapped on my potential contract.

"So I get to be paid to have ODYSE read my mind and slowly formulate a way to kill me?"

"Nothing but the best."

"…Thanks." I raised my mug as a toast and clanged it into the mug in his hand. I sipped.

"You have hesitations."

"Darwinn, two men just tried to kill me, and I watched as they got butchered. I'm having a hard time breathing, let alone signing my life away."

"I know, I get it. In fact, I watched your every movement and the lovely guests' reactions to your presence."

"They all looked ready to join in if they could. I'm just wondering if there is a smarter way."

"This is the best way. Because we make our own path here," Darwinn said.

I raised my brow.

"I saw who you met out on the balcony," Darwinn said. On a screen levitating in the air, Darwinn replayed me bending down to pick up a tulip petal and looking at Vale.

Except Vale was not there.

"Impossible…" I said.

"Fear not. I know Vale was there."

"What happened to him?"

"He's been in a period of growth. Learning how to control Ragg and the Deus… it's not so easy. At least that's what he tells me."

"You talked to Vale? He's alive?"

"Very much so." Darwinn opened a drawer. He pulled out all the tiny 'bot models that were on the dashboard of my Crown Victoria.

"I had buried these!"

"Vale told me this was his best shot at convincing you," Darwinn said. "Don't tell me I dug these up for nothing."

"Then who was dead in my living room?"

"A Morte, died in the same way as Shyla Dalton and Crony… Vale told me so, at least."

My mind swirled in a million directions. I stood up and turned away from Darwinn, trying to digest his words. "I suppose he told you about his childhood."

"He did. And to you in your dreams."

"Vale knew Os and Shyla this whole time… He's never connected to cybernetics."

"How did you think he was exempt? I told you my sister became a monster, but she was just as much a victim—and it all started with Mr. Vale."

"Why did Vale not tell me this in person?" I asked.

"You know why. Same reason Elara had me keep an eye on you to protect Vale."

"That was you at the station!"

"See anyone else in a golden blazer?"

"I would have moved on."

"Not with your history in the Northeast Quadrant."

"Why not?" I snapped. "I did for everything else."

"Mr. Price, the most destructive evils are unseen." Darwinn stood up, only slightly taller than me in my seat, reached across the table, and shook my shoulders. "As long as we exist, they too will roam. We created the White Eye. And at many points throughout history, we created every little fragment of Ragg that exists today. We let it happen because we normalized fear. We didn't make up hate, just reinvented how to. And we'll do it again. Because while fear's existence is unsettling, fear's timelessness is horrifying—we've targeted humans for many reasons beyond genetics!"

"Really? We've oppressed people besides lessers?" I said, furrowing my brow, unable to think of what else could possibly cause this amount of hatred.

Darwinn shook his head. He let go of me and fell back into his chair. "You embody ignorance. A weapon more lethal than anything tangible."

I reflected on how my prejudice helped form the world that derailed Vale. The realization shook my body. "I understand."

"No, you certainly do not. Because I hardly do with this lab." Darwinn hopped off his seat and paced around the office. He sipped the dark roast from his mug and continued. "In fact, all I've been doing lately is tracking imperium on my satellites, specifically imperium we label as the emotion *hatred*. And my new results have been… rather surprising. You see, they strongly suggest we don't just die, and our soul crosses over into the Deus in milliseconds, but rather ascends at different rates throughout our life."

"You mean we don't just die and go to the spiritual world?" I asked.

"The thorns of curiosity, Mr. Price! My research suggests that many people's souls start to leave when they are young and completely cross over decades before they are pronounced physiologically dead."

"Why?"

"Hatred, Mr. Price. Its imperium runs rampant in the Deus and has a habit of sucking our soul out of our body, little by little."

"But the world's a hateful place," I said.

"Precisely!" Darwinn stomped his foot. "And when our world sets up a system to allow people's fears to be justified comfortably, we think it's normal or even beneficial to hate. Then what happens? The world loses sight of how to live. Even though our bodies remain upright, our souls leave, getting dragged away by our hatred. We're dead... gone! And in the U-S-of-A in particular, over the past century, every year we are dying sooner..." Darwinn's eyes looked possessed, burning into my soul. He turned away, staring through the clear glass at the crowd in the ballroom. "If you don't pay attention to your hatred, you just might up end up here, nothing but bones and skin, a member of the... *Party of the Dead*."

In the background, the crowd from the ballroom shouted, "*Four... three... two... one... Happy New Year!*"

I jumped.

Darwinn's family coo-coo clock struck twelve over the door as Horo flapped his feathers. Papers flew off the grandfather clock it nested on.

"Horo! Where did you get those? I had been looking for them!" Darwinn said, jumping to the other side of the lab, waving his arms.

One of the sheets landed by my feet. The paper was actually a photograph featuring a young Darwinn, standing next to Nana, with slicked-back gray hair in a ponytail, radiant emerald dress, and diamond errands. Shyla stood on the adjacent side, her thick black curls dangling past her shoulders.

An older gentleman stood behind the three. His face looked like an older image of Darwinn, balding, gray hair sticking out to the side. Sleek frames rested on his nose, and he wore a button teal sweater.

"Pardon the family photo."

I furrowed my brow. He did not look like the grizzled, hard-nose auto mechanics I had imagined. "Forgive my ignorance, but I thought your father was a mechanic?" I asked.

"An aerospace mechanic, Mr. Price—think spaceships."

Questions poured into my mouth, but before I could let anything out, Darwinn cut me off. "And worst, after hatred sucks all the life out of us, ODYSE is synthesizing medication to inject, to enhance our sensation to the Deus, in theory to create *more* imperium."

"From Crony's work?"

"Exactly. It could never end! An endless amount of imperium from one's soul in the Deus would lead to an endless amount of data for ODYSE. Absolute control in our dimension and the afterlife. Now, if you'll look this way."

Automatically, I turned to the levitated screen at the end of the desk. Colors of red, orange, and yellow hovered over the city like smog. "These are my satellites detecting the Deus. Part of everyone's souls leaves this world—some much faster than others as we suffer. Hatred is the biggest part of the equation."

"I guess I'm just about all in the Deus then."

"And I'm right there with you. It's nothing to be ashamed of. It's part of fighting through life. The problem is you and I are now aware parts of our souls are missing as we walk this planet amongst the dead. It's vital we have each other's backs and push forward. Or else we just might be dead with them if we aren't already. Do you think you are?"

My head was exploding. "This is crazy."

"Our world is killing us in unforeseen ways. And it is our job to understand why and fix it. But make no mistake, we are just pieces to this puzzle. This battle will revolve around the chosen *two*."

"Two?"

"Mr. Vale and Marie…"

My brow furrowed.

"A regular human is born with their soul in our universe, only to drift into the Deus at their own hateful pace. Marie, she was born with her soul in both already. Her soul could go back and forth between both universes independent of her body."

"How do you know this?"

"My niece has been contacting me through the Deus, manipulating my satellites in ways I could never fathom. A brilliant soul, and the great joy of my day," Darwinn said, with a genuine smile, one I had not seen from him. "And oh, of course, she has locked Ragg into the physical world. Vale is containing Ragg in his body now. If he dies, who knows where it goes and what it can do, now more than ever, with ODYSE so blindly wired in. I fear how Ragg could control the 'bots through the Deus."

"Was that Marie's order to kill them?"

"No. She can have some control over Ragg, but then it takes liberties to customize the order. Please, it's Vale's body! He would need to agree to some extent. I'm sure both Vale and Marie want to protect you. What you witnessed was Ragg's interpretation of the wish. I imagined you can only have so much authority over pure evil."

I shook my head in disbelief, and after a few moments to process, I asked, "What could I possibly do to help?"

"By doing the same thing as me. Give them every possible bit of energy to support them before it's too late, and every human dies when they are born, artificially hanging on thanks to ODYSE's injections, so their souls can be mined for data. Of course, I have a few other small tasks."

"Name them."

"You would be my associate field researcher, as well as my guard twenty-four seven."

"I'll need whiskey," I said.

"You can have as much as you want." Darwinn glanced down at his desk at his contract on the blue screen.

"Where is Vale now?" I asked.

"Following a path laid out to him by Marie from the blood room. I do not know where. But you can ask her... She has been listening to this conversation through my encrypted satellites."

A wave of adrenaline coursed through my body.

Before I could ask how, a voice boomed from the ballroom. "Ladies and gentlemen, may I have your attention. It is our delight to bring you the beloved founder of ODYSE, who put America back on track to be the best nation on both planets..."

"...The voice of the dead," Darwinn muttered during the dramatic pause.

"*Os,*" the announcer said. The crowd roared in applause.

My blood boiled in my veins. I turned away and placed my finger on the dotted line at the bottom of the electronic page. I signed while I braced myself for Os's voice to fill the office.

Darwinn curled his lips in a grin, raised his mug of the two tin cans, and forcefully clanged it back into mine on the table.

On the levitating screen next to me, a text appeared.

MESSAGE FROM:
MARIE: "Welcome."

CPSIA information can be obtained
at www.ICGtesting.com
Printed in the USA
LVHW080026210922
728906LV00016B/729

9 781958 729830